Revolution

BETHANY A PERRY

ISBN: 978-1-7344692-3-3

This one goes out to my Alpha and Beta Readers. I couldn't do any of it without you.

Reclamation 2: Revolution contains an on-the-page depiction of sexual assault.
Chapter 43

Also included are the mental repercussions of this assault.
Chapters 44, 45, 49

I have included a note at the end of the book with resources (phone numbers and websites) for survivors of sexual assault.

THE ISLAND

CHAPTER 1

Adelaide's feet pounded the ground on the other side of the driftwood, spraying sand and leaves into the air. Not missing a step, she sprinted into the copse of trees ahead, pulling a breath through her nose and exhaling through her mouth.

Hot on her heels, her pursuer cleared the same driftwood just after her.

Listening for the feet to slip, hoping really, she twisted at the last second to avoid a scrubby bush in front of her.

Came out of nowhere, that thing.

Zigzagging, focused on pulling breath in through her nose and blowing it out through her mouth, she Listened again for her pursuer.

Silence behind her.

Ducking behind a stubby tree, she crouched and peeked around it.

Nothing moved.

Nothing breathed.

The ocean, too far away to hear, salted the air with humid heat.

The middle of summer here was about the most awful torture she could imagine. Thick, heavy air crowded her lungs, filling all the space for breath. Water dripped from the air, as though she could take a handful and squeeze it.

Feet shuffled over sand twenty feet to her left. Here she'd been thinking about the damn weather and almost gotten snuck up on.

Dashing from behind the tree, she set her sights on a brick square. Could have been a store, could have been a house, could have been a who cares. It was more cover. Better cover.

With no way to not be seen ducking in, she settled for getting there first. Stretching her legs to their burning limits, she sprinted for the building.

And where there had been clear ground in front of her, there wasn't.

Ankles catching the staff that had materialized, she tucked her shoulder as she fell. Landing flat on it instead of rolling, she exhaled a quiet *woof.*

Coughing, she rolled to her back and stared at the sky, cheek covered in sand. Hair in her mouth.

Sand in her teeth.

Of course.

"Score one for me," said a soft male voice. He leaned over her, angular cheeks curved in a smile.

"You son of a bitch, Yasuo," Addy said. "About broke my ankle."

Holding the end of the staff out to her, he laughed. "You should take better care of your surroundings, then, shouldn't you?"

Snatching the staff, she pulled herself up and brushed away as much sand as she could. Spat until her mouth felt like the bottom of a dog's foot, and frowned. "I thought you were back there. How'd you get in front of me?"

His smile fell. "Back where?"

"Back over," she said, pointing behind her, "there. That. Wait, that wasn't you?"

"You'd have to get up pretty early in the morning to get ahead of me, pupil," Yasuo said, leaning on the staff.

"Oh, stuff it. You're what. Three years older than me? Two?"

"Adelaide, I may look youthful. But in reality," he said, leaning over the staff and whispering, "I am over six hundred years old."

"Shut up." She kicked at the staff, catching it with a toe before he got it out of the way. "If that wasn't you, then what—"

The bubbling began, not five feet away. Stumbling through a bush, a Dead Head tripped over the lower branches and fell on its face.

Yasuo raised the staff.

The 'Head crawled toward them, feet tangled. Blackened fingers gripped handfuls of loose sand, clawing through it. Creeping closer, buzzing and growling, it could have been frustrated at its slow progress.

Addy knew better. There was no one home. Not anymore.

Unsheathing her machete, she glanced at Yasuo.

He frowned.

"I know," she said, looking at the blade, "you don't want me to bring blades for training. But you expect me to just walk around naked. No weapons." Hacking at the 'Head, she silenced its buzzing in one stroke. "I mean, what would we have done here? Just left it?"

Shaking his head, Yasuo picked up the staff and turned. "How will you ever learn how powerless you are if you don't *let* yourself feel it?"

"Yaz, wait, it's not about that," she said, reaching for his shoulder.

Stopping, he took her hand. A sad smile lifted the corners of his mouth. "Adelaide," he said, "let me know when you're ready." He walked around the building and disappeared.

* * *

Returning to Harkers Island, Addy searched the dock as she berthed her canoe.

Not that Dad and Dean would come back this way, but she could hope. It'd been six weeks since she'd seen either of them.

Several boats took up space at the dock, Mike's among them, but not their little silver skiff.

She trudged to the Big House, limping over her sore ankles. Probably needed ice later.

Scott had requested a report from the mainland. Even when she repeated she wouldn't be his lieutenant, he treated her like she was his number one. That whole "not good with women" thing was a clever façade. The leader of this island was quite good with whomever he chose.

Hand on the doorknob of the Big House, weathered wooden sprawling monstrosity that it was, her fingers slipped off as someone opened it from inside.

"Oh, girl, I was coming to find you," Celia said, smiling through heavy-lidded eyes.

"Celia," Addy said, pulling her into a hug. "I'm glad to see you."

"You too, Addy. Hey," she said, backing up and tucking a stray hair behind her ear, "Scott's looking for you."

"I was just coming to see him," Addy said, stepping into the cool shade of the house. Lazy fans spun on the ceiling, mixing hot air with not as hot air.

Sighing and fanning her face, Addy frowned. "What does he need?"

Celia shaded her eyes and grinned. "You'll see."

Before Addy could open her mouth to ask, Celia pulled the door closed.

"Good talk, Cee," she mumbled, following the twisting, turning halls. The stuffed mallards on the walls pointed the way, if you knew how to follow them. At the door to Scott's study, she knocked and crossed her arms. She rehearsed what she would say after giving her report, whispering under her breath. "I can't do this job for you, Scott. I'm not telling you again, I—"

Slight squeak of the hinge.

Expecting to see Scott there, with his silver hair, she couldn't process the man in the doorway until he stepped through it and wrapped his arms around her.

Dean lifted her and spun in a circle. He buried his face in her neck. "Oh man, am I glad to see you," he said, his breath warm on her collarbone.

Grinning from ear to ear, stretching her face so hard it hurt, she squeezed him back. Eyes closed, she held the back of his neck and head and breathed. He smelled like campfires and ocean.

He sat her down, beaming.

"You're back. I didn't see your boat. Is Dad here?"

"Adelaide," Dad said, leaning in the doorway.

"Dad," she said, hand trailing away from Dean. "Are you OK?" Brow cocked, she looked him over.

"Yeah, baby girl. I'm alright." He kissed the top of her head and gave her a one-armed hug.

"Adelaide," Scott called, somewhere deep in the study, "won't you come in? Bring your father and Dean, please."

Dad crossed his arms and cocked a brow, just like she'd done. "How's that not being his lieutenant going?"

Frowning, she stalked past him and into the study.

Though the fireplace was dark today, every single lamp glared. Scott sat at his desk, his young face beneath a head full of grey hair, surrounded by books. Catching her eye, he frowned. "It gets so horribly dark in here with no windows. For today, we need the light." He motioned to the two chairs in front of the desk. "Please."

Ignoring the man dance behind her, Addy took a seat and waited for Dean and Dad to finish fighting over who got to stand.

After a few tense moments, Dean won. He draped his arm over the back of her chair and stood as Dad took the other seat.

"Scott, I—" Addy began.

He held up his only hand. "Adelaide, your father has important information. You'll want to hear this. Mr. Cooke?"

Dad cleared his throat and shifted. "Sorry, baby girl."

At least he could be polite for Scott when Scott clearly couldn't do it for himself. Was he incapable, or did he just not care?

"As I was saying before you got here, Addy," Dad said, angling his knees so he faced the space between Addy and Scott, "I think we've finally found the location of the Emerald Isle survivors."

Addy sat forward. A headache began behind her left eye. It always made such a nice accessory for the heavy cloak of guilt lying over her shoulders. Somehow she'd transferred the fact that her mother had been responsible for all the experimentation and death on that island onto her own conscience.

Dean leaned over the back of the chair. "We had the hardest time finding them. After everything went down and they disappeared, it took us most of the time we've been gone just to pick up their trail."

Glancing up at him, she smiled with tight lips. "It was thousands of people, Dean. How could you miss a trail that wide?"

He frowned, brow creased above flat eyes. "Addy, it was like they just disappeared. Vanished into thin air."

"I remember, I went back to the island the day after we left."

"They were just gone. Like they'd been picked up and taken in the middle of their meals," Dad said, turning to Scott.

Addy shivered. The pinprick of headache expanded into an ice pick. "It made no sense."

Dad sighed. "And knowing what we did about the experiments being done, the work on the vaccine, we had to find them."

"And you think you have," she said, rubbing her forehead.

From behind her, a warm hand gripped her shoulder. A single-handed massage.

Too long since she'd felt that hand. Too long. The butterflies in her stomach threatened to flutter up into her eyes and become tears. Instead, she opened her eyes and stood. "So, where are they?"

"That's where it gets tricky," Dad said, turning back to Scott. Not before giving Dean a laden glance, steely blue eyes flashing in the lamplight.

Dean sat and leaned on the desk. "This isn't something we ask lightly, Scott, but we need more people."

Scott nodded. "Of course. Whatever you need," he said, looking between them.

"We've also discovered Iridium Flare might have had something to do with this," Dean said, pitching his voice low.

Addy crossed her arms, back against the mantle. Dean's company, IRF, was involved in all this, too. He'd never let it lie. "When are you going back out," she said, voice flat, more of a statement than a question. The butterflies resettled in her stomach, but they weren't happy, fluttery butterflies anymore. They were *I think I'm going to throw up in your lap* butterflies.

Spinning in the chair, Dean tensed to stand.

Dad held a hand out to him. "We can't lose them again."

Arms uncrossed, Addy leaned on Scott's desk and stared into his eyes. "I cannot do this job. Not one more day. Not one more report. I am done."

Throwing a glance at her father and her, what? Boyfriend? After one date? Didn't you have to spend time together to be in a relationship?

Good lord, who knew.

She slammed the study door behind her.

* * *

Jack flinched as the door slammed.

He didn't mean to make her angry. But here he was, taking her man away, again, after they'd just arrived.

"Hey, Dean, I think I can get this. Why don't you go after her," he said, jerking his head toward the door.

"You sure?" Without waiting for Jack to answer, Dean followed her.

Jack leaned on the desk. "I think he should stay here. Take care of Adelaide. I'll be fine without him."

Scott shook his head. "Mr. Cooke, if there's one thing I've learned about your daughter in the last six weeks, it's that she needs no one to look after her. In fact," he said, leaning back and curling his hand under his chin, "she's been learning new combat skills while you've been away."

Not for the first time, pride gripped him. She was so much better than he could ever be. "Has she now?"

"Yes. I believe she's made very good progress. Her instructor, Yasuo, has been on the island for many years. He's young but wise beyond his years."

Jack nodded. He'd like to meet him, but the longer he sat in this office, the less sure he was he'd be here long enough to meet anyone.

Scott nodded as if he'd spoken. "Now, to the business at hand. You need men?"

Jack's stomach fluttered. The men had been Dean's idea, but Jack didn't want to be responsible for anyone else. Last time he'd been responsible for people, they'd all ended up worse than they'd begun.

Gerald, dead. Elizabeth, the woman Gerald loved, the one who'd ripped his throat out.

Andrew, twisted into some sort of human/Dead Head hybrid. Even almost two months down the road, Jack could still smell the gunpowder in his nose when he closed his eyes at night. Still see that final bullet finding its home.

He swallowed. "Sure. Just about half a dozen. Whoever you can spare. We need eyes more than anything," he said, handing Scott a folded paper from his pocket. "Dean and I made a list of the things we think we'll need."

Scott examined it, eyes narrowed. "Mmm. Some of this we don't have. The night vision glasses, for one."

"I was afraid of that. If we have to go without them, that's fine."

Scott nodded, going back to the list. He angled his missing right arm. "We may be able to scrounge some up. Let me ask around. In the meantime," he said, handing the list back, "take that to Christian. He'll help you with the rest."

The bartender. Of course.

Maybe he could also help Jack with some things that weren't on the list. The bottom of a bottle, for instance.

Jack slid the paper back into his pocket.

Scott shrugged. "What about more weaponry? An archer, perhaps?"

"The only archers I know are Celia and my daughter," Jack said. "And you need them both here."

"That's not entirely true, Mr. Cooke. Your son's girlfriend, what's her name? She has been learning, so Celia tells me."

The bottom of a bottle sounded like a good place to find, all of a sudden. He opened his mouth to say her name but produced a croak instead.

He cleared his throat. "Has she?"

"She's been going out with Celia almost every day." Scott leaned on the desk. "I'm not sure what else Cee is teaching her, but I'm certain it'll be useful in the field."

Jack stood, heartbeat in his temples. His forehead tight, stomach in knots, he shook his head. Cleared his throat again. "She. Uh, she's not coming with us. Thank you, Scott," he said, walking to the door on legs like stilts. "Let me know if you find those glasses."

Scott snapped his fingers. "Jane. Her name is Jane."

Without another word, Jack pulled the door closed behind him.

Jane.

She couldn't have really been in love with him. He was twice her age. Her best friend's father. She couldn't have.

And if she hadn't really loved him, it begged the question of how he'd felt. If he could just let her walk away like that… Were there an award for asshole of the year, he'd take it home for the next twenty and still not make up for it.

He looked up.

In an unfamiliar hallway somewhere deep within the house, he tried to get his bearings.

My god, Jack, get it together. You can't go around berating yourself all day.

Fine, but how do I get out of this hallway?

Someone touched him on the shoulder.

Jumping halfway out of his boots, he spun and drew his knife in one motion.

Melinda leapt back, hands raised. "Whoa, Jack. Just me."

He sheathed the knife and crossed his arms.

"Welcome back," she said, smiling with that lopsided grin he'd loved for so many years. A lifetime ago. "How's it going out there?"

"Fine."

She twisted a toe. "OK. Um. How long will you be back?"

"Don't know."

"Well. It's good to see you," she said, reaching for his shoulder.

In his mind, he flinched away from her hand. Rather than dull the pain of what had happened, rather than forgive her for what she now said had been a long series of errors in judgment, being away had only brought resentment. Bitterness.

But how much of that was her, and how much of it was him?

He let her grip his arm.

She squeezed. "Let me buy you a drink?"

"I've got to go see Christian anyway," he said, following her out of the hallway.

At least she knew her way out of here.

CHAPTER 2

Addy had made it almost back to her house before Dean caught up to her.

His feet hit the ground behind her, not quite a run. "Adelaide," he called.

Butterflies in her stomach, again, she stopped with one foot still in the air. Rather than lower it, she practiced her balance like Yaz had shown her.

As she spun on the ball of one foot like a ballet dancer, Dean stuck a hand out to catch her.

She wobbled a bit, but her balance remained true. She smirked.

He smiled and dropped his hand, looking her up and down.

Blushing, she turned back around. "Hey, Dean. I was just going back to the house. Walk me?" She stuck out an elbow.

Taking it, he fell into step next to her. "Addy, I'm sorry we were gone so long. It's been kind of a wild ride."

"Dangerous?"

"Not exactly. Dead Heads we can handle. But when there was any indication of other people, your dad, well, he got a little squirrely."

She stopped, eyes widening. "*My* dad. Squirrely?"

"I didn't really know him very well before all this, but the guy I met back home and the guy he is now, they seem like two different guys."

Tugging his arm, she started walking again. "I think whatever Tim did to them was pretty bad. I don't know all the details. Jane won't hardly speak to me."

"What? Why not?"

"I don't know. I told you, she doesn't talk to me." She glared at the ground, the truth of her heartbreak over Jane's unexplained silence trapped behind her lips.

Dean steered her around a hole in the road. "Maybe we ought to go see her. See if we can find out what's up. You guys seemed really close."

"We were." Whether she wanted it to or not, a tear slipped down her cheek. She batted at it with a finger.

"If it makes you feel any better, your dad doesn't really talk much, either."

"He's not much of a talker." She grinned. "I think if one were to describe him, he'd be the strong, silent type."

Dean grunted. "True. I mean, he's said a little. I think the thing with Andrew, that really messed him up. And I can't quite put my finger on it, but there's something else. He's playing it pretty close to the vest."

Brow creased, Addy pulled his arm. "Why didn't you guys ever call?"

"Couldn't," he said, stopping.

She shuffled a foot. "Why not?"

"Addy. We're actively spying on IRF. We can't use their cell towers to make calls to report back about how we're spying."

Cheeks flaming, she glanced up at her house. "Wanna come in?"

Dean held out a hand. "After you, milady."

She all but skipped up the walk. The little black cloud of doubt and fear that'd settled around her heart for the last few weeks lifting, she walked on air. Unbolting the locks, she invited him in and closed the door behind him.

When she faced him, he hemmed her between his body and the door.

He locked the bolt with one hand, staring down into her eyes and smiling. The corners of his eyes crinkled. He pressed into her, leaning so close, his scent filled her nose. The campfires and ocean and some kind of unidentifiable sweet fragrance. Like sweat but also a bit like magic must smell.

Insides floating in some sort of pink, cloudy concoction, she twisted her arms around his neck and pulled him in.

Arm around her waist, he lifted her off her feet and kissed her so deeply her toes curled.

Tightening her grip around his neck, she leaned into him and forgot everything. The only thing in existence the two of them.

Tiny claws scrabbled across the kitchen floor and raced through the living room.

A soft lump plowed into her shins.

Dean jumped back, hand going for his gun.

Grinning so hard it hurt, again, she glanced down.

A tiny ball of chocolate fur and ears jumped on her, teeny claws catching on her pants leg.

She bent down and snatched up the golden-eyed furball to nuzzle his cold puppy nose.

"Dean, meet Data. Data, this is Dean."

Releasing his gun, Dean scratched the puppy's ears. "Cute. What is he?"

"Who knows? Little bit lab, lotta bit uncoordinated mess."

"Oh, perfect. They say pets are like their owners."

She kicked him. "Not funny," she said, laughing.

He chuckled. "It's good to see dogs again. The last time I had a dog I think I was six."

"I didn't have many animals when we were out there," she said, making her way to the couch and pulling Dean along with her, "so this is new to me. It's weird. But I like it." She sat the wiggling puppy on the ground.

Dean threw an arm over her shoulders and pulled her close. "I missed you so much," he whispered into her hair.

Shoving the thought of how quickly he'd be leaving aside, she told the fear to take a walk. Instead, she wrapped both arms around him and kissed him again, the way she'd dreamt of doing so many times while he'd been gone. Long, and slow, and gentle.

He cupped her jaw with one hand and ran the other up her back, pressing his body into her until she leaned back into the couch.

What she wouldn't have given to have this, just this, all the time.

* * *

Straddling a stool at the bar, Jack slid the list across to Christian.

The bartender opened it, his shiny bald head nodding. After a glance, he stuffed it into his breast pocket. "A week. Maybe a little more."

Jack cursed. "That long?"

"Takes time to get things like a grenade launcher."

Another of Dean's ideas. Jack wasn't even sure what they'd do with it, but Dean had insisted.

He slumped. "Fine. Get me a shot of vodka then."

Christian lowered his brow. "Yeah?"

"It's been a long six weeks. And this next week will be the longest yet."

From behind him, Melinda's laugh echoed.

He frowned. It was impossible to remember the last time he'd felt so bitter. Angry. Even after Melinda died, he hadn't felt quite so hopeless. Now that she'd returned from the dead, he was alone. More alone than he'd been, even then.

Christian set the shot on the bar in front of him and stood with his arms crossed over his round belly.

Jack downed it.

Burning his throat, it slid down to his stomach and disappeared. He considered. "One more."

The laconic bartender poured.

The second shot going down smoother, Jack's eyeballs jumped once. Back of his tongue tasting of fire, he nodded and sat the glass on the bar, top down.

Christian leaned on the bar, hiding the bottle beneath it. "Anything you want to talk about?"

Jack shook his head. Talking about it would accomplish nothing. Dead friends stayed dead. The only true healing of a broken heart was time. And there just wasn't enough of it.

"Let me know if you change your mind," Christian said, frowning and walking to the end of the bar.

The liquor wormed its way from Jack's stomach to his brain. It'd been so long since he'd had any, he'd forgotten how quick it was to make the leap from one to the other.

"Drinking early, huh, Jack?" Melinda sat on the stool next to him, leaning close.

"Five o'clock somewhere," he answered.

Laughing, his not-so-dead wife raised a finger. "I'll drink to that."

Christian reappeared, and as she ordered her drink, Jack faced the rest of the bar.

In the mid-afternoon, about a dozen people sat around, playing cards, smoking, and knocking back a drink or two. The atmosphere jovial, they bonded in tight little groups over the things people bonded over. Fighting together, drinking together, fucking together.

A smile touched his lips, a sad little affair with the corners of his mouth drawn down. If people could still be like this with each other, even after everything, humans would probably be alright after all.

Melinda leaned a little closer. "Drink with me," she said, handing him a glass.

"What is it?" He tilted the glass, spinning the ice cubes. Pretty little cubes of frozen water. Still his favorite thing about the return of civilization.

"Rum."

"Oh, ew, Melinda. You know I hate rum."

"You have no choice. And all the rum is well aged at this point." She tapped her glass to his. "Drink."

Turning back around, he took a sip.

Yeah, it was awful. But it slipped down his throat easier than the vodka. Lit up his belly. His eyeballs jittered.

Fishing an ice cube out, he sucked on it.

"What have you and Dean found?"

He shook his head, sucking on the cube and staring at a spot on the bar. "I don't think that's something we ought to talk about."

"Why not?" She bumped his shoulder with hers.

He leaned away. He might have been getting drunk, but he knew flirting when he saw it. Especially from her. "I don't think you're to be trusted." He turned his head, making eye contact. "If I had my way about it, you and all your men would be in jail."

Frowning, she stared back. Hazel eyes hard, she squinted. "Lucky for us, you don't always get your way." She glared at her glass. "The virus had a ninety to ninety-five percent mortality rate. Jackson, in the US alone, it killed at least three hundred million people."

"Your point."

She sat her empty glass on the bar and pointed a finger at it.

As Christian refilled it, Jack finished his and got the same.

"Things are different now, Jack."

Different. She was right. So many things were different.

He closed his eyes, covering his forehead with the palm of his hand. Jane's green eyes filled his mind. Her cocky smile. The scent of flowers. The taste of her.

He knocked back the drink in one go, his eyeballs tilting behind his closed lids.

Edges of his brain fuzzy, he opened his eyes just as Melinda finished her own drink. She'd always been able to drink him under the table.

He might want to slow down.

Glancing in the mirror behind the bar, he narrowed his eyes when the door opened and filled the room with light. In the glare, he couldn't see who walked in until the door closed.

His son. And his girl.

His girl, not mine.

He pointed a finger at Christian. More drinks required.

"Dad," Mike said, hand falling on his shoulder.

Plastering a smile to his face, Jack stood to embrace his boy. "Michael," he said, "good to see you, son."

Mike squeezed him, patting him on the back. "You too, Dad. Mom," he said, releasing Jack and hugging Melinda.

Jane stood back, shifting from foot to foot. Her deep red hair hadn't grown back enough to touch her ears yet, but she reached up as though she were tucking a strand behind her ear and glanced at him.

Say something, Jack. Anything.

"Um. Jane," he said. *Smooth.*

"Hi, Jack," she said, ghost of a smile appearing and disappearing faster than a shooting star.

"Do you, um, you want a drink?"

Eyes flitting to Mike, she shook her head. "No, thank you."

Blood rushing to his spinning head, he sat back on the stool and swallowed around a lump in his throat.

Melinda stepped over to give Jane a brief hug. "Celia tells me you're learning the ways of bowhunting."

"I'll never be as good as Addy," Jane answered, crossing her arms, "but Celia's a good teacher."

"Scott mentioned that," Jack said.

"You were talking about me?"

"He brought it up."

"He should keep his handsome nose out of things that aren't his business," she said, green eyes flashing.

Jack smiled. There was that attitude he missed. "He's kind of in charge around here."

Jane cocked a brow and raised a finger. "That so? You tell him—"

"Jane," Mike said, "don't."

She sighed, dropping her hand. "Jack. Melinda. Excuse me. See you later, Michael." Stalking away, she jerked open the door and was gone, leaving the scent of flowers in her wake.

* * *

"Jack, my friend, you don't have to go home—"

Jack finished Christian's sentence for him. "But you can't stay here."

The bartender smiled. "You got it."

Jack pressed his eyelids together. His head swam. It'd been a long time since he'd had this much to drink. "I have no idea what I was drinking about, Christian," he said, leaning over the bar as he stood.

"I hope it leaves you alone for a while, Jack. It'll be there when you wake up." He glanced over Jack's shoulder.

Jack followed his eyes. Uneven as he turned around, like a top losing speed, he stumbled.

Melinda caught him before he fell over. "Hey, Jack. Why don't we get you laid down somewhere."

He jerked his arm away and overbalanced. Sticking his hand out at the last moment, he caught the top of a stool. "You're. No. I can take care of myself, thank you. I remember what I was drinking about now. He was one of my best friends. Look what you made me do." Closing his eyes, he told the world to stop spinning.

Of course, it didn't. It just spun on and on. Without his friends. He ought to be the one not feeling it anymore, not them.

Yet here he was. Feeling every bit of it.

"I'm sorry, Jack. I'll say it as many times as you need."

And here was this woman, tears standing in her eyes, mother of his children. Apologizing for the horrific things she'd done. Been a part of. Been in charge of. For authoring his pain, killing his friends, and breaking his heart.

He hadn't found it in him to think of forgiving her.

As the tears fell from her eyes, the ice in his heart melted. Maybe it was time to consider it.

He wobbled, and she reached out to stabilize him again. One arm curled around his waist, she steadied him with her fingers caressing his hip.

Fire hit his belly again, but not related to alcohol. His brain reminded him there were other ways to obliterate thought.

Frowning, disapproving of his own reaction, he tried to step away.

She gripped him, yanking him closer. "We need to get you out of here, now," she said. She pulled him toward the door.

Ricardo, just a kid really, one who had tried to help him, held it open for them. "Mr. C., will you be OK with the general?"

He opened his mouth to respond, but Melinda beat him to it. "I'm not a general anymore, Ricardo. He'll be fine." She smiled at Jack. "Won't you?"

Grimacing, he took in her lopsided grin. Those brown hazel eyes.

Eighteen years they'd had together. The least he could do was try. "Yeah, Ric, I'll be alright." He let her help him out the door and down the stairs. Overhead, a quarter of the moon made its trek across the sky.

Melinda breathed deep. "Gorgeous night."

"Too warm," Jack said, clutching her hand and pushing it off his waist.

"Walk with me a while," she said. She laced her fingers through his.

He exhaled. Her stepping away a small comfort, his skin began to cool from the inside.

One foot almost went out from under him. Stopping, he closed his eyes. The world spun on. "I think I might have drank too much."

She chuckled. "Wouldn't be the first time."

"I haven't drunk like that since before all this began," he said. "I'm not sure what I was thinking."

She tugged his hand. "You were thinking this island is safe. You were thinking about your friends, the ones who died. You were thinking it's all your fault. You were thinking you miss me."

He peeked at her from beneath heavy lids. "Most of that is true."

She looked at her shoes. "Do you have a house yet?"

"No. I was just going to camp."

"Well," she said, tugging his hand again, "let me take you to mine."

"Melinda," he began.

"You can sleep on the couch, Jackson. Scout's honor," she said, holding up three fingers.

He put one foot in front of the other, stumbled, and grabbed her shoulder. "You weren't a scout."

"Sue me," she said, ducking under his arm. "Let's get you home."

Pulling him down the road, stopping once so he could throw up in someone's bushes, she dragged him to her house.

Leaning on a post, he waited as she unlocked the front door.

She opened it wide and stepped in.

He stood on the porch.

"Well, Jack, are you coming in? Or are you going to sleep on my porch?"

"Melinda," he said, eyes closing again. Wavering, he opened them. "What do you want from me?"

She stepped back out onto the porch and took his hand with her cold fingers. "I want you to forgive me. I want us to move past this. I want to be your wife again."

"I can't promise you those things."

She looked off the porch. "I know. But maybe, we could try?" She kissed him on the cheek.

He glanced at her. Her round eyes. Full mouth. Upturned nose.

Closing his eyes, he tried to take in her scent, but all he could smell was the puke from earlier.

This was a terrible idea.

He turned to leave.

Grabbing him before he got all the way around, she pressed against him and kissed him. Curling her fingers in his hair just how he liked. Wrapping an arm around his waist and pulling him closer. Another thing he'd always liked.

His alcohol-addled mind gurgled that maybe he should make her stop.

Instead, he pulled her closer, twisting a hand in her hair. Followed her when she backed into the house.

Closing the door without stopping to lock it, he yanked at her shirt before he had time to think.

She unfastened his belt, weapons clanking to the floor with his pants.

He tripped, falling in an attempt to remove his boots, and she knelt to help him, shirt hiked up around her neck. Though his vision blurred and trebled, he caught flashes of silver scar tissue in the low light.

He stopped, one hand running over the latticework of gouges and bite marks. Her skin buckled and puckered from more bites than he could count. "Mellie," he whispered, looking in her eyes.

Her lopsided grin turned down on one side. "It's OK, Jack. They're all healed now."

As he ran his hand up the side of her ribcage, her scars bumpy and uneven, his stomach turned. But not from the alcohol. "You did this for us. Killed yourself for us." He cupped her jaw. "They missed your face."

Shrugging, she leaned into his hand. "Lucky, I guess."

Rather than finish the job of taking off his boots and disentangling his ankles from his pants, he twisted a hand in her hair again. Kissed her like it was the last time. The goodbye kiss he never got a chance to give her.

And not that she'd asked what he wanted, but he found it spilling from his mouth before he could stop it. "I just want to forget everything, baby." His voice trembled.

She straddled him. "I can help you with that."

And for a while, his brain got what it wanted.

Obliterated thought.

CHAPTER 3

Dean's snores from the couch woke Addy from a dream. More of a nightmare, really. Her dad had taken Dean back out.

They'd never returned.

Shivering under the covers, she curled into a ball. Hot, humid breath in the hollow space between her knees and chest brought her back down from the ledge. Slowed her heart rate.

They were here right now. Right now was all they had. Yasuo had taught her that. Reminded her daily.

Right, Yaz. Was the sun up?

She peeked. Pink light streamed in the windows.

Sighing, she threw back the covers and stumbled to the kitchen. Coffee now. Yaz could wait.

Little feet hit the floor after hers, tiny claws scrambling to keep up with her.

"Morning, Data. Sleep well?"

He yipped and tripped over his food bowl.

Laughing aloud, she poured some food in and set him on his feet. "OK, genius. Coffee now," she said, filling the press and lighting the fire under the kettle.

Elizabeth, after she'd recovered some, had shown her how to use the press. Though they didn't see each other often, and Elizabeth wasn't exactly the wordiest person in all of existence, they talked about her dad some. Seeing him from Liz's perspective put a whole new twist on things. Even after everything that'd happened over the last few months, Addy had come to find it difficult to accept her dad was a real human being with real human problems. He'd always seemed like some kind of superhero.

She carried the puppy into the yard and stared at the sunrise as he did his thing. The rising star stamped bright silhouettes of itself against the backs of her eyes, and she considered whether or not parents being humans was acceptable.

Data scratched to be let back in. She followed onto the porch and opened the back door.

It hit someone.

"Shit, Dean, I'm sorry," she said, easing through the half-open door.

Hand over his face, he gave her a smile from behind it. "Should've expected that."

The kettle whistled.

Brushing his uninjured cheek with her lips, she turned off the stove and poured the water. "You sleep OK on the couch?"

"Yeah. You have a knack for finding comfortable furniture." He cracked his back in three places, wincing.

"Sorry about that," she said, frowning at the coffee press. Grounds floated in the water, doing their dance.

He slid an arm around her waist. "Sorry about what?"

Her stomach fluttered. The sweet scent of magic overpowered the bitter coffee.

Facing him, she smiled. "Making you sleep on the couch."

"Adelaide," he said, leaning back, "you're calling the shots here. You've got nothing to apologize for."

She smiled wider. "You can stay on my couch as long as you're here."

Kissing the palm of her hand before letting her go, he sat at the table. "I don't know how long that'll be. I think your dad wants to get going as fast as we can."

"Do you have any idea why? What's going on with him?" She sat their coffees on the table and took the seat across from him.

"Honey, I don't know," he said. "Think I slowed him down a bit, though." Sipping, he grinned with one corner of his mouth, a twinkle in his eyes.

Someone getting the best of her dad? Maybe he was human after all.

She grinned. "What did you do?"

"Talked him into asking for a grenade launcher."

She spat coffee on the table, slopping some of it onto her hand. "Ah shit, that burns."

"Here, come here," Dean said, standing and holding out his hand.

Cheeks flushing, she gave him her burned hand and let him pull her to the sink.

Running it under cold water, he massaged her fingers with his thumb. "What do you got going on today?" The corners of his eyes crinkled.

The cool water flowed over her skin, tingling her nerve endings.

Closing her eyes, she exhaled a contented sigh.

Plans.

What plans?

Her eyes popped open. "Yasuo." She turned the water off. "I've gotta go, Dean."

"Yeah. I've got some things to do, too." He nodded with a frown.

She shifted from foot to foot. Considering his lies about IRF, she wanted him to tell her everything, even the mundane. But she found it impossible to ask him for honesty. He had to volunteer it.

After a few seconds of silence, she tugged her hand loose. "Well," she said, twisting a toe. "Let me know when you're free."

* * *

Cracking his eyelids open, Jack squinted against the pink light of sunrise.

Rays of light jabbed into his brain, screaming against the inside of his skull.

Holding his head, he sat up. The covers fell from his chest, pooling around his hips.

His bare hips.

Oh, crap.

Stomach in free fall, he glanced over.

Melinda slept, hair splayed on the pillow, hand underneath it. The smallest bit of a smile on her cherry red lips.

Jesus, Jack. What more could you possibly fuck up?

Sliding out of the bed, displacing as little area as possible, he snagged his shirt from the bedroom floor and stood, searching for the rest of his clothes. The inside of his head pounded, his sinuses plugged.

Water. Water would be good.

Instead, he crept into the living room to seek out the rest of his clothes. Tiptoeing around the room, he found his pants still twisted around his boots, weapons spread in a semicircle around it all.

Grimacing, a stone settling into his gut, he sat and attempted to untwist his pants. His gun clunked against the floor.

He froze, wide eyes searching the bedroom door.

Don't wake up, don't wake up, don't wake up.

No movement from the bedroom.

Removing the belt, he rested the weapons on the floor. Untangling the pants easier without all the extra weight, he slid them and his boots on. He stepped to the front door, stringing weapons back into their places.

"Last time I drink, I swear," he mumbled, holding the loose belt closed and pulling the door open. They'd never locked it.

On the other side, Ricardo stood on the porch, hand raised to knock. He goggled.

Shit.

"Uh, Mr. C.," Ric stammered. "Morning. Um."

Jack tried on the most winning smile he could find. "Hey, Ric. Morning."

"Good morning, Ricardo," Melinda said.

Jack glanced over his shoulder.

She stood in the door to the bedroom, holding a single sheet over her otherwise bare breasts. Smirking.

I think I might puke.

Turning back to Ricardo, watching the boy's eyes flit from him to Melinda and back again, his stomach lurched.

No really. I'm going to be sick.

"Jack," she said, stepping into the living room. "Leaving?"

Fastening his belt, he stood as tall as he could. "I have to go see Scott about our supplies. If you'll excuse me, Melinda," he said, stepping onto the porch. "Ric." He nodded to the boy.

A smile turned up one corner of Ric's mouth. "Be seeing you, Mr. C."

Grimacing, he took one stair at a time as he stepped into the already warm sun.

Behind him, Ricardo stepped into the house. "Mrs. C.," he said, closing the door.

Stopping, Jack leaned over and held onto his knee. He closed his eyes and inhaled the sour, fishy odor of the sound.

Swallowing his gorge back once, twice, three times, the urge to throw up passed.

The slick feeling in his stomach remained. This was going to be all over the island before morning was over.

"Well, Jack," he said, straightening, "nothing for it, now."

* * *

Jack raised a fist to knock. Lowered it. Raised it.

Knocked on the door.

Paul opened it. His soft white hair blew in the breeze. "Friend Jack," he said, swinging the door wide, "come right on in."

"Thanks, Paul," Jack said, dipping his head and smiling.

"Join me for some tea," Paul said, leading him to the kitchen. "I got the kettle on already."

Tea sounded like just the thing for his head.

Paul sat, and Jack followed suit. Wooden chair creaking under him, he smiled again. "I hear some thanks are in order."

Paul shook his head. "What are you talking about?"

"I heard what you did for me. On the beach."

"Oh, that. Wasn't nothing. Don't think on it."

He grasped Paul's hand. "Performing CPR, saving my life when I almost drowned. That's not nothing."

Paul stood and busied himself with making tea, getting out a cup for Jack. He spoke with his back turned. "Wasn't nothing you wouldn't do for me."

Jack nodded. "True. Still. While I was here, I wanted to come say thank you. I owe you one."

Paul leaned on the back of an empty chair and narrowed his bright blue eyes. "Owe me one, huh?"

"You're damn right I do."

As the fire heated the kettle, the nothing scent of hot water floated through the room. Soft beams of sun falling through the window, kettle ticking, the kitchen had a homey feel Jack hadn't seen in years.

For no particular reason, he thought of his own dad. A man he hadn't considered for so long it was amazing he still remembered his face. Of course, his dad had listened to oldies like Black Sabbath and Led Zeppelin and Pink Floyd. While smoking weed. But, he'd also been a tea man.

"I want to come with you, friend Jack."

Jack shook his head. "No. No way. No."

Paul sat, even as the kettle began to whistle. "I want to come with you," he repeated.

The kettle's whistle rose to a shriek.

Hairs on his neck raising at the loud noise, Jack stared. Steam poured from the hole in the spout, little wisps escaping from around the lid, and it vibrated with bubbling, boiling water.

The bubbling.

So like a fresh Dead Head.

Almost like Andrew had sounded. Just before Jack put a bullet in his brain.

"Paul, are you gonna get that?"

"Let me come with you," Paul answered, immobile.

The kettle bubbled and shrieked.

Jack sighed. "Fine, fine. Come with us." Just please take the kettle off.

Smiling, Paul stood and removed the kettle from the heat. He dropped loose leaf tea into a couple of strainers and set a cup in front of Jack. The hot water sucked color from the tea leaves. Brown strings of tea, arms made of swirling heat, oozed from the strainer and into the water.

"Sorry there's no sugar," Paul said. "Not something I really need at my age. Can't afford to become diabetic. Not these days."

Nodding, Jack shrugged. "I got so used to not having it. It's not even a thing anymore."

"You don't really owe me," Paul said. "You got us out of the prison. We woulda died there, weren't for you."

Jack shook his head. "I don't know. I think my daughter had more to do with that than me."

"She's a good woman, your daughter."

Pride, and a healthy dose of fear, gripped him. Someone people could look up to, she also was all but grown. "That's my little girl." The water in his cup homogeneous now, he removed the tea strainer and sipped. It slid down his throat with heat that soothed rather than burned.

"Good tea."

"Thanks, friend Jack. I do like good tea."

Jack sat the cup down. "Look. I don't want you to come out there. You're, well, you're—"

"I was younger than you are now when all this started. I might be old, but I'm still quick enough to pick up what you're laying down."

"That's not, well, that's not exactly what I was going to say."

Paul laughed. "You kids and your attitudes. You think you can just lie right to my face and I won't notice?"

Jack flushed, red creeping into his cheeks. He took a gulp of tea. The thought of his own father flashed through his mind again. If he'd had to work less when Jack was a teen, maybe Addy and Michael wouldn't exist. But still, it might've been nice to have seen more of him before he had his own family to work for.

"No. That's not what I think. I'm sorry. I didn't mean it."

He nodded. "Accepted."

"I just," Jack paused, forming his mouth around the right words. "I don't want to be responsible for you getting hurt out there."

Throwing back his head, Paul laughed until his face turned an alarming shade of purple.

Unable to do otherwise, Jack laughed with him.

Sucking in a breath, the laughter tapering down, Paul wiped his eyes. "Son, ain't no one but me been responsible for me in more than forty years. Don't reckon I'm going to start looking for someone else to hang that responsibility on now."

Still grinning, Jack nodded. "Alright, Paul. If that's the way you want it. You're on the team."

CHAPTER 4

Addy steered her canoe at the floating platform next to the swamp. The spot where she'd first stepped foot on Harkers. After a long morning of meditation with Yaz out by the lighthouse, it seemed the best way to re-greet the island. Stepping out with caution, she gazed across the marsh. Though the corner of her mouth lifted, her stomach rolled thinking of dragging Dean across the wooden walk and into the hospital.

The first time she'd walked this way, her mom was dead and Jane was her best friend. Now, she and Jane hardly spoke and her mom was alive. Changed, but alive. Addy still couldn't untangle her feelings about that one.

A loose board popped up beneath her feet. She fell to her knees on the wooden walk, gripping the side. The scratchy, weathered wood repaid her for her trouble with a splinter.

"Ah, hell," she said, sitting on the walk. She sucked on her palm, working the splinter, and stared at the trees.

Where she caught movement.

Forgetting the splinter, she stood and unsheathed her machete. She crept along the boards, careful to put one foot in front of the other, heel to toe, outside to inside, silent.

Entering the canopy of trees, she sniffed. Listened.

On that long-ago night when she'd arrived, Oren had told her they rarely got 'Heads on the island. That they usually got so waterlogged they just washed ashore with no feet. No hands. Sometimes, no legs. Even without heads. The sound made the best natural barrier she'd ever seen.

The only scent on the air that of the brackish marsh, she caught no odor of decay. Still, it paid to be cautious.

Hiding behind a tree, she waited.

The footsteps—purposeful, human steps—approached the other side of the tree.

Machete raised, she stepped from behind it.

"*Jesús Cristo*, Adelaide," Mike said, throwing both hands in the air. "Don't jump out at me like that."

Grinning, she sheathed the blade. It'd been too long since she'd seen the jerk. "Hi, Mike. What're you doing out here?"

"Oh, you know. Just walking." He shrugged, plunging his hands deep in his pockets. "Walk with me?"

"Sure," she said. "Which way we going?"

He shrugged again. "That way?"

"You didn't point. Which way?"

"Does it matter?" He started walking.

She fell into step next to him, her stomach doing a dance again. More and more, lately, he'd been almost surly like this. Such a shift from his usual jovial nature, she just about didn't recognize him on the few occasions they'd run into each other. "You got a sucker for your sister?"

"Just root beer."

She gagged. The worst flavor. But, giving out candy had always made him feel better. Supposedly it was to make others feel better, though she'd figured him out long ago. "I'll take it."

Shrugging again, he fished one out of his black pouch and handed it to her.

Brushing sand from it, she unwrapped it and stuck it in her mouth.

Just as terrible as ever.

"Oh, hey, check it out," she said, tucking the paper in her pocket, "got my pouch back this morning." She wiggled the black pouch, identical to his, where she'd attached it to her belt.

"From where?"

She pointed with the sucker. "Out by the lighthouse where I lost it. Yaz found it."

He frowned. "Awesome."

She stopped, gripping his shoulder. With Jane avoiding her, she couldn't take it anymore from Mike. "Michael. You've been weird lately. Are you alright?"

Staring left of her, he shrugged. Again. "I guess."

"Is everything alright with Jane?"

He laughed. "Jane? Never better. Never better, Addy. Jane's great."

"I mean, you guys are OK, right?"

He started walking again, pulling out his own sucker.

So. He wasn't completely different. Just a little sideways. Maybe it was Mom.

"Yeah, Addy. We're fine. Everything's fine. Listen," he said, stopping. "There's something. Can we come over later?"

"Sure thing, Mike. Just say when."

He nodded. "Right. OK. After sunset. I, we, need some advice. Ideas."

The hackles on her neck rose. The last time he'd asked her for advice, she was six. "Yeah. OK. No problem."

"Thanks, Addy. Thanks," he said, popping the sucker back in his mouth. "I'll see you then."

Wandering off through the trees, he rounded a bend in the path and was gone, leaving Addy alone in the shadows.

* * *

Addy walked past the Big House. Someone called her name.

"Wait up, honey," Mom said, catching up.

Addy sighed. Tried on a smile. "Hi, Mom."

"Hey, baby," Melinda said, pulling her into a hug.

A warm, Mom hug. No matter what had happened, she always smelled like Mom. Felt like Mom. And her hugs were always warm.

"Where are you headed?"

Addy shook her head. "Just getting back from seeing Yaz. Thought I might shower then head to work."

"Oh?" Mom fell into step next to her. "Where are you working these days, when you're not out running about for Scott?"

"I quit that job, Mom."

"Did you? Good for you. I know you hated it."

Addy chuckled without humor. "That's one word for it." Tucking a hair behind her ear, she frowned. "These days, I've been working over in the nursery, learning to change diapers and whatnot."

"Really?" Mom smiled, touching her on the shoulder. "Are you thinking of having one of your own?"

"Mom."

"Sorry. You don't like me asking. I forget. Just want to know when I can expect to be a grandma, is all."

Addy's stomach lurched, lip lifting. Much as she might love her Mom, having her near babies still sent an icy spike through her. Mom's experiments with the vaccine were aimed at babies, in large part, and for all her protestations, Addy wasn't sure she'd given up on her research.

"I don't want to talk about it."

Melinda blew a breath out her nose. "On a related note, how are things with Dean?"

Blood rushed into Addy's cheeks. She crossed her arms. "Good. They're good. He's. He's good."

"I'm glad. He seems like a nice guy. Honey," she said, stopping Addy with a hand on her arm, "things aren't like they used to be. With dating and everything."

"I don't know how things used to be, Mom."

"Right. What I mean is, I know he's been out with your dad, and they don't really get in as much as we'd like." She bit her lip, staring into the distance.

"Mom?"

Brushing a hair from her face, Melinda turned.

"What's going on with you and Dad? Are you, I don't know, are you working things out?"

A sunny smile popped up on Mom's face. "I think we just might, kiddo. I think we might."

Nodding, Addy started walking again. "I just want you both to be happy."

"I want that too, sweetheart."

"So," Addy said, "what is it you're doing for work these days?"

"Oh, I joined the fishing team."

"Fishing? Cool. I never learned to do that well enough."

"I'll teach you. It's easy."

Addy smiled, though her heart ached. "That sounds fun. The last time we did anything like that I think I was ten."

Melinda laughed. "You mean when I taught you to catch rabbits bare-handed?"

"More like when you taught me to fall face-first on the ground."

"Come on, you caught some hair."

Addy burst into laughter, covering the guffaws behind her cupped hand.

After a moment of confused silence, Mom joined her. "Pun not intended," she said, chuckling. She shook her head. "Hey, listen. There's a place I want to go, it's not far from here. Want to come with me?"

Addy's stomach flipped. Yes. But no. "Where?"

"Just a museum down the coast. Saturday?"

She cocked a finger, winking and clicking her tongue. "You got it."

Mom winked back and watched her, arms crossed, as she walked up the sidewalk and into the house.

CHAPTER 5

After spending hours gathering supplies, Jack found himself in front of Scott's study door again as the afternoon took to smelling like evening.

"Mr. Cooke, please," Scott said, red rings around his eyes.

"Scott," Jack said, entering the study, "look like you could use some rest."

"There's no rest for the wicked. You know that."

Jack nodded, sitting in front of the fire. Though summer baked the ground outside, the depths of the Big House always seemed chilly. The fire warmed the tip of his nose, his knees, his shins. The headache had disappeared throughout the day, till it was no more than a dull spot of red beside his temple. Small blessings.

"What can I help you with this evening?" Scott took the other wing-backed chair next to the fire, propping his socked feet on the hearth. One sock had a hole in the toe.

"Christian says it'll be a while before the supplies are ready," Jack said.

"Mm. Yes. The grenade launcher."

"Dean's idea."

"Indeed."

Jack cleared his throat. "Yes. Anyway. Paul has expressed an interest in joining the team."

"The old man from the prison?" Scott sat up, forearm across his knees.

Nodding, Jack agreed. "He's insistent."

"If you approve, I have no choice," Scott said. "It's your team."

The slick feeling he'd become accustomed to settled in his stomach. "Sure, but the final decision is yours."

"I have some others who have expressed interest while you've been away. Would you meet with them?"

Sighing, Jack nodded. They needed more men, like it or not. He leaned back, watching the fire. One of the logs split, squealing as it was consumed. Sparks rose into the chimney, spiraling up and away. "Something else."

Silence from Scott.

"It might be nice for me to have a place to lay my head when I'm here. Nothing big. Just four walls and a bed."

Scott cleared his throat. "Oh. I thought you had decided to stay with your wife."

Heart knocking in his chest, threatening to break his ribs, he sat up again and faced Scott. "What makes you say that?" Careful to keep his voice mellow.

Scott cleared his throat. "Everyone thought so. It didn't take long this morning for that intelligence to reach my ears." He crossed one leg over the other. "This island isn't very big. People like to talk."

Yes the fuck they did.

Not like it mattered what Jane thought, but what would Jane think?

Shit, what would the kids think?

He sat back, sinking into the cushion of the chair. One hand scratched under his beard in need of a trim. Let the rumor mill do its thing. He couldn't control it. "My own house is fine, Scott."

"Then I have just the place for you," Scott said. He gave Jack one brisk nod and made his way to the desk. "I have the key here, and the one for the outer fence."

"It has a fence? I haven't seen many homes with fences on this island."

"Oh yes, Mr. Cooke. Better than lead people, I know people. And I know," he said, producing a tinkling key chain from the desk drawer, "you enjoy fences. Locks." He shook the keys, picking three off the ring and holding them out. "Security."

One corner of his mouth turning up, Jack took the three keys and the extra key ring Scott offered. Sliding the keys onto the ring, he bobbed his head. "I do like fences, you're right about that."

Another brisk nod. "You're all the way on the west end of the island. Here, let me show you," he said, pulling a map from the top drawer. "Here's you." He pointed at a spot on the map. "Your daughter is here," he said, a finger hovering over another spot, "your son and his girlfriend are here," he said, just a block from Adelaide, "and you know where your wife is."

Jack pointed her house out on the map. Cleared his throat. "She's not my wife, Scott. That was a long time ago."

Scott's grey-blue eyes skipped from the map to Jack and back again. He folded it. "Yes. Well. That sounds like something for the two of you to work out."

Jack nodded. It did, indeed.

* * *

Closing the door to the Big House, Jack stared into the road.

So, the island had been talking about him. He'd been here less than forty-eight hours and already he'd become the subject of rumor and speculation.

Not for the first time, he wondered if rebuilding society was really the right thing to do. Or if he wanted to be a part of that.

Facing the sunset, he began the trek across the island, missing his little electric ATV from the village in Arizona. The last time he'd seen it was when he'd pulled up to Ger's house, checking in on some Dead Heads they'd found.

They'd been loaded into a truck from there, along with Jane, and everything had changed.

Ah hey, you haven't hardly thought of Jane all day, Jack. Remember her? How you took advantage of a young girl? Thought she loved you? Ha. What a joke. She couldn't love you. Not someone like her. Too young, too pretty, too alive.

The phone in his pocket buzzed.

He leapt ten feet in the air if it was a day. Even with the ringer off, the buzzing of the phone sounded too much like a 'Head.

Sliding his hand in his pocket, he pressed the button on the side of the phone to silence the buzzing. Pulling the phone, he flipped it open. Ancient thing.

"Cooke," he answered.

"Hey, Dad," Addy said, voice crackling. "Dean and I wondered if you wanted to come by for dinner?"

"Hi, little girl. I don't know, I—"

"Just while you're here. You know. Come and see me."

He smiled. "You got it."

"Great, see you soon." Her smile came through the phone.

He flipped it closed, staring at the slick little plastic thing warm in his hand. A thing he thought he'd never see again. Their time away from technology had been long. Hell, he'd had almost as much time without it as he'd had with it.

When he knocked on Addy's door, Dean answered, flushing as he smiled. "Sir," he said, sticking his hand out.

Jack shook his head. "We don't need to stand on ceremony, Dean, just because you're seeing my daughter. I already knew about you two," he said, taking Dean's hand. He leaned close and lowered his voice. "If I didn't approve, you wouldn't have made it back to the island."

Dean cleared his throat, leaning back. "I don't know if I should be happy about that or not." He smiled with one side of his mouth.

Laughing, Jack dropped his hand. "I'm just giving you shit, Dean. Besides, you should probably be more afraid of my daughter than me."

Addy walked in from the kitchen, frowning. "Dad. Are you giving Dean a hard time?"

"Yes."

She chuckled, motioning to the couch. "Have a seat. I'm just getting things ready. Hope fish sounds good." Even as she said it, the scent of frying fish wafted into the living room.

"Of course it does. We're on the ocean." His mouth watered. "Hot food, cooked indoors? You spoil me, baby girl," he said, sitting.

She smiled, perching on the arm of the couch. "Dean, get him a drink."

"Coming up."

She watched him leave, her smile fading. "Dad," she said, sitting next to him, "what do you think?"

"About?"

"Dean."

"Honey," he said.

She held a hand out. "Be honest. Please."

He patted her knee. "I would say he's probably the second-best man I know. One of the best I've ever known."

Her eyes widened. "Who's the first?"

"Your brother."

"Ha. Good one." She wrinkled her lip and brow.

He laughed. "Sibling rivalry aside, Adelaide, your brother is a good man."

"Only because you raised him," she said, standing. "I gotta finish the fish." Without giving him a chance to argue, she disappeared into the kitchen.

He rested one foot on the coffee table. His other pants leg jerked.

Jumping, heart racing, he glanced down.

A little brown puppy tugged on the cuff of his pants, growling.

He chuckled, reaching down to scratch the pup behind his ears. "Hey, little guy."

The puppy sat and started scratching as Jack hit a ticklish spot.

Grinning, he sat back and took the cold and clear water Dean had returned with. The couch faced the west windows, and he considered the sunset as he sipped. Faded orange and pink, the clear horizon mellowed its colors.

Dean sat on the arm of the couch, arms crossed.

They watched in silence as the last arc of the sun sliced beneath the horizon. Dean did well at silence. Not a bad thing.

Jack took a swallow of the cool water. No ice. "I've gotten a house from Scott," he said.

"That so."

"It's on the west end."

"Good. A house is a good thing to have."

"What about you, Dean?"

He started, arms uncrossing, and lost his balance on the couch arm. Putting a hand down, he stood. Shuffled a foot.

Jack locked the smile behind his lips. Face neutral, he waited for Dean to speak.

"Well. I, um. It's— We aren't going to be here for long, you know?"

"Yes and no. Why?" *Like I don't know, Dean.*

Dean pointed. "Well, sir, you're, um. You're sitting on my bed."

And the details Jack had failed to take in popped out. The pillow scrunched into the arm. The blanket folded over the back. Dean's book on the coffee table, open and flat on the spine.

He shook his head, allowing the smile to show itself. "It's alright. Really."

"I'm sleeping on the couch. I swear to god, Jack."

"Dean. I don't expect to have this conversation again. It's. Fine."

Dean opened his mouth again, but before he got a word out, Addy shouted from the kitchen. "Shit. Dean!"

Without a word, he dashed away.

Smiling, Jack finished his water. Some things never changed. No matter the circumstances, getting approval from a girl's father would always be nerve-racking. Terrifying, even.

Something he'd never gotten from Melinda's father.

And Jane. Well. That was different altogether, wasn't it?

Knock.

Pause.

Knock-knock.

Standing to answer the door, head swirling, he didn't stop to consider whose knock it was until he opened the door.

Michael.

His breath caught in his throat.

And Jane.

She murmured under her breath, but Mike didn't notice, and Jack couldn't hear what she'd said.

Addy called from the kitchen. "Ah hell, is that Michael?"

He stepped through the door. "Yeah, we're here."

"OK, come in, alright?"

Jane stayed on the porch, arms crossed and gripping her elbows.

Heartbeat like a hummingbird in his throat, Jack stepped back and held the door wide.

She glanced up, making eye contact.

His heart might have stopped. His breath did. For a moment, the only part of him that existed in the world looked back into her green eyes. Green flecked with gold.

Mike walked into the kitchen, speaking over his shoulder. "Jane, are you gonna stand on the porch or come in?"

"Come in, Jane," Jack said, paralysis breaking. He pulled the door as wide as it would open and stood behind it. Hid behind it.

Dipping her head, she stepped through the doorway.

He closed it behind her.

Think of something else to say now, Jack. Anything else to say except "Hi."

Clearing his throat, he locked the door and leaned against it. "How are you?"

She covered her nostrils with a slender finger. "Been better. You?"

"Rough day."

"I heard."

Motherfucker. "Yeah. Well. I'm getting a team together. We'll be gone soon."

She nodded. "I thought you might. Who's going with you?"

"A handful of people from the island. Scott's working on it."

"Dean's not going back out?"

"He doesn't know that yet. I want him to stay here with Addy."

Jane smiled. It wasn't so bright as the sun, but it did hold the same understated silver of the full moon. "She'll like that. But she'll be worried about you."

"I know," Jack said, smiling back, all but lost in the tiny wrinkles at the corners of her eyes. "But that's the way it's gotta be."

"The way it's gotta be," she said, copying him, "yeah. Sometimes things are that way." Eyes lowered, she covered her nostrils again. Her skin turned a delicate shade of green. She swayed.

"Jane," he said, eyes wide, reaching for her without thinking, "are you alright?"

Nodding, eyes closed, she let him lead her to the couch and perched on the edge.

As he opened his mouth to ask again if she was alright, Addy, Mike, and Dean walked in from the kitchen.

"Food's ready, guys," Addy said.

Jane, eyes still closed, lips pressed together, nodded.

Stomach in knots, Jack teetered between standing over her or sitting next to her.

Mike sat on the couch next to her, rubbing her back. "Are you alright?"

"Fine, Michael."

Mike nodded and glanced up. "Uh, listen. I'm glad you're here, Dad. Before we eat, I need to talk to you. You and Dean, too, Addy," he said, looking over his shoulder at his sister.

Jane opened her eyes and flashed them at Jack. She frowned, a fine line between her brows, and leaned toward Mike. "I think maybe we should wait."

Jack dropped his eyes. Couldn't look at her anymore.

This was so stupid. Why hadn't he just told her? Weeks and weeks ago. It was her he wanted, not Melinda. Of course, she could've asked him. They were adults after all.

The blood rushed up his neck. His palms started to sweat. He swallowed. Damn shame he'd drunk all the water.

Michael spoke. "No, I think now is a good time. Dad can help us, too. Listen guys," Mike said, standing, "we have a slight dilemma. We need your help keeping something from Mom. Not forever, obviously, but we need a plan."

Addy frowned. "Sure, Mike. Whatever you need. What's up?"

Jack's stomach sank. A stone settled that might never find its way out. Her wan complexion. The way she covered her nose to block the strong scent of fish wafting from the kitchen. The ringing in his ears began before Mike could even utter the words, could pound the final nail in the coffin.

"Jane's pregnant."

As Addy jumped up, exclaiming and hugging her brother and then Jane, Dean smiled and shook Mike's hand.

"Congratulations, Mike," Dean said.

Mike shook his head. "Congratulate Jane."

She stood, glancing at Jack again, and hugged a bouncing Addy.

Jack couldn't hear the form of the words. The ringing in his ears drowned them out. Heart pounding in his throat, he took a moment to consider what his reaction was supposed to be.

Hug the boy.

He did.

Alright, Jack. What next?

Oh, right. Congratulate the mother.

He'd lost her. She no longer stood in front of the couch.

As Addy, Mike, and Dean chattered, he searched the room.

Jane stood in front of the windows, cupping her elbows again, her back to them.

Either talk to her or leave. Those are your choices.

"Jane," he said, stepping across to her. The ringing in his ears subsided, and he couldn't feel his heartbeat anymore. He took a deep breath and touched her on the shoulder.

Spinning a slow circle, she met his eyes.

"I'm happy for you. I know it's what you wanted."

She covered her nostrils again. "Jack." She paused. "I…I think I'm going to be sick," she said, covering her mouth. Voice muffled by her hand, wide, wet eyes peeking out from above it, she excused herself and dashed to the bathroom.

Swallowing his pride and the last vestiges of hope he'd held for getting her back, he sat and helped Addy, Mike, and Dean plan against Melinda's interference.

CHAPTER 6

*K*nock.

Pause.

Knock-knock.

Addy, mostly clothed yet asleep on the couch and pressed up against Dean, awoke with a start. As she slid backward into the floor, he curled his arm around her and stopped her descent.

She smiled. "Thanks," she said, burying her face in his shoulder.

"Is that Mike?"

She nodded into his chest. "Yeah. I'll just..." She rolled, falling off the couch anyway. "Right. Hang on, Mike," she called. At least she'd avoided hitting the coffee table.

Mike spoke as the door opened. "He's gone."

Rubbing her eyes, Addy let him in. "What do you mean?"

"Dad. He left. He's gone."

Dean, retrieving weapons from where they'd been unceremoniously dumped in the floor, stopped. "Dammit."

Addy frowned, pushing hair out of her face. "Alright. Have a seat, Mike. I'll make some coffee."

Little claws scrabbled in from the kitchen. Data launched himself at Mike, taking a pant leg in his tiny teeth.

Mike grinned. "I'll take the little guy out," he said, scooping the puppy from the floor. "Maybe you want to put those away. Or on," he said, nodding at the couch.

Forming her lips around the question, Addy followed his eyes.

Her pants lay across the back of the couch.

Her cheeks had probably not turned quite this shade of maroon for months.

Data walked, coffee poured, Addy sat down with Dean and her brother at the kitchen table.

"So," she said, "Dad left. Without so much as saying goodbye."

"I can't believe he would do this," Mike said.

Dean shrugged. "It's weird he didn't say goodbye to you guys. But"—he glanced at Addy—"we kind of expected him to leave early."

Addy winced. It wasn't anything they hadn't talked about. But the hurt on Mike's face still socked her in the gut.

Mike goggled at them both. "What? Why?"

Mike's wounded face turned Addy's sympathy meter up to eleven. The back of her throat hurt.

"He's not been too good with people since the whole thing at the prison," Dean said. "I knew he was going to try and go alone." He grimaced, swallowing a mouthful of coffee.

Addy squeezed Dean's hand. "You've got to go after him."

Mike stood, bumping the table, and leaned on the kitchen counter, back to them both. "This is just all so dumb. I don't get it." He crossed his arms. "We find out, after all these years, Mom is alive. But here we are months later, and we're still not a family like we used to be, and Jane—" He broke off, staring out the window.

Stomach taking an unexpected twist, Addy frowned. His drooping shoulders were out of place. She couldn't process the negativity baking off him. She joined him at the counter. "Jane what?"

He grinned. Or tried to. "I don't know. Pregnancy hormones, I guess."

"Is she OK, Mike?"

"She's fine. She's out with Celia right now."

Dean stood. "I heard she goes out with her a lot."

Mike chuckled. "She's been learning all kinds of stuff. She rivals you with a bow, Addy," he said, nodding at her. "Also, recently, she's been bringing home stuff she 'picked up' out there to cook for me. It's, um"—he paused, face breaking into a wide smile—"different."

Addy laughed aloud, trying to picture Jane cooking.

"Yeah. Well. She's trying," Mike said, laughing.

"Hey Mike, about Mom," Addy said, once she'd let the image of Jane cooking go, "she's optimistic about Dad." She shrugged. "I guess, give them some time?"

"Did he tell her he was leaving?"

"I don't know. Let's," Addy said, pausing. What? Go see her? Much as she wanted to be that twelve-year-old girl again, with the perfect mother, she wasn't. Would never be.

Dad wasn't the only one with human flaws, Addy had found. Mom had them, too, and in spades.

"Adelaide," Mike said, "let's what?"

She shook her head. "We're going out in a couple days. I'll talk to her then."

Mike sat, taking a sip of coffee. "Sounds fun. Hey, you got any sugar for this?"

Setting the sugar jar on the table, she joined him.

"Spoon?"

"Good lord Michael, so needy," she said, leaning over and pulling a drawer out. With her arm fully extended, she rocked to two legs on the chair.

Dean inhaled, a sharp breath drawn through his nose.

"I'm fine," she said, not looking. Wobbling a bit, she pulled out a spoon, shut the drawer, and clunked back onto all four legs. "See?"

He grinned. "Sometimes, baby, you got it. Sometimes, not so much."

"I always got it."

He shook his head, taking a sip of his own coffee.

As Michael stirred the sugar in his coffee, they sat, each considering their own steaming cup. Mike broke the silence first. "So, you said you're going after Dad, Dean?"

"Yeah, man, I am," he said, glancing at Addy.

Her heart twisted. Dad couldn't be left out there alone, not after what Dean had said about his behavior. But having Dean here had been nice. And too brief. She sighed. "Do you know where he went?"

"Oh," Mike said, jumping, "he left a map."

"He thinks I won't follow him if someone else can," Dean said.

Addy smirked. "You got to know him better than you think."

"I'll get out there as soon as we're ready," he said, swallowing the last of his coffee and standing.

"How long?"

"Well. I guess we don't *need* the grenade launcher. Two days, probably." He kissed her on the forehead. "I've got to go see Scott. Check in with IRF. Mike, how are the towers coming?"

As Mike and Dean talked about the towers and the report Dean would make to IRF, mostly to curb any suspicions they might have about him, she frowned out the window. Her coffee, lukewarm now, left a sour aftertaste.

The puppy snored under her chair.

* * *

Dean got the supplies together faster than he thought, and a day later, he stood in Addy's bedroom doorway, speaking into the phone in hushed tones.

"Mm-hmm. Yeah, no, I understand. Round everybody up. I'll be there soon."

She pretended to sleep. Maybe if he thought she was asleep, he'd stay.

The side of the bed depressed. "Adelaide," he said, whispering in her ear.

"Adelaide's not awake right now. Please wait," she said, rolling her face into the pillow.

He massaged her neck. "It's time."

She shook her head.

"Let's have coffee first," he said, patting her arm. "Come on."

Sitting at the kitchen table with him, steaming cup of black ambrosia in front of her, she sighed. "I don't know whether to ask you to stay or force you to leave."

"If you want me to stay, I'll stay."

Her eyes prickled. "No. He trusts you. He can't be—" She swallowed, blinking a tear. "He can't be out there alone."

He reached for her hand.

Curling her fingers, she slid it away.

"Sweetheart. Come with me."

"That's," she said, shaking her head. That's what? Crazy? A great idea?

Not the right thing to do. Despite the weirdness with Mom, and with Jane, and with Michael, she had to stay. The fact was, people had begun to look up to her, whether or not she stayed Scott's lieutenant. Also whether or not she deserved it.

Dad would understand. She had a duty here.

Dean frowned. "I hate to think about leaving you again."

She stood, the chair bumping into the back of her legs and tipping. She let it fall. As it clattered to the floor, she stepped to the back door and cupped her elbows, laying her forehead against the door and peeking out the tiny window.

"Just go."

"Addy, you know I lo—"

"Go. Please."

After setting her chair right, he left the kitchen. He paced around the living room for a few minutes, gathering his gear and packing his bag. Tiny claws followed him around the room. *Click-click-clicking* on the wooden floor.

He zipped the bag closed. His feet stopped moving.

Forehead pressed into the door, the hairs on the back of her neck and arms tingled. She imagined him standing there in the doorway, shifting from foot to foot, debating on speaking.

He mumbled. "Take care of Mom, Data."

Back to him, she listened as he clomped across the living room.

Oh, this was stupid.

She hurried into the living room just as the door closed.

When would he come back through it?

It could be weeks.

It could be months.

It could be never.

Dashing to the door, she tore it open.

He stood at the end of the walk, staring at his feet.

"Dean?"

Head snapping up, he dumped the pack on the ground and rushed up the sidewalk. Bounding onto the porch in one jump, he enclosed her in his arms. When he kissed her, heat rushed from her toes to the crown of her head.

He pushed her back. "Adelaide," he said, "I love you. Don't ever doubt that. Don't ever forget it."

"I love you back," she said, wiping a tear from his cheek. Smiling, she grabbed a handful of his shirt and pulled him back through the door, slamming it behind them.

Tugging his shirttails free, she kissed him, sliding her hand under his shirt. She laid her palm over the bite mark on his abdomen.

He smiled, breaking the seal of her lips on his. "Sweetie, I'm going to be late."

Burying her face in his neck, she inhaled the scent of his magic deep into her lungs. Cheeks on fire, she fumbled with his belt. "They can wait. I can't."

When his breath stopped, she glanced up into his emerald eyes.

He smiled, corners of his eyes crinkling the way she loved, and he kissed her with such tenderness she thought her heart might melt and drip right out the soles of her feet.

Not unlike the way the blood oozed from the soles of a 'Head's foot.

Blocking those thoughts before they gripped her, she pulled him to the couch.

He was kind, and he was gentle, and he gave her all the things she asked for. And some she didn't know how to ask for, or even to want to ask for.

There came a moment when he stopped, staring deep into her eyes. "Are you sure?"

She shuddered. The ache inside her was more than physical. She needed to be close to him. To hold him, in her arms and inside of her, to melt into him and let herself go in a way she had never really considered until this moment. It was all she could do to answer him, and she did it in a whisper. "I love you so much, Dean. I've never been more sure of anything." With a trembling hand, she guided him in, closer to her than anyone had ever been. A part of her, the way only he could be.

She found there was something in the world that made her feel more alive, more human, more complete, than killing the dead.

If she was never going to see him again, she wasn't going to let him forget her. And she'd carry the memory of him within her for as long as she lived.

CHAPTER 7

Pulling the stale fish smell of the sound into her nostrils, Addy waited at the dock for her mom.

Dean had been gone twenty-four hours. A lifetime already.

"Hey, baby girl," Mom said.

Addy jumped like she'd been goosed, her heart racing. "Morning, Mom."

"Morning yourself. Ready?" She gave her half a hug.

"Yeah. Where are we going, exactly?"

"Down the coast a piece to what used to be called Wilmington. There's a museum I wanted to visit."

"A museum? The last time we even saw one of those I was," she paused, casting her memory back.

A warm and fuzzy one, that memory. They'd found an art museum. Many of the pieces had been damaged by passing hordes. Some had been inexplicably spray-painted. But they'd found a whole wing untouched, full of dioramas and paintings on ancient scrolls.

"You were ten," Mom said. "We were in Phoenix."

"Oh yeah," she said, following Melinda down the dock. "What were we doing in such a large city?"

"Needed supplies. Your dad broke his leg. Remember?"

"Jesus. No. How did that happen?"

Mom stopped. "You don't remember?"

Shaking her head, Addy cast her memory back again. They'd stayed in one place for quite some time when she was that age. It'd been a zoo. She'd wondered what had happened to all the animals.

"Dad broke his leg? I don't remember that at all."

Melinda chuckled. "Funny what you don't remember. I thought he was going to die for a while there. I was scared out of my mind. I found a library in Phoenix and there were medical books. I set his leg myself," she said, smiling. "You and I went back into town for antibiotics, painkillers, stuff like that. That's when we found the museum."

"Oh," Addy said. "I remember a vase. The little placard said it was five thousand years old."

Mom nodded. "From China. Yeah, I remember that." She smiled again. "Jack was furious when we showed back up. We were gone at least twice as long as I'd said we were going to."

"He thought we were dead."

"Course he did. And he never liked feeling impotent, unable to help. But he couldn't even stand on that leg. Much less come after us."

Addy frowned. "He left."

Melinda sighed through her nose. "I know."

"Did he say anything to you?"

"Your father only talks to me if I make him." She stopped in front of a speed boat easily three times bigger than the canoes Addy had become accustomed to. And with a motor.

"I don't know how to drive one of those," Addy said, pointing.

Mom patted her shoulder. "You look just like your father when you do that. I'll teach you." She stepped into the bow and held out a hand.

Reluctant, her stomach in knots, Addy took her hand. Last time she'd been in charge of driving, they'd plowed straight into the middle of a horde. Visions of Dean's train, silver like his skiff, danced through her mind, bound up in a twist in her stomach.

Stepping into the boat, her eye fell on a cube in the back with rail handles. "Generator?"

Mom nodded, sitting in front of the steering wheel. Which, Addy would learn, was actually called the helm. "You're going to have to help me lug it once we get there."

"What's it for?"

"You'll see." She started the engine and backed away from the dock. Cruising through the sound, the island slipping away, she kept the motor in a low gear.

Addy watched the mainland approach as the deep shadows over it lightened.

"Mom," she said.

Mom grunted.

"Why doesn't he talk to you? I thought you guys. Well." The sun hadn't quite breached the horizon yet, and the flush in her cheeks was probably not visible. "The whole island was talking about how he went home with you."

"The whole island? Really."

"Well," Addy said, facing front again, "yeah. And we all thought maybe, you know, you'd worked it out."

"Addy, honey, your father was drunk."

Addy's stomach turned. What did that even mean? And had she ever seen him drunk?

Mom answered the question she hadn't asked. "I mean, he wouldn't have, um"—she cleared her throat—"wouldn't have spent the night with me if some part of him didn't want to. But. Well. It's complicated."

Addy nodded, watching the compass in the dash wobble. "Like I said before, I just want you both to be happy. Whatever that looks like." She faced her. "It's weird. Realizing your parents are people."

Melinda chuckled. "Yeah, sweetie. It can be." She kicked the motor into a higher gear.

Further thought along the lines of parents and mistakes and sex didn't invite Addy along. She sat back and let Mom show her how to work the boat, the wind blowing her hair back as they sped away from Harkers.

Eventually, Mom steered the boat around a point with another old lighthouse, this one not painted but instead made from some sort of yellowish brick, and pointed the bow north.

"We went the long way, but it's the easiest way to go if you don't know how to get out of here. Just in case you need to know," Mom said, slowing the boat to a less breakneck speed.

Addy, memorizing the lighthouse, watched land slip by on both shores. "Are we in a river?"

Mom nodded. "Cape Fear."

Uncertain what to make of the name, Addy kept silent.

They rode up the river for several miles, eventually pulling into a dock for larger boats. Maybe eight docked here, a couple of them listing to the side, their paint flaking off the fiberglass hulls and into the river.

"Are there people here?"

"A few. One of them was supposed to leave us a handcart." She scanned the dock. "Let's go take a look." The boat bumped into the pier. She cut the engine.

Once she'd found the handcart in a nearby shed, Addy helped her load the generator onto it, and they rolled it through silent streets. Derelict houses and businesses listed in overgrown lots.

Addy's heart rate doubled as the buildings grew closer together. Sweat popped on her brow. "Are you sure we have to do this, Mom? Cities make me—"

"Nervous?"

"Yeah."

"Me too, sweetie. But I've got lots of intel about this area. Remember, I've lived basically next door for years. It's safe. As safe as it can be, anyway."

Addy shuddered. Safe or no, the half-crushed dreams of a society lost loomed over her. Staring. Waiting for her to join the darkness within them.

"I know you haven't seen many old cities, honey," Mom said. "This is what most of them are like."

"How do you know what I have or have not seen? It's been over a decade since we saw each other." Addy stopped, glaring at her feet. With effort, she met her mother's eyes. "Don't pretend like you know me, Mom."

Melinda's jaw trembled. "Yeah. Sorry. You're right. I should've. I didn't think it through."

Grimacing more than grinning, Addy took the handle for the handcart and began to push. "I know. I'm sorry. Just, let me push this beast for a while."

Mom stopped her when they arrived at a large brick building toward the middle of town. "Here we are. I think you're really going to dig this, honey." She tugged the handcart up the front stairs. Inside, she pulled out her flashlight and stopped to look at a giant map made of plastic and glass, shining the light from here to there. It showed the locations of several exhibits, one of which was a history of the islands they now lived on.

"That'd be cool to look at," Addy whispered, pointing.

Melinda nodded, still searching the map. Finally, her flashlight landed on lettering that read "Coming Soon," and she took off in the direction of it before Addy had a chance to see what else it said.

Somewhere, deep within the museum, Melinda stopped in front of a bank of electrical panels. "Leave the generator and go in there," she said, pointing with her flashlight to a door they'd passed. "I'll get this working." She handed Addy a second light.

The sound of her mom banging around with the generator, cursing its firstborn and the cretins who birthed it, receded into the distance the farther Addy got into the room. She pointed the light at a bunch of blank, black screens. Also a few things that looked like robot arms and long, yellow gloves behind glass. All very interesting, and even more interesting it was all still in one piece, but why had Mom brought her here?

Mom shouted with glee.

The lights came on, screens flickering into life all around Addy.

Filled with pictures of astronauts in space suits. A space station, the one Mom had told her about. Other satellites. The moon. The stars.

Pictures and pictures and pictures of the stars. In ways she'd never seen them. Full-color, full-spectrum, breathtaking photos of nebulae. Close-ups of their own burning star. Of supernovae, blowing out their energy. Enveloping everything around them in a cloud of shimmering light and color.

Melinda bumped her with her shoulder.

Addy couldn't raise her voice above a whisper. "Oh, Mom. It's beautiful."

Melinda smiled, starlight twinkling in her eye. "Yeah, it is, jellybean."

They spent the better part of the day playing with the interactive exhibit. Ogling pictures of stars like they were supermodel spreads. Talking about the vastness of space and how somewhere, in some other solar system or some other galaxy, was a world like Earth.

A world that was whole. Hadn't been swallowed by the dead.

* * *

Shivering as the day slunk below the horizon, Jack covered his tired legs with a blanket and stared out the window. It'd taken just over a week's worth of walking to get here, outside the five-mile radius of Emerald Hills. Last time they'd been here, he and Dean had found this tar paper shack in the middle of the woods. No explanation. No drive. No nothing. It hadn't been on any map. It was just there. As though it'd been waiting on them.

The view from the window didn't have much to show, as he let himself sink into guilt over not saying goodbye to the kids after a few hours' fitful sleep, but the summer woods buzzed with life, even beyond sunset. Fireflies lit the air with their twinkling yellow butts.

He sighed, closing his eyes, ghostly yellow flashes lighting his memories. Not unlike the flash of the gun, the split second between Andrew's last breath and the bullet that stole the rest of them.

Shaking his head, he threw off the covers and stood. He buckled on his weapons and stepped outside the shack.

A firefly lit up in front of his face.

Reaching up with his fingertips, he lifted his hand just under it. It alighted on his index finger, its feet the lightest breath of air on his skin. He brought it in front of his face, and let it crawl onto his other palm. Cupping his hands around it, he peeked in the hole created by his thumbs.

It lit up, blinding him.

Which was the perfect moment for a stick to break from the other side of the shack.

He opened his hands, the firefly buzzing away. He drew his knife.

Someone whistled through their teeth. Twice, pause, once more.

Even though Dean had changed up Mike's knock, it still made him think of his son.

He whistled back.

Dean came around the shack, four men behind him. One loomed over the rest.

"No. You," Jack said, pointing to the large Japanese man. "You get out of here. I don't care where you go, but it won't be here."

The big man, the one Jack had come to think of as His Guard at the prison, held up both hands, palms facing him. "I knew you'd say that. Look, I owe you," he said. "I was… What I did…" He cleared his throat. "I'm sorry. I was scared and angry and did what they told me to."

Jack stepped into his face, ignoring his hands and glaring up at him. "So, you were just following orders? That's your excuse for what you did to Andrew?"

"You can hit me if you want."

Ricardo stepped next to him, the teen dwarfed by them both, and held an arm between them. "It was my idea to bring him, Mr. C. He's a good guy. He just wants to help."

Jack, glaring at the boy, stepped back. "You've got to be fucking kidding me." Everything within him vibrated. He stared at the woods, arms crossed so tight across his chest he could barely breathe.

Dean stepped up next to him and lowered his voice. "Maybe we could talk inside? There's room for everybody. Even though it'll be a little cramped."

Jack sighed. Maybe some people deserved a second chance. This world was rarely simple. Shoulders drooping, he glanced at the others. Paul, Oren, Ricardo, and the big guy. "Let's get inside."

"Even Renzo?"

"That his real name? Tim called him Bull."

"Yeah, um. Don't call him that. He hates it."

Jack laughed without humor. "Figures. Yeah. Even him."

CHAPTER 8

Addy stepped onto her porch and sniffed the air flowing in off the sound.

Dean had been gone a week, and the air still smelled a little stale. Not that one had anything to do with the other, but Addy made the association anyway.

Frowning, she exhaled through her nose and locked the front door.

"Come on, Data, time to learn a leash." She tugged it.

His little tail thumped the porch. He jumped on her leg and yipped.

"No," she said, shaking a finger in his face. "No barking. Quiet puppies are good puppies."

All four feet, growing bigger each day, landed back on the porch.

Grinning, she walked him down the stairs.

Well. She walked. He tripped, butt in the air, face in the steps. Then kinda scooted feet first down the next two.

She scratched his ear. "Yep. That's my dog." She pulled his leash to take him right. Past the spot where Dean had dropped his pack.

Her cheeks flushed. "Come on, boy."

He followed, wagging his little tail and sniffing at the ground. Once, he yipped and hid behind her leg when a seagull landed in front of them. She scratched his ears, shooed the bird, and tugged him forward again.

The sun warmed the part in her hair. Felt like ants crawling along her scalp.

* * *

The sun hits your little head, heating it up at the part. Feels like ants on your skin.

Mom is picking tomatoes and putting them in a baske—

* * *

"No, Adelaide. No," she said, whispering under her breath. "That time is over and done. Over and done."

"Hey, Addy," Jane said, from behind her.

Addy jumped two feet if it was a day. "Jane," she said, heart racing. "I didn't even hear you. Damn but you're sneaky these days."

Jane nodded, short and shaggy hair swaying in the breeze. "Celia's a good teacher."

Tugging on Data's leash, Addy swallowed. Couldn't hurt to ask. "Walk with me a bit?"

Jane nodded again, cupping her elbows. "So, um, how old is your puppy?"

"Data? He's about ten weeks. Celia's friend Elicia bred him. She's been working on quiet dogs for about ten years, I guess. Cee said she's pretty good."

Data yipped at another seagull as it took off in front of them. Addy sighed. "We'll see."

"So, he was born about the end of April?"

"Jane? I'm impressed. You used the name of a month," Addy said, goggling at her friend.

She frowned. "Yeah. Well. Probably ought to keep track of time at least a bit." Her hand snuck to her belly, rubbing the top of her pants.

"That's so cool," Addy said, a large grin crossing her face. "I'm so happy you found your fit."

Jane cleared her throat, nodding. "Thanks. That's… How's Dean?"

The grin on Addy's face widened, if it could, and she lifted a thumb to the sky. "He's aces. I mean, he's gone now, but, aces."

"Adelaide," Jane said, stopping, mouth open. "No. No way," she said, voice going up an octave. She slapped her on the shoulder. "You didn't."

Addy blushed so fiercely she thought she might actually burst into flames. Even the top of her scalp burned, and not from the heat of the sun.

Catching her in a tight hug, Jane leaned right and left, taking Addy with her. "Oh, Addy. I'm so happy for you."

She stepped back, the first true smile Addy had seen on her face since, when? The village? Whenever, it was good to see. Like the sun coming out.

"I," Addy started. She cleared her throat and tried again. "I didn't know what you meant about love before. I do now."

"Neither did I," Jane mumbled, cupping her elbows again.

And just like that, the sun was gone.

She bumped Jane's shoulder and started walking again.

After a pause, Jane joined her. "So, where did Dean go?"

"You didn't hear?"

"Celia's been teaching me to sleep in trees. I haven't been on the island much this week."

"He took a team to go find my dad. Help him do whatever it is he's doing out there with IRF and everything."

Jane stopped again. "I see. Well," she said, twisting a toe into the ground, "I gotta get home. Subject Michael to more home cooking. Excuse me," she said, retreating before Addy could open her mouth.

"It was good talking to you, Jane," she called to her back.

Jane raised a hand over her shoulder.

Data yipped.

After scolding him again, Addy kicked a rock. Uneven as it had been, talking to Jane had been nice. For a moment there, it had almost been like it was. For a moment.

Data ran out to the end of his leash and tugged Addy's arm with more strength than a puppy that little should be able to. Jerked forward, she glanced up.

Yasuo sat on the sidewalk, a piece of bacon in his outstretched hand.

Data barked.

"No, bad dog," Addy said. She glanced at Yasuo. "Bad Yaz, distracting my puppy."

"Addy," he said, standing and sweeping the dirt off his pants, "the world is itself a distraction. He must learn to not be distracted."

"Well, you're not helping."

He broke the bacon in half, popping one-half in his mouth.

Addy held out her hand.

He fed the other piece to the puppy.

Frowning, she tugged Data's leash and walked around Yaz. "I was just coming to see you."

"That so?" He walked next to her, hands in his pockets.

"Yeah. I was wondering if you'd teach me some more staff moves."

Yaz scratched his hairless chin. "I think that could be arranged."

"Right now?"

He nodded, cheeks dimpling in a grin. "We'll go to my house."

Once they arrived at his house, complete with its own mini-Dojo in the garage, Addy put Data in the backyard.

"What, you don't think he'll get along with my cat?" Yaz asked as Addy stepped into the garage.

She shook her head. "I think Cliff'll kick his ass," she said. "I used to have a cat. Beverly. I wonder how she is."

Yasuo handed her a staff. "What happened to her?"

"I had to leave her behind. We left my old village kinda sudden."

"Such is life in the world. Powerless over events. Cats are smart," he said, picking up his own staff. "They can make their own way."

She nodded, bringing her staff up. "That they can." The pile of feathers with its bloody quills flashed through her mind again.

Without so much as a warning, Yaz crouched and swept his staff low.

Addy jumped, too late.

The staff hit her in the ankle, sweeping her feet from under her. She fell to the mat, all the air pushed from her lungs in a gushing *woof*.

She coughed. "Son of a bitch, Yaz."

He held the staff out to her. "Need to be quicker."

Grasping the end of the staff, she stood. "I am quick," she said, lashing out with the leading end of her staff. It sailed for his hip.

He blocked, shoving her staff away. "Alright. Enough. Let's do this for real."

"Fine."

Backing several paces away from each other, they bowed. Yaz played the part of the aggressor, while she blocked and backed away. When he struck low, she almost forgot to lower the staff. Just in time, she got there, and he swung for her again.

After going through the routine until he didn't knock her down at the end, but almost taking her head off at least twice, Yasuo paused when she put her hand up.

"Water," she panted.

"You know where it's at."

She leaned her staff against the wall and got the pitcher out of the little fridge he kept out in the garage. Two cups on top, one white, one black, sat top down. She glanced over her shoulder, eyebrow raised.

"Sure," he said.

Sitting crisscross applesauce across from each other, they drank.

"Hey Yaz," she said, emptying the cup and rolling it in her hands.

"Hey Addy."

"We talked about being powerless. I think I get it."

"Oh?"

She nodded. "Yeah. I mean. I can't control people. I can hardly control a puppy."

"So. What can you control?"

"My reactions?"

"Is that a question or a statement?"

She cleared her throat, staring at the cup. "A statement. The past couple weeks, my dad, Dean, my mom. If I needed proof, that's been it."

"Good. We can move on, then."

Her head snapped up. "We can?"

He smiled, cheeks dimpled again. "There has to be balance. Now that you've found the balance in powerlessness, we can move on to discovering how to balance your relationships."

She blew a stray hair off her forehead. "Ha. Sure," she said. "Not many of my relationships are really working right now. I think they're all broken."

"And what part in those relationships do you play?"

"Uh. I don't understand."

He nodded. "Here. Let's learn some more spins," he said, standing. "And you can think about your part. And about how for all the dark, there is light. Equal," he said, standing, "balanced."

"Oh my god, Yaz. Do you always have to talk in circles?" She stood, taking his cup and setting them both on top of the fridge.

"A circle is a perfect shape," he said, grinning.

She sighed. "Teach me this new spin."

* * *

Jack stood at the tallest point of the ridge, staring down into the valley through the telescope Ric brought, his face sore from squinting through the eyepiece.

"Hey, Dean," he said.

"Yeah."

"Have you seen this? Is that a hospital? What's that marking on the front?"

Dean leaned into the telescope. After a few moments of fiddling with the knob, grumbling something about Jack getting his eyes checked, he nodded. "Yeah. I see it. What marking?"

Jack pointed. Not that Dean could see him doing it. "Just to the right of the front door. There's some kind of mark."

Grunting, Dean squinted harder, side of his face wrinkling. "OK. I see it. Like we thought," he said, pulling back from the eyepiece, "it's an IRF symbol." He leaned back into the scope.

"Must be killing Talus Crest that IRF got their people," Paul said.

Jack glanced at him, grinning with the corners of his mouth turned down. "Yeah, it must."

Considering what intel had told them about Melinda's former company, that probably didn't bode well for the people. Two companies in competition for a test population like that? It—

"Shit." Dean stood back from the telescope. "There's a problem." He pointed at the scope. "That man is called Burke. He's one of the highest-ranking commanders in IRF."

Fiddling with the focus, Jack sighted in on the tall white man in fatigues, mind racing. IRF had their own hospital out here in the mountains of Virginia, with one of their highest-ranking commanders in charge of it. Well, that wasn't foreboding at all. "Dean."

"Yeah. I know."

Paul stood, using the tree he'd been leaning against as a handhold. "I know I'm quick, gentlemen, but I have to ask. What do we know?"

Jack's stomach turned.

Andrew. Chained to a bed, arms a pincushion for fluids that were, at best, questionable. In the end turned into some kind of human-Dead-Head hybrid.

Jane in the chair, paper gown stretched over her, half her long, thick hair shaved. Electrodes taped to her.

She had come off damn lucky, in the end. The vaccine hadn't killed her. She'd suffered no ill effects. And clearly, it hadn't ended up affecting conception down the line, so.

Well, that's where that thought train stops.

He cleared his throat. "If it's anything like the last hospital we saw," Jack began.

Paul gripped his arm. "We have to know. We have to know now."

Laying a hand over Paul's, Jack grimaced, brows knitted. He glanced across the valley. "If Talus Crest believes these people belong to them, don't you think they'll come looking? And what is IRF doing? The same thing Talus was? Or are they protecting these people from Talus?" He clenched one hand into a fist. "Too many questions. I don't even know who's the good guy."

"If there even is a good guy," Dean said.

Paul pointed a finger at him. "Got it in one."

Jack sat, soft summer grass a green cushion under him. "One of us needs to get in there."

Dean and Paul sat on either side of him.

"Want to ask the others for volunteers?" Dean asked.

"Nonsense," Paul said. "Obvious choice is the frail old man."

"It's not nice to talk about me like that," Jack said, grinning with one side of his mouth.

Mouth wide, Paul laughed. "I'll report in twice a week," he said, blue eyes twinkling.

Jack held a walkie out to him. "Watch your ass, old man."

CHAPTER 9

Between road trips with her mom, at least one of which involved running from Dead Heads, training with Yaz, and raising a puppy, four months on Harkers Island passed quicker than Adelaide realized. Sometimes she and Melinda went out with Michael, sometimes it was just the two of them. It was hard to stay guarded. Especially when Yaz kept reminding her to focus on her feelings.

One moment, Mom had been the shiny, fuzzy memory. Perfect.

The next, she'd become a deeply flawed individual. Idealistic still, but leaving a lot to be desired in the execution department.

And then, she'd become Mom again.

Mom, who was heartbroken over Dad, but tried not to let it show.

Still, it made sense. They were different people. Dad had become so much more since they lost Mom. He'd learned how to be gentle and sweet. He'd learned how to teach them math and science. He'd learned how to kiss a boo-boo.

And Mom had hardened. Despite being one of the first people ever cured, she'd become bitter. Angry. Ambitious.

Either way, Adelaide did what she could to get to know this new person from this new perspective. She still had sweetness. She still had dreams. She still talked endlessly of the stars and life in the universe besides theirs. Of exploring its vastness. And how she still had hope for humanity.

Meanwhile, Yasuo taught Addy the complete suite of spins and attacks with the staff. The day he gave her her own staff to take home was a shining memory with sparkling edges. His serious face, her skipping heart. He'd trusted her enough to not only teach her but to set her free to learn on her own.

And even though they still hardly spoke, she watched Jane's belly grow. Every time she saw her, she had a hand on her belly. Like she was trying to hold the baby. She kept learning from Celia and even went out to the range with Addy a couple times. As Mike had said, her bow skills rivaled Addy's. She was a quick study, and her growing baby never got in the way. Never shook her concentration.

She'd always been someone Addy had enjoyed, but now more than ever, Addy admired, even looked up to Jane. She'd changed from the girl Addy had known in the village. Overnight, it seemed. Though she was far more serious, she carried a full richness to her Addy hadn't seen before. She glowed with more than just pregnancy hormones.

But there was something missing, something Jane wouldn't tell her. They'd always been the ones to tell each other everything. Now Jane held back. Locked whatever it was behind her lips. Frowned a lot.

It hurt to be shut out. For seemingly no reason. Had she done something wrong?

As Yasuo suggested, Addy tried to figure out what her part was in the hurt. At first, it wouldn't come.

Yaz had her meditate on it, both of them sitting in front of the crashing surf.

And she pinned it down, much to her own surprise.

She expected Jane to talk to her. Counted on it. When Jane refused, it scared her. Though change was constant, she hadn't been prepared for her relationship with Jane to change. It made her angry.

"What isn't love is fear." Yasuo repeated it so many times, Addy thought about that statement almost every single time she said the words "afraid" or "angry."

She tried to alter her expectations. She couldn't control people. Only her reactions.

And she kept working for Scott. Of course.

* * *

"Hey, Christian," Addy said, leaning across the bar. Making a fist, she bumped the side of her hand to his. Their official handshake. "How's tricks?"

He grunted. "Depends. You here as Lieutenant Adelaide or sister Addy?" He nodded to the opposite end of the bar.

Michael sat, head hanging, four empty shot glasses in front of him.

Brow wrinkled, she leaned closer. "What the hell? It's the middle of the day."

Christian nodded, sliding a glass of water to her. "You got me. Your brother's a pretty good dude, always open to conversation. Not today." He shrugged. "Just drinks."

Frowning, she thanked Christian, snagged her water, and headed down the bar. "What's up big brother?"

Without looking up, he held out a sucker. Sour apple.

Her favorite. Whatever it was, it was serious.

Taking the sucker, she sat on the stool next to him and unwrapped it. She stuck it in her mouth and bumped his shoulder with hers. Repeated her question.

Glancing at her, he tried on a smile. With his brow still wrinkled, it looked painful. Like work. A Herculean effort.

"Baby sister. I think I fucked up."

Pulling a breath in through her nose, swallowing her pounding heart, she took a swig of the water. He never, ever used language that severe. She asked Christian for a beer, her duties as lieutenant over for the day. Michael clearly needed her more than the island did.

Taking a pull from the bottle, she frowned. "Tell me what's going on."

He sniffled, stealing her water. "I'm an idiot. I was stupid."

"What, like, right now? Or all the time?"

Laughing without humor, he pulled out his own root beer sucker. "Both."

"Shit, it was supposed to be a joke," Addy said, stomach churning. He always gave away the root beer ones. Sharing his favorite made him happy.

"I know. I know. Life's full of jokes."

Making an attempt at aloof, she rolled her eyes. "Oh my god. Out with it, Michael."

"I told Jane I love her."

Her heart fluttered. "Why would that be a problem?"

He glanced at her again.

For the first time, she noticed his eyelashes were wet. Oh, boy.

"It's not my baby, Addy."

Standing so fast the stool fell over, she shouted. "What do you mean? What the hell?"

Conversation in the room stopped, all eyes on her.

Nervous smile playing across her lips, she raised her hand to them and picked up the stool. "Sorry. Go back to your games."

They did.

Sitting back down, she leaned closer to her brother. "What do you mean? Has she been cheating on you?"

That would explain so much about her behavior.

He laughed. A genuine, smiling chuckle. "No, bean. She wouldn't."

"Then how do you know?"

Giving her a sad smile, he shook his head. "If you must know, I've never touched her."

As though she'd been punched in the stomach, the wind fell out of Addy's mouth. Her mind a fog, she leaned back and polished off her beer. Signaled for another. "You what?"

"She let me kiss her once. Then she cried for an hour."

If he'd shown up with a boot stapled to his head, she wouldn't have been more surprised than she was right now. Jane? Crying?

"Mike," she said, "I think you need to tell me the details."

He nodded, sipping her water and eating his sucker. "When we first got here, we went on that date she promised me. It went good, though she seemed a little down. Which made sense, given all that had happened."

Losing her parents. Being kidnapped. The vaccine. The fight with the horde. Andrew. Yeah. It had been a lot.

"You know me. I didn't let it get me down. I tried to cheer her up. We skipped rocks at the duck pond. Had a little knife practice. Did some sparring. You know, stuff she likes." He looked at his hands, twirling the sucker. "We went back to my house, sat on the porch swing, and talked for a bit. That's when she let me kiss her. And then she just…closed up like a clam. And cried." His shoulders sagged. "I thought she'd run away then. You know she doesn't like to be emotional in front of people."

Addy nodded. She didn't think she'd seen Jane cry the entire time she'd known her. Not once. Not even when she had to kill her own father. "I know. But why did you let everyone believe the baby was yours?"

"Oh Adelaide," he said, the smile stretching his mouth so sad it threatened to break her heart. "Because I love her." He downed the rest of the water and wiped his face. "She came back around a few days later. Asked if she could hang out. We watched TV together most nights for a couple weeks. Usually in silence. But at least she was there. Sometimes, briefly, I saw the old Jane."

Addy couldn't feel her stomach. She poured alcohol in it. The fire worked its way through her gut, but it didn't take the edge off his story.

"She did some knitting once in a while. I thought she'd be OK, just needed some time." When he looked up, more tears stood in his eyes. "A few weeks after that first date, she showed up on my doorstep one night, crying. Again."

"Jane, what's wrong?"

Her face was a mess of snot and tears. She wore loose pajama pants and a half-buttoned flannel shirt, like clothes had been a second thought.

"Come in," Mike said, ushering her in. His heart leapt to his throat, on the verge of tears himself just seeing her this way. "How can I help?"

Curling up on what he'd come to think of as her end of the couch, she pulled her feet under her, buried her face in her knees, and sobbed.

He perched next to her, but not too close. Years of knowing her told him she wouldn't talk if pushed. But if he let her come to it on her own, she might not run away from it. He wanted to crush her in a hug and tell her it was OK. Whatever it was.

After a minute, she raised her face. He'd never, ever seen such a look in her eye. The utter despair, the hopelessness, it threatened to pull him in with it.

But her mouth turned up at the corners. "I'm pregnant, Michael."

She could have curled a fist and rammed it through his diaphragm and it would have had the same effect. After he thought he'd been making progress, finally, here she'd been seeing someone else.

But, babies were good. They needed babies. He smiled. "Well, that's good then, right? What's the matter?"

Then she cried again. He'd never seen anyone cry so much. It twisted his heart the way a tornado they saw when he was a kid had twisted the trees into knots. Protecting her, making it better, it was all he could think about. After her tears subsided, he again asked her what he could do.

For a moment, she stared at him with a line between her brows. Her mouth hanging half-open. Then she looked around the house. "Can I come stay here? With you?"

He sighed, glancing at Addy from the side of his eye. "I couldn't say no. She needed me."

Even for all the work she'd done on expectations, on her side of the street, the flames of anger wormed through Addy's gut. Why hadn't Jane told her this? Why had she suffered alone? What the hell, exactly?

"She ever tell you who the father is?"

He shook his head. "No. I asked her once. About a week after she moved in and we were making her bed together. She told me if I ever asked her again, not only would she have my balls for breakfast, but I'd never see her again."

Addy grinned. That, at least, was exactly something Jane would say. "This is crazy, Mike. Crazy. I can't believe she would do this to you."

"Oh no, bean," he said, taking her hand. "She never lied. She never led me on. Except for that first date, when I think she really tried, I never thought—" Dropping her hand, he faced the bar. He spun the empty water glass in circles and sighed. "I mean, I hoped. I'm not going to lie. But I never really thought. She didn't make me think we were anything more than what we are. Friends. She needed me. I decided to help. That's all. Don't be mad at her."

He glanced up again. "The last few weeks, it's been nice. I've seen a lot more of the old Jane. And we were joking around, and it just… It slipped out. I said I love you." He peeked at Addy. "She got this funny look on her face and told me to leave her alone for a while. So," he said, signaling Christian, "here I am."

Christian set the drink in front of him. Another shot of some evil-smelling amber stuff.

He downed it, grimacing. "Ask me, she's still in love with the guy, whoever he is. They're not together, and who knows why. But he still has her heart. The lucky son of a bitch."

"Well," Addy said, stuffing the sucker in her mouth and standing, "I'm going to go ask her."

* * *

Dean's phone rang.

Jack looked at him like he'd grown two heads. The phone hadn't rung in weeks. Dean had come up with some clever story to keep IRF off the horn for a while.

"It's Adelaide," Dean said, frowning at the ringing phone.

The fire crackled, acrid smoke crawling up Jack's nose. Jack and Dean sat on the ridge, Renzo between them, waiting for Paul to check in. He'd been in the city for more than three months. The intel he'd returned invaluable, he'd decided to stay until Jack wanted to get back to Harkers.

Assuming Jane would be showing a pretty large pregnant belly by now was all the encouragement Jack needed to keep sleeping in the woods in Virginia.

"Answer it," Renzo said, stoking the fire. "Even if she's not supposed to, no, especially if she's not supposed to. Your girl calls you, you answer."

Dean glanced at Jack.

Jack gave him one curt nod.

He flipped the phone open. "Addy, why are you calling?"

All Jack's ears could pick up was tinny buzzing. Sounded like a 'Head underwater. He shivered.

Dean sat up, almost kicking the fire. "What?"

Heart pounding the inside of his ribcage, Jack took slow, deep breaths. Apparently his daughter hadn't called with good news. Either something had happened to Michael or Melinda, or—

No. Please no.

He closed his eyes.

Jane's OK. Jane's OK. Jane and the baby are OK.

He said it over and over, so many times it became gibberish inside his head.

It seemed even the passing of months hadn't completely healed the wound. Just the thought of her being in danger enough to rip the healing scab right off, he held his breath through the pain.

"Fuck," Dean said. "Yeah. Yeah, he's right here." He held the phone out. "She wants to talk to you."

Exhaling, Jack opened his eyes and held out his hand.

Dean slid the phone into his fingers. Plastic warm where he'd gripped it.

"Hi, baby girl, are you and Mike alright?"

"We're OK, Dad. But it's Jane."

Fuck. No, no-no.

"Oh? What's up?" Nice and even.

"She's gone."

He sat up, almost kicking the fire as Dean had. "What do you mean, she's gone?" His heart raced. Gone? Or *gone*?

"I was talking to Michael, that's a whole other story, and when I went to talk to her about it, we found this note. Her weapons and pack all gone."

His heart rate slowed. She left. Alright. That he could deal with. He exhaled, holding his forehead.

"Dad?"

"I'm here, baby girl. What did the note say?"

"It was very Jane. It said, I'm quoting, 'I made a mistake. I'm sorry.' Then she signed it and left it on her pillow."

He replayed the six words in his head. Made a mistake? What did that mean? Did it mean she still...

He stopped the thought and instead, asked if Addy knew where Jane went.

"No. But someone saw her boating across the sound a few hours before we found the note. It's been almost a full day. We're going after her, a few of us. Celia thinks she might be able to track her."

"Might? Celia's the best tracker I know."

"Yeah. Not anymore."

He couldn't help it. He smiled. Jane was a hell of a smart woman. He cleared his throat. "Keep us posted. We'll meet you if you come this way."

"OK," she said, sighing.

"What's up?"

"I'm scared. Can you meet us anyway?"

His little girl didn't scare easy. And she didn't ask for Daddy lightly. Ever. "Of course. We'll find a place in the middle. We're leaving now."

"Hey, Dad, I love you."

"I love you, too, baby girl."

"Can I talk to Dean again, please?"

Glancing up, he caught Dean's eye. He'd pretended not to be listening, but Jack knew better. That man heard everything. He cleared his throat.

Dean glanced over, nodded, and snagged the phone. He smiled into it as he spoke to Addy, corners of his eyes wrinkling.

They'd gotten a lot closer, he and Dean, and Dean was never happier than when he spoke of Adelaide. He lit up like a Christmas tree. It was a sight to see.

Dean cleared his throat and tried to speak softly. "Yeah. I love you, too," he said. The blood crawling up his neck and into his cheeks, visible even in firelight.

Renzo chuckled.

Jack glanced at him. It wasn't so much that the man reminded him of Andrew, but he had the same way of moving his muscular frame through the world without disrupting it that Andy had possessed. Much as he hated to admit it, he'd liked the guy once he'd gotten past the past.

"Hey, Renzo," Jack said.

He raised an eyebrow.

"We have to go meet my daughter. My son, too, most likely. You want to come with us or stay here?"

Renzo shrugged massive shoulders. "Whatever you decide, Jack."

"Why don't you come with us then. Ric and Oren can stay here, take the next few reports from Paul."

"We need to let Paul know, Jack," Dean said, pocketing the phone.

The radio crackled. *"Base camp, come in, over,"* Paul whispered over the high-powered walkie.

"Perfect timing," Jack said, pressing the button.

Paul relayed another four days' worth of information to them.

Over the course of three months, he'd managed to get himself into both the hospital and their detention facilities. He was now doing what they called "civic service" for his petty theft of two vials of Cure.

The hospital, he said, was state of the art. Only he said it in caps. State Of The Art. Nicer by far than the one Talus had run, even the maternity ward. He'd managed to stumble into their nursery, just like he had at Shanti Station. In fact, he was some kind of genius about getting into places he wasn't supposed to be.

He said they had a neonatal intensive care unit and everything. The most advanced birthing unit he'd seen since his own kids had been born in the early two-thousands.

Of course, there'd been a wing he shouldn't have been able to stumble on. And of course, he had.

He hadn't found anything like what had happened to Andrew, and no Dead Heads strapped into torture rooms. But there were scientists, microscopes, clean rooms. Vials labeled "Cure." A room full of refrigerators stacked with blood samples.

Their running theory was these IRF people were doing the same thing as Talus, but they were using blood samples for their tests instead of living subjects.

"Not much to report, friend Jack," Paul said. *"I got a job. Mopping the floor of some dive bar. Great place for intel."*

Jack nodded.

Fool, he can't see you nod.

"That's a big 10-4. Learn anything yet?"

"I'd forgotten how heavy full kegs were."

He grimaced. The old man had probably thrown his back out. Again. That was how he'd gotten to the hospital in the first place.

"Anything else?"

"Not really," Paul said. *"These people are a little Stepford, if you ask me. But I don't have anything more concrete to tell you."*

"What does he mean by that?" Renzo asked. Dean explained as Jack caught Paul up to speed.

"So you're going to give your next few reports to Ricardo and Oren, it looks like."

"Be careful out there, friend Jack. I know she means a lot to you. Don't do anything stupid."

Jack's stomach curled in on itself. Of course, he'd forgotten. Paul always saw more than he let on, and he'd seen plenty in the prison.

He flashed on sleeping next to Jane, her arm stuck under the barred door between them. Rubbing her hands and arms, leaning on the door just to be a little closer.

Getting knocked out by Renzo here, trying to defend her honor.

Yeah, Paul had seen plenty.

He glanced at Dean to see if he'd overheard. Head down, Dean carried on explaining the Stepford reference.

"You got it, Paul. You watch your own ass, old man."

"I'm rubber and you're glue, whippersnapper. Over and out."

CHAPTER 10

Adelaide walked along the train tracks, machete drawn.

Behind her, Celia laughed at something Mike had said. Likely trying to make him feel better.

Melinda brought up the rear, no doubt frowning at Celia. She'd never cared for her.

One foot caught on an uneven railroad tie. Before Addy fell over, she planted her staff and steadied herself.

"Still my baby sister," Mike said, laughing. "Some things never change."

"You be quiet. I've gotten a lot better, thank you. Just ask Yaz."

"Convenient he isn't here to ask."

Celia chuckled.

"Stow it, jerk. He'll be back with my dog and some fresh rabbit soon." She glared. "Let me take a look at that map. How far are we?"

Mike pulled a paper from his back pocket and knelt to lay it on the tracks.

"Is that the map Dad left?"

"No, I couldn't find that one," he said. "That's OK, Dean told me how to find them." He stopped, staring at the paper. "You know Dad once told me they had maps on their phones? Maps of everything, everywhere. Man. That'd be nice. Anyway. We're here." He pointed.

Catching up, Mom crouched with them. She'd come, she said, because she didn't want both her kids and her grandchild out here alone. Addy hadn't the heart to tell her about the baby. Mom had seemed so happy about becoming a grandparent. Maybe once they caught up to Jane and figured it all out, maybe then.

Mike grinned at Mom and continued. "Alright, so we've followed the tracks to here"—his finger traveled up to a road labeled #40—"where we should intersect with Dad and Dean. Dean says there's track there that's not on the map."

"Convenient," Mom said, hand on her chin.

Addy nodded. Unease tensing the muscles in her shoulders, she breathed deep. "Celia," she said.

Celia stared down. "Adelaide."

"Are we still on her trail?"

The small woman raised her hands and lowered them in a shrug, slapping one leg. "I guess? I'm telling you, Addy, I've never in my life had such a tough time tracking someone. I knew she was smart, but damn. I can't believe how well she covers her tracks."

Addy nodded. Leave it to Jane. "When we meet up with Dad and Dean, we'll come back down and see if we can start over with fresh eyes."

"Better be soon. Trail's getting cold as we speak. She still has at least most of a day on us. Pregnant ass moves quick."

"I bet Data could help," Yaz said, appearing from the trees. "Look what he hunted down." He held up a rabbit by the back feet.

Data snorted. A few weeks ago, that would have been a bark, and Addy beamed, taking the dog's leash from Yaz. "Who's a good boy?" She knelt to hug him. He nibbled her chin, and she scratched his ears, slick chocolate fur warm from the sun. As a six-month-old, he was about three-quarters the size Elicia said he'd get. And a snuggle bug.

Her knee resting on the rail, she felt the thrumming before she heard it. "Train's coming, guys," she said, stepping off the tracks. Data and the rest of the group followed her. She flipped her phone open, catching the sun on it and reflecting it at the train as it rounded the corner ahead.

It slowed, coming to a stop about ten feet ahead of them. The back door opened, and Dean stepped onto the tiny porch. His eyes fell on her. He smiled and opened his mouth, then looked at the dog. "Is that Data? You got big, boy." Skipping the last two stairs, his feet hit the dirt.

Addy crossed her arms. "It's been what, almost four months, and you say hi to the dog first?"

Dean grinned. "You have to admit, he's a pretty dog."

Opening her mouth to throw another smart comment out of it, she didn't get so much as a syllable out before Dean caught her around the waist and spun her, holding her in the air and kissing her with enough passion to take her breath away. His scruffy beard tickled her face. She couldn't feel her toes when he set her back on her feet.

Data danced in a circle around them both. Yaz caught his leash and pulled him to sit.

Dad cleared his throat. "Little girl," he said, descending the steps, "good to see you. And you, Michael. Yasuo. Celia."

Mom scuffed a rock with her foot, frowning and crossing her arms. "Jackson."

"Melinda."

"I'm glad you're OK," Mom said.

"Likewise."

The air between them crackled. The tension palpable, Addy stepped back. "Um. Dad. Can I talk to you?"

"Sure, baby girl."

She caught Dean's hand and tugged. "You too."

He winked. "As you wish."

She led them off the side of the tracks and down toward the trees. "Listen," she said, when she thought they were safely out of earshot, "only Michael and I know at this point, but well." She paused, looking for the right words. It might not be easy for Dad to hear either, and he'd most likely be furious, but she needed his help, and he needed to know.

"Out with it, little girl," he said. He swallowed. "Is she alright?"

"We're still on her trail, though I think we have to backtrack a bit. But that's not what I wanted to say. What I wanted to say," she said, peeking at Dean.

He squeezed her hand.

"I wanted to tell you. Um. Mike's not the father."

Not only did the air escape Dad's mouth in a rush, his knees almost buckled. He put a hand on her shoulder and steadied himself. "Exactly what do you mean by that?" Eyebrows drawn, expression inscrutable, he narrowed his flinty blue eyes and stared into hers.

She related the story from finding Michael in the bar to their discovery of Jane's note. Dad went paler and paler by degrees, two high spots of color on his cheeks, just discernible under weeks' worth of scruff.

Turning to her own unshaven man, she searched his eyes.

They flitted back and forth. "Do you have any theories?"

She nodded. "Maybe? I asked around before we left, no one ever saw Jane with anyone. The only other man I can even think about her being around was Andrew. But," she said, glancing at her dad, "I never got the feeling he was that into girls."

Ignoring her altogether, Jack held a hand to his mouth and stared out into the trees. The two spots of color flamed outward.

"What do you mean?" Dean asked, tilting his head.

Addy glanced at her dad again. "I mean, I always thought, um. He kinda favored—" She broke off, tilting her head at her dad.

"Oh." Dean's eyes widened. *"Oh."* He nodded. "Well. Who can blame him?"

"Anyhow," Addy said, "it's a mystery. But we should catch up to her in about half a day if we go quick. We can ask her then."

"Half a day?" Dad turned, giving the first indication he'd heard anything she'd said since she finished the story. "What are we waiting for?"

* * *

Jack and the others wound through the forest, still on Jane's trail.

"Jack," Celia said, walking next to him, "tree."

Coming out of his reverie, he stepped right of the tree, frowning. He could tell the others what he suspected, but that'd take a lot of talking. Besides, it did no good to bring it up without being sure. No, best to get Jane alone once they caught up to her and find out the truth. In private.

A truth he couldn't dare to hope for. That after all this time, her heart still belonged to him. As his did to her. There wasn't any denying it now. Some people came into your heart and left a mark that never healed. He'd thought it had been healing, but as Adelaide told her story, a fire ignited in his belly and reached up to lick the edges of the hole that was still, inexplicably, shaped like Jane.

Glancing over his shoulder, he caught sight of Melinda walking between Addy and Mike. He'd thought there'd never be another like her. And there never was. Just like the kids she walked between, no two loves were equal.

But Jane had captured his mind, body, and soul in a way no one had ever come close to. And now, the possibility that she carried a child of his overwhelmed his senses. Celia had to keep pointing out the trail, even though he was a decent tracker on his own.

"Jack," she whispered, as though on cue, "do you see that?" She stopped, pointing at a depression beneath a tree.

He knelt. "Footprint?"

Celia nodded, kneeling beside him. "Not only that," she said, moving a fallen leaf with the tip of her knife.

Blood. Bits of rotted flesh splashed outward from the insole.

The stench seeping into his nostrils, he glanced at the nearby trees. A bit of dark blood here, a piece of flesh there. A bright splash of red blood just down the trail, stippling the side of an oak.

He stood, following the dripping 'Head blood.

Celia took a sniff of the red blood on the tree. "Human."

"Fuck."

She nodded, eyes roving over the ground.

They followed the bright splashes away, toward the north. The blood wove between some saplings, pooling up on the other side of a towering elm. Ten feet away from the elm lay a disembodied arm. Skin mottled and brown, it stank of maggots and trash heaps. Or spoiled, soupy vegetables left in the bottom of the crisper drawer for too many months.

He covered his nose, wide eyes glancing at Celia.

She kicked the arm with a boot and shrugged.

Frowning so hard his forehead hurt, he picked up the trail again. The bright red splashes began to dry up, become less.

Jane had slowed the bleeding. Good.

Addy caught his shoulder from behind, pointing ahead.

He stared into the still woods. A body lay ahead, half leaned against a tree.

Quickstepping through silent underbrush, pushing through a patch of poison ivy, he knelt next to the body.

An arrow protruded through one eye and deep into the tree. A drying smear of red blood the shape of a fingertip on the end.

Celia chuckled. "Definitely her."

He stood, glancing around the forest floor. "Which way? I can't find the trail."

"Dad," Mike called, twenty feet to his right. "This way."

"Are you sure?" He trotted over.

Mike nodded, pointing with his forehead.

Another body lay splayed on the ground, knife protruding from its eye.

Jack yanked the knife free, cleaned the blade on the 'Head's ragged shirt, and slid it through his belt. She'd want that back.

Ahead, the trail became easier and easier to make out. She'd begun bleeding again, and the underbrush had been trampled by who knew how many rotting feet.

Breath short, the sense of the others following him far away, he rushed along the trail. A fallen 'Head here, arrow protruding, another there, knife sticking out of its temple.

How many knives did she even carry? He'd never asked.

Crashing through the trees, running over her trail like an eighteen-wheeler with no brakes careening down a mountain, he came to two trees that had grown together as one. A splash of red blood in the shape of a hand smeared on the bark.

He rounded the trees, and there she was, just outside a dappled shaft of light falling through the canopy above.

Buried under four or five Dead Heads. Three more lying on the forest floor in a semicircle around her, arrows sticking from several places each.

Nothing moved.

To say no thought went through his mind as he ran to her would be an insult to lack of thought.

Sliding on his knees through the dirt and leaves, probably shouting, who knew, he ripped the 'Heads off of her. Threw them aside like rag dolls. She'd killed them all, her porcelain skin soaked in their curdled blood.

She didn't move, as still as the bodies.

Gripping the back of her neck, he lifted her head from the forest floor. It lolled above his hand. With his shirttail, he wiped her face clean of the blood and dirt smothering it.

He waited for her to move. Open her eyes. Say his name.

Something touched his hip.

Jumping, eyes wide, he glanced down.

The baby kicked again, rolling. It kicked again and again, the skin of her belly jumping out.

Holding his hand in the air above her, he swallowed around the lump in his throat. The saliva, what there was of it, hurt going down.

The baby rolled, kicking out again.

He laid his hand over it. "Ssh, baby. Ssh. It's OK. She's alright."

The baby continued to kick, right under his hand. He stared into Jane's face.

So still.

Shaking her by the back of the neck, he tried to speak, but his heart had lodged between his breath and his mouth. He swallowed it. "Jane, come back now, OK?" When she didn't stir, he leaned close, laying a scruffy cheek against her smooth one. "Jane," he whispered, "baby, I need you to come back to me now."

He leaned back and watched her eyes.

They rolled under her lids.

He exhaled, lights dancing in front of his eyes. How long had he held his breath?

Pulling a labored breath in through her nose, she opened her eyes. Gaze falling on his face, her mouth fell partway open. She exhaled a sigh.

As though his life depended on it, as though hers did, he kissed her.

Curling her fingers into his hair hard enough to hurt, she kissed him back, tiniest of moans escaping her.

The baby stilled.

Jack's every nerve ending exploded with white light. His very skin vibrated.

So this was what coming home felt like.

He pulled away, staring into her eyes and smiling so hard he thought his cheeks might split. Salty tears rolled into the corners of his mouth.

"I'm sorry," she said, frowning, a fine line between her brows.

Shaking his head, he opened his mouth and paused.

Someone shifted behind him.

"Cat's out of the bag," Jane whispered.

* * *

Between her brother and her mom, Addy followed Jane's trail through the woods. Celia and Dad took point, and the others followed somewhere behind. Dean had taken Data, who snuffled through leaves, trying to chase rabbits instead of Jane.

As they came upon more and more blood, the trail got easy enough for even Addy to follow. Tracking hadn't really been her thing, she was more the gatherer, but the pieces of Dead Heads and eventually whole bodies made it impossible not to follow Jane's path of destruction.

The woods ahead dead silent, Addy's stomach flip-flopped. Whatever they were going to find at the end of the trail might not be good. Even a tough person like Jane would have trouble with what looked like a mini-horde.

She glanced over her shoulder at Dean.

He frowned. "She'll be alright."

"How do you know that?"

"She has to be."

Rather than agree as she'd expected him to, Mike huffed and walked farther ahead. Her dad sprinted ahead.

She quickstepped to keep up.

As they rounded two trees that had grown together, everyone stopped. A hushed silence fell over them all, Yasuo and Renzo bringing up the rear and staring.

Addy's heart caught in her throat. Her face numb.

The air around them slowed, dust motes dancing in the sunbeams breaking the canopy, but Dad didn't hesitate. He sprinted through the small clearing, shouting her name the way Addy had once heard Jane shouting his. Echoing across the grassy fields, she'd screamed his name as though it came from her toes. He did the same now, falling to his knees next to her and ripping the lifeless 'Heads away from her body.

"Oh my god," Mom breathed. "Is she dead?"

"I don't—" Addy began.

She'd seen Jane with several boyfriends over the years, especially once they'd moved to the village. There was always one or two hanging around. As Dad laid his hand over her belly, though, it came to her. She'd never seen anyone touch her with such a sense of intimacy.

A tumbler fell.

Jane stirred, opening her eyes.

"Thank god," Mike said, voice thick.

When they kissed, Addy's mouth fell open. Her mind struggled to place the last few tumblers.

"Well," Mike said, beating her to it, "that explains a few things."

She turned to him, eyes just about popping out of her head. Tried to form her mouth around words, but none seemed adequate.

Mike smiled with the corners of his mouth turned down. "Yeah, bean. It does." He walked around the double tree and vanished.

Dean chuckled.

Staring, using the sight of his crinkled eyes to center herself, she found her voice. "Did you know about this?"

One hand holding Data's leash, one stuck in his pocket, he nodded. "Yeah. I did."

"Wha...how? Did he tell you?"

"No. It wasn't in what he said, it was what he didn't say. In all the months we've been out here, he never said her name. Not once, even when we talked about her and Mike. And the way he looks at her. Well. Two and two, Addy."

All the unfocused feelings swirling around her head coalesced into anger. She spat it in Dean's direction. "You could have fucking told me."

"Whoa," he said, "I didn't *know* know. Just had a feeling I couldn't put a name to." He held up both hands, fighting the overgrown puppy jerking his leash. "And only that for a few weeks."

"I. When did. Oh shit, Mom."

Melinda turned away, hands covering her face. She didn't walk off like Michael had, but her legs trembled as though they wouldn't support her. The sounds of either laughter or tears echoed off her palms. With her face covered, it was impossible to tell. They sounded so similar.

Glancing back at her father, Addy melted just a bit.

Dad hadn't smiled like that in months and months. Probably longer. She might've been a kid last time she'd seen him smile so big. And he was crying.

Melinda sniffled.

Torn between her parents, Addy couldn't move either foot. What finally got her moving was the sight of Jane, curling her fingers in Jack's hair, flushed and smiling. Tears on her cheeks, too.

God, no wonder she hadn't said anything. How the hell would she have explained this?

"Fuck's sake, Jane," she said, kneeling next to them both and glancing at her dad, "are you OK?"

Licking her lips, Jane swallowed and tried to sit up, but her belly got in the way. Gripping Jack's shoulder, she slid her hips back and lifted to sitting. "I think so. Shit, they came out of nowhere. I did good for a while there, but then I ran into that tree over there, and I must've hit my head." Gripping her head with the hand Jack wasn't clutching, she frowned. "What about you?" She glanced at Jack, then back to Addy, brows raised. "Is this, um, are you OK with this?"

"I mean, it's weird, but…wait," she said, voice rising. "Jane, are you bit?" She snatched Jane's forearm and pulled it close. Just beneath her wrist, in the soft flesh, a small chunk of skin had been ripped away. The imprint of a few teeth scraped the edges of the wound.

"Damn, I guess I am. I hardly felt that. Was like a bee sting," she said. "I thought getting bitten would hurt a lot more."

"You're lucky," Jack said, taking her hand and turning it over. He stroked her palm with a thumb and inspected the dirty wound. "A few inches to the left and it would have caught the artery. Did you bring your dose?"

She shook her head. "I haven't carried one in months. Melinda said—"

"You can't give her the Cure, Jackson," Melinda said.

Dad's mouth pinched into a white line. "I thought I told you to stay away from the babies."

"Good thing you're not the boss of me. Besides, you give her Cure now, you'll kill them both."

Jack stood, brushing the knees of his pants with precision.

Stomach a mess of slick knots, Addy backed up next to Jane. "This might get ugly."

"You're telling me," Jane said. "Should we, I don't know, tell them to stop?"

"Won't do any good. I think maybe we should back away." She chewed a nail, teeth slicing into her cuticle.

Jack folded his arms. "What, exactly, are you saying? Won't they both die without it?"

"She's had the vaccine. You can't double up on vaccine and Cure. Besides that," she said, glancing at Jane's belly, "studies have shown a dose of the Cure to have a worse effect on a fetus than alcohol. It can even be fatal." She pointed at him and sneered. "If that's your child, do you really want to take that chance?"

Hands clenched and stuffed into his elbows, Jack opened his mouth.

With stunning alacrity, Jane bounced to her feet. She gripped Jack's shoulder and pulled him down to speak in his ear.

Addy couldn't hear what she whispered, but Dad's expression softened. He almost smiled.

When she'd wished for him to be happy, this wasn't exactly what she'd meant. But it was good to see, nonetheless.

"You're right," he said, smiling at Jane and taking her hand. He glanced at Mom. "You better be right about this vaccine. I won't soon forget this is your fault." They walked out of the clearing, holding hands.

"Neither will I," Mom said, staring after them.

* * *

Once they'd left everyone else and were out of earshot, Jack stopped.

Jane stopped with him, green eyes turned to his, the little golden-brown flecks dancing next to her irises. She bit her lip. "I was afraid you'd hate me if you found out."

So many thoughts floated around his head, he had trouble capturing one of the balloon strings and pulling it in. "What were you doing out here?"

She tugged a paper from her back pocket and unfolded it.

The map he'd left behind.

He studied it. "I should never have let you go," he said. "It was stupid."

"I don't think either of us did this right. I just knew I couldn't be the reason you weren't with your wife." She stuffed the map back in her pocket. "Even so, I was going to tell you about the baby when you came home. But when I saw you, you were with her. And then you, um."

"I went home with her that night," he said, remembering that day on the island. Not for the first time, he saw it from Jane's perspective.

"Yeah," she said, frowning, "so, I thought—" She cut her eyes to the side.

"That's something you don't have to worry about. Listen," he said, brushing a leaf out of her hair, "I could never hate you."

"Do-over?"

He caught her eyes again. Said what he should've said forever ago. "I love you, I want you, I don't want anyone else." A rock the size of a boulder rolled off his heart and disappeared into the woods.

Tears standing in her eyes, she smiled up at him. "I love you, too. It's your baby."

Even expecting it, his breath caught. "You're sure?" Dumb question. Too late to pull back in his mouth.

"I haven't been with anyone else. Not in months before you, and not anyone after. Not at all," she said, kissing the back of his hand. "How could I even want to?" Her eyes fluttered closed. "When I saw myself having kids, I didn't think—"

"Didn't think it'd be with someone my age?"

She laughed. "I didn't think I'd be in love. Let's be honest," she said, glancing up at him, "I don't have the best track record with people close to me. They tend to end up dead." The tears lining her eyes fell. "I sometimes thought I must've done something to deserve it. So I kinda just shut everyone out of my heart."

At a loss, surprised by her honesty, all he could do was gape at her.

"You," she said, poking him in the chest, "you son of a bitch. You got in there anyway."

Lifting her chin with two fingers, he kissed both eyelids and then her lips.

Still, after all this time, she smelled like flowers. Like a whole bouquet of blooming roses. Tasted like the sweetest ambrosia made for the gods of Olympus.

Resting his forehead against hers, he exhaled. "I'd apologize, but I'm not sorry. Not now." He laid a hand on the baby again. "My baby, huh?"

Laying her hand over his, she chuckled. "Yeah. Pain in the ass already, I'll tell you that. Aren't you, baby?"

The baby kicked hard enough to bounce both of their hands.

Jack laughed. Almost twenty-four years since he'd felt the little butterfly kicks of a baby in utero, it still amazed him as much as it had then.

Sticks broke behind them. Data came charging through, Dean following. He stopped, yanking on the leash.

"Hey guys, you see a rabbit? Data seems to think one came through here."

Jack shook his head. "No, no rabbits. Hey Dean," he said, attempting to lift his hand from Jane's belly. She didn't release him.

Which was fine. Nothing had ever been more fine. But questions begged to be asked.

"How's Adelaide?"

Dean shrugged. "She'll be OK. She's a smart woman. She loves you both. I don't think you need to worry about her."

"I wonder how Michael is," Jane said, chewing a nail. "I didn't mean to hurt him. I thought he was alright, but then he told me he loved me, and I realized how stupid I'd been to think that."

"Michael will be fine," Jack said, frowning. "He's strong. It'll take him some time, but I think he'll be alright." Smiling at her again, he took her hand. His cheeks ached. "We should get you home. Get you to the doc. Make sure you and the baby are OK."

Jane nodded. "Did you bring that train of yours, Dean? I could use some time off my feet."

"I did. Should be about an hour from here, as the crow flies."

"Well, hell," she said, taking a step. She coughed, covering her mouth with a slender fist. "We should," she coughed again, dropping Jack's hand and gripping her belly. "Should," she tried again and doubled over coughing.

"Jane?"

"I'm fine," she said, standing and grasping his shoulder. "Just a catch in my throat. I'm—" Her eyes rolled up in her head.

Before she collapsed to the forest floor, Jack got an arm under her. Heartbeat in his temples and throat, he laid her on the ground and screamed for the first person that came to mind who could help.

"Melinda!"

It must have been the note, hell the symphony, of desperation in his voice. The whole group of them came running. Melinda dropped to her knees next to Jane and felt for a pulse.

"What happened?"

"I don't know. She started coughing and collapsed." His voice shook. "Is this a normal reaction with the vaccine?"

"Well," Melinda began.

All the happy butterflies in his stomach curdled like spoiled milk. "Well?"

"Uh," she said, not meeting his eyes, "it's hard to say. We don't have data."

He stood. "What do you mean? You mean you don't know?"

"That's what I mean."

Jane began to shake. Somewhere between the shakes an infected person would get and a seizure.

Stomach in free fall, Jack dropped to his knees next to her again. He laid a hand over her belly and found it hard and unforgiving. "Melinda, is she having a contraction?"

Melinda cleared her throat. "It could be. Or it could be Braxton Hicks. It could be any number of things. I can't tell you yet. We need a hospital. And I need blood tests to find out what's going on with the vaccine and the bite."

"Let's get her to the train, Jack," Dean said. "I can get her to Emerald Hills in a little more than an hour."

Glancing around the circle of faces, he grimaced. "Can you all help me build a litter?"

Without hesitation, Addy gave directions, pulling out her machete and cutting down the nearest sapling. The others gathered cloth to string across, and someone else chopped at another tree.

"I need your watch, Jack," Melinda said, holding out a hand.

He glanced away from the flurry of activity. "What?"

"Your watch," she repeated.

Slipping it off his wrist, he laid it in her palm and curled his legs under him. He settled Jane's head in his lap and brushed the hair from her face. As she went in and out of the shakes, he held her limp, clammy hand and whispered to her that she'd be OK.

THE HILLS

CHAPTER 11

Hanging over Dean's shoulder, Adelaide watched the map screen. The little red dot representing the train flashed faster than she'd ever seen. "Dean," she said, "how fast are we going?"

"Don't worry about it. Just keep an eye on that map. It was clear when we came down a few hours ago, but if anything new showed up on the tracks, it's going to come at us in a hurry. I need you to be my eyes."

She swallowed. "You got it." Staring at the screen, she eavesdropped on the conversations behind her.

"So, you grew up on the island?" Renzo asked.

"Basically," Yaz said. "My parents went there after Charlotte fell. I guess they'd vacationed on the island a couple times. Rode the ferry, whatever. Scott's people were already getting set up."

"Crazy. My parents came up from Brazil. I don't remember my mother, though. My dad used to be some kind of mixed martial arts fighter, I guess."

"Guess that's where you got all that muscle." Yaz laughed.

Addy grinned. Yasuo could make friends with a rock. Without moving her eyes from the screen, she listened for Michael.

He spoke in a quiet voice. "I mean, even given everything, I forgot how quick life can change. Six, seven months ago, I had no idea what was coming. Crazy, right?"

"This is why I don't get close to people," Celia said, her voice muffled by what sounded like a sucker.

"Oh, shut up. That's a lie and you know it. I've seen the way Oren looks at you."

The sound of a hand slapping a shoulder. "You're gonna stop talking now, Michael Cooke."

"Melinda," Dad said, voice pitched high.

"Just keep her head from hitting the floor. It'll pass."

Addy sighed. "Jane's having another seizure, Dean."

"I'm going as fast as I can. Any faster and we'll fly this bucket right off the tracks."

"I know, I know. Just. We can't lose her."

Without looking away from the screens, he laid a hand over hers. "I know, sweetheart. I know. We'll get there."

"This is the settlement, those people from Mom's island?"

He nodded.

"What are you going to say to get us in there? How do you know about this hospital?"

"I'm working on it. We've got a man on the inside. Shit, that reminds me. Hey, Renzo," he said, speaking over his shoulder.

"Yeah, Dean," he said, stepping up on the other side of the Captain's Chair and hanging onto the back.

"Somehow we've got to get in touch with Paul. We don't have the radio, so you've got to find him once we're in. I don't know what's going to happen, except getting Jane to that hospital, pronto." He glanced at Addy. "I'm gonna try and silver tongue our way in there. But if we get arrested, I need you to run. Get to Paul. Think you can do that?"

"You got it."

Dean nodded and punched a button.

Addy rocked forward.

Dad called from the back. "Are we there, Dean?"

"Going up the last hill before we descend into the valley. Ten minutes." He faced Addy. Corners of his eyes crinkled. "Thanks, Addy. Go help him now, I got it."

"You sure?"

"Wait. Kiss me, doll."

Puckering her lips, she blew him an air kiss. "Dad," she said, kneeling next to him, Jane stretched out in the floor, "what can I do?"

He glanced at Melinda.

She shook her head, one hand on Jane's unbitten wrist.

"Not much, right now, baby girl. Help me keep her stable if she has another seizure." His voice wavered, just this side of breaking.

Struck in the heart, as though a tiny little seamstress used it for a pincushion, she hugged him. "It's going to be OK."

"I hope you're right."

"She is," Mike said, kneeling on his other side. He glanced at Jane. "Jane's tough. She'll make it."

Jack hung his head. "Thank you. Both of you." A tear tracked down his cheek, and he threw an arm around each of them. "You guys are my best thing."

"You did good with them, Jack," Melinda said.

"Hey, guys," Dean said, train slowing, "we're here."

* * *

Jack stared out the side window as two armed guards in uniforms, hats pulled over their eyes, flashes of pale skin showing at their necks and wrists, approached. "What's the play, Dean?"

"I'll show them my credentials. I'm a supervisor, remember?"

"Do you have access to a place like this? Isn't this off the map, even for you?"

"Well. I'm not terrible at bullshit," Dean said, clapping Jack on the shoulder. "I'll get us in." He winked.

Not heartened, Jack stepped back from the window. "I've got a bad feeling about this."

"Nonsense," Dean said, pulling papers from a compartment under the driver's seat. "Be right back."

Before he closed the back door, he called out to the guards. "I'm IRF, guys. Papers are in my hand."

Ducking, Jack made his way to the back. His woman still lay on the floor, unconscious, with Melinda taking her pulse. His beautiful children on either side of her, Addy brushing the hair from Jane's face.

"Hey-hey-hey!" Dean shouted, followed by thumping on the side of the train.

"Shit," Melinda whispered. "I don't think they're going for it, Jack."

He peeked out the window.

One guard held his gun trained on Dean's back, while the other spoke into his radio, both of them frowning. The one pointing the gun shifted from foot to foot.

"It doesn't look good," Jack said.

"You there," the one holding the gun shouted, "you stay inside the train. You're not supposed to be here."

Jack sat on the bed, staring at Jane. What could be going on inside her? What kind of war was her body waging with the virus?

Vaccine or no, her immune system was already compromised, just by being pregnant. The first time Melinda had been, he'd done a little reading on the subject, when he wasn't working or studying. From what he could remember, pregnancy was a constant battle between the woman's immune system and the baby.

Could Jane fight the baby *and* the virus? Someone had to come out on the losing end.

Melinda stood and peeked out the window. "It's going to be alright." She smoothed her hair, straightening her shirt. "How do I look?"

"For what?"

"Surrendering."

"What?"

Rather than answer him, she stepped to the back door and flung it wide. "I'm coming out with my hands up, boys. Please don't shoot."

"Stay there, ma'am," the one with the radio called.

"Melinda, what the fuck are you doing," Jack hissed.

"You boys recognize me, don't you?" she asked, stepping down.

Jack tiptoed to the back and peeked around the doorjamb.

The one with the radio slapped the other on the shoulder. The gun wavered. "Holy crap, dude. It's General Thibodeaux. We're supposed to be on the lookout for her."

A slow smile crossed Melinda's lips.

Even from what he could see in profile, Jack shrank from that grin. He'd been on the receiving end of it enough times to know these boys were going to get more than they bargained for.

"That's right, my boy. I'm here to surrender. But," she said, pointing at the train, "I have conditions. I will discuss them with your commanding officer. Before that, you must follow my first condition." She glanced over her shoulder, hazel eyes round, and drew her brows together.

Jack held his breath. The rubber was about to meet the road.

"There's a girl in there who must be taken immediately to the hospital. Give me access to a doctor and facilities to treat a prenatal emergency. Once she's taken care of," she said, turning back to the boys, "you may take my full surrender."

* * *

Dean steered the train through town, slowing at crossings and blowing the horn.

Squished onto the bed with Michael on one side and Celia on the other, Addy frowned. "Thibodeaux? Isn't that your maiden name?"

Dad glanced up, brow wrinkled. He opened his mouth, closed it, and went back to watching Jane.

Exhaling through her nose, Mom nodded. "Dean," she said, staring at the watch in her hand, "can we go faster?"

"What's wrong?" Dad asked, back tensing.

"She's getting thready. We need to get her some oxygen. Get the baby on a monitor. Get the blood work done. We need the hospital, Jack."

Addy's stomach dropped. Most of what Mom said about the hospital made little sense. Hospitals weren't something she knew much about, except that the pharmacies could be helpful if they hadn't been picked clean. Seemed like most of the time what you wanted was a simple damned aspirin and all they had was expired opiates.

Either way, there were people at this hospital who could help Jane. And the baby.

Mike groaned.

"Are you alright?" Addy asked, eyeing him sideways.

He shook his head. His skin a faint shade of green, he gripped the underside of the bed.

"You got any suckers?"

"No," he said, still shaking his head, "gave the last one to Celia."

Addy stared, eyes wide.

Celia chewed on the paper stick, peeling pieces of it away in layers as they softened with saliva. "Sorry." She glanced at Mike. "I didn't realize it was your last one."

Shrugging, he closed his eyes.

"We'll revisit this conversation later," Addy said, bumping his shoulder.

She glanced at one of the guards, his gun pointed in the vague direction of Dean. They'd been hesitant to take Mom's deal, even after talking to their commander. But once they'd stepped onto the train and seen Jane, pasty pale with her sweaty hair stuck to her forehead and her belly rolling, the one with the radio had taken action, pulling his partner onto the train and telling Dean to take it away.

Data bumped Addy on the back of the heel.

She leaned over. He hadn't been crazy about the train and had curled up under the bed. The atmosphere within couldn't be helping. "We'll be there soon, boy," she said, scratching him behind the ear. His tail thumped.

The one with the radio stood, swaying to Dean. He leaned over, speaking in his ear.

Dean sighed and glanced over his shoulder, making eye contact with Addy.

She rocked sideways, into Mike, as the train slowed.

"Dean, what's going on?" Dad asked, eyes closed.

"Gotta make a stop, Jack," Dean said, glancing at the guard. "We'll get going as quick as we can."

The train rolled to a stop in front of a two-story, blocky brick building.

"Alright," the guard said. "Everybody off but these two and the driver." He pointed to Melinda and Jane.

Dad didn't argue, but he also didn't move.

Addy grinned. Good luck getting him off the train, poor, unsuspecting guard. She grabbed Data's leash. "Come on, boy. Let's go for a walk."

Stretching, Data oozed out from under the bed and stood, wagging his tail and grinning up at her.

She scratched his head again, at least some of her anxiety melting through her fingertips as she did.

Tugging him, she stood by the back door and glanced at Dean.

He puckered his lips and blew a kiss, the way she'd done to him earlier.

Stomach flipping, she turned to go out the door.

"Let's go, you too, man," the other guard said, poking Dad in the back with the sight of his rifle.

Jack didn't open his eyes. "Poke me with that again, boy, and you'll find out how it feels up your—"

"Jackson."

"I'm not leaving, Melinda."

"I know, just, god, don't make it worse. Look," she said, releasing Jane's wrist and standing. She spoke to the first guard, the one with the radio. "Can I talk to you? What's your name?"

"Matt."

"Matt. Dear. This man is the father of that baby. You cannot ask him to leave. He won't, and I guarantee you'll have to shoot him if you hope to force him."

The boy shuffled a foot. "But Commander Burke said—"

She laid a hand on his shoulder and squeezed. "I don't care what Commander Burke said. If you force this man off the train, our deal is off. If she dies while you stand here hemming and hawing about what your commander said, our deal is off. And then"—she glanced down at Jack, who'd begun to shake when she suggested Jane might die—"that man is going to kill you. I've known him for nearly half my life. Trust me when I say I know what he's capable of."

Without waiting for an answer, she sat and took up Jane's wrist again. "We need to hurry, gentlemen."

"Fine," Matt said, waving his gun, "you guys all get off." He stepped around Addy with a grimace and opened the door.

As she stepped off the train, Addy glanced back at her dad.

So she really was going to be a big sister.

Mike shoved her. "Move," he mumbled, tripping down the stairs. He puked on the ground next to the train, leaning against it with one hand.

Yasuo came down last and patted Mike on the back. "You alright?"

Mike shook his head.

As Addy stood there, slack-jawed, Data snuck to the end of his leash and lapped up the puke.

"Oh, Data," she said, yanking him away, "gross."

The train's horn blew, and it pulled away.

"This way, everyone," Matt said. "The commander would like you to get settled. We'll help you with your supplies."

Five armed men emerged from the building in front of them.

Raising the hand not holding her dog, Addy frowned. "This isn't real helpful, Matt."

"Just a few questions first. If you would, everyone, please." He motioned to the door.

Shuffling sideways, Renzo inhaled.

Addy remembered Dean's request.

"Hey, Matt," she said and kicked him in the shin.

"Son of a bitch," he said, hopping on the other leg and lifting the gun to the sky.

Renzo took off. Before the guards even knew he'd gone, he was down the hill and into the trees.

Scowling, Matt glanced at the rest of them and lowered his foot. "We will find him. Anyone else tries that, I'll shoot you myself. Inside, now." He yanked the door open and waved the gun.

One by one, they filed inside.

* * *

Addy stepped into the cool building, one hand held above her head. Data's nails clicked on the floor as they walked in.

"You can lower your hands," Matt said, pulling the door closed. It whooshed, latching into place. "Bulletproof glass." He knocked on the window in the door. "You'll be safe here."

Data slipped on the glossy floor, jerking Addy down with him.

Somehow, she kept her footing in this shiny, citrus-smelling hallway. Reaching down to scratch his ear as he regained his feet, she glanced around. Looked like it might have been a school once. "Tell me, Matt, who are you?"

He stepped closer and removed his cap. With the shadow off his face, he appeared older. Closer to her age than she'd thought, bright blue eyes peeked from beneath dark brows. "I'm afraid I can't really tell you that right now. But if you'll follow me and my men," he said, pointing to two men behind him, "we can get down to some questions I have for you."

Glancing behind her, she eyed her brother.

His complexion back to normal, he nodded. "What could it hurt, Addy?"

She snorted, nodding to the group. "Watch your asses. I'll see you soon."

Matt's men took her friends and Mike and led them down the hall. Sunlight bounced off the waxed linoleum floor and into her eyes as she tracked them. They disappeared into a room halfway down.

She turned back to Matt.

He smiled, lines ingrained on either side of his lips like a pair of parentheses framing his mouth. He held a hand toward the room behind her. "After you."

Going ahead, she walked into the classroom.

Gone were the desks it must've once held. It'd been a long time since she'd seen an actual classroom, but she remembered whiteboards and desks and carpet from 1986.

This room, grey and barren, shone from the coat of spit shine these guys must've put on it. In the center stood a table and two chairs. No other furniture or ornamentation.

Like Matt's slick smile, it felt just a little too perfect. All the edges too square. Everything just a little too clean.

"Please," he said, "if you'd have a seat, we can get these questions out of the way."

Sliding the chair out on its silent feet, she sat hard. It didn't squeak.

Unnerved, she smiled at Matt. Two could play the smile game. "So, Matt, can I ask questions of my own?"

"Sure. I might not answer them. But you have to answer mine first," he said, slinging his rifle over the back of the chair and sitting across from her. He produced a small notebook, flipping it open and grinning again.

She started. "So, you're IRF, right?"

"You already know the answer to that. My questions first, Adelaide. That is your name, right?"

She swallowed. "Yeah. How did you know?"

"Adelaide Cooke, yes? Daughter of, let's see…" He flipped a few pages in his notebook. "Ah. Jackson Cooke. No picture available. Is he with you?"

"No."

"Don't lie," he said, lines appearing in his cheeks again.

"No, not right now. He's on the train."

"I see," he said, bending over the notebook and writing. "That's his baby in there." He glanced up. "The baby will be well taken care of. We have a top facility here."

She crossed her arms. "Huh. Tell me about that."

"Ms. Cooke, procreation is the number one priority. Surely you must realize that."

"You sound like Jane."

He made a note in his book. "And she is?"

"Probably dying."

He frowned, flipping another page in the book. "Oh. The pregnant woman. So, uh. How are you acquainted with General Thibodeaux?"

She smiled, leaning on the table. "Ah, there it is. That's what you really wanted to ask about, isn't it?"

He cleared his throat. "Well. Um. Also, have you ever been bitten, that sort of thing."

"Yeah, once," she said, waving her hand.

He flipped the notebook closed. "I'm afraid that's all the questions I have, then. We'll escort you and anyone else in your group who's been bitten to the edge of town and ask that you leave."

Watching him stand, stomach twisting, she crossed her arms. "I'm not leaving without my dad. Jane. Dean."

Matt smiled, disarming blue eyes twinkling. "I'm going to have to insist," he said, holding his hand toward the door. "Our population here is pristine. Untouched. With formerly infected here, we run the risk of contamination. I'm sorry," he said, stepping around the table, "but we can't take the chance you would pollute them." He gripped her arm.

She sprung up, Data following her and growling, and yanked her arm. "Don't you touch me. We're not going anywhere, not without my family."

He frowned. "Miss Cooke, I don't want to hurt any of you. But you can't be here." He tightened his grip.

Heart in her throat, she blurted the one thing she knew would work. "She's my mother, alright?"

"Say again?"

"The general. She's my mom."

He jerked the notebook from his pocket and dropped it on the floor with a splat. Cheeks red, he picked it up and flipped through pages and pages of notes. "She's not. It doesn't. I don't have notes about her having a family."

"We thought she was dead. Until about six months ago."

"She…" He trailed off, glancing up at her. "Oh. You look just like her."

Heat sprang up in her cheeks. "I've heard that." Data walked around her legs, wrapping them in the leash.

Fighting to maintain her balance, she peeked over the top of the notebook as Matt scribbled.

"So, we can stay?"

"Well, we can't kick you out now. This deal with the general is far too important. My commander has been waiting a long time for a break like this."

"I hate to jinx it," she said, sitting back down, "but why is he being so compliant to her?"

Matt grinned and sat opposite her again. "The commander is more of a chess player than a bulldozer."

"That makes no sense."

"I just mean, he must want something from your mom. And you get more ants with honey."

CHAPTER 12

Jack wandered back into Jane's hospital room with two cups of coffee.

"You're a lifesaver," Melinda said.

Frowning, he handed her the cup and sat on the opposite side of the bed. "That's as a thank you. I appreciate what you've done." He glanced at Jane's sleeping face. "But I'm not sure I like you being here. In a hospital."

She sipped. "You're welcome."

He exhaled through his nose. The coffee sloshed, burning the side of his hand. He cursed and sat it on the bedside table, drying his hand on his pants.

Jane's eyelids flew up like window shades, and she tensed every muscle.

"Oh god, finally," Jack exhaled.

Without moving her head, she looked at him. With the intubation tube rammed down her throat, she couldn't speak, but she moved her lips and the tip of her tongue flashed out. She tried to wet her lip and jerked one hand. It'd been buckled into restraints. She wrinkled her brow, fine line appearing between them.

He took her hand. "I'm sorry. You kept trying to pull out the tube. Melinda," he said, "can we get this thing out now?"

"Let me get a nurse," she said, sipping her coffee and walking out the door.

Jane moaned, exhaling through her nose. Squeezed his hand.

He freed her arm, insides doing a complicated dance between sorrow and happiness. He leaned over her, laying a cheek on hers.

She exhaled and stilled, her thumb stroking the back of his hand.

Melinda and a nurse came in and went through the sickening process of removing the tube. Jane coughed six or seven times, and the nurse handed her an oxygen mask as they sat her up in bed.

He kept her hand, watching her eyes as she sat up. Waiting for them to roll up again. Waiting to lose her.

Instead, she glanced down at her belly. Exhaling, spit coating the inside of the oxygen mask, she ripped her hand from his, unbuckled her other one, and curled up around the baby. Pulling her knees as close as she could get them, she rocked with her face down.

"She's alright, Jane," he said. "You're both OK."

Rolling her forehead against her knee, she pulled the mask down around her neck. "She," she croaked.

He smiled. "Yeah, she. Doc did an ultrasound."

Tip of her nose turning red, she grinned and reached for him. As he took her hand, she tugged.

He moved his ass from the chair to the bed.

Clearing her throat, she opened and closed her mouth several times before words followed. "I thought I was dreaming. Was I dreaming? Are you here?"

"I'm here, Jane," he said, "I love you, and if I have to tell you a thousand times a day so you're sure, I'll do it."

Sighing, she patted his cheek. "Damn right you will."

"I'll just, um, I'll be at the nurses' station, Jack," Melinda said, shuffling a foot.

"Melinda, wait," Jane said, sitting up. "I wanted to thank you." She cleared her throat again.

Jack slid the water cup into her outstretched hand.

She drank, cleared her throat again, and inhaled. Exhaled. "I don't remember a lot. It's a blur. But I know you helped me. I owe you."

The corners of Melinda's mouth raised, eyes narrowed and warm.

It lifted a weight from Jack's heart he hadn't known was there. She may not have granted anyone such a sincere smile since she'd come back from the dead.

"I'm glad I could be there. It was my people who did this to you, the least I can do is help."

"How long have I been here?" Jane asked. "How long since I was bitten?"

"A week," Jack said.

Jane laid back into her pillow. "A week. And I'm not infected. Or dead. I think your vaccine works."

Again, Melinda's smile touched the corners of her eyes. "I'm grateful none of this killed you. You, um"—she cleared her throat, crossing her arms and staring at her feet—"you seem to mean a great deal to my family. And to Jack."

"I'm glad it didn't kill me, too," Jane said. "Do you know what happened after I was bitten? What caused this?" She gestured at the hospital bed.

"We're still trying to determine exactly what happened. More blood tests would—"

"Melinda," Jack said, "no. No more tests. Not right now."

She cleared her throat. "That's. You're right. We will need to eventually." She glanced at Jane. "But for now, I think we have what we need. There is a small matter, though."

Jack frowned. The words she used said "small matter," but her tone implied something else.

Jane clutched his hand. "Is the baby going to be alright?"

Melinda glanced up again, unable to maintain eye contact. "We're not sure."

Taking a bare moment to be thankful he was already sitting, he slid his arm around Jane and pulled her close. "Of course she'll be OK. Right, Melinda?"

"Uh," her voice shook, "we're really not sure, Jackson. This is kinda new territory for everyone. We don't know exactly how the interaction of the live virus with the vaccine will play across the placenta."

"Fuck's sake, Melinda." His throat tight, the curse came out more like a whimper.

Melinda made eye contact with Jane and held it. "I know this is my fault. I'm going to do everything I can to save this baby. You have my word."

Closing her eyes, Jane leaned into him. "I'd like to be alone with my. With Jack, please."

Melinda stepped into the hall and pulled the door closed behind her.

Words failed him. There were none he knew to fix this. None.

Jane pulled her knees up and scooted so he could slide farther onto the bed. She tugged.

Though the bed was a twin, she made room for him by lying on her back. He lay with her, plastic rail digging into his back, one hand on the baby.

"Hi," she said, eyes dancing. "I missed you."

"I thought I might lose you again. I don't know what I would've done."

"Carry on, just like you always have."

He shook his head, burying his face in her hair. It'd almost gotten to her shoulders already. "Maybe," he said, "but I don't want to."

"If there's one thing I know," she said, fingers sliding around the back of his neck, "the last few months have only reinforced: Enjoy the moments you have." She paused to kiss him, cradling the back of his head. "You never know when they might be the last ones you get."

The baby launched a kick so hard his hand flew into the air.

Jane cursed. "Pipe down in there, you." She rubbed her belly.

He chuckled. "I imagine she'll be using throwing knives before she's out of diapers."

"I wish I could've seen the ultrasound."

"Oh, wait," he said, jumping up. "Here, there's a thing." He leaned into a cabinet next to the bed, digging through supplies. He'd watched the nurse put it back in here somewhere. It even had working batteries. When Paul had said this place was bright and shiny, he hadn't been lying.

"What are you doing in there?"

"Ah, got it," he said, snatching up the little white box and the mystery gel that went with it. Sitting back on the bed, he grinned.

"This was my favorite part with Michael. I didn't get the chance with Addy. Here," he said, giving her shoulder a gentle push, "lie back."

"What are you doing?" she asked again, lying back with a frown.

"Hope it's not too chilly," he said, pushing her gown up over the baby. Eyes closed, he kissed the warm skin.

The baby kicked him in the face. Maybe it was an elbow. Either way, he sat up and squeezed out a bit of the goop onto Jane's belly the way he'd seen the nurse do. He turned on the little machine. Jane watched him with wide eyes as he lowered the wand.

Muffled bumps echoed out of the box. He moved it in small circles as he'd watched the nurse do four times a day for a week.

"What—" Jane began.

A fluttering, hummingbird-quick whooshing emanated from the box. He stopped moving the wand and closed his eyes, smiling and listening.

"Jack," she whispered.

He peeked at her.

Her eyes filled with tears. She laid a hand on her stomach, opposite from the wand. "It's so fast. Is that the baby's heartbeat?" The tears spilled over, a few collecting in the cup of her ear.

"It is. It's supposed to be fast. That's her, Jane. That's our baby." Light-headed, he closed his eyes again.

She took his other hand, and they sat, listening to the baby's heart. Stretching the moment as far as it would go.

* * *

Addy sat on Dad and Jane's couch, watching her dog as he gave the room a sniffing. "How is everything, boy?"

Nose to the ground, he wagged his tail. It cleaned the coffee table.

"Shit," she said, jumping up. Catching her half-full water glass before it fell, she set it back in the middle of the table. She swept books up from the floor, elderly things without covers, and stacked them back on the table. The top title said something about pregnancy and birth.

Jane walked into the room, speaking over her shoulder. "Yeah, I'll bet you do." She wobbled a bit and shot Addy a glance. "Don't look at me like that. I'm not waddling yet." With a grin, she perched on the couch and pulled her feet up under her. "Nice digs, huh?"

"Compared to literally anything I've ever seen, it may as well be a mansion," Addy said. She leaned forward. "Isn't it a little weird, though? Out here in the middle of the mountains, all this," she said, gesturing in a wide circle. "And I told you what Matt said about the bulletproof glass. It all feels wrong."

Jane nodded, picking up her knitting. This time, it was a tiny little hat. A pink one.

"Jane," Addy said, "I thought you hated pink."

She smiled with the corner of her mouth, eyes flashing. "I did. I guess it's not so bad. Under the right circumstances."

"About that," Addy started.

Jane lowered the knitting to her lap, staring at her knees. "Addy. I—"

"You don't have anything to apologize to me for, Jane. Really," she said, squeezing her knee.

Glancing up, Jane tried on a smile. Her brows wrinkled in a question.

"He makes you happier than I've ever seen. And you do the same for him. An idiot could see that."

Red raced from Jane's neck to her hairline. "I didn't plan it that way." She pushed hair from her face with the flat of a hand. "Are we OK?"

Addy swallowed. "I'm working on it." Not that it would ever be what it had been. Years of kicking around together, whispering secrets. All of it undone. Complicated by life.

"Please don't be mad at me, Addy. I couldn't stand that. I really couldn't take it."

She smiled. "I'm not mad at you, Jane. Yasuo and I have talked a lot about balance and how powerless I am over people, places, and things. It's good, Jane. It's different. But it's OK."

Grinning, Jane went back to her knitting. "You remember that night I got all mad at Michael?"

Addy chuckled. "Which one?"

"The night you met Dean."

The cat water. Mike sitting on Jane's feet. Gerald getting bitten. Dean in his pea green army jacket. Dean and his crinkly eyes. His immediate regard for her.

"I remember. You wouldn't tell me why you were so mad."

She sighed, putting the knitting down again. "Oddly, I've thought a lot about that over the last few months. I'm still not a hundred percent, being honest, but I think… After you and Dean left to go tell Jack about the 'Head, Mike kinda tried to put the moves on me." She pulled her mouth into half a frown. "You know, in Mike's own special way. He'd never done that before. Did you know that?"

"I could've guessed."

"Yeah. Well. I was going to let him. Didn't we all kind of accept that's the way it was going to be?"

"Did we?"

Both corners of Jane's mouth pulled down. "I was alright with it. In my head. Mike's a good guy."

"The best."

Jane nodded. "The best. All these other guys, I just, you know. It was whatever. But when it came down to it, I couldn't be that way with Mike. I didn't feel that way about him. I never have. I couldn't lead him on."

"Then why were you mad at him?"

She sighed. "I was mad at me. Look, I didn't realize it at the time. I wanted Mike to be someone he's not. I made that mistake more than once."

"I'm confused."

"So was I. But I can tell you one thing. After I had to kill Bi— my dad, when I found out Jack was in trouble, nothing was ever more clear. I had to help him. I didn't even think. I just went."

Addy flashed on running to Dean through the surf. No thought. Just feeling. Uncomplicated and clear.

The last tumbler fell.

"Wow, Jane. Wow."

"Bad wow?"

Shaking her head, Addy leaned on her knees. "I get it. I do." She gave Jane's knee a squeeze again.

"Ouch, son of a bitch," Jane said, flinching.

"Sorry, what," Addy said, yanking her hand back as though she'd stuck it in a fire.

"Oh, not you, sorry. This baby just hauled off and punched me in the liver or something."

Addy chuckled. If there were ever two people who were tougher fighters, she'd never met them. And here they'd gone and made a baby. "I don't know what you expected, considering her parents."

Rubbing her side, eyes closed, Jane nodded.

"Sorry," Jack said, walking in. "I'd carry her for you if I could, Jane."

She nodded, eyes still closed. "You'll get your chance, love."

He flushed, sitting in the chair across the table.

He'd never looked more human.

They had a good night, laughing, talking, just being generally happy. It'd been a while since Addy'd had that, with either of them, and it was a welcome change. She wasn't about to make it weird or get up in arms about something that made two people she cared so much for deliriously happy.

Life was weird, sometimes.

* * *

After prying Data away from a corner in the kitchen, where he must have sniffed out a mouse or something, Jack shut the front door on his eldest daughter and her dog.

Sitting on the couch with Jane, he sighed. Being this content, it was unusual. So foreign, there must be something wrong with it.

"You alright?" Jane asked, needles clicking. She sat with her bare feet on the couch, back to the arm.

He peeked at her. The lamp shone from behind her, giving her already glowing skin a halo. He'd thought she was beautiful before. Now, she was like a living angel. Cliché as it was, a gift straight from the heavens.

Impossible. Something had to be wrong. Feeling this good shouldn't be allowed.

Her brow creased. "What's wrong?"

"Nothing," he said. "Nothing."

She grinned, setting her knitting on the coffee table. Sliding close, she nudged his back with a foot.

He leaned up, and she slid her leg behind him, throwing the other over him.

His toes tingled.

Leaning on the back of the couch, she brushed a hair from his forehead and ran her fingers through it.

He shivered, the feeling rolling down his spine and resting in his stomach, curling at the edges of his toes and sending heat all the way back up.

"Jack," she whispered, "I need you to kiss me."

He did as he was told.

Not that it could be, but every kiss was better than the last.

He buried a hand in her hair and slid the other under her shirt. The skin of her back smooth, like light made physical, he pulled her closer. Her belly pressed into his leg.

Breaking away, he grinned and glanced down.

She lifted her shirt, rubbing the compact little belly. "She's hiding in the back tonight. Tap dancing on my liver."

Covering her hand with his, he caught her eyes. Watched as the golden flecks danced. "My god woman, you're breathtaking."

The blood rushed to her cheeks. Pulling her leg from behind him, she straddled him and kissed him like her lips were on fire. Yanking his shirt off, she kissed every inch of his neck and chest until she couldn't bend any farther.

He returned the favor with her shirt, reveling in the feeling of her warm skin on his. Something he'd thought he'd never feel again.

As they undressed and he fell completely in love with her all over again, he couldn't shake the feeling something had to be wrong. Waiting for him to look away before it came to drag him into the dark again.

"Jack, where did you go," she said, cool fingers cupping his jaw.

Swallowing, he wrapped his arms around her waist and drew her closer. "Don't let me go again, Jane."

"You're here with me, right now," she said. Gripping both sides of his head, she turned his face up and stared into his eyes. "You hang onto that, honey."

He nodded and stretched to kiss her, her silky lips light on his, her round belly squished between them.

With a muffled groan, she leaned back and stood. "Take me to a real bed for once, love." She stretched out her fingers for him.

Grasping them, he followed her upstairs and onto the bed, fresh sheets smelling of a hint of lavender and a bit of sunshine. He didn't think his feet touched the ground once. And lying back, he could hardly feel the bed. He could only feel her. When she straddled him again, grinning down at him, he stared in disbelief. At the sheer luck of her being here.

And when she finally slipped him inside, he had to restrain what wanted to be instant. What cried to let go. Desperate to stretch the moment, he almost couldn't look at her.

But she went slow, her hips moving in a gentle rocking. She let him savor the moment, let him hold onto it for as long as he could.

* * *

Addy wandered through town. A few lights on here and there, her footsteps echoed in the quiet streets. She couldn't see her breath, but winter was fast on the heels of fall.

In the week they'd been here, she'd met probably half the people from Emerald Isle. It was the same story with them all.

Innocents. Most of them had never even seen a Dead Head. None of them carried weapons. Although they knew about the Cure, they acted as though the thought of using it was a strange, distasteful thing. Especially the younger ones, the ones Addy's age. Like they were immune to the virus.

In a way, she supposed they were. If they'd never even seen a Dead Head, the virus may as well have never existed.

They didn't know what death smelled like. What it felt like when it reached for you with its black claws. Its breath on your neck. The blood curdled in its eyes. Gnashing its teeth in your face.

"Adelaide, what are you doing out so late," Matt said, stepping out of a shadow.

Heart in her throat, she yanked Data's leash before he barked. "Fucking hell, Matt. Scared the shit out of me. What the fuck?"

"Sorry."

"The hell were you doing lurking there anyway, crazy stalker?"

He took a bite out of a hunk of beef jerky. "Just waiting."

"Uhm."

"No," he said, laughing, "not like that. That's not. Alright, let me start over."

She nodded, crossing her arms.

"Good evening, Miss Cooke. I'm here waiting for my girlfriend. We walk together every night. Won't you join us?"

Laughing, Addy exhaled. "Sure. When will she be here?"

Data growled, low in his throat.

"Matthew," a voice said, rounding the corner, "why is there a…oh."

Addy stuck out the hand not holding the leash. "Adelaide Cooke."

The willowy blonde crossed her arms and raised a brow. "Mm-hmm. Matthew?"

"Ella, sweet pea, this is Addy. She's. Her family just got here," he said, giving Ella a peck on the cheek. "Addy, this is Ella."

"Just got here? That's odd." Ella took in Addy and Data with a raised brow, lips pursed.

"I can't really say more, cupcake. Security stuff."

She blew a breath out her nose. "You and your security stuff." Hooking her arm through his, she pulled him down the sidewalk.

Addy tugged Data and positioned herself on Ella's side. She tried a few conversational gambits in her head, but none of them seemed to work in the face of Ella's eyebrows.

Ella sniffed. "Adelaide."

"Yeah."

"I assume this is your dog?"

Addy smiled, scratching him behind an ear. "He is. His name is Data."

They crossed under an orange streetlight, and in its glow, Ella frowned. "That's an interesting name."

"Thanks." She folded her cards close to her vest and tried to tease some of Ella's loose. "Do you have any pets?"

"I do not. Pet hair is impossible to clean."

"That's true." She laughed. "Data is impossible in a lot of ways. But he's a decent tracker, and he's better at making friends than me."

Matt chuckled.

"What's funny?"

"Nothing. You seemed to have plenty of friends when you got here."

Ella stopped. "Tell me about that, Matthew. A whole group of people came in that I knew nothing about?"

He shook his head, scuffing his heel on the sidewalk. It rasped against the sole of his boot. "I told you, muffin. Security stuff."

"You act like I'm a child. He never tells me anything," she said, leaning toward Addy.

"I used to have that problem with my boyfriend, Dean." Addy frowned. "He's better now. Although," she said, glancing at Matt, "your boyfriend here locked him up and won't let me talk to him."

Matt rolled his eyes.

Ella pulled her arm free. "You what?"

"Pumpkin," he began.

"Don't you pumpkin me! You let that woman see her boyfriend!" She stomped a foot.

Addy smirked. This Ella might prove useful.

"It's not that simple, Ella-belle," he said, reaching for her.

"Matthew Aaron Lyburn, it is that simple. You're the head of the guard. You do what you want."

Oh, ouch. All three names. Addy grinned wide, scratching Data between the ears, and watched the couple argue.

She wanted Ella to win. She hadn't seen Dean since they got off the train. He'd been locked up as soon as Jane was at the hospital, for trying to access a restricted area. Mom hadn't been able to do anything without risking Jane's health. Addy couldn't do anything for the same reason.

But she hadn't even been able to look at his face. See his smile. Make sure he was alright.

Ella twisted her lips in a sour frown. "Adelaide, you don't worry about Matthew. If he can't help you," she said, hooking her arm under Addy's and pulling her along as she started walking again, "I'll get you in there. Commander Burke is my father."

Addy glanced over her shoulder and grinned as Matt jogged to catch up.

CHAPTER 13

Sun creeping through the window snuck under Jack's eyelids. He rolled to his back and stared at the ceiling, relishing the first night they'd spent together in a real bed. Even the quiet moments in the cold dead of night, when Jane woke him with nightmares.

He eased his arm from under hers, slid out of bed, and located the closest pair of pants. When the powers that be had set them up with this house, they'd also brought in a whole closet full of clothes. Even had the right sizes.

He might be over the moon, but he wasn't stupid. All these things were some kind of trick. Some sort of ploy.

And why had they given them their weapons back? He'd taken a stroll with Matt, the head of the guard, around the perimeter of the whole compound. Most of it ringed in twenty-foot tall steel-reinforced walls, there seemed little to worry about.

But who even was he without worrying?

Strapping on his belt, settling his weapons into place, he glanced at the sleeping woman in the bed. What was it she'd said last night?

"I thought we'd just be a fling. Just a little bit of nothing fun. I didn't know how hard I'd fall. This is crazy."

Crazy. What was crazy was that despite all the seeming differences, the more they talked, the more he found they had in common. And the more grateful he was that he didn't let a little thing like an age difference that only mattered to the society he came from before all this bar him from finding someone who was so perfectly suited for him.

He crept down the cold stairs in his bare feet and sought out the coffee. If there were clothes in the closets, surely there'd be coffee in the cabinets.

And so there was. He set to making it.

Glass broke outside. "Dad!"

Adrenaline dumping into his legs, he dashed to the living room and peeked out the front window.

Michael stood in the yard, listing as he clutched the porch railing. Glass at his feet.

He opened the door. "Mike? You OK, buddy?"

"No, I'm not fucking OK. No. I am not."

Jack stepped out onto the porch. Bare feet and bare chest freezing in the October morning. "Come inside. Tell me what's wrong."

Mike stumbled, falling on the frosty grass. He pointed a finger. "You know. You know what's fucking wrong. I *loved* her." Eyes closed, he rolled to his knees and tried to stand.

Jack glanced at the broken glass. Amber liquid glistened on the shards. "Please," he said, holding up a hand and stepping around the broken liquor bottle, "come inside. We'll talk."

Grimacing, wiping his wet face with a shirt sleeve, Mike shook his head. Clenched his fist. "I never even had a chance. Never." He stepped into Jack's bubble, wobbling. His breath stank of alcohol.

Emptiness engulfed Jack's heart, popping sweat on his forehead in the chilly morning. His little boy was heartbroken, and it was his fault.

"You took her away, *Jack*," Mike spat. "You're supposed to protect me, and you took her away."

"I understand," he said, not breaking a whisper. He cleared his throat. "I understand if you hate me. I don't know what else to say but I'm sorry. I didn't mean to. I didn't plan it."

Lowering his voice to a fierce whisper, Mike crushed him. "I wish I could hate you," he said, red-rimmed eyes cast down.

"Michael," he said, reaching for his son's shoulder.

Mike slapped his hand away, and when he looked up, features twisted into a scowl Jack had never seen on his face, tears dropped from both eyes. He pulled back his arm, balled fist at the end of it.

Jack closed his eyes and dropped both hands.

Mike's fist connected with a glancing blow to his jaw.

Stars lit the inside of his head. He stumbled but kept his feet. If his son wanted a target, the least he could do was provide him with a standing one.

Another fist connected with his right eye.

He locked the shout behind his lips. Swallowed it down into his throat. His eyes burned and his chest ached, but not from being hit.

Another fist knocked him in the temple and sent him stumbling again.

Fighting to maintain his footing, he crunched down on the broken glass. The bottom of his foot seared, glass grinding into the heel. Slipping, he opened his eyes and fell.

Glass ground into his palms, and he teetered sideways, landing on more shards.

With any luck, one of them would be large enough to puncture a lung or something. He'd done this, thinking with his cock instead of his brain. His fault. Every bit of it.

Mike kicked him in the gut.

The smallest of exhales escaped him. He gripped his stomach, slick, bloody hands sliding across his abdomen.

"Michael," Jane shouted from the front door. "Michael, stop!"

Bare feet slapped the wood, tripping down the stairs.

"Jane," Jack tried to say. All the wind knocked out of his words, he tried again. "Jane, it's OK."

"Watch out for the glass," Mike said, stepping between them. "You'll cut yourself."

"Get out of my way, Michael. And stop this. It's not his fault."

Mike sniffled. "He was. He's. You're wrong. He did this to me."

"No, he didn't. I love him. I love him. I'm sorry it couldn't be you. But it's not because of him, alright?"

"He took away my chance," Mike said, voice small. Like a boy.

Jack snuffled, the fresh copper scent of blood sliding down his throat. Tried to speak again. Tell his little boy it was OK. Tell Jane it was OK.

"No, he didn't." She stepped around the shining shards of glass, some now tipped with red. Sunlight glinted off each of them, deflecting tiny little yellow pinpricks of light.

"I never felt that way about you, Mike. Never. I love you. But not like that. I'm sorry," she said, kneeling next to Jack. "Come on, baby." She tugged his arm.

Jack sat up, trying to open both eyes. The right one had swollen shut.

Without another word, Mike wobbled out of the yard.

Jane tugged and pulled when Jack lacked the strength to stand on his own. Working together, they got him up.

Ducking under his arm, she guided him back to the house.

He limped up the stairs, leaving bloody footprints on the porch like a Dead Head would.

* * *

Matt unlocked the back door to the jail. "Now look," he said, glancing over his shoulder, "don't tell Ella about this. I can't afford for her dad to find out."

Arms crossed, Addy grinned. "What are you going to tell her, then?"

"You let me worry about Ella. Just try to make it quick." He opened the door.

"Yes sir," she said, sketching a salute. Slipping past him, she stepped into a cool, dark room. Bars across the high, small windows. Eyes widening as he closed out the morning light, she asked about the inside lights.

Voice low, he grabbed her just above the elbow. "No lights, not right now."

"I can't see anything," she said, unease fluttering in her gut. Alone in a dark room with a strange man with a gun. Not the best place in the world to be. Dad would kill her if he found out she'd taken such a stupid risk.

"It's OK, Addy. It's just right here." Light edged the bottom of a door and glowed through a frosted window at head height.

He could be putting her in a cell. That was possible.

The door before her opened, light flooding her eyes.

She squinted.

"Oh thank god," Dean said. "Matt, you came through."

"Fine, yeah, whatever. Just don't tell anyone. Five minutes, you guys."

The door behind Addy closed as her eyes were still adjusting. A Dean-shaped blur approached her.

She blinked. Before her vision cleared, he wrapped her in a hug.

Pulling a breath deep in her lungs, she smiled and hugged him back. His scent was as much a balm to the soul as freshly fallen rain.

"I have been so worried about you," he said, cupping her face in his hands, corners of his eyes crinkling.

"I'm fine." Running her hand over the beard taking hold on his jaw, she frowned. "I hadn't realized your beard had so much red in it."

Still holding her face, he bent to kiss her.

Her feet suddenly too close together, she fell backward.

Wrapping an arm around her, he reached out with the other and stood them both up against the wall, kissing her neck.

"Dean," she said, smiling, "we only have five minutes."

"Long enough," he said, kissing the other side.

She closed her eyes. "Ha-ha. No really. We've got to get you—"

He covered her mouth with a kiss. "They're listening," he whispered, lips less than half an inch away from her ear. Moving to the other side, he kissed her jaw. "They're always listening. Always," he said, pulling back.

As he moved to step away, she gripped the back of his head and pulled him close again. "Don't you think Matt would have diverted their attention?"

His warm breath tickled her ear again. "Can't be too careful." He went to pull away again.

Hooking an ankle around his leg, she laughed. "You can't escape me that easy, mister." She kissed him, forgetting about everything for a bare few moments.

After what could have been their entire five minutes, she broke away. Sliding her hands down the back of his head and neck, she spoke into his ear. "We haven't been able to find Paul or Renzo."

Frowning, he leaned in. "Try the west wall. Sunset. Tonight. He should be there." He kissed her neck, down to her shoulder.

Giving him a playful shove, she smiled, eyes darting around the room. If they were listening, they could be watching, too.

"Here, have a seat." He motioned to a steel chair bolted to the wall.

"Nice digs."

"Mmm. Yeah. Well. They feed me, at least." He sat cross-legged on the floor in front of her. "Hey, I did have a question for you."

"Shoot."

"Is your dad OK?"

Shifting gears, she frowned. "I just saw him and Jane last night, so, I assume so. I mean, they seemed plenty fine when I left. Why?"

"I heard something, that's all."

"What something? When?"

He leaned forward, laying his forearm on her leg. Took her hand and kissed her palm. "The guards were talking about it this morning. I guess news travels fast around here."

She chuckled. "Like Harkers. Yeah. What did you hear?"

"I hear he and Mike got into it."

And just like that, the sun was gone out of the day. "Ah, fuck," she said, standing. Crossing her arms, she paced the cell. "Anything else?"

"That it was less of a fight and more of a beating."

"Jesus Christ. Fucking hell," she said, leaning over. Gripping her knees, she closed her eyes and breathed. "We all said Mike would be OK. We didn't even worry about him. Goddammit, Dean. How could I be so stupid?"

He rubbed her back. "It's not your fault, Addy. Hell, it's nobody's fault. It just is."

She stood. "However hard Mike is taking it, my mom is taking it six thousand times worse. Hell. I need to check on them."

As though on cue, Matt opened the door in the back of the cell. "Time's up, guys."

Clutching Dean's arm, she pulled him close again. "I need you out of here."

"I'm doing all I can, Addy," he said, kissing her on the nose. "Remember what I told you."

"I love you, too," she said, wrapping him in a real kiss.

Matt cleared his throat. "Adelaide, we gotta get you out of here before the guards come back."

"Sweetheart, go," Dean said, giving her a push. "I'll see you soon."

Releasing his hand, she backed up to the door.

He held his breath. "Addy, you're going to trip."

She smiled. "No faith." Blowing him a kiss, she spun and just about smacked into the side of the door.

Matt caught her before she rammed into it face-first. "Miss Cooke, your coordination skills are legendary."

She snatched her arm away and walked through the door, scowling. "The hell is that supposed to mean?"

He slammed the door, covering them both in darkness again. "I brought a flashlight this time," he said, clicking it on.

CHAPTER 14

After leaving Matt outside the jail, Addy mulled Dean's intel and walked to her mom's.

Who had been given a huge house. So odd. Dean, an employee of the company in charge here, had been thrown in a jail cell. Mom, basically public enemy number one, had been given her own house.

Two armed men on the porch, two more round the back.

Not that it wasn't its own jail, but it was still a hell of a lot nicer than what Dean had.

Shoving her hands in her pockets, she dragged her feet up the walk. On the porch, she nodded to the guards and knocked on Mom's door.

"Second," Mom called.

Addy shrugged at the guards. "You guys hear about my brother?"

One of them frowned. "Heard he was pretty drunk. Whole neighborhood saw him beat up your dad."

When had Mike become a day drinker? Hell, when had he become a drinker at all?

"Does my mom know?"

The talkative guard shrugged.

"Adelaide," Mom said, opening the door. Her hair in a ponytail, she'd thrown on a button-up shirt and shorts.

"Morning, Mom. Got some extra coffee?"

"Sure, baby girl, come on in," she said, stepping back. "How's your father?"

The guard cleared his throat.

Frowning, Addy shut the door behind her and latched it. No bars, though. So what if the glass was unbreakable? The doors would still give eventually.

She followed her mom to the kitchen.

Leaned against the counter, a tall, tanned man in military fatigues sipped coffee. The lip of the cup raised to his grey eyes, he narrowed them as he drank.

"Ah, my own personal guard," Melinda said, sitting at the table and drawing up a leg. She rested her arm on her knee. "Adelaide, this is Commander Burke. Casey, this is my daughter, Adelaide."

"Commander Burke? Really?" Addy stuck out her hand.

Standing to his full height, which was a foot more than Addy if it was a day, he smiled and shook. "Your mom's told me a lot about you," he said, voice gruff.

"Has she?" She sat next to her mom. "And what's she been saying about me?"

Mom gave her a steaming cup of coffee and slid over a slice of freshly baked coffee cake.

"That you're smart, strong. A good leader."

Blood rushed to Addy's cheeks. "I don't know about all that. It's probably closer to the truth to say I'm clumsy and I can swing a machete." She took a bite of the coffee cake. Good lord, had Mom made this? "I only hit myself with the blade once out of every ten times. Not bad, I guess."

"Mothers are prone to exaggeration." He cut his eyes at Mom and lifted one corner of his mouth.

Which, by the standards Addy had already accepted about him, was a downright huge smile.

She took another bite. "So, commander, can you tell me what IRF is doing all the way out here?"

Mom spat out her coffee. "Adelaide!"

She shrugged. The sweet cake filled her mouth, and she downed it with a bitter swallow of black ambrosia.

"She's direct, Melinda, I'll give her that."

Addy smiled. "And?"

"I'm afraid I can't answer that, Miss Cooke. Privileged information and all. You understand."

"No, commander," she said, taking another bite, "afraid I don't. Oh, by the way." She smiled over the top of her cup. "I met Ella last night. What a lovely girl."

It was Burke's turn to spit out coffee. "My Ella?"

"Tall as an Amazon, skinny as a pole, long pretty blonde hair? Yeah," she said, grinning, "I'd say I met her." And once she'd established they wouldn't be in competition for the same man, Ella had taken quite the shine to her. Still, she chuckled. "Nose so far in the air she'd drown if it rained. But, lovely all the same."

Burke set his cup down on the counter. "General, if you'll excuse me," he said, bowing. "Miss Cooke"—he stuck his hand out again—"good to meet you."

She shook, smiling. "Hope to see you again soon, commander."

Melinda smiled at Addy after he was gone. "You're craftier than you used to be."

"You learn a thing or two here or there. No big deal. I really did meet Ella last night."

"You make friends fast, too. The right sort, even."

"Dad taught me how to make allies," she said.

Mom closed her eyes. "You didn't answer me. How is your father?"

"Nursing some injuries, from what I hear."

"What?" Her eyes popped open.

"Michael."

"Ah, hell, sweetie. Where is your brother now?"

"Don't know," she said, downing her last swallow of coffee. She grimaced. Why was the last swallow always ass? "But I came here to see how you are."

Mom frowned and drank some coffee. The steam had stopped rolling off of it, and if Addy's was anything to judge on, it was lukewarm at best, now. She stared at a spot on the table. "Some days are better than others."

"Mom, I'm an adult over here. You can talk to me, you know."

She patted her knee under the table. "I know, sweetie. I know. It's hard. All the years I thought about getting you guys back, I didn't think…" Trailing off, she glanced out the window.

"Didn't think he wouldn't want you back, too?"

A tear falling, Melinda nodded.

"He did, Mom. For a long time, he did. But, you were dead. Dead and gone. We all had to move on eventually."

Inhaling through her nose, Melinda wiped the single tear off her cheek and smiled. "I know that, honey. I get it. I'm just glad you and Michael still like me."

"Oh Mom," Addy said, reaching for her hand, "he still likes you. He just doesn't. Well. He's just human."

Mom sniffled. "Aren't we all."

"Yeah. Even you," Addy said. She picked at the cake, crumbs falling on the plate. "We need to help Mike. I'm worried about him."

Melinda nodded. "He's had it rough these last few days. That's for sure," she said. Under the table, she patted Addy on the knee again. "I'll take care of him. It's what moms do, right?"

Addy nodded and stuffed the last bite of cake into her mouth. Nothing about this sat right.

* * *

One eye open, the other a slit through which some light fell, Jack stared at the ceiling. It'd taken Jane the better part of an hour to clean up his wounds and dig out all the little shards of glass from his hands, feet, and sides.

He could've gone to the fancy hospital. They had all the things he needed there, including doctors. But to be honest, this was the first time he'd even thought about the place. As Jane fussed over him, tweezing out even the smallest sliver of glass, he'd felt strangely warm.

Michael's feelings were nothing to be happy about. He'd had his heart broken by the one person who was supposed to keep him from being broken in the first place.

But being fussed over by his woman. That was something Jack hadn't had in ages. Above and beyond the talking, and the sex, and the closeness, the depth of care she showed as she tweezed and plucked glass from his skin, some of it buried fairly deep, touched him on a level he'd forgotten. After giving and giving, to his kids, to the village, to the cause, someone was giving back rather than taking. No matter the reason she had to do it, he'd be damned if he'd pass up the opportunity to appreciate it.

Pots and pans crashed in the kitchen. A cacophony of clanging metal.

He sat up, wincing and clutching his middle. "Jane?"

More clanging.

Flipping on the light next to the bed, he glanced at his wrist.

Oh, right. Melinda had never given his watch back.

Whatever. Jane didn't use clocks anyway.

"Jane?"

He tiptoed to the door of the bedroom.

Silence.

She'd hung his machete from the back of the door handle. He grabbed it and limped down the stairs.

Glasses clinked.

So someone was still in the kitchen. Someone, or *something*.

Rounding the newel post, a board creaked under his foot. He stopped, held his breath against his aching guts, and Listened.

Someone breathing in the kitchen. Nothing more.

He lowered the machete an inch. Probably a person.

Sunlight streamed through the window as he crept into the kitchen. Jane sat in front of the cabinet where Data had been sniffing, pots and pans strewn in the floor behind her. She stared into the depths of it, head tilted.

He laid the machete on the table.

At the sound, she spun like a round little top and frowned. "Hey, honey, just rearranging some stuff in here. Whoever put these pots and pans in the cabinets did not know how to stack things." Something false in her voice. Like she was forcing a smile.

Limping around the table, he held a hand out. "Let me help you then."

She took his hand and stood. Fingers light on his waist, she kissed him under the jaw. "Thanks, honey." The smile in her voice didn't actually reach any part of her face. Her eyes, still and sincere, flicked right.

Following her gaze, he saw she'd pointed a single finger at the cabinet.

He began to bend, but she caught his arm.

"How do you feel?"

"About as good as I look."

"This can probably wait," she said. At least her voice sounded like her again. "You need more rest."

He floated about two feet off the ground. Kissing her fingers, he smiled. "I can help you with this first. At least get these put away."

Nodding, she steeled her arm and helped him lower to the ground, muscles of her forearm standing out.

Unable to resist, he grinned up at her and eyed the smooth bulge of her belly from down here. He couldn't see her face.

She leaned over, smiling. "What are you grinning at?"

"Nothing, nothing," he said, shaking his head. He leaned into the cabinet.

Indeed, Data had sniffed out something lurking in there. But not a mouse.

A tiny little microphone.

* * *

Addy kicked a rock down the sidewalk. It rolled into a storm drain.

The west wall. Really fucking specific, Dean.

As the sun set, pink light soft over the tops of the trees, she frowned. Since being in the east, she'd not seen a single sunset comparable to the ones out west. Pretty, sure. Every sunset was pretty. But they still didn't compare.

A bird tweeted.

Behind the house in front of her, the wall rose fifteen feet. A good, sturdy wall. And of course, mountains beyond that. IRF may have stolen these people from their safe little space on the island, but at least they'd provided some sort of fortress here in the middle of nowhere.

"Psst."

She ducked, unsheathing her Bowie knife and taking cover behind a bush.

"Adelaide, it's me, Renzo," he hissed. He whistled again. It hadn't been a bird tweeting at sunset after all.

Following the tweeting, she crept toward the wall.

She found him behind an empty house, its windows intact but shingles and siding slipping into the yard. The windows staring, black.

"Renzo," she said, sneaking up. "Glad to see you. Did you find Paul?"

"I did, he's just over here," he said, standing and stepping from behind trash cans.

If no one lived here, why would the trash cans be standing? They should have blown over and rolled away long ago.

"Where have you been hiding?" she asked, following him through the back yards, up against the wall.

"I don't think you'd believe me if I told you. Maybe you should just come talk to Paul."

She followed him through three more yards and over a couple fences. Coming to a drainage ditch, a ditch that smelled of fresh grass and stale water, they stopped. Renzo hopped in the ditch and held out a hand.

She took it and followed him. "So. Now what?"

He ducked under the wall and began to crawl.

She bent over and peered in after him.

Crawling away from her, down a large culvert, his knees and elbows scraped along the uneven cement. The dying light hardly illuminated anything inside, but she caught the outline of bars at the far end of a twenty-foot tunnel. Water trickled along the middle.

A radio crackled, static buzzing off the inside of the tunnel.

She shivered.

Well, Addy, no alternative. Either crawl down there or go home.

On her knees, she followed Renzo into the culvert but found it easy enough to crouch-walk since she wasn't as big as him. Her knees and elbows muck-free, she took her time inching down toward the end. Dad had always been twitchy around tight spaces, and though they didn't bother her as much, creepy darkened tunnels weren't high on her list of favorite places.

"This is alpha team, come in zed," the radio crackled.

"Zed here, over."

Paul's sure, happy voice echoing down from the end kicked her butt into gear. He'd once saved Jack's life, administering CPR when he'd drowned. A throwback from Dad's world, he was one of her favorite new people.

The radio crackled. *"What do you got to report? Over."* Oren. Red mustache bouncing, no doubt.

Addy sat next to Paul and touched him on the shoulder.

He took in her face. Smiled. "Hey, Lou. How's tricks?"

She see-sawed her hand. *So-so.*

"Gentlemen," Paul said into the radio, "our lieutenant has just joined me for report this evening."

A pause from the radio. *"Tell her hi from us,"* Oren said.

She pushed the talk button herself over Paul's hand, pulling the radio in front of her mouth. "Hey, Oren, good to hear from you."

"Is Celia with you?"

"No, not this time."

"You tell her"—the radio crackled with static—*"next time it's her turn to sleep in the woods while I drink champagne and eat caviar."*

Addy chuckled and released Paul's hand.

"That's a big 10-4, Oren," Paul said.

As he gave his report, Addy found a dry place to sit.

A few things about the place became clear as he spoke.

One, not all of the residents had been happy about the relocation.

Two, not everyone agreed that IRF was in charge.

And three, everyone knew about their arrival, the baby, and the general. Her mom. And, likely, every bit of gossip they could get their hands on. With only about a thousand people on Harkers, gossip was a good sixty percent of how they spent their time. Even with two to three thousand people here, Addy didn't suppose it was much different.

"Same bat time, same bat channel guys. Over and out," Paul said, lowering the radio. He smiled at her. "How are you, Adelaide? How's your dad?"

"Bat time?"

Chuckling, Paul shook his head. He clipped the radio to his belt and began to crawl out of the culvert. "Need to educate you. I'll come over later, we'll look at some ancient films on the pop culture history of this land."

Following him, she laughed. "Sounds good."

"You didn't answer me about your dad." He stood at the end of the tunnel, straightening and popping his back.

Renzo crawled out, holding a hand out to her.

She took it, brushing her knees. "Where are you staying anyway?"

"Easier if I show you. Stop avoiding the question."

"He's fine, Paul."

"Not what I heard."

"Good lord, you people and your gossip," she said, hands on her hips.

"Adelaide," he said, hand on her shoulder, "you need to know what people are saying. Knowledge is power."

She dropped her hands, hitting herself in the thighs. "Fine. What are they saying?"

He glanced over her shoulder at Renzo.

Renzo shrugged.

"Walk with us. We'll show you where we're staying. I'll tell you all about what I've heard."

CHAPTER 15

"**I** always half expect to see fires in trash cans when I come down here," Paul said over his shoulder, sliding down an embankment. About a dozen people had congregated under a bridge. With the cold drawing down, they hugged their coats closed, leaning into each other.

"I don't know what that means, Paul," Addy said.

"Good. Anyhow. Let me introduce you." He tugged her arm.

Following his introductions around the circle, Addy shivered. She hadn't planned on being out this late. Her coat wasn't equipped for the bone-chilling cold of an October night in the mountains. She tried to learn their names, but the cold sucked everything out of her.

"Why are you guys out here?" she asked, containing a shiver.

"We ain't exactly welcome," a stout Black woman said.

"Why not?"

"It's complicated," Paul said. "But they came from outside."

Furrowing her brow, Addy looked around again. "You guys snuck in? And they don't know you're here?"

"There's a few holes in their surveillance, yeah," a pale man said. Frizzy hair stuck out from beneath his 'boggan cap and his nose was red from the cold. He shuffled a foot. "Getting food's no easy thing, but we manage."

"Why stay, then? Why not find somewhere else?"

The stout woman stuck her nose in Addy's face. "These are *our* walls, alright? *We* built them. With our own hands. They can't kick us out of our homes."

The frizzy-haired man tugged her arm. "Don't get mad at the girl. She didn't know."

Addy raised both hands. "I'm sorry. I didn't. I thought IRF built all this. That's what Matt—"

The woman spat. "That boy. What a piece of work he is."

Paul's radio blipped once. He grabbed Addy's arm, waving to the others. "See you guys tomorrow," he said, dragging Addy away from the bridge. Renzo followed.

"Wait, Paul, where are we—"

"Shh. I'll explain in a minute." He dragged her into a nearby brick building. It may have been a factory at one time, but now all the windows sported wood instead of glass and the doors had been ripped off. "Be quiet. Wait here. Patrol's going by." He gave her a gentle shove and crouched inside the door. Renzo flanked her, and they copied Paul.

Radios crackled outside. The high whine of a battery-powered engine grew louder.

Her stomach flipped. A fugitive from justice? That was a new one. Dean would've been proud. She held her breath until the guards passed, Listening to their conversation.

Just regular stuff. Girls, gossip, machismo.

Paul gave it at least two minutes after the sound of the guards passing had eased. "We've got a sympathetic guard, but no one knows who he is. There's times when they should come right through the middle of us, but they go around. Sometimes, we get a blip on the radio. Other than him, though," he said, scratching his chin, "we don't have any friends here."

Addy glanced out the door. Night had come on thick, leaving the streets pitch black. Dry October breezes blew colored leaves across the empty streets. "Are you telling me there's a whole community here they don't know about?"

Renzo shook his head. "No, just about a quarter of the original settlement. The rest of them are farther up in the mountains. Keep to themselves. But they want their home back."

"IRF came in about eighteen months ago, told them they'd provide food, supplies, weapons, protection. Gave them the bulletproof glass. Reinforced steel. Materials for the wall. All they asked for in return was a few teams to work the towers, and the railroad lines," Paul said, helping her to her feet.

"What happened?"

"IRF kicked them out in the cold." Paul sighed. "Moved in the people from Emerald Isle."

She shrugged. "So, what now?"

They walked out of the building. The rest of the group had disappeared, probably gone to wherever it was they holed up. Paul walked out to the road, checking it both ways. "It's like Renzo says. They want their home back. But they don't want to hurt these people IRF has moved in. These people, they're soft."

"I know. Most of them don't even carry weapons."

Paul frowned. "For all your mom's company did on that island, they wouldn't know the real world if it came up and bit them in the ass." He sighed. "I know a lot about that jail. It'd be best if we get Dean out, but he's about as safe as he can be while he's in there." Linking his arm in hers and smiling, the kind of smile someone's grandpa would probably give her, he lifted his brow. "You gonna tell me about your dad now?"

She sighed. "I haven't seen him today. But I heard Mike laid into him. Probably about Jane."

"Definitely about the girl," Renzo said. "Surprised your dad didn't hurt him."

"Dad would never hurt Mike." She paused, considering. Sighed. "Well. Not physically."

Paul patted her hand. "I'm sure you're right."

Addy's shoulders fell. "Speaking of complicated."

Renzo shrugged. "I saw them at the prison. Complicated it might be, but they were already together by then. Even if they didn't know it."

Paul nodded. "Funny old life."

A tangential thought hit her. "Hey, do you guys know anything about Burke's daughter, Ella?"

Paul laughed. "That girl is something else. Her dad has kept her insulated from everything. She's green. Why?"

"I think I made friends with her."

Paul doubled over, his laughter echoing off the darkened houses and empty windows. When he stood, tears lined his eyes. "Good luck to you then, sweetheart. You're going to need it."

* * *

Jack opened the door to his daughter.

She flinched, eyes roving over the patchwork of bandages on his torso.

Pinching his button-up shirt closed, he ushered her in. "Addy, what are you doing out?"

"I've got to talk to you, Dad." She perched on the couch.

Not here. Not here, baby girl.

How to tell her that?

Widening his eyes the best he could—Jane had gotten some of the swelling down with a foul-smelling poultice—he held a finger to his lips. "I know, I look awful. Trust me, I've been worse," he said, limping to the couch. Spinning on the foot without bandages, he wobbled and sat. "If this is about your brother—"

Jane breezed in from the kitchen. "Hey, Addy, you like the new threads?" She turned a circle, her maternity shirt flying up. "These guys loaded the closet, and some of the shirts are so comfy." She tapped her ear and pointed to the kitchen.

Jack watched his keen daughter.

Narrowing her eyes, she gave the barest of nods. "Yeah, it's about Michael," she said, shaking her head.

With a grimace, Jack stood. Hobbling around the block with his little girl sounded a bit like torture, but it would be nice to get out of the house for a few minutes.

Jane crossed to him and laid a light hand on his chest where his shirt had fallen open again. "Jack, I think you should rest. I'm sure Addy and I can talk about M…her brother." She retained eye contact. "Don't you think so, Addy?"

He frowned. "I really think this is a conversation she and I should have. I'll make sure and tell you all about it." Buttoning his shirt, he wobbled.

"Let me," she said, buttoning it. Standing on tiptoe, she kissed him on the cheek and whispered in his ear, "You goddamn well better."

Shivers slipping down his spine, an unbidden grin crossed his lips.

He limped to the door and patted Addy on the shoulder. "Let's take a walk, little girl." Shifting his weight from foot to foot, he found he could put more weight on the injured one than he could a few hours ago. More of Jane's foul-smelling poultice. She'd learned more than bow and arrow from Celia, it seemed.

Preceding him onto the porch, he caught Addy smiling in at Jane before pulling the door closed. It was good they'd made up, at least a bit. He could see wavering discomfort on both their parts, and regret seized him that their friendship had to suffer. But as Jane had pointed out to Michael, it hadn't been all him. Hard as it was for him to shake guilt, she'd reminded him over and over through the day she was quite capable of making her own decisions, thank you. They were a two-way street, no matter how much guilt he wanted to lay on himself.

"So baby girl," he said, clutching the rail and limping down the stairs. He stepped onto the walk up, pavement cool under his feet.

"Dad, are you sure you don't want help or something? Jane and I really can have this conversation."

He gritted his teeth and limped along the walk. "Whatever it is you really came over for, I do also want to talk about Michael."

"If you insist," she said, sticking her arm out. "At least let me help my old, broken Dad." The corner of her mouth turned up.

Gripping her arm, he let her walk him out to the street. The black pavement even cooler than the sidewalk, he stretched his toes.

May as well get this part out of the way, then.

"I'm sorry about Mike," he said, "I didn't intend to hurt him."

"I know, Dad."

"He hates me."

She sighed. "No, he doesn't. He could never hate you."

He stopped. "Adelaide, look at me."

She stared, frowning at his swollen eye.

Wobbling, he closed them both. Swallowed around the lump forming in his throat. "I don't know if I can fix this."

Addy tugged his arm. "No, you can't."

Inhaling, he opened his eyes. She was right, of course. Mike would never forgive him.

"Time can, though. It'll be alright. It's Michael. He just needs time," she said, shuffling a foot. "You'll see."

Frowning, he began walking again. "I hope you're right. I'm sorry you had to see me like this."

That's it, Jack. You find that guilt wherever you can pile it on.

"It's a little jarring," she said, smile in her voice, "but I know. You'll live."

Rounding the corner, the house falling out of sight, he peeped at her with his good eye. "What did you really come about?"

"Did you know about the people, the ones who originally lived here?"

"The what?" With a rock sinking into his gut, he listened as Addy explained what Paul and Renzo had told her.

At some point, they began walking again, his head spinning. So many things to pin down. Strings to catch. "Is there anything we can do to get Dean out of jail?"

"I don't even know why they're holding him."

"Fuck. He would be pretty useful in this. Well," he said, pausing, "how do we want to split this?"

She scratched her head. "I could probably find out who the sympathetic guard is."

"How's that?"

Grinning, she explained Matt and Ella. "I think Ella likes me. I bet she could get Dean out of jail if I really wanted."

"Nice job, baby girl," he said. Cunning. This Ella could be useful in so many ways. "Let's start with the guard. See where we can go from there. If he's sympathetic to the residents, he might also give us intel about IRF's real purpose here."

"I assumed it was the vaccine," she said, brow drawn.

The very mention of the vaccine clouded Jack's heart. The vaccine, Melinda, and Jane inextricably tied. Wrapped around the baby as though it were the cord wrapped around its neck. Tightening and tightening, squeezing all the hope and life from it.

He shook his head. "Best not to assume."

She started walking again. "What about you? What are you going to do?"

"I'll see what I can find out at the hospital. I'll be in and out of there with Jane over the next few months. Melinda said—" He stopped, cleared his throat, and tried again. "Melinda said the baby may not survive because of the bite and the vaccine. They're going to have to keep an eye on her."

"Oh, Dad. No." Addy's voice dropped an octave. Tiny. Scared.

He patted her hand. "It'll be fine. I know it will. In the meantime, I also need to find out more about the original residents of this place. What they know. What their plans are. They're not going to just sit out there forever."

Eyes flicking back and forth, thoughts sped through his brain. It took a while to get rolling sometimes, but once it did, it raced like they used to burn fuel around tracks. Loud and hot. "Once we figure out what's going on with IRF, I'll bet those people can help us get them out of here. Drive them back to the hole they came from. You," he pointed, "focus on building that relationship with Ella and Matt, finding out which of Matt's guys is sympathetic, and why."

"And freeing Dean."

"Of course. Now I just have to figure out how to tell Jane all this. Hey," he said, a speeding idea striking him, "can you bring Data over again? He sniffed out a mic in the kitchen. It'd be nice to know where the rest of them are."

"Sure thing, soon as he sniffs them out in my house."

His chest tightened. "Be careful. They can't know you know. I don't know why they're listening, but it can't be good, I can tell you that. Once you find the mics, stay the hell away from them. Don't touch or move them."

She nodded. Frowned. "What about Mom?"

"What about her?"

"She's. Well. You've been gone. Me and Mike, we kinda patched things up with her."

"I wouldn't trust your mother any farther than I can throw her." Not that he had a choice when it came to the baby. She was the only one who knew anything about what they'd injected Jane with back on that godforsaken island. Even still.

Tugging her arm free, Addy crossed them both. Kicked at the ground. "Yeah. You're right."

"Adelaide."

She glanced at him, looking over the bandages and his swollen eye again.

"Addy, I know I don't always make the right decisions," he said, gripping the dull ache in his side, "but please listen to me about your mom. I don't trust her. Don't tell her anything about this. Not one word."

"You got it, Dad. Not a word."

Watching her eyes shift did nothing to soothe his nerves. But his daughter knew how to keep her word.

He glanced up. They'd rounded back to the house.

"I'm glad you came over, baby girl," he said, finger under her chin.

She grinned. "Me too." One-armed, she hugged the side without bandages.

He locked the flinch on the inside and hugged her back. "We're going to be alright."

*   *   *

Jack peeked out the window in the front door. "It's Yasuo," he said, speaking over his shoulder. He swung the door open. "Come on in, Yaz."

Needles clicking, Jane watched him as he walked in.

He wobbled under a large wooden box. "Hey, guys. Got a little gift for the happy couple." Setting it on the coffee table, he stepped back. Tapped his ear. Pointed to the box.

Jack closed the door and sat on the couch. Leaning back, he held his breath and steeled himself against the week-old ache of bruised organs.

"You're looking better than last time I saw you," Yaz said. "What was that? Few days ago?"

"Yeah. You and Addy were training in that big field next to the tracks. I see she earned herself a staff."

Yaz chuckled. "Eventually."

"What is that thing, Yaz?" Jane asked, angling her chin at the box. Her needles paused.

Yaz flipped the lid of the box back. "My parents used to have one of these. Man, I loved that thing. Got Addy one, too, Jack," he said, opening a door on the side. "Even brought you something to play on it."

At first, the flat envelope he pulled from the side didn't compute. Jack hadn't seen one since he was probably ten. At least. Yasuo pinched its contents and tugged, and the black circle slid from its paper case.

A record.

"Check this out," Yaz said, laying the record on what Jack now realized was a record player.

He sat up. "Yasuo, I haven't seen one of these in…more years than I care to mention," he said, glancing at Jane.

She sat the blanket she was knitting on the couch and leaned up, pushing into the back cushion for leverage. "What's it do?"

Grinning, Yaz turned it on and lowered the needle. Tinny and scratchy, the sound of trumpets wafted from the box.

"Billie Holiday," Yasuo said, leaning over the spinning record.

Jane's warm hand snuck over and gripped Jack's knee. "What is it?" Her voice soft, full of wonder, eyes wide.

Glancing at her partially open lips, Jack grinned. "Blues."

"It's beautiful," she breathed. "I've never heard anything like it."

"Oh, sweetie," Jack said, smiling with her. "Wait till you hear jazz. Rock and roll."

She flapped a hand. "I've heard music, Jack. Just not this."

Reaching into the player, Yaz turned a knob. The music got louder. Louder. Louder. So loud, Jack could hardly make out what Yaz said when he pointed at the knob. Tendons on his neck standing out, he strained. "Volume control." Tapped his ear again.

Oh, of course. Hard to hear what they were saying over the music.

Handy, since the microphones were in every room except the bathrooms.

The one in the bedroom gave Jack the creeps, but it turned out Jane had a bit of an exhibitionist streak. Not that he minded her being more emotive and vocal.

Focus, Jack.

Frowning, he stood and turned the volume down. "Any other records in there?"

Yaz grinned again. "You're going to love this," he said, sliding another record out of the side. "Check this out."

Taking the proffered cardboard sleeve, Jack flipped it over and took in the front cover. "You're kidding," he said, grinning. "Jesus, Yaz. I haven't heard Amy Winehouse since I was a teenager. My mom loved her." He clapped him on the shoulder. "Thank you."

"I thought you'd appreciate it. I don't know many who would." He shuffled a foot. "Well. You guys enjoy. I have more cheer to spread." He headed for the door.

Stopping him before he left the porch, Jack squinted into the afternoon light. "Yasuo," he said, pulling the door almost closed, "have you seen my son?"

"No, Jack, I haven't. There's talk, though."

"Oh?"

"Not many people have seen him at all," Yaz said, "but he's been seen in the company of his mom when they have."

"Dammit."

"Yeah. Addy said she'd try to talk to him, though."

Clapping Yaz on the shoulder again, he smiled. At least it didn't hurt to smile anymore. "Thanks again."

"One thing, though."

Jack's stomach sank. It was always that one last thing that got you. He frowned, waiting.

"No one's gotten any candy from him since Celia took his last sucker on the train. I don't know if that means anything, but Addy thought I should mention it when I saw you."

He clenched his jaw. "It's not good. I can tell you that." With a frown, he walked back inside.

Back to him, Jane swayed in front of the player, Amy singing about what a losing game love is.

Sliding his hands around her waist, he pressed against her and leaned his face into her hair. Inhaled the scent of flowers deep into his aching lungs. "This song is a little bang on the nose, don't you think?"

Swaying, she reached over her shoulder and curled the tips of her fingers in his hair. "It's lovely."

"Here," he said, spinning her, "something my mom taught me." One hand on her waist, her other hand in the other, he adjusted around the baby and guided her hips.

"Oh lord, Jack. I can't dance."

He shushed her. "Close your eyes. Feel it with me," he said, swaying. Guiding her in a simple box step, he spun her around the living room in a slow twirl. Even losing more and more coordination every day, she kept up well. And hey, she was light on her feet when she did step on him.

Amy sang on about the losing game, and he tried hard to think about anything other than the truth of it.

So many things they could talk about with this player turned all the way up to eleven.

Just not right now.

CHAPTER 16

Hooking her arm into Addy's, Ella guided them into the street.

"So, Adelaide," Ella said, smiling at the sun and sliding on a pair of sunglasses, "where are we headed?"

"Need to talk to my mom," Addy said, frowning.

"If we must. Have you seen Matthew today?"

Odd that Ella should have to ask her. She didn't seem the kind of girl to lose track of her boyfriend. Obsessively so. Addy shook her head.

Ella frowned, scrunching up her lower lip. "Me neither. I hate these kind of days."

Standing up straight, Addy pictured the way Ella threw her hair back as she spoke. "What kind of days?"

"Some days I just don't get to see him very much, and he's been especially absent lately. I'm sure it's head-of-the-guard-type things, but it's still frustrating."

"Sounds like."

"Oh, but who am I to talk?" Ella stopped, tugging Addy's arm. "You haven't seen Dean since you got here, have you? You poor thing. You must be just dying."

In her head, Addy replayed Ella's words, "you poor thing." Good lord. She shook her head. "It's rough. But at least I know where he is."

Laughing without humor, Ella started walking again. "You don't know how right you are. That, sister, is a blessing."

Sweeping through the great concrete barriers blocking the hospital, Addy tried to hold in her puke.

"Are you sure my daddy can't help get you in to see him?"

Matt's admonition floated through her thoughts. "*…don't tell Ella about this. I can't afford for her dad to find out.*"

She shook her head. "I don't know. I don't think so."

"Ridiculous."

Addy opened the steel front door. "After you." Following Ella, she hugged her elbows.

Rubbing her own arms, Ella shivered. "I don't know why they keep it so cold in here."

"Subtle torture."

Giggling, Ella glanced at her. "Where do you think your mom is?"

"Let's ask this guy," she said, pointing at the desk clerk.

A young boy, within spitting distance of puberty, sat back in the chair. His eyes flitted between their faces. "What can I help you ladies with?"

Addy leaned on the desk, holding eye contact. "My mother, please. Where is she?"

"I don't, uh, I don't know who—"

"Oh, please," Ella said, flipping her hair over her shoulder and sitting on the desk. "Don't pretend you don't know who her mother or my father are."

He cleared his throat. "I can't, um. I'm not supposed to, uh." He glanced at Ella, tried on a smile, and stuck a nail between his teeth.

Addy's own hand snuck toward her mouth. She balled her fist and crammed it in her elbow.

Ella leaned forward. "Don't fuck with me, boy. Tell me where her mother is. Now."

"Lab six, fourth floor and to the left. No entry restrictions." He cleared his throat again. "Ma'am."

Leaping from the desk and snagging Addy's arm again, she frowned. "Be quicker next time." With a shake of her head, she led Addy to the stairs.

One thing Dad had mentioned after they left Shanti Station and the Hospital of Doom was the stairwells. How they'd smelled of cat piss and death. How even with all the bright lights and seeming innocence, the stairwells had set his teeth on edge from the first moment he stepped foot in them.

These stairs, clean and shining, mopped and beautiful, gleamed with the fluorescent light shining down from the fixtures. Radiated cleanliness. The only scent that of floor cleaner and maybe an undertone of antiseptic as it crept into the stairwell from the rest of the hospital.

"Ella," she said, the girl bopping up the stairs in front of her, "how long have you been here?"

"Probably about six months or so."

"And your dad?"

She shrugged. "About eighteen months, I guess. Matthew too." Stopping, she frowned. "That was a long year."

That fit with the timeline Paul and Renzo had given her. The question then became why had they begun to set up this place a full year before Addy and the people from Harkers had destroyed Shanti Station?

Had they already planned on taking these people?

Did they have another group of their own?

What was their plan for the original residents?

Ella continued up the stairs. "Why?"

She rounded a banister. "No reason. Just curious."

Stopping on a landing between floors, Ella shook her head. "I liked it where we were before. Daddy says it used to be called California." She rolled the word out like it had been made of French. Foreign. An unfamiliar taste in her mouth. "It was nice there." Her eyes drifted over Addy's head. "Have you ever been in an earthquake?"

"A what?"

Locking her eyes on Addy's, she grinned. "An earthquake. The ground shakes, feels like it's going to shake you right off like a dog shaking water off its back. It's like the only time I'm not in control." She sniffed.

"I'll bet," Addy said, smiling. If that didn't tell her all she needed to know about Ella.

Ella bounced up the next two flights and propped the door open, waiting for Addy to reach her.

Breathing hard, Addy held the door and waved her into the hallway. "Sorry," she panted, "just gotta. Whew. The elevation, you know?"

Ella breezed into the hall. "He said it was on the left?"

Addy peeked in the first window. "I can't see anything."

"Look here," Ella said, pointing, "it says lab six. Just like mister boy downstairs said." Without waiting, she pushed the door open and charged in.

Sighing, Addy followed. On its pneumatic hinge, the door whooshed closed with less of a slam and more of a whimper. A partition stood between the door and the rest of the room. Considering what she'd seen at Shanti Station, she thought about stopping. Turning around. Running away.

Can't do that, Adelaide.

She rounded the screen.

Mom sat at a bench across the room, bent over a microscope. Whatever was under the eyepiece had been projected onto the whiteboard at the end of the room. Squiggly lines moved about in the sample.

Next to Mom, Burke sat far inside her bubble, feet propped up on her stool, knees open. Leaning on an elbow and smiling. He murmured something only Melinda could hear.

She giggled.

Mom. Giggled.

The hell?

"Mom?"

"Daddy," Ella said, sweeping across the room.

Burke stood, setting the stool rocking. He caught it and backed away from Melinda. "Ella, sweetheart, what are you doing here?"

"Well—"

"She came with me, commander," Addy said, stepping up to him. "Came to see my mom, actually. What are *you* doing here?"

Mom turned around, crossing her arms. "Adelaide, I told you. He's my personal guard. I can't seem to get rid of him." Her eyes smiled, even if her mouth frowned.

"Hmph," Addy said, narrowing her eyes at Burke. "I'd like to understand more about why Dean, a loyal employee of yours, I might mention, is still in jail, but my mom here, an admitted member of Talus Crest, is basically free to do whatever."

Burke narrowed his eyes. "Is that why you're here?"

"No. But it's a damn good question."

He frowned, crossing his arms. Mouth closed.

"Daddy," Ella said, hanging on his arm, "can't you let Addy see her boyfriend? I can only imagine how I'd feel if I couldn't see you. Or Matthew." She tugged.

He glared at her.

"Addy, I'm glad you're here, sweetie," Mom said, touching her arm. "Let me show you something."

Addy spun on a slow heel, narrowed eyes not leaving Burke's face. Slippery bastard.

Stay away from my mom.

"Yeah," she said, leaning onto the desk between the commander and Mom. "What's up?"

"Look up at the screen," she said, pointing. She leaned back over the microscope. The picture shifted as she moved the little glass plate.

"I don't think I've ever been this close to a microscope," Addy said, angling her forehead at it.

"Oh honey, they're not as cool as telescopes. But they're useful in their own way," Melinda said.

"Ew. What is that?" Ella asked, lips twisted. She stared at the screen.

"That's what I'm trying to show you guys. Look, that's the virus."

Addy jumped, pulling her arm away from the microscope like the thing had just exploded white-hot shrapnel into the room. Without warning, a gagging sound emanated from deep in her throat.

"It can't hurt you like this," Mom said, eyes still fixed to the scope.

"That's. You should warn people, Mom."

Melinda sighed. "Look at the screen, Addy."

Another squiggle, shaped like the other one, overtook the first one. The new squiggle wasn't exactly the same color, but it was close.

It began to shift, taking on more of a bubble shape.

"What's going on?"

"That's the Cure, attacking the virus."

Corners of her mouth turning up, Addy felt for the stool, eyes glued to the screen.

Burke pushed it closer.

Nodding, she sat, never taking her eyes off the screen.

The Cure ate the virus, puffing into a circle and changing color. Turning white. After floating for several seconds in the fluid that had to be blood, it began to break into pieces.

"If we watch long enough, you'll see it has dissolved the virus in a relatively short amount of time. It then dissolves itself. It's a scientific marvel, really, and as close to perfect as it's going to get."

"It's amazing," Addy said. The little pieces of the circle broke into more pieces, dissipating. The evil little squiggle had been eliminated.

Watching it work, her insides floated. Like they'd been filled with white light. Magic. Fairy dust.

"Yes." Melinda removed the slide. "It's not perfect. It leaves a residue. Over time, even the residue dissipates. But it's never gone." Picking up another slide, she frowned. "You'll never be rid of it, sweetie."

As if on cue, her shoulder ached. Though it had no reason to, not six months later, the bite still itched from time to time.

Placing the new slide, Melinda leaned over the scope again. "That's part of the reason why it only works so many times. We're narrowing down the formula. But. Take a look at this, baby girl," she said, pointing at the display again.

Addy watched. As it came into focus, she saw only red. Then it cleared, and the red resolved into little blobs. "What's that?"

"Those are healthy red blood cells."

"OK," she said, squinting. "Where's the virus?"

"This blood," Mom said, looking up, "was infected with the virus after being treated with our current run of the vaccine."

"It's," Addy said, leaning over the table, "it's not there. It's not there at all."

"You're damn right it's not," Burke said.

"Wait." Sitting back, Addy put a hand to her chin. "Mom. You're working with the vaccine? I thought you gave that up." She glanced at Burke and Ella. "That's, um, that's what you told me and Mike."

Mom looked at her feet.

Standing up so fast her thighs knocked into the stool, Addy stepped away and cursed.

The stool clattered to the floor.

"Ms. Cooke," Burke said, "it's my fault. I forced her."

Arms crossed, Addy paced halfway to the door. "That's not a fucking excuse. Mom, you could have refused."

Someone sucked in a breath. With her back turned, Addy didn't know who it was.

Burke cleared his throat. "I threatened her. And her family. If she didn't comply."

"Daddy!"

He exhaled through his nose. "I'm sorry, peanut, but it's important."

It's important. Heard that one before.

Fuck.

"I can't, Mom. This isn't OK. I don't care what he said," she said, spinning and pointing at the commander. "You make your own choices. Your own choices."

"Addy, honey, I," Mom started, crossing her arms. "I couldn't let them hurt you. I'm sorry."

Shaking her head, Addy left the room.

Ella followed behind.

* * *

Ella tugged Addy's arm. "Sorry about your mom. That's shitty she lied to you."

Addy favored her with a glum nod. "It's something, alright."

"If it makes you feel any better, I can't control Daddy either."

"It doesn't."

Ella sniffed. "I wish I could help."

Rounding the corner, Ella's house came into view. A giant magnolia stood in the yard, evergreen leaves still clinging to the branches, its limbs creaking against the house.

"Addy, is that your friend?" Ella asked, pointing.

Addy squinted. Sure enough, there sat Yaz. Sitting on the porch swing and talking to—

"Matthew!" Ella shouted. She ripped her arm free and took three quick steps, looking for all the world like she was going to run to him.

Whether she'd hit him or not when she got to him was in question.

But she did neither.

She stopped, straightened her hair and shirt, and frowned. Mounting the porch ahead of Addy, she curled two fists and put them on her hips. "Matthew," she said as he stood, "where have you been?"

"I'm sorry, cupcake." He kissed her on the cheek. "I had some administrative stuff to take care of. And I do have to take a watch from time to time."

"I don't think we've been formally introduced," Yaz said, stepping up to Ella and holding out a hand. He ducked, making himself shorter than her, and looked up from under his brows with his eyes wide.

She softened, taking his hand and shaking.

Addy cringed. Ella's handshake was worse than a dead fish floating rotten in the surf. It made her stomach slick just to look at it happen.

Yasuo took it like a champ, though.

"I'm Ella Burke. You're Adelaide's friend, Yasuo. Right?"

"Got it," he said, dimples deep in his cheeks.

She smiled back. How could you not?

"Well, Yasuo, I need to speak with Matthew. Adelaide," she said, dropping Yaz's hand, "lovely to see you as always. Please do drop by tomorrow. You've just got to help me try on my new nail polish."

Now it was Addy's mouth that was worse than the dead fish. Nail polish?

Yaz bumped her shoulder. "She'd love to. Right, Addy?"

Without consulting her brain, she nodded. "I'd love to."

"Nice talking to you Matt," Yaz said, stepping off the porch.

Sketching a wave, Addy stumbled down the porch steps and followed Yasuo to the street.

The sound of Ella's front door closing brought her back from wherever it was her brain had run off to. "The hell, Yaz?"

"Oh, Addy. You could use a friend."

"I have friends."

He grinned and started walking. "You have allies. Not the same thing."

"I. That's. What about Jane?"

"Yes," he said, stopping with his hands clasped behind his back, "what about Jane?"

Ice sliced into her heart. A valid question. For which she had no answer.

He narrowed his eyes. "You've got lots of people you care about. People who care about you, too. And I wouldn't say you're without friends. But there's a hole," he said, poking her in the chest, "right here. And you refuse to see it. Much less fill it."

"Goddamnit, Yaz. Stop it." She started walking again, crossing her arms and watching one foot eat the pavement in front of the other. "I've got to tell you something."

He jogged to catch up with her. "What's going on?"

She stopped, looking around the street. For once, that feeling of being watched had subsided. Still, she leaned close. "It's about my mom. And the vaccine."

CHAPTER 17

Ella opened her front door and stepped back. "Addy." Her breath fogged out onto the porch. "How are you this morning?"

"Fine, thanks," Addy said, stepping through.

"Thanks for coming over," Ella said. Twisting her hair between two fingers, she checked the street before closing the door. "Something to drink?"

"Hell yes."

She flounced off, and Addy followed her down the hall, glancing into the rooms they passed. Addy and Celia's house was large, as was Dad and Jane's, but they were shacks in comparison to this mansion. Such large houses were all but indefensible. Too many entryways. Windows, doors, and with a big enough horde, even the walls would give. With the exception of the barracks back in the village, she'd never seen so many large houses being lived in.

The kitchen gleamed so clean it made Addy's teeth hurt. She squinted as Ella waved her to the table.

"Sit, let me get you a drink."

"Thanks," she said, scooting an immaculate chair away from a spotless table. She did her best to pretend not to be looking everywhere at once.

Gleaming appliances, like they were new. Shiny silver and copper pots and pans hanging over an island in the middle of the giant room. Perfect countertops, probably made of marble or quartz. Paintings on the walls like some of the ones Addy had helped box and store back in the village. But these hung in their

167

gilded frames, opening the arms of their artists' visions out onto the world like some sort of divine gift.

Warm and fuzzy from all the clean, pretty things, Addy swallowed and concentrated on hiding the pure admiration behind neutrality.

Ella sat a long-stemmed glass in front of her.

Addy wrinkled her brow. "What's this?" She picked up the glass with two fingers and sniffed what looked like orange juice. "Is there no coffee? Is there…"—*sniff*—"is this"—*sniff*—"is there…what is this?"

"Daddy says they're called mimosas. My mother used to have them. So when I was old enough, I made him let me drink them too." She sipped, frowning.

Addy took a sip.

OK, that is definitely not just orange juice.

"Why does it taste like ass?"

"That's the champagne. You think it tastes like ass?"

"What's champagne?"

"It's like wine," Ella said, grinning and taking another sip. "In all honesty, we're not supposed to have alcohol. But whatever. Daddy hasn't been home, Matthew keeps disappearing, and you're the only one who keeps coming by. So, here we are." Draining the glass, she sat it on the table.

Addy winced as it clinked against the table. The little stem was so fragile.

But it held, and she exhaled. "I don't know if we should be drinking this early, Ella," she said, pushing the glass away.

Ella slid it back in front of her. "Drink it. I'll make more." She pulled the juice and champagne from the fridge again and set to work, mixing more than was likely prudent in a large pitcher.

As Ella mixed, the sinking feeling in Addy's gut telling her she was about to get drunk with Ella, she remembered the first night on Harkers. Dean dragging her to Celia's, tucking her in.

Taking her out to the ocean the next morning. What a day that was.

Plunking the pitcher in the middle of the table, Ella pushed her glass closer again. "Girl, drink. I am not drinking all this by myself."

Nodding, Addy took another sip. Her taste buds had already begun to forget about the champagne, and the drink took on the sweet flavor of orange juice. But with bubbles in, and less bite than orange juice usually had.

Back up.

"Ella, what do you mean I'm the only one who comes around? Don't you have friends?"

She sighed, pouring more into both glasses. "I grew up on the ocean, but once Daddy started working for IRF, we've moved around a lot." Resting her chin on her hand, she gazed out the window. "I just haven't really tried here. It's so much work."

Finishing off the glass, Addy poured more for them both. It might be too soon to throw this line out, but hell. As Mom had taught her, you couldn't catch fish if you didn't throw out the bait. "What's your dad doing here?"

Brow wrinkled, she shrugged. "I don't know. Here." She stood and grabbed the pitcher. "Let's go in here."

Addy followed her, not wobbly on her feet but not a hundred percent steady, as Ella flounced slower than usual through a room with nothing but a large, shining table and chairs, through another room with more books than Addy'd ever seen in one place, and into a room with three large couches, two chairs, and a giant TV.

"Jane would love to see all those books," Addy said, choosing one of the three overstuffed chairs.

"Would she?" Ella filled both glasses, handed one to Addy, and sat the pitcher on a palatial coffee table. "Tell me about her. Are you guys close?"

Addy cleared her throat. "That's a long story."

"We've got time."

"What do you have to watch?"

Flapping a hand, Ella leaned back into a couch covered in some sort of flowery pattern. "You don't want to watch what I have."

But it turned out what she had was Trek.

Hardly able to believe her luck, Addy forgot for a while about time and thought about space. The acrid scent of nail polish assaulting her nose, she drank mimosas and told Ella about Dean, and eventually about Jane.

"I don't know if it'll ever be the same, Ella." She sniffled.

Ella nodded, inspecting the polish on her index finger. "Because we move around so much, and because of Daddy's job, I haven't had any friends like that."

"Ever?"

"Ever. But Matthew has been, up until the last few weeks, the best friend I've ever had."

Addy smiled. "That's good. Is he a good guy?"

Ella smiled and polished off her drink. "He's been my personal guard since the day we met. If that tells you anything."

Unsure what she was supposed to get from that answer, Addy finished off her own drink. Leaning to set the glass back on the table, she fell off the couch. Her head smacked into the coffee table and the world went white for a second.

Giggling, Ella helped her up. "Maybe we should cut you off."

Addy's eyes rolled in her head. "Think that might be a thing." She stood, clinging to Ella's arm. "Inna get home. Sleep some of this off."

"You can sleep upstairs. We have like six bedrooms."

And though the thought of crawling up the stairs and passing out on what would no doubt be the most comfortable bed she ever slept on tried to convince her to listen to Ella, Addy shook her head. "Feel like I should go home. I'm living with Celia, she'd probably worry about me. But thanks." Stumbling toward the hallway, she laughed. "It's been fun, Ella. Oh shit."

"What?"

Addy lifted her hand to her face and inspected her nails. Voids crossed the thick red polish on them. "Think I fucked up the nail polish."

Arm clamped around her shoulders, Ella steered her to the door. "We'll fix it when we're sober."

With a laugh, Addy pulled the door open. Before she thought about it, she threw an arm around Ella and pulled her in for a hug. "Thanks. Thanks again." She backed through the door, leaning on the screen.

"I had a good time, Addy." Ella looked into the street, her breath puffing out as it had in the morning. "Still cold. Get home quick before you freeze to death."

Addy clicked her heels together. "Yes, ma'am."

Shaking her head as she shut the door, Ella smiled. "I'm not your ma'am."

Still laughing, Addy wobbled down the porch steps.

One of the bushes near the door rustled.

She stopped. "OK. Now I *know* someone is there. Who the hell?"

Yaz stepped out. "Sorry, Addy. I didn't want to disturb you, but there's things I have to tell you." He held his arm out. "You look like you could use some help getting home."

She took his arm as tiny granules of ice began falling from the sky. "So it's your turn for news?"

He nodded. "I think we need to do something about the people who used to live here. Sooner rather than later."

* * *

"You know someone dropped off new shoes the other day," Jane said, standing on the porch with her arms folded as Jack pulled the door closed.

"No shit." He took her arm as she wobbled down the stairs. "Watch the ice."

"Yeah, after I said. Crap." Slipping, she gripped his arm with both hands and stopped.

"You said crap?"

"Ha. Ha. Funny man. No," she said, stepping onto the sidewalk.

Dusted with white granules of snowy ice, it presented an image of safety but was slicker than greased ball bearings. He'd be lucky if he wasn't the one going ass over teakettle. But Jane needed him to be her anchor, so he planted both feet and imagined himself wide and strong as a granite pillar.

Putting one foot in front of the other, feet she said she couldn't see very well anymore, Jane wobbled down the walk.

"Remember I said my shoes didn't fit? It was a while back. Just after we found the you-know-whats."

He nodded, lips pressed together. The microphones. "Sure."

"They brought me more shoes."

"Jane," he said, leaning over, "we know they're listening. All the time, in every room."

"Probably outside, too," she said, glancing over her shoulder. Her foot slipped.

He caught her, almost fell himself, and righted them both. "That could be. I've thought of it. But dammit, we have to talk sometime. I have to assume they're just too busy to physically spy on us twenty-four seven."

She nodded. "I'm sure you're right. I guess. Anyway. It's still creepy."

Through the crisp air, they walked to the hospital. Only about six blocks or so, Jane still stopped twice. One of those times, she stood rubbing the forearm where she'd been bitten and pulling in one labored breath after the other.

Goose bumps raced across his arms in painful rows. "Are you alright?" Was there still a war being waged between the virus, the vaccine, and the baby?

According to Melinda, that was entirely possible. It was the reason for today's checkup.

Covering her mouth with the back of her hand, she stood and nodded. "Need to get knitting those damned mittens. My fingers are freezing."

He looked her over. The tip of her nose was red, wisps of hair stuck out from under her hat, but otherwise, she looked good. Her complexion ruddy, not pale. He wrapped her hand in his.

"Let me warm them up."

"Your hands are freezing too, Jack."

Tugging, he pulled her in and kissed her. "Not that kind of warming, then."

She smiled, and a snowflake landed on her eyelash. She caught a flake on the tip of her tongue.

The baby rolled and punched him, even through the heavy jacket.

"Ouch," Jane said, walking again. "She's being a little jerk lately."

"Well, let's get you both to the hospital before we get stuck in the snow," he said, throwing an arm over her shoulder.

Through thickening snow, they walked up the hill, another block, to the hospital.

"Those barriers look different," Jane said, pointing as they walked through the opening in the perimeter wall.

He glanced over, but all he wanted to focus on was getting her into the hospital, where it was warm. "You sure?"

She shrugged.

"Let's get inside before all three of us freeze to death." He fought chattering teeth and held the door open for her.

As they wiped their feet, the boy at the desk leaned over. "Snowing?"

"No," Jane said. "Confetti."

Jack snorted.

The boy sat back, chair creaking. "Go on up, they're expecting you, Mr. and Mrs. Cooke."

Jack's stomach flipped. Twice. Heart in his throat, he swallowed. "That's—"

Jane spoke at the same time. "We're not—"

They both stopped.

Jack's cheeks flamed. A natural enough mistake for the boy to make. But not even something he'd considered.

You really should have, Jack. You really should have.

And if he had? If he'd considered it for a moment? A second? Stopped to think about what he wanted out of this? What she might want? Here he'd just been running on instinct, just like the last twenty-five years. So fucking blissful in the moment, he hadn't even considered the future. Or what it should even look like in the world the way it was now.

Letting the thoughts run themselves as they'd do with or without his interference, he followed her up the stairs. One hand held out behind her, but where she couldn't see it and get upset he was being overprotective. He followed her up the stairs the same way every night, and while she'd probably caught on, she didn't say anything. Just let him pretend he wasn't ready to catch her at any moment.

On the fourth floor, they turned right at a T intersection and headed down a long, windowless hallway.

"Wasn't it room 415?" Jane squinted at each sign on their right.

"I think so." He checked the signs on the other side.

A man in fatigues burst from a room in front of them, almost mowing Jane down.

Jack opened his mouth to tell the guy to watch out.

"Open your eyes, asshole," Jane said, beating him to it. She glanced up and frowned.

Following her eyes, Jack glared at the man. Half a foot taller than him, greying hair, silver leaf on his collar, and Burke on his name tag.

"You must be Commander Burke," Jack said, holding out a hand. "I'm surprised we haven't met yet, but—"

"Jackson Cooke," he said, eyes on Jane. He shook Jack's hand. "Yes, I'm surprised myself." Dropping Jack's hand after two firm pumps, he took Jane's and kissed the back of it.

Jack kept his blood from boiling out his eyes by sheer force of will.

"You must be the lovely Jane I've heard so much about," Burke said.

Lips pressed together, she slid her hand out of his. "Must be."

He nodded, frowning. "Yes, well. Good to meet you both. This way." He held a hand out toward the room from which he'd barreled.

Jane threw her head back and marched through the doorway.

Rather than follow her, Jack crossed his arms. They'd been here the better part of a month now, and this was the first time he'd seen the commander, outside that moment in the telescope. He had so many questions, it was all he could do to pick something to say. "Commander, if I can have a moment," he said, "I'd like to ask you about the wall around this place. It's pretty impressive."

"It is," Burke said, crossing his own arms.

"Did you find it that way, or…"

"That's not something I care to discuss."

One corner of Jack's mouth lifted. "Alright. How about the people here. Seems like they're pretty quiet. Just find them here too?"

Burke glared, jaw bunching.

"Right. How about what you're doing here. In this hospital. With Melinda."

Sardonic grin crossing his lips, the commander nodded. "That's what this is really about, isn't it?"

Jack cocked his head. "What what is all about?"

"This conversation. It's about your wife, isn't it? I think she's perfectly free to—"

"Ex-wife. What she does is no concern of mine," Jack said, narrowing his eyes and holding Burke's gaze.

Burke cleared his throat. "That's right. So, what can I help you with?"

"What. Are. You. Doing. In this hospital. Research?"

"Also not something I care to discuss."

Jack stepped into his bubble, craning his neck to maintain eye contact. "I think you and I should have a talk sometime. About Melinda. About what she was doing when I found her. What she's capable of."

"Oh, I think I know what she's capable of."

Whether he asked it to or not, the blood rushed to Jack's cheeks. He stepped back and studied the man.

Projecting an air of confidence, using it as a shield against being read, Burke continued to glare.

"Listen, commander," Jack said, uncrossing his arms, "this has nothing to do with her and me. That's water under the bridge. Air through the engine. But it does have everything to do with how dangerous she is."

A smirk crossed Burke's features like a ripple. "It's under control, Mr. Cooke. Now please, the doctor is waiting." He held a hand out toward the room again.

Jack took a step and stopped, staring up at the commander's eyes again. "You know, I wish I could believe that. But I just can't. And I hope you don't, either."

He left Burke in the hallway and joined Jane in the ultrasound room.

* * *

Addy sat up and blinked at the sun slanting at a hard angle through the west windows. Celia hadn't questioned her when she'd come home a few hours ago, wobbling and mumbling about Ella, orange juice, and Yasuo.

The blanket Addy had tugged off the back of the couch and covered her shoulders with now stretched all the way to her toes. Which had been freed of their shoe prison.

"Celia?"

The empty house ticked, settling as the sun released it from the day.

Grabbing a bite from the kitchen, she packed what she thought she'd need for a quick trip deeper into the mountains. Yaz had said it'd be about a day's walk to get to the rest of the people who used to live here, including their leader, and it was likely to be chilly. There might be a river crossing or two.

When Celia returned, she'd ask if she wanted to go. Maybe Renzo, too.

Restless, she wandered out of the house and down the street. The afternoon snow gathered around the edges of fences and trees, sucking all the heat from the air. She clutched her jacket and headed toward the jail.

It'd be nice to see Dean before she left. She wouldn't be able to whisper everything she needed to him, at least partially because she wouldn't be talking for most of it, but also because it just wasn't possible to whisper so much information without looking suspicious.

But mainly because of the first thing.

Good lord but she needed to be touched.

Ah, dammit, Adelaide, pull it together.

She passed Dad and Jane's house.

Through the window, with the curtains open, she could see them dancing. The soft sounds of music drifted into the yard.

Smiling, they talked and laughed, Dad twirling her around as best as she could twirl.

Addy hadn't been to see them in a couple weeks. Telling herself she was just too busy, she'd come up with one reason or another to never go over there.

No doubt Jane thought she hated her. Which wasn't the case. Probably.

She slipped away, continuing to the jail. She considered the way the town was like a jail. The wall out there, out of sight. Tall. Unclimbable. Unbreakable.

And then there was Mom. Maybe she'd overblown the whole vaccine thing. If Burke really had threatened her and Mike, Mom would've really had no choice other than to cooperate.

And all this she had to leave so she could go play diplomat with the people whose home had been stolen by IRF. Keep them from a plan Yaz said would bring them down into this valley to retake their home. With deadly force.

She looked up. The sun had sunk below the horizon. She'd stopped in front of the jail.

At the door, she tugged the handle, but it remained closed. Locked tight.

Hands cupped around her eyes, she tried to peek in, but the one-way glass yielded nothing but a close-up of her own nose. She knocked. "Hello? Anyone there?"

A high-pitched whine from beside the door invited her skin to leap off and run down the street.

Holding it together, she glanced over as a voice emanated from a small panel.

"Can I help you?" It crackled with static.

"I'd like to visit a prisoner. Um. Dean Ross, please."

Silence.

She tapped a foot.

More silence.

Maybe they were thinking about it? Calling someone to get approval?

The static crackled. *"Push the button if you want to talk."*

Crap.

She pushed the button and leaned into the little panel. "My name is Adelaide Cooke. I'd like to visit a prisoner, Dean Ross, please."

The intercom squealed in her ear as she released the button.

Standing back, she rubbed her ear and frowned when the voice came back and told her no.

Heart in her throat, she pushed the button again. "Why not?" Why had they rebuffed her so quickly?

"Sorry, ma'am. No visitors for Mr. Ross. Commander's orders."

"Why not?" she asked again. Sighed. Pushed the button. "Why not?"

Static squealed. *"He didn't say."*

Pushing the button, she considered her next move. Breath coming in short, sharp inhales, she blinked several times. "Is Captain Lyburn available?"

"One moment, please."

Her heart rate inched up again. What would she say to him? She couldn't tell him she was going. Couldn't talk about Dean right here in front of the jail. Why had she even asked for him?

"Addy," he said, opening the front door, "what are you doing here?" Looking over his shoulder, he stepped through the door and latched it. He grabbed her upper arm and led her away from the jail.

Heart pounding, she allowed him to drag her into the shadows.

"You shouldn't come here," he whispered, letting her go and crossing his arms. The streetlights glowed, casting an orange hue over his sidearm. He rubbed his forehead and stood his hair on end.

"Sorry. Sorry. I think Ella fed me too much alcohol earlier. I just wanted to see Dean."

"You were with Ella? How is she? Is she OK?"

"Not that you care, but yeah, she's fine."

"What do you mean, not that I care? I care."

"You sure don't show her."

He laughed. A struggling, painful thing. "I tell her all the time."

Addy laughed back. "You have to show a girl, Matt. Telling her doesn't mean shit if you don't back it up with action. When's the last time you just went to see her for no reason?"

He opened his mouth. Closed it. Opened it again. "Fine. Whatever. Don't come here, Addy. They won't let you in to see him."

"So they said. Why would Burke say he can't have visitors?"

"I can't say."

"Bullshit. Tell me why. Tell me why my boyfriend is in jail and my mother is practically running this place. Tell me. Or I'm going back to Ella and so help me—"

"Oh god, whatever it is, don't do that." He rolled his eyes. "Look, here's the thing. The official story is that Dean hasn't been checking in with the company like he was supposed to, alright? He fed them some line of shit about having to go off the grid for a while, but when they checked in with his guys, a couple of them didn't line up with his story. And then he showed up here. It looks bad."

"Ah, hell. So then what?"

"So then, they're trying to get the story out of him."

"What's he said?"

"Nothing. That's why he's still in jail."

A surge of pride rode through her, her cheeks blazing with heat. With that one little sentence, all the time he'd spent in this stupid jail was worth it. His loyalty was sound. Just like he'd said.

Backing up his words with action.

The grin that stretched her face split her cheeks so hard she thought they might break. "Thanks. That's all I needed to know."

"Fine. Fine." He sighed. "Just don't go saying things to Ella she doesn't need to know."

Addy laughed. "You ought to give her more credit. Or one day she's going to kick your ass and I'm going to get popcorn."

He hung his head. "Her dad would kill me if I told her half the stuff I want to say."

"I'd be more afraid of her if I were you."

Laughing, he nodded, blue eyes dancing. "You sure you're alright?"

"Yeah, yeah. Just gotta sleep off a few hundred mimosas."

Guffawing, Matt started for the door. "Sounds like my pumpkin pie, alright. Thanks, Addy."

She flapped a hand. "Sure. Thank you back."

Waiting for the door to the jail to slam home, she turned her feet. Walking around in this place, thinking about the wall surrounding it, not on one hundred percent high alert, was an odd feeling. Even after a few weeks of it, after a few years of this so-called "civilization," she couldn't get used to the feeling of not having to worry twenty-four seven.

Sometimes she wondered if she was making mountains out of molehills so she could feel better.

CHAPTER 18

Paul stepped onto Jack's front porch, gave him a brief squeeze, and watched the sunrise with him.

Jack sank his hands into his pockets and wiggled his bare toes on the freezing boards with Jane's most recent creation wrapping his neck. "You're up early."

With a nod, Paul narrowed his eyes at the rising sun. "Need to talk at ya."

"We can't talk inside."

"I know it. But I heard there's some records and the chance at dancing with a pretty young lady." He exhaled and stared at the row of hedges to the south. He lowered his voice to a whisper. "Because we can't talk out here, either."

Jack nodded. He stepped toward the door.

Paul laid his hand on his arm. "Talking to you on the radio all that time, I hadn't realized it'd been so long since I'd seen your face."

The beating, several weeks old now, had faded to dull yellow in most spots. The bad cut over his eye had taken a while, though, and the busted blood vessels in the eyeball itself had made him look more half 'Head than anything for weeks.

"You didn't miss much," Jack said, glancing at his feet.

"Looks like I missed a fair bit. Your little girl caught me up on most of it." He shuffled. "I sure am sorry it had to be that way."

"You and me both," he said. "I didn't. I mean, I don't. Well. It can't be helped."

"Got that right. Alright if I tell you something? Then we'll drop it?"

Jack's stomach clenched. Either he was about to get laid into, shamed, or humiliated. Probably all three. He nodded, tongue stuck to the roof of his mouth, heart in his throat.

"You're right. It can't be helped. But you need to shuffle off some of that guilt I see hanging around your heart."

Jack shook his head. "With all due respect, Paul—"

"Don't you all due respect me, boy. You listen," he said, pointing a gnarled finger into Jack's chest.

He snapped his mouth closed.

Nodding, Paul went on. "I seen you two, soon as you got to the prison. You was already head over heels then. And I don't know much about women, but I know what one looks like when she loves a man. I know that." He stopped, staring off across the yard. His mouth twitched, and he rocked from side to side.

Opening his mouth to prod him to continue, Jack paused.

Paul's eyes had glazed over, and when he blinked, it was long and slow.

Folding his arms across his chest, he waited for Paul to return from his memory trip. Sometime, he'd have to ask where he went.

Inhaling through his nose like he just woke, Paul glanced around. "Sorry about that, friend Jack. Lost me for a minute. Anyway. Where was I?"

Jack cleared his throat. "The prison."

"Right. Right. Now look," he said, facing Jack, "You went through a hard time on the way. Y'both of you did. Going through shit like that together changes things. Changes people."

He stopped trying to argue. Maybe Paul had a point. "What is it you're here about?"

"Let's talk inside. I'm freezing my nuts off, friend Jack."

Jack opened the door and ushered him inside. The warmth of the house washed over his cold toes. His feet tingled.

"Ah, there's that pretty lady," Paul said, settling on the couch next to Jane. "How are you and your tiny human?"

"We're good." Smile in her voice. "What about you?"

"Can't complain. Well," he said, pausing long enough for Jack to mouth the rest of the words with him, "I can. But I won't."

She chuckled.

Paul leaned close to her, inspecting the needles in her hair, which had grown back so fast. Like a magic trick known only to pregnant women.

"Those are something else," Paul said.

Nodding, Jane pulled the needles out.

Once, she'd made chop suey out of a 'Head's brains with those things. So Jack wouldn't get eaten. He'd only just begun to pay her back for that.

"My hair's not really long enough yet. But it was nice to be able to stick 'em in there again." Points down, she impaled the table with a woody thump.

A board creaked under Jack's foot.

Glancing up, she smiled. "Jack, take your coat off. Stay awhile."

He did as he was told. Behind him, Paul asked if she'd show him their records.

"Oh, look at this." She eased up and crossed the room. With a smile, she pulled a record from its sleeve, laid it on the turntable, and turned it up.

Billie Holiday lit up the room.

Nodding, Paul glanced at Jack. "That'll do, pretty lady."

"Here," she said, holding out a hand, "my honey taught me how to dance."

Paul raised a brow at him. "May I?"

Jack held out his hand. "Not my call. The lady said. Better do what she asks."

After taking a moment to place his hands, Paul twirled her around the room. Whispered in her ear.

Whatever it was he had to tell her didn't sit well. As the song went on, Jane's expression fell by degrees.

Jack's stomach fell with it.

* * *

Having fed Paul breakfast and ushered him out the door, Jane sat on the couch and took up her needles and yarn. She began knitting so fast Jack couldn't see the needles. Just a blur.

"Jane?"

"Yeah, honey." Smile in her voice, not on her face.

"What are you making?"

Slamming the needles into the table, she stood. "Nothing. Let's go for a walk."

He put his coat back on. Shoes. Scarf.

She wobbled, pulling on a pair of boots.

"Jane, let me—"

"I got it, Jack."

Holding up both hands, he backed away.

Paul's news had been worse than he imagined.

She was out the door and halfway down the street before he could catch her. He put an arm around her shoulders. "What did he say?"

"Fuck's sake. What didn't he say?"

Alright. Um.

"Start at the beginning?"

"No. Let me start at the middle. You remember we heard about the people who lived here before?"

"The people who built the wall?"

"Yes. Them. They want their home back," she said, frowning. "Before they have to spend the winter freezing their asses off out there."

"Not surprising."

"Yeah, well, your daughter is going out there to talk them out of it. She's already gone."

"She what?" He stopped walking, gaping at her. "Is she going alone?"

"I don't know," Jane said, slapping herself in the leg with a hand. Rubbing her belly with the other. "I just know she left."

He chewed his lip.

"Why didn't she come tell me?" She put her back to him, arms crossed. "She hasn't come to see me in weeks. Do you think she hates me?"

"No, I don't."

"Why not?"

Even with her shoulders curled around her arms, arms curled around her belly, back to him, he stepped closer. Didn't lay a hand on her, but stood close enough for her to feel his breath. "She doesn't, OK? She's been busy."

"Making new friends. You told me about that Ella girl."

"Smart allies, that's all, Jane."

Nodding, she dropped her arms. Her shoulders drooped. She faced him and stuck a hand out for him to take.

He did.

"Michael has been seen with his mother. And with no one else."

Jack cursed. "Addy said they'd kind of patched things up with her. Guess he's done more than just patch it up."

She shrugged. "I'm worried about him," she said, tugging his hand. "He should've stayed on the island. Far away from me."

"What do you mean?"

"Jack, I've done nothing but hurt him. As long as I've known him." Staring in his eyes, she sighed. "I tried to get some distance. Get him away before I could hurt him again. But he came along anyway."

Though his stomach knotted around itself, Jack smiled. "I'm sure Addy couldn't have gotten him to stay on the island if she'd tied him down. You were in trouble."

She freed her hand. "I was alone. There's a difference."

Shifting from foot to foot, he tried to straighten out his brain and say the right thing. It wasn't usually this hard with her, and his mind just didn't want to cooperate. "When we found you—"

"I was fine," she said, stepping back. "I'd killed them all, in case you forgot, and I was fine. I was not in trouble." She crossed her arms again. "Just because I'm pregnant does not mean I'm made out of fucking glass."

Opening his mouth, he hesitated. The image of her eyes rolling up in her head played itself, in Day-Glo colors, across the back of his retinas. Like it was tattooed there. Now might not be the most strategic time to bring that up, though. Instead, he changed topics again. "What else did Paul say?"

She exhaled through her nose. Spun on a heel and kept walking. "You were right about her and Burke."

"What do you mean?"

"Seems like your wife—"

"Ex-wife."

The corner of her mouth lifted. "Ex-wife. Seems like she's pretty damn chummy with the commander. If you know what I mean."

"You what?"

"Yeah. And they spend a lot of time together up at the hospital."

So the man in charge of this place, though he worked for IRF, had fallen under Melinda's thumb.

He shouldn't be surprised. They'd already had their suspicions. That little conversation in the hallway had been as much a giveaway as anything. But to hear it out loud…

He frowned. Their children might have the ability to forgive her, but he still couldn't fall all the way to sleep without seeing Andrew's eyes before oblivion took him down. He couldn't look at Jane without thinking of the room where they shaved her head and injected her with this poison that might kill his baby.

And now she was in control again.

$$* * *$$

After traveling most of the day using a crude map Renzo had drawn, he, Addy, and Celia arrived high in the Virginia mountains. Yaz and Renzo had spent time with these people while Addy had been painting nails with Ella, and when they arrived, one of the guards recognized Renzo. His quick talking earned them accommodations in an old camp of some kind. What seemed like a hotel but wasn't.

Addy fell asleep before her head hit the pillow.

Two seconds later, a rooster crowed and daylight peeked into the room.

Pulling her eyes open, sand caught in them both, she rolled over and scratched her dog. He'd decided the floor was too cold at some point and had since commandeered about half the twin bed.

More than half.

Smashed against a wall partition, she elbowed him.

He grunted, rolled to the floor, shook, and wagged his tail.

Scratching him between the ears, she sniffed. Coffee. And bacon.

Oh god, bacon.

Her mouth watered. "Come on, boy, let's go find us some of that breakfast."

Head in her hands, Celia sat on the edge of her own twin bed. "Thought you were never going to wake up."

"I could sleep for two more days." Addy stood on wobbly legs and knocked on the wall. "Renzo."

Silence.

"Zo?" She pulled back the partition.

Empty room.

Celia peeked over her shoulder. "He already go down?"

"I guess?"

"OK. After you," Celia said, pulling the door open and motioning into the hall.

Addy walked out into the small hallway, looked both ways, and went left. They'd come up one set of stairs, but at the opposite end, another set descended. Little wider than her hips, the stairwell smelled of old wood and dust, mixed with the coffee scent. Every single board on the way down creaked, as did the floor once she'd reached the bottom level. There'd be no sneaking in such a building.

Renzo called from the next room. "Addy, that you?"

Data loped through the door and Addy followed.

In her head she looked like another one of those cartoons Mom had shown her. Where the character would float along the scent of something enticing. Feet in the air, eyes closed, nose in the lead.

It led her to the coffee, an enormous plate of bacon next to it.

She grabbed a handful of strips and a black cup of the good stuff.

"So, Renzo," she said, sitting next to him. A tawny-skinned woman with wide-set, round brown eyes and a smile that lit her whole face sat on his other side. Also at the table with him sat a couple white dudes and a Black man with light skin and mellow green eyes. Mason, if she remembered right. He'd been the one to let them in after recognizing Renzo as a friend.

They all held a handful of cards and took turns slapping them down in various places.

"What is this you guys are playing?"

"S'called rummy," Mason said, grinning and laying five cards down in front of him. He laid one faceup on the pile of them and clutched one in his hand. "And I am kicking ass this morning."

"Anything like gin? My dad taught me that one." She smiled, sipping the coffee. One bacon strip for her, one for Data.

"Addy needs to see man today, Mason," Renzo said with a nod, laying down three cards of his own and discarding one.

"Sorry we couldn't do it last night. But this morning should be fine," Mason said. "We'll take a walk here in a bit." He dropped her a wink as he laid down his last card. "Read 'em and weep!"

The others groaned, and Renzo picked up the cards. He handed the deck to the woman, whose large eyes smiled at him.

Mason stood. "You stay here. I'll take her down."

Flushed, Renzo cut the deck. The woman next to him dealt.

Feeding the last strip of bacon to Data, Addy hopped up, and Celia materialized at her elbow. "What are we waiting for?"

"Indeed what," Addy said.

"This way, ladies," Mason said, nodding to them.

Mason opened the back door, Data dashed out into the yard, and they all stepped outside.

A volleyball game, a heated one, played out on the court. Down the hill, kids played on playground equipment. A grill smoked, some sort of fresh meat slow cooking.

Addy's stomach, though full of bacon, grumbled at the smell of meat cooking over a fire. Heart light, she smiled at the kids playing and laughed when someone got the volleyball spiked in their face.

Mason followed her eyes. "Yeah, it's a good morning. Trying to get all our fun out before it gets cold. Hear it's snowing back home already."

"Back home?"

He faced her with a slow half turn and stared. "You hafta ask?"

Addy's stomach dropped. Right. Stupid question. "I'm sorry. I wasn't thinking. It's not that far away, weird that it's not snowing here."

"Oh, it will, soon enough. Gonna get real cold."

Shuffling a foot, Addy shoved her hands in her pockets and watched Data run circles around the playground. "So, this man."

Mason chuckled. "No. Mann. Two Ns. Laurel Mann. She's in charge here."

Addy's eyes widened. "Oh. Oh! Alright," she said, smiling.

Thought about it.

Frowned instead.

"Where is she?"

"Let's go on down there," he said, angling his chin. Without waiting, he struck off down the hill.

Adrenaline kicking into high gear, Addy followed him down. She'd been thinking about and talking about this meeting for days, building herself up to it. Now, she began to back away, toes curling.

What the hell was she supposed to say? What could she say to get these people to alter their plans?

Did she want them to?

The hill dropped like a stone, down into the valley below. A small valley, no doubt carved by the little creek that now ran through the bottom of it. Deciduous forest topped the mountains to either side. A large house sat on the left side of the road, hidden behind two huge maple trees.

Mason mounted the front porch and knocked.

A small child opened the door. The tow-headed girl sketched a salute. "Hi, Mason." She gave him a sunny grin.

"Hey, Dora. Your grandmommy around?"

She looked over Addy, Celia, and Data. Her eyes lit up as they landed on the dog. "Oh, whose doggy?"

"Mine," Addy said, kneeling and throwing an arm over him. "His name's Data. You want to pet him?" She scratched his ears.

The girl knelt on his other side and laid her head on him. "Hi, Data. Good doggy," she said, closing her eyes. She inhaled. "I had a doggy back home. Her name was Princess. I hope she's OK."

Celia leaned on her knees. "You want to go throw some sticks for him? He likes to run and chase things."

The girl looked up, eyes wide.

Addy smiled. "While I go and talk to your grandma."

"Come on, Data!" Dora hopped off the porch, dashing into the yard to find a stick.

Celia followed, cutting her eyes at Addy. No doubt trusting her to do the work of peacemaking.

Addy slapped Data's haunch. "Go on, boy. Make friends."

He ran after the girl.

Grinning, Addy winked at Mason. "So. What are we waiting for?"

With a smile, he led her into the house and closed the door. "This way," he said, taking her up the stairs.

The staircase had no banister, and Addy held her hands out to either side as she climbed. At the top of the stairs, three doors stood before them.

Mason opened the one on the right. Light streamed into the hallway. "Ms. Mann?"

"Yes, Mason."

"I'd like to introduce you to someone."

She sighed. "You're lucky you're pretty."

He chuckled, hanging off the doorknob.

"Show them in, then."

Not looking, he waved Addy over and stepped into the room. "I'd like to introduce Adelaide Cooke. Addy, Laurel Mann."

Addy stepped half into the room and addressed the silhouette standing before the window. "Ma'am." She smoothed her hair.

"She wants to talk to you about home."

Mann blew out a breath.

Mason turned those mellow green eyes on Addy and gave her a short, sharp wave.

Addy came around the door into the bright room, squinting at the light framing Mann.

About the same age as Mom, her flowing brown curls streaked with white, she leaned on the window. She frowned, half her tanned face turned to them. "So. You want to talk about Magnolia."

"Ms. Mann, it's good to meet you," Addy said, crossing the room. She held out her hand. Her mouth dry, she tried to smile.

Mann took her hand and shook. A good, strong, not-too-hard shake. The faint scent of soap drifted off her grip. "Mmm. Sure."

"It's called Magnolia?"

Mann nodded, lips pressed together. Deep frown lines framed her mouth. "Named it that for the giant magnolia in front of my house."

The way she caught and held Addy's gaze sent the only message Addy needed. Only being direct was going to get results. She stabbed right into the heart of the problem.

"You're planning on taking it back by force, aren't you?"

"You here to stop me?"

"I just want to talk. There's a lot of people there. People I don't want to see hurt."

Pressing her lips together again, Mann crossed her arms and stared down into the yard. "You met Dora on the way in." She angled her chin.

Stepping up to the window, Addy nodded. "That's my dog and one of my best friends she's playing with. She's your granddaughter?"

Mann closed her eyes. "Follow me." She walked out of the room.

Addy followed her through the house, hardwood floors creaking. Through a sitting room, a kitchen with an ancient stove, and onto a screened back porch with a swing. Without hesitation, Mann led her outside and down past a pond large enough for swimming. They also passed a couple chicken coops and a barn. A cow lowed. Some pigs rooted in a small, fenced yard.

"It's beautiful here," Addy said. "But where are we going?"

Mann grunted. "A mile or so. Alright?"

"Sure, Ms. Mann."

"Call me Laurel," she said, glancing at Addy's side. "Nice knife."

"Thanks. That revolver of yours makes me think of someone I used to know."

"That so? They dead?"

"No. Yes. Kind of."

"Which is it," Laurel said, stopping and putting a hand on her hip.

"She's not who she used to be. But she's alive."

"Good for her." She began walking again, glancing at Addy from the corner of her eye. "That staff of yours looks pretty useless, though."

Addy grinned, watching her feet skim over the cold ground. "It's more useful than you'd think."

They followed two wheel ruts through a few fields and into the woods. Eventually, a path angled off to the left and up a hill. They took it, climbing to the top.

Addy, out of breath, leaned over her knees as Laurel knelt next to a tree with a wooden box chained to it. Reaching in, she pulled out a pair of binoculars and stared into the next valley.

Following her gaze, Addy narrowed her eyes. The valley held some fencing, from what she could tell, and a larger blob of something toward the other end.

A gust of wind pushed up the hill and into Addy's face.

It stank of rot. Spoiled blood. Congealed life.

Fighting a retch, she wiped her mouth. "Laurel. What's down there?"

Without a word, Mann held out the binoculars.

Addy took them. Fumbled. Dropped the staff and caught them. Aimed them at the larger blob.

A horde the size of a small city.

Dropping the binoculars, stomach turning inside out and lungs locking the breath in, Addy stumbled back and into a tree. She sat on the ground, teeth clacking together so hard she just about bit through her tongue. "Laurel," she said, wheezing, "that's the largest horde I've ever. Ever seen."

Arms crossed, she nodded. "You see those fences?"

Sliding on her ass through dried, wet leaves, she snagged the binoculars again and raised them to her eyes. Dirt ground against her cheek.

Two sets of chain-link formed a tunnel. Pieces of meat hung from the sides at intervals. One or two 'Heads munched on a piece, and another shuffled past, heading for some hanging farther down. Where the tunnel ended, it opened into a large, fenced area, and 'Heads roamed there, bumping into one another.

She couldn't hear the buzzing. The sound like a beehive. Like a cadre of cicadas risen from the dirt to mate.

But it was there.

"We herd them down into the valley," Laurel said.

Flinching, Addy lowered the spyglasses from her eyes and wiped her face. "Why? Why not just kill them?"

Mann sat next to her, picking up the binoculars and wiping the dirt away with her scarf. Short, careful strokes, teasing off each granule of dirt without scratching the glass. "Dora. The girl you met."

"Yeah."

"Her mom, my daughter. She's part of that horde. Her uncle, his wife, my son and daughter-in-law. Their three children. My grandchildren. They're all part of that horde."

"Oh god, Laurel. I'm sorry." How did this woman even stand under that kind of pain?

She glanced up, lips twisted in a grimace. "Dora is all that's left of my family. We built a clan. A life. Everything. Back home."

And just like that, Addy knew the rest of the conversation was pointless.

"Then those bastards with IRF came with their materials. And their promises. And their requests for help. And we helped them. They helped us."

Clearing her throat, Addy watched the horde. Forced herself to look at it. To take in the stench rising from the valley. There had to be thousands of them down there.

"Then they came back. And with their guns, and their boys in uniforms, their grenades. Murders. They forced us from our home and brought in new people. People I've since learned," she said, sniffing, "I've since learned they have no business here. They've never seen the world the way it is. They have no idea." Her voice husky, she cleared her throat but didn't go on.

"That's not their fault."

Mann stood and looked down at Addy. "They don't deserve our home. We don't deserve to sleep in some busted, barely heated, worn-out girl scout camp for the winter. That's our home and nothing you, them, or anyone could say will change that."

Addy stood, folding her arms. "I can't begin to know how you feel. Or express how sorry I am. But Laurel," she said, laying a hand on her arm, "there's women and children and people's families back in Magnolia, too. My own family. I'm going to"—she cleared her throat—"I'm going to be a big sister for the first time soon. Just a couple months now."

Though she didn't move away from Addy's hand, Mann stared at the horde. "Well then in the morning you get out of here. You get back to them. And if you want them to live through this, you get them to leave." She turned, narrowing her eyes. "This horde is going there. It'll take some time, they're slower in the cold. But they're coming. Me and this army, we're taking Magnolia back."

CHAPTER 19

Addy mumbled to herself as she climbed the secret ladder back into Magnolia.

Placed at uneven intervals so they didn't appear planned, short crosspieces had been welded to the wall on either side of a support beam. Taken individually, they looked like nothing. Taken together, they made a ladder of sorts. Little more than toe holds, but they got the job done.

Placing each toe with care, she crawled to the top of the wall and looked down.

Twenty feet. A sheer drop straight to the bottom. Could Mann's "army" really make it over this thing?

She scanned the roofs next to the wall. Some still perfect. Some dipping where snow had collected.

"Coming down?"

At least she'd had a hold of the wall. Containing a shout, she glanced down.

Yasuo stood beneath the wall, squinting up at her.

With a sigh she made sure he could hear, she climbed down the other side. Once both feet landed on the ground, she slid the staff out of her pack and leaned on it. "Are you the welcoming party?"

He nodded. "How'd it go?"

She shrugged. "Too soon to tell. This Mann woman is interesting. A little crazy, but I get it."

Leaning on his own staff, he walked out to the road. "You're missing some people. And a short, brown one."

"Celia and Data are cozying up to Mann's granddaughter. Renzo made some friends. They stayed back to see if maybe they could turn some people since Mann's not budging."

"Renzo fascinates me."

"Why?"

He glanced at her from the corner of his eye. "Now that you know your part, guess what you get to do next."

"Oh good. What now?"

"You get to make amends."

"Apologize? The hell do I have to apologize for?"

He stopped. "No, Adelaide. Make amends. It's more than a simple I'm sorry." He smiled. "Take Renzo. He was a guard in that prison where your dad was taken. Heard he did a lot of shit he regrets. But what's he doing about it? Is he going around, blaming a bunch of people for his mistakes?"

She pictured him. Hulk of a man, but with gentle eyes. Quiet about his past but constantly going about the business of making up for it. Making different choices.

"Besides," Yaz said, walking on, "amends aren't for other people. They're so you can work through your bullshit. And sometimes it's more of a living amends, like Renzo's doing, than really saying 'I'm sorry.'"

She nodded. "Do you have any suggestions about where to start?"

"Where do you want to start?"

With a shrug, she stared across a football field as they passed. An old school stood crumbling next to it, trees growing out the windows. As she watched, two guards walked around it.

They angled across the field, and one of them resolved into Matt. Must have been taking a watch, like he said. As they got closer, the other guard went to raise his rifle. "What are you doing here? This is a restricted area."

Matt frowned, hand on the barrel of the guard's rifle. "I don't think we need that." He nodded at them. "Addy, Yasuo, how are you guys?"

Yaz smiled and leaned on the staff. "This is a restricted area? Why?"

"Oh hey, Addy," Matt said, turning to her, "Ella wanted me to invite you over for Christmas."

"For what now?"

His mouth flapped a few times.

The other boy grinned. "You don't know what Christmas is?"

Matt shifted on his feet. "Uh. Christmas. There's uh. You really don't know?"

Addy shook her head.

He smiled. "Bring gifts."

* * *

Shifting the small boxes to her hip, Addy opened the screen and lifted Ella's door knocker.

She paused. A wreath smelling of fresh pine hung around the knocker, adorned with bows in green, red, and white. It had to be one of the strangest things she'd ever seen.

The door opened, yanking the knocker out of her hand.

She stumbled, reaching for anything that could help her stay upright.

"Miss Cooke," Matt said, catching her flailing arm. "Didn't mean to knock you down." He waited for her to balance and released her. "Ella said you were here, sorry about that. Come on in."

She stepped in, pulling the screen closed behind her. "Thanks. What the hell is that on the door?"

He smiled, parentheses framing his mouth. "She made that wreath herself. Got sap all over the kitchen." Leading her down the hall, he called out to Ella.

"Back here. Just getting the drinks."

Addy laughed under her breath. "Of course." She cleared her throat. "So you didn't have a watch or any of that other stuff Ella thinks is more important than her?"

He peeked over his shoulder. "It can wait. This is probably the most important holiday in Ella's life."

Before Addy could ask any more, they walked into the kitchen.

Ella stood over a giant bowl on the table, stirring. "So glad you could join us, Adelaide." She looked up with the warmest smile Addy'd ever seen from her and glanced at the gifts. "Matthew, take those in and put them under the tree, please."

He tugged the presents.

Addy released them and stood across the table from Ella. "What's this? It's not mimosas."

"Something I only make once a year." She lifted the ladle and held it under Addy's nose.

A variety of spices Addy could only term "riotous" assaulted her nose. She'd had cinnamon exactly twice, but you couldn't forget that scent. The rest, however powerful, were unrecognizable. But there was also an undertone of something…vaguely…

"It's got bourbon in it." Ella smiled and tipped the ladle toward Addy. "Taste."

Addy sucked a bit off the ladle, trying not to slurp the creamy concoction. It had some kind of weird taste in the middle of her tongue, but the spices she'd smelled dulled most of it, and the bourbon cut through the sweetness.

Hand under the ladle to catch drips, Ella watched her. Eyes wide.

"What is it?"

"Do you like it?"

Addy shrugged. "It's different, I'll give you that. Never had anything quite like it." She licked her lips, tasting the inside of her mouth again. "What is it?"

"It's called eggnog and it only comes at Christmas. Carry the glasses, please." She sat the ladle in the bowl and picked it up. "Let's take it in the living room."

Addy followed her through the dining room and past the books. She stopped when they got to the living room and stared at the front window. "You've got a tree in the house, Ella."

"Please put the glasses here on the coffee table," Ella said, setting the bowl down.

Of course, the coffee table wasn't where it had been because everything in the room had been rearranged to accommodate the giant fucking tree standing in the window.

A fire crackled in the fireplace, the scent of oak floating into the room with its mellow, almost neutral odor.

"It's called a Christmas tree," Matt said from the couch, his feet propped on the table. He wiggled his toes. "That's a nice fire, baby."

"OK," Addy said, setting the glasses down. "It's called a Christmas tree. So this is Christmas?"

Ella poured them all a tumbler full of eggnog. "Yes. Here." She picked up a glass and held it out to Addy.

Matt leaned forward and snagged his off the table. He and Addy both went to take a sip.

"Matthew, Adelaide. You can't drink without toasting. Not on special occasions." She held her cup aloft.

With a smile, Matt stood and held his aloft as well.

Addy stared at them both, wondering what toast had to do with drinking. She hadn't seen any bread.

Ella widened her eyes. "Raise your glass."

She did.

"To Christmas," Ella said, tinking the rim of her glass against Addy's and then Matt's. "Now you."

They clinked glasses the way Ella had done theirs.

Addy frowned. "When do we drink it?"

"Now," Ella said, smiling. She tipped the glass back and sipped.

Taking in a mouthful of the thick drink, Addy swirled it in her mouth. She got a bigger dose of the cream, which gave what could have been an overpowering experience of spices and alcohol an almost pleasant feeling. She wondered what other drinks Ella was hiding up her sleeve.

She sat on the couch and sipped again. "Please tell me why the tree is here. What's all over it?"

Ella sat next to her and smiled at Matt as he came around and squeezed between Ella and the arm of the couch. He threw his arm around her and pointed at the tree. "Popcorn on a string. Don't ask me how long it took."

"Why popcorn?"

He shrugged, leaning against Ella. "She said string popcorn. I strung popcorn."

Addy smiled. "It's different. I like it."

Setting her glass on the table, Ella stood. "Presents." She walked to the tree and pulled a hat from behind it. Pointy and red, it had a white ball at the top, and when she settled it on her head at an angle, the ball fell down to her shoulder.

A thousand questions running through her mind, Addy decided to stay quiet and watch.

Ella pulled packages out from under the tree and handed one to each of them.

"I brought you one, too," Addy said, pointing.

Ella shook her head and sat on the coffee table. "I'll get to it. Open them."

Wrapped in rough, plain brown paper with a ribbon made of fabric wrapped around it, Addy's present had a vague, rectangular shape. She flipped it over and found it secured with tape in the back.

Knife unsheathed, she slit the tape and did the same with the pieces at the ends.

Matt chuckled.

"What?"

"You just rip it. Like this." He tore the paper on his, exposing the present beneath. He held up his new book. "*Welcome to the Universe: An Astrophysical Tour.* J. Richard Gott, Michael A. Strauss, Neil deGrasse Tyson." He grinned. "Thanks, sweet pea. This sounds amazing. I think I've heard of this Neil guy. Did he write any other books?"

She nodded. "This one almost didn't get published. It came out in 2016."

They sat in silence. The year the virus had happened. Before any of them were born.

Not for the first time, Addy considered what it must have been like before. People publishing books, making TV shows. Driving cars to jobs that, according to Dad, did nothing but give them money. Money they used to buy the books and shows and cars.

Weird.

She pulled the paper off her own book. The back of the book faced her, so she turned it over to inspect the cover.

It had Data, the android, on it.

She gasped. "Ella, what is this?"

"It's a book about Star Trek. I thought you might like it."

The grin started somewhere under her nose. By the time it finished, she could hardly feel her tightly stretched cheeks. "It's amazing. A whole book about Trek?"

"It's called *Metamorphosis*, and apparently it's about Data. Do you like it?" She leaned forward, her breath caught in her throat. Eyes wide.

Addy's cheeks started to hurt. "I love it. Thank you." She clutched the book to her chest.

And that was how she spent her first Christmas. Reading her new book in front of a fire with a tree inside the house, eggnog in her cup, and friends by her side.

Mann and her horde forgotten. For just a moment.

* * *

"I can't believe we never celebrated this before," Jane said, legs beneath the massive blanket she was knitting.

Jack frowned. "Didn't seem much of a reason to celebrate, I guess. With the world the way it was."

She shrugged. "It's always been this way, far as I'm concerned."

"True. I guess I disliked the holiday, to tell the truth. Too commercial." He fingered his new necklace. A resin pendant, poured with some of Jane's hair inside, strung on a leather thong. Probably the most thoughtful gift he'd ever received. "I guess it's a little different these days."

She grinned. "I'm glad you like it."

He nodded. "These new socks are pretty amazing, too. Where did you get such soft yarn?"

"A woman has to have some secrets."

With a chuckle, he stood and walked to the window. Thick snow blanketed the ground, coming down in sheets even now. A fire crackled in the fireplace, and he could almost feel at ease. Almost.

Jane's belly pressed into his back. She hadn't made a sound crossing the room. "Let's go look at the snow. I can wear these gorgeous, warm new boots you got me. How'd you know my feet are always cold?"

"You have to ask? You put them on me every chance you get."

She laughed and stepped to the door. Sliding her feet into the fur-lined boots, she pulled his jacket off its hook and held it out to him.

He shrugged it on, wrapped his scarf around, and tugged on the new hat she'd made him. And his gun squeaked against the new leather holster. Hand-stitched. She'd been busy.

The inside of his gut bubbled with warmth. No one had ever given him so much. Not in so many years, he'd forgotten what it felt like to receive rather than give.

She opened the door and stepped onto the porch. "Damn. That's cold." Her breath puffed out in front of her face. She lifted her scarf and tightened it against her mouth and nose. "You promised to teach me to make a snowman."

He laughed. "Right you are. But here, let's pile it up and I'll show you how to sculpt people instead."

For several minutes, they piled snow up and up and up, until it was almost as tall as him.

Fingers soft on the snow, he teased out the general outline of a person sitting on a pedestal.

Jane stood, arms crossed on top of her belly, and watched. "What do you think about these people out there in the mountains? That horde?"

He shrugged, brushing snow away from the head. "Sounds like Addy has done all she can for the moment. With Celia and Renzo still out there, at this point, I just have to hope something can break our way."

"You really think that'll happen?"

He shook his head.

She stepped closer, carving a line through the snow person's face to make a chin. "You think you should go out there and talk to them?"

He considered, frowning, as he carved a swath out of the back of the person, giving them short hair. He glanced at her.

Her eyes red and wet, she stared at the sculpture. He couldn't see her mouth beneath the scarf, but it was probably a thin, straight line.

Twist in his gut, his heart beat in time with her quick blinks. He stopped sculpting and beat his snowy gloves against his legs. Picking up her hands, he squeezed them and stepped into her. "Do you want me to go?"

Blinking, snow in her lashes, she shook her head. "But holding that horde back is important."

"So are you."

She sniffed and met his eyes. "Thanks." Her voice wavered.

Pulling her in, he kissed the side of her covered head. "I'm not going anywhere without you. Not now. Not when you can't leave here."

She nodded against the side of his face. "You don't worry about the horde?"

"Of course I do. Who would I be if I didn't worry?"

She chuckled.

He pushed her back and took her in, belly and all. "But there are times you have to figure out where to put your heart, where to put your effort. And my effort, my heart, is here." One side of his mouth turned up. "I'm not going to spend all my energy worrying about some Dead Heads. Dead Heads I can handle. Something happening to you, or the baby…" He trailed off and tugged the scarf away from her mouth.

She smiled. Before he had a chance to say more, she kissed him, gripping the front of his jacket and pulling him in close.

Light filled him. The horde might be out there, a shadow on the horizon, but in this moment, he knew there was no better place to be. And that, against logic, everything was going to turn out fine. That it had to.

Leaning back, she lifted the scarf again and covered her mouth and nose. "Let's finish building this person and then we can get back to that fire inside."

CHAPTER 20

A knock at the door shook Addy from a reverie in which she imagined Dean had been let out of jail. They'd been here, what, four months almost? And still nothing. Despite the reason he remained in jail, she almost wished he'd just cave and tell them something so she could see him.

She opened the door.

"Hey, Addy," Matt said. "You ready?"

Snagging her jacket, she checked her weapons. "I think so. Just let me grab the juice. Come in for a second?"

He stepped in and closed the door.

Pulling her jacket on, she walked to the kitchen. "You don't have to stand by the door," she said over her shoulder.

But no sound followed her into the kitchen.

She shrugged. He could mill about by the door while she got the party supplies Ella had asked for. It was no skin off her nose.

Spinning, she ran right into him.

He steadied her. Again. "Where's your dog?"

Ah hell. She shouldn't have let him in. "Celia took him for a walk." She shifted on her feet, bouncing the jug of juice.

He narrowed his eyes. "Haven't seen Celia in a while, either, come to think of it. Was she here for Christmas?"

Addy fought a nervous swallow. The skin on her forehead tightened. He could probably hear her heart pounding, he stood so close. "I've known Celia forever. As long as I've known Jane, almost. I can't believe she didn't at least tell me about Christmas."

With a shrug, he glanced at the counter. Still standing entirely too close, but at least he seemed distracted now. "We taking this stuff to Ella's too?" He pointed.

She stepped away, reaching for the plates she'd gathered. Ella had promised quite a spread for the New Year's party. At least New Year's was something she'd heard of, but never had she been to a party.

Her front door rattled with a knock again.

Eager for the distraction, she stuffed the juice into his arms and rushed around Matt. "Yeah. Can you get that stuff? There's a bag on the table."

She peeked through the peephole in the door.

The bottom of Renzo's chin met her eyes.

Shit. Hadn't Matt threatened Renzo last time he saw him? What was he doing all the way in town?

Her heart leapt up her throat, still pounding, and socked her in the chin. She tried to swallow around it. Hand on the knob, she checked over her shoulder.

Matt's back to her, he worked to get the plates and things stuffed into the bag.

She opened the door a crack and stuck her face into the cold. Voice low, she frowned. "What're you doing here, Zo? You can't be seen here." She lowered her voice further. "The head of the guard is in my house."

He ducked, eyes darting to the window. "You gotta come, Addy. You gotta."

She tried to swallow around her heart again. "Is it…is it the…" Unable to finish, the thought of the horde too big in her mind, she trailed off.

"Mann's in town. You gotta get her out of here."

White spots danced in front of her eyes. Mann? In town? Good Christ. With a nod, she shut the door and returned to the kitchen on stilts. Now, the question was how to escape from Matt and Ella's party?

She picked up the juice from where Matt had sat it on the table. "Can you take this ahead? I have to go see someone right quick."

He hefted it, along with the bag of plates and utensils. "Sure. Who?"

"Just a friend."

Walking toward the door, he spoke over his shoulder. "Pretty sure I know all your friends, Addy."

"Either you're insulting me by saying you've got me all figured out or by saying I don't have many friends."

Stopping, he turned on a heel. "Neither. Sorry. I just meant. Isn't everyone coming to the party?"

She opened the front door and pushed him out onto the porch. "I'll be right behind you."

"Don't take too long. Ella doesn't want you to be late." He stopped on the stairs. "I know I said Christmas was important, but the last time she got to throw a party was probably three years ago. Don't tell her I said this, but I haven't seen her this excited since." He trailed off, slight smile playing across his lips before it soured into a frown. "Well. It's been a while."

"If you promise to make up a good lie about why I'm going to be late."

"I think I've got you covered." He turned left at the end of the sidewalk. "See you soon?"

"Yeah. Shouldn't take too long."

* * *

Addy approached the same bridge where she first met the people who used to live here, Renzo on her heels. "You left her here? Right here?"

"She might be in the—"

Someone whistled.

She stopped and looked for the source in the old industrial buildings.

A face peeked through one of the empty windows.

Addy couldn't help but smile. Eyes darting from side to side, she inched up to the window. "Cee. Good to see you. What are you doing back? What's going on?"

She shook her head. "She's in here."

Creeping closer, Addy checked the other windows. No one leaned out, but the space behind them seemed to breathe. Someone was definitely watching.

She edged through the empty door. "Where's Data?"

Celia shrugged and detached herself from a shadow. "With the little girl. Speaking of her, she keeps asking for you."

"For me? I hardly know her."

"Data's her favorite new person. You made an impression."

Renzo leaned close. "You do tend to do that, Lou."

One corner of her mouth turned up, whether she wanted it to or not. "Hell, maybe I can make some kind of impression on Mann. Lead the way, Cee."

Without a word, Celia cupped her elbows and led them into the dark building.

Towering monoliths and broken conveyor belts littered the path. Celia stepped around them with confidence, the grey sunlight filtering through what windows weren't covered with plywood enough to use for navigating. A time or two, she pointed ahead of them in silence and sidestepped a hole in the floor or some fallen equipment.

Who knew what they used to do here. But it didn't matter now.

Addy dismissed the images of workers slaving away at whatever menial job they did here, workers who would go home to their families and do whatever it was people did before they had to fight for their lives every day.

Instead, she glanced ahead of Celia, attempting to make out shapes in the shifting shadows. "Zo says she wants to bring the horde. Is that what you think, too?"

Celia nodded. She spoke over her shoulder. "She's desperate."

"What's she planning to do?"

She shrugged. "Ask her yourself." Stopping, she held her hand out, palm up.

Addy stepped around her, resting her hand on the pommel of her knife and running her finger along the handle in a well-worn track.

Someone sat in the shadow against the back wall of the factory. No chair, no light, little protection from the cold besides the brick walls.

Addy motioned with the hand not fidgeting with the knife. "Mind if I join you?"

"If I said yes, would it stop you?"

She shook her head, snakes in her gut. "No."

Mann's voice rasped. "Then sit." She cleared her throat but didn't follow it with words.

Addy sat next to her and leaned against the wall, staring off into the darkening factory. A catwalk crossed the ceiling, no longer complete all the way across. "What are you doing here?"

"Came to look in on my home. Make sure these people aren't mistreating my land."

"What would you call a mistreatment?"

"Pretty much what they're doing to it." She pitched a rock into the dark. It clanked against something metal and fell in water, the echo from the splash falling flat against the walls. The fading light reflected off the white streaks in her curly hair. Mann's shoulders hunched, and she pulled her knees up and hugged them.

"Laurel. What's really wrong?"

"I'm sick of it, Addy. The way they look at me when I come up to the camp. The way my granddaughter plays with your dog. The way they all know I'm failing them."

"What do you mean?" She scooted closer as the light faded. The impossible cold would follow.

"They're going to spend the entire winter out there instead of in their own homes because I couldn't get off my ass and take our land back. So I came down here to take one last look at it before I sic my horde on it. It's not going to look the same after."

Addy shivered. Either from the cold or the hardened note in Mann's voice as she spoke, she didn't know. She'd failed to figure out who the sympathetic guard was, and she hadn't been able to see Mike. He refused to see anyone except their mom. And if Addy couldn't keep this horde out of town…

She fought to keep the desperation out of her own voice. "Before you do that, let me come see my dog again. And that cute grandkid of yours." Standing, she held out a hand.

Mann glared up at her, eyes narrowed. "You're not going to talk me out of it. My people deserve to have their homes back. I intend to see it through."

"I know," she said, still holding her hand out. "I know. I just want to see my dog."

And talk you out of it.

Laurel sighed and took her hand. Pulling most of her weight up on her own, she gave Addy's hand a quick squeeze. "I never thanked you for leaving your dog." Her eyes skipped to Addy's, but she couldn't maintain eye contact. "I was so angry at you for leaving him."

"I can't keep up with you. If you're angry, then why—"

"I *was*. I'm not anymore." She met her eyes again, the corners folded in what looked like the most painful, unwitting smile Addy had ever witnessed. "Dora needed something after we lost her parents. And I couldn't be that something. I didn't know where to even begin." The smile worked its way to her mouth. "Data has been what she needed. If for nothing else, I'm grateful to you for that."

Addy smiled. "Let's get back to them, then."

CHAPTER 21

Sighing, Jane stood and walked to the window, cupping her elbows. Her arms raised so high above her massive belly they almost crossed under her chin.

"You OK?" Jack asked, lowering his book from directly in front of his face. Like it or not, glasses were probably on the horizon.

"Can't get comfortable." She swung her hips side to side.

"You've had this problem all day."

"Goddamnit Jack, I've had this problem for months. You have no idea how uncomfortable I am." She lowered her head, back still to him. "I can't sit properly, I can't sleep without getting kicked in a fucking kidney. I can't lay on my stomach. I can't lay on my back. I can't sit in a wooden chair without my tailbone feeling like it's going to fall off." She spun, scowling. "I'm a fucking mess."

He laid the book on the table and crossed to her. "I'm sorry, baby. Just a couple more weeks."

"Oh Jesus Christ," she said, stomping off into the kitchen.

He wanted to grin, not that it was wise. This baby girl was his, and she was Jane's, and she was trouble already.

He wouldn't have expected any less.

Following Jane into the kitchen, he eyed the record player.

Yasuo had brought a couple reports from the wall. No change. Not yet. Addy had been gone two weeks.

And whoever the sympathetic guard was, they hadn't made it easy to figure out. This man was a master of shadow and disguise.

Even so, there'd been at least twice Jack had caught him from the corner of his eye when he and Jane had been outside. There might not be twenty-four-seven surveillance on them, but that guard was there at least part of the time. Who knew what he was hoping to discover, but he was there.

Jane's annoyed cursing floated down the hall. "Ouch!"

"You alright?"

"Yes. No. I don't fucking know."

He eased into the kitchen.

Leaning against the counter, she rolled her head, eyes closed. Long, graceful neck slick with sweat. One hand rested on the top of her belly. "This warm snap has done nothing for me staying cool. I'm hot all the time." Scrunching up her face, she squeezed her eyelids together. "And my back is freaking killing me."

Tripping into double-time, Jack's heart lodged itself in his throat. Last time he'd seen all this cursing and back pain, he'd had to deliver a baby in their makeshift home of an old car garage.

"Um, Jane," he said, approaching with a hand out, "I think maybe we should go down to the hospital." He slid the hand across her belly and the other around her back.

"Mmm. That's nice, though," she said, swiveling at the hips to lean her forehead on his shoulder. "You just do that. I'll be alright."

Her back muscles clenched, bunching into knots. Her belly hardened under his other hand.

Just remember, Jack. This isn't your first rodeo. You can do this. She's got all the hard work to do anyway.

"Jane, really. Let's get you down to the hospital."

Nodding against his shoulder, she threw an arm around his neck. Ran her fingers up into his hair. "Give me a second."

Her back muscles relaxed.

He let out the breath he'd been holding and cupped her cheek. "You're going to be fine. She's going to be fine. I'll be right there with you both, OK?"

"Promise?"

"Always."

Tightening her grip, curling her fingers in his hair hard enough to hurt, she grinned. "Kiss me, love."

He did as he was told.

With almost as much passion as the very first time, but with the flavor of familiar, he crushed her to him. Her delicate, satiny lips danced over his. That bit of playful joy she always had in her kisses lighting a path from his brain to his toes.

Eyes still closed, she pulled back and stroked his cheek. Smiled. "I love you, Jack. Don't forget."

"How could I? Jane," he said, laying his hand over hers and leaning into them both, "I'd do anything for you."

Her eyelids fluttered open. "Then get me to that hospital."

* * *

Six hours in, Jack dabbed Jane's lips with a moist cloth, squeezing to release a few drops into her mouth.

She closed her eyes and swallowed. "I'm so thirsty."

Brushing the damp hair from her forehead, he glanced at the bedside table. "We're out of ice. When the nurse comes back, I'll have her get some."

"You could go outside and get me some snow."

"It's melting. Also, I'm not leaving."

Eyes still closed, she smiled. "I'd be alright."

Lips pressed together, he nodded even though she couldn't see it.

The door creaked open on hinges that needed oil.

"Oh good, nurse Elinor, could you bring us some ice chips, please?"

"I'll be happy to ask the nurse on my way out," a male voice said.

Jack started, unexpected men in the room not a surprise he'd asked for today. Glancing down at Jane, whose eyes had popped open, he stood. "Who are you?"

"Forgive the intrusion, Mr. Cooke. Doctor Leonard Huxley." He stuck out his hand, one or two age spots forming on the pale skin there.

Leaving a hand on Jane's shoulder, Jack shook with the wrong hand.

It threw the doctor off balance. But he recovered well, taking the sides of Jack's fingers and pumping his arm up and down in some sort of awkward curtsy.

Adaptable. Smart. Jack remembered his quick adjustment and filed for later use. "So, doctor, why are you here? Are you delivering the baby?"

The good doctor turned a subtle shade of green, pressing his lips together and shaking his head. His white hair, splayed about his skull like a dandelion, bounced and waved. He adjusted his black-rimmed glasses. "Oh, dear me, no. No. That's not my area." He flattened a hand on his chest. "I am one of the foremost experts on *Neuromuscular Zombipomorphism*."

Jack's ears did their best. He blinked. "I'm sorry?"

"Ahem. NMZM."

Narrowing his eyes, Jack glanced at Jane.

She shook her head and reached for his hand. Her breath shortened.

"Breathe, baby." Another contraction was building. He side-eyed the doc. "What's NMZM?"

"The virus."

Jack's eyes widened. He took the man in again. Tall, thin, official-looking lab coat. "So, why are you here?"

"Miss Doe here is a unique subject, and her baby—"

"And mine."

"Your, um. Yes. The baby is important to my research."

Jane exhaled, pulled a long breath in through her nose, and exhaled again. She squeezed Jack's hand hard enough to leave marks. "I don't give a shit, doctor. You don't get to—" Breathing through the contraction, she stopped again.

Staring at the wall, studiously ignoring the woman in labor, the doctor waited for her words to return.

"You don't get to turn her into one of your lab rats," she finished, releasing Jack's hand a micrometer.

The blood rushed to his fingers. Pins and needles.

"Miss Doe, that's not my intention. At all. I simply study the disease. Through clean, sterile, detached ways. Like a few drops of blood. Nothing more."

"That why you're here, doc?" Jack asked, holding Jane's hand and stepping close to Huxley. Though the doctor had several inches on him, he stared up into his face and narrowed his eyes. "You want to get to the point now, mister expert."

Huxley waved a hand over his shoulder.

A nurse appeared in the door, tote full of vials and needles.

"I need a blood sample from Miss Doe. I'm afraid I have to insist."

The thought of doctors touching her again, sticking needles in her, examining her for the virus, it all sent his heart into overdrive. His stomach roiled. He glanced at her.

She pressed her lips together. "Make it snappy then, doc. Let's get this over with before another contraction comes."

He waved the nurse in.

She uncapped her needles and vials and set to work.

Jaw bunched, Jack watched. Roiling stomach or no, it wouldn't do to not pay attention to what was going on here. He'd been ignorant enough throughout the last few months. Complacency was a luxury he didn't have, and should never have indulged in.

Blood spurted into the tube. The nurse switched it for another.

"Jack," Jane said, squeezing his hand.

Catching her eye, he smiled. "She's almost done."

"Another one coming," she said, closing her eyes and exhaling through tight lips.

"I'm all done," the nurse said, bright voice bouncing off the wall behind her. The rubbery strap she'd wrapped around Jane's arm came off with a pop, and she labeled the vials. Sticking them in her tote, she scurried around the foot of the bed and headed toward the door.

Huxley caught her arm, lowering his voice. "Wait for me. Don't leave the room with those samples."

She nodded.

"So, Mr. Cooke," he said, turning back around.

Jane exhaled through her nose. Short, sharp breaths.

Glancing between the two of them, Jack tried to pick one. Jane, suffering through labor. This doctor, full of no doubt valuable information. He sighed. "Yes, doc."

"I want you to know your family's contribution to my research is absolutely invaluable. Invaluable. I cannot overstate how grateful I am you've come to this community." He laid a hand on the bed. "I would be years behind where I am now if it weren't for you."

Scrunching his brow, Jack stared. "After the baby comes and we're all good, you're going to have to explain that to me in a bit more detail."

Jane moaned, locking what wanted to be a scream behind her lips.

Shoulders knotted, Jack glanced at her.

Teeth clenched over the inside of her lips, her mouth had turned into a white line. Head tilted back in the bed, almost as though in the throes of passion.

"I'm sorry, doctor. You're going to have to excuse us," he said over his shoulder.

"Of course. I'll send in the obstetrician."

Jack didn't watch him leave. Didn't watch the other doctor and their labor nurse Elinor come in. Didn't watch all the commotion, the cradle rolling in, not any of it.

He watched Jane. Never took his eyes off her.

After all the years of being alone, just him and his growing kids, and all the time being lonely, just him and his sinking thoughts, finding her light in the dark was like some kind of miracle. And here she was, bearing his child. With grace. With strength. Suffering under the weight of the work her body was going through, without complaint. Without exclamation. Facing it down. Just like she did to the hordes and their stinking masses. No fear.

The contraction eased. Opening her eyes to slits, she eyed him. "What are you grinning at?"

Gripping her hand, he kissed her. Her scent, flowers times ten, overpowered the antiseptic smell of the room. He floated about three feet off the bed. Breaking away, he leaned his cheek on the rail next to her. "Do people even get married anymore, Jane?"

She shook her head, closing her eyes. "I don't know, Jack. Maybe?"

"Then, marry me."

Eyes popping open, she flushed, her mouth flopping. She squeezed his hand tighter than she'd done before. Like iron bands wrapping around his fingers. Before closing her eyes again and rolling with the contraction, she glanced in the corner and frowned.

Taking his eyes from her for the first time since Huxley had been in the room, he followed her gaze.

Melinda stood in the corner, arms crossed. Scowling.

As he opened his mouth to ask her just what the fuck she was doing here, Jane shouted, arching her back. From her toes, she screamed, "Yes!"

And then there was pushing. And the doctor commanding her when to stop and when to push and Jack stroked her forehead and told her how great she was doing and lost all feeling in his hand as she gripped it, and nearly lost all his breath when his third child was born.

Another daughter. A perfect little girl. She came out silent.

He held his breath as they waited for her to take her first one. When she did, and began to cry as they laid her on Jane's chest, he cried with her. His own hot tears sliding down both cheeks, he leaned onto the bed and kissed both of them. Even as the baby nuzzled for Jane's breast, he kissed the back of her fuzzy little wet head.

"She's perfect, Jane," he whispered, glancing up at her. His warrior woman.

She smiled down. "She looks just like you."

"Oh god, I'm sorry," he said. "Hopefully she'll get your brains, at least."

She slapped him on the shoulder, scrunching her neck to glance down and position the baby where she could get her first real meal. The nurse stepped over to help.

Allowing Jane a moment to get this whole nursing thing started, he glanced over and found Melinda again. Deep in conference with the other nurses and the obstetrician.

He cleared his throat, trying to swallow the heart in it. The question needed to be asked. "Is she OK?"

"The baby," Melinda said, frowning, "needs to be tested."

"What kind of tests?"

"Just a little prick of the heel. For now." She took one step toward the bed, stopped, and crossed her arms again. "I, uh. I need to supervise. Make sure they label the samples properly." Fidgeting, she swallowed and made eye contact for a fleeting second. "This was harder than I thought." Tears lined the bottom of her eyes.

He slid closer to Jane. "I didn't ask you to be here." Harsh tone hitting his ears, he softened. "You shouldn't have come."

"You're not wrong," she said, pointing to the closest nurse. "You. Get those samples. We need to test her. Make sure she's clear of the virus."

The baby shifted with a small whimper as they poked her heel and drew out tiny droplets of blood onto a sliver of glass.

Jane cuddled her, cooing she'd be alright.

Approaching the bed with three shuffling, hesitant steps, Melinda clipped the slivers of glass into a tray, which she then snapped closed and cupped her hands around. Without glancing at Jack, she began to walk out.

Jack frowned. "That's it, then?"

"That's it. We might have to come back later."

"Will it be you, or…" He trailed off, glancing back at Jane.

Eyes slitted, the gorgeous new mother glared at his ex-wife.

Back to them both, Melinda shook her head. "I think I have all I need. I can send someone else next time." Without another word, she stalked from the room. The door eased closed behind her, latching with a whimper.

A couple nurses and the obstetrician stayed, helping Jane finish with the placenta and getting the baby cleaned and settled in the bed with her.

Once they were gone, Jack sat next to the bed again, smiling at them both.

Jane grinned, one side of her mouth turned down. "Thank god that's over."

His stomach turned. "Yeah. Melinda shouldn't have been here."

"Oh, not that." Disentangling an arm from the baby, she reached for his face. Stroked his cheek with a thumb. "You're mine, honey. I know that."

Goose bumps racing down his spine and both arms, he grinned like a fool.

Huffing out a breath, she leaned her head back into the pillow and trailed the hand down his arm. "No, I mean labor. Good lord, Jack. I don't think I've ever done something so difficult. Short of losing you."

Gripping the hand on his arm, he frowned. Words could go here, but he'd lost them all. Instead, he sat and tingled, exhaustion coming over him in waves.

"Ah hell," she said, lifting her head.

He fought his heavy eyelids. "What?"

"What are we going to name her?"

CHAPTER 22

Jerking awake, Addy clutched the bark beneath her ass. Stomach leaping into her throat, she inhaled.

"Careful. Remember, you slept in a tree," Celia said.

"Oh god. No wonder I can't feel my legs," Addy said, tongue stuck to the roof of her mouth. "Never again, Cee. Never again." The tree ground into her spine as she stretched, dropping a leg over each side of the huge branch on which she sat.

Celia chuckled. "Need me to help you get down?" Wrapping up her rope, she glanced over with an elvish grin.

"Probably," Addy muttered, gathering up and coiling her own rope. Before throwing anything down, she checked the ground below. If they'd had Data, they could've continued through the dark hours. But after tromping through the woods for two weeks with him and Dora, playing kid games and trying to win over half the camp, Addy had decided he should stay with the girl. They seemed pretty attached to each other, and he'd already made friends with the other half of the camp.

Returning to Magnolia without him, Celia had deemed it best to stop at night, and Addy had agreed.

Having never slept in a tree before, she didn't know she ought to just keep walking. It would've been preferable to the agony her back was currently in. "Never again," she repeated, inching down the tree.

Celia waited at the bottom. "Just get your ass down here so we can go. I don't—"

Like some sort of stinking, crawling magic trick, a 'Head appeared from behind the tree. It buzzed like two branches of old, dead wood scraping against each other.

Jumping back, Celia unsheathed her knife and stabbed at it.

As she did, Addy hopped the last five feet or so to the ground.

Landed on her foot wrong.

Though she rolled to minimize the strength of the impact, the tendons in her ankle twisted at an unnatural angle. The bones didn't snap, but they screamed against each other as she clenched her teeth.

Knocking the 'Head over, Celia brought her knife back. At the last moment, its head twisted and she missed. "Son of a bitch."

Bubbling snuck its way into Addy's ear and drilled into her brain.

She stood, sprained ankle buckling. "There's another one coming," she said, unsheathing her Bowie knife.

"Handle it," Celia said, weaving through the 'Head's grasping, clawing, blackened fingers.

"No shit," Addy said, heat rising into her cheeks. Of course she would fucking handle it.

She wobbled, facing it. Her ankle was not going to get her very far. Still, she lifted the knife and waited for the 'Head to come through the trees.

It and two of its friends.

"Celia, more."

She stood, cleaning blood from her knife. Blood that had all but dried to dust. Glanced at Addy. "Are you alright?"

Addy swayed, nodding. "Twisted my ankle."

With a chuckle, Celia launched herself at the closest one.

Addy raised her knife and braced herself on her good foot.

The next 'Head reached for her, bubbling and buzzing. Its teeth gnashed. Red flesh still caught between them.

The bubbling, though. It was fresh. No more than a day old. If Mom was right, someone on the verge of losing all their memories but still able to see everything through crystal-clear vision. Still able to remember the meal they just finished. Be it a woodland creature or someone's kid.

She swung the knife, aiming for the temple. The 'Head shifted at the last moment, grasping for her, and her swing went wild. The blade stuck in the side of its head.

The 'Head wobbled but continued to buzz.

Adrenaline burst into her thighs, warm and prickling, and she fell back onto her good foot. Shifting her weight to remain standing, her hand slipped on the handle of the knife.

Another bumped into the 'Head, pushing her back a step.

Her balance shifted. About to go down whether she liked it or not, she turned so they'd fall away from Celia.

Ankle screaming, she went down. Both 'Heads came down on top of her. The handle of the knife hit the ground and popped free, the gash it'd created in the 'Head's skull dripping blood and bits of grey matter. Soupy, stinking brains. Its teeth chomped in her face.

She dry heaved.

"I swear to god, girl," Celia said, kicking the one on top to the ground. She stabbed the one lying on Addy in the base of the skull. "Some days, you work magic with that thing." She pointed her forehead at the knife. "Some days, it's like you were born with ten thumbs."

Dry heaving again, stomach in knots, Addy rolled the dead one on top of her off and sat up on an elbow. Crunchy leaves scratched her arm. "Today is one of the latter." Without changing her tone, she glanced behind Celia. "It's getting up."

Rounding on the last one, Celia kicked it in the face and sent it sprawling onto its back.

Like a tortoise, it lay on the ground and kicked its legs. Flailed its arms. Snarled and bubbled. Its blackened fingers fighting for purchase, it could not get itself up.

Not before Celia stood over it, staring into its face with her lip curled. "Don't you let me die like this, Adelaide Cooke." Kneeling next to it, she pushed her knife through its eye.

With a last bubble, it stilled.

Massaging her ankle, Addy frowned. "I'll do what I can, Celia."

* * *

Staring up the wall, Addy leaned on Celia. "I cannot climb it. Not like this."

Celia shifted the arm wrapped around Addy's waist and hefted her farther up her shoulder. "I can't leave you out here. Your dad would kill me, first of all."

"I really don't think I can climb it."

"I can't get you in no other way," Celia said, ducking from under her arm. "You can make it. You're tough." She grimaced. "There's no other way, Addy."

"Can't we go in the way we came out? That tiny little secret garden door?"

"No, I'm sorry, we can't. It only opens from inside."

"That's the dumbest door I've ever heard of," Addy said, putting weight on the bad ankle. It didn't support her.

Celia gripped a handhold on the hidden ladder. "You'd rather walk in through the front door?" She began to climb.

"Yeah, and then tell them how we got out. Sure." She put a hand on the ladder. Inhaling, she lifted herself onto it with her hands and hopped her good foot onto the first rung. "Let's hope my arms hold up," she said, hopping to the next rung.

One down. Nineteen to go.

Then there was climbing down the other side.

Sweating, cursing, and with cramped hands, she reached the bottom of the other side about ten minutes after Celia had finished. With ginger care, she stepped down, unwrapped her aching hands from the last two beams, and sank to the ground.

"You want to go check in on your dad?"

Peeping up at Celia, she frowned. "What I'd like to do is sleep for four days."

Celia stuck a hand out. "So, check on Jack it is."

Sighing, Addy took her hand. Her good leg shook with the effort of standing. "I don't know if I can make it all the way back to town, Cee. That was rough."

"Let's wrap that ankle a little tighter. Then you can lean on me. We'll get you there."

Taking five or six breaks, they approached Jack's block. Addy's energy waned at an alarming speed as they approached. Bad ankle throbbing, good leg shaking like the earthquakes Ella talked about, she clenched her teeth and pressed forward.

Just before Jack's block came into view, someone shouted her name.

Someone she knew. But it couldn't be.

"Addy!"

Releasing Celia, she spun, stomach somewhere near her feet. Or throat. Or floated off to do its own thing.

Dean approached at less than a sprint but more than a walk. Once he got close enough to speak instead of shout, he grinned. "I couldn't find you at home, so I thought I'd check your dad's." Without a pause, he scooped her up and lifted her, cradling the back of her head and burying his face in her neck. "I am so unbelievably happy to see you," he said, breath hot and wet on her neck.

Her cheeks stretched so tight she couldn't feel her face, she wrapped both arms around his neck and held on. "They let you go?"

"Yeah," he said, moving to set her down.

"Careful," she said, wobbling as he put her on the ground.

His grin widened and he looked her up and down. "What'd you do this time?"

"She fell out of a tree," Celia said.

Addy scowled at her. "I jumped. Trying to save your ass."

He laughed. "That's my girl." He tugged her sleeve. "Hey."

Turning back to him, she opened her mouth to ask what. Before any sound escaped, he covered her lips with his own and squeezed her again, this time around her waist. One hand reached up her back.

The butterflies, the ones she hadn't felt in far too long, raced up her spine and into her brain, fluttering behind her eyes and rushing back down to pool in her stomach. Head light, she heard herself let out a moan as she pressed against him. Cupping his strong jaw, she inhaled through her nose. He smelled like all the best parts of cedar and sweat. The strong, full, middle of the nose scent of male.

He released her, and she reeled, trying to get her overworked legs back beneath her. She'd forgotten their existence.

When she stumbled, he caught her. "I got you," he said, muscled arm snaking around her waist.

Stroking his face and gazing into his green eyes, she tried to remember what it was her brain had told her to ask. Working through the cotton candy in her head, she shook it. "Dean, why did they let you out?"

He returned the head shake. "I don't know. Matt came and said I was free to go. Even gave me directions to you and your dad's places."

"Did you tell them anything?"

"Course not."

"Matt said one of your guys didn't back you up. That made them suspicious of you. Do you know who it could have been?"

He frowned. "I didn't know that. No, I don't know." Closing his eyes, drawing his brows into a V, he put a finger on his chin. Shaking his head, he opened his eyes. "No. I don't think so. But I think it's pretty clear I don't work for them anymore."

Addy nodded. An unexpected twist, to lose their insider information. But not a surprise, not at this point. "Well. Let's get to my dad. I just got back. There's a lot to catch you up on." She leaned on his shoulder.

He kissed her just below her jaw and shifted her weight on his hip. "How is Jack, anyway? Jane? Mike?"

"Oh, Dean. So much to catch you up on."

"Adelaide!"

"Fuck's sake, what now," she said, hopping around. Dean helped her turn.

Paul jogged up from the direction she and Celia had come. "Welcome back, ladies. Where's Renzo?"

"He stayed," Celia said, crossing her arms. "Think he found a girlfriend."

"And your short, four-legged friend?"

Addy sighed. "He made new friends, too."

Paul nodded. "You three need to come with me. Hi, Dean."

"Heya, Paul. What's going on?"

"I think it's best if you come with me. I don't think we should talk about it out here." He looked around the street.

Addy glanced behind her at the empty street. "Where are we going?"

"To the wall."

CHAPTER 23

"Just one day in the hospital, if that, and here we are again," Jack said, opening the front door.

Smiling, swaddled baby in the crook of her arm, Jane stepped past him and into the house.

He closed the door and put his arms around both of them, kissing the baby on the nose. "Welcome home, little Katherine."

Flushed, Jane kissed him on the cheek. "She's so beautiful, Jack."

"She's perfect. Just like you." He'd forgotten how sweet they were when they were born. Nothing but sleeping and eating and changing diapers. Seemed like the best time was this, right here.

Settling into the couch, Jane propped her elbow on the armrest and unwrapped the baby. "Hey, Katie," she whispered, "you hungry little angel?" She maneuvered her onto the breast, grumbling under her breath about how breastfeeding was harder than it looked, and sat back, eyes closed.

Allowing her a few moments of peace, Jack headed toward the kitchen to get her a glass of water. Cold, sweet water from the tap. Maybe with a few cubes of ice. That miracle of refrigeration.

He filled the glass with both. "You know," he said, heading back down the hallway with her drink, "before the world went to shit, I never even liked ice." Sitting the glass on the side table, he sat on her other side and stared over her shoulder at the baby.

"I don't know, honey." Jane leaned her head on his. "This doesn't feel like a shitty world."

He closed his eyes. "No. No, it doesn't." It felt warm. Happy. Comfortable.

The door rattled with a knock.

Sitting up straight, he glanced at Jane.

She shrugged, pulling the baby close. "Maybe Addy's back."

They knocked again.

Jack's lungs constricted. It didn't feel like Addy's knock. Removing his gun from its holster, he peeked out the window in the top of the door.

Michael's curly hair bounced in the breeze.

Sliding the gun halfway into its holster and exhaling, Jack hesitated. "It's Mike."

Jane pressed her lips together. Cuddling the baby, who'd fallen back to sleep, she pulled her shirt down and nodded. "Let him in, before he freezes to death out there."

Dropping the gun the rest of the way into the holster, he inhaled to the bottom of his lungs. Held the breath. Opened the door.

His son smiled at him. "Hey, Dad."

"Michael," he said, exhaling. Blood rushing to his face, he pushed the screen open and let Mike in the house. Though he'd lost several pounds and carried dark circles under his eyes, it was good to see his smiling face.

"Jane," he said, crossing his arms and standing across the coffee table from her. He glanced at the baby. "How are you feeling?"

"Have a seat," Jack said, touching him on the shoulder. He'd rather hug the boy, but he wouldn't unless Mike offered. Didn't want to invade his space.

Mike jumped, glanced at Jack's hand, and perched on the overstuffed chair, brow furrowed. "What did you name her?"

Jane answered. "Katherine."

"Wasn't that grandma's name?"

Taking the chair next to Jane, Jack nodded. "She hated it. But yeah. That was Mom's name."

"I wish I'd known her better," Mike said, frowning.

"Wish you had too, son." He'd never even been able to make sure his parents were dead. Though why wouldn't they be. Six billion people had died. The fact none of those six billion had been himself, Melinda, or Michael was its own miracle.

Scooting over to the couch, Mike sat just outside the middle cushion and peeked at the sleeping baby. "She looks like you, Dad." The side of his mouth lifted in half a smile.

Jack nodded, watching him. Though he had an even tone and was more like Michael than he'd been last time they'd seen each other, the dark circles under his eyes did not suit him. The missing pounds didn't, either. He glanced at Jane, trying to gauge how she was feeling about the whole thing.

Her round green eyes held every bit of empathy he'd ever seen on her. Though she liked to project cool, distant, and aloof, she had more empathy for others than anyone he'd ever met. Showing it on her face, however, was not a thing she did. Especially not to the object of the empathy.

"Do you think I could hold her?" Mike asked her.

Though Jack's stomach somersaulted, Jane handed the baby over. Showing him how to cradle her head, she slid her into his arms.

He stared down into her face. His chin trembled, and he blinked six or seven times. "Hi, little Katie. I'm your big brother," he said. His brow furrowed and smoothed. His lips worked their way into a smile.

Jane glanced at Jack. Fine line between her brows.

He held his hand out to her.

She took it, flashed a smile at him, and glanced back to Mike.

Who cleared his throat. "She's immune."

Jane's fingers tightened into five little vises. "What did you say?"

Mike cleared his throat again and looked up. A tear rolled down his cheek. "Your baby. She's immune."

Jack's heart skipped and then took off at a gallop. "One more time?"

"Probably the first baby with immunity ever born, Mom says. The first one she's ever heard of."

Curse words bunched behind his lips, but when Jack opened his mouth, all that fell out was breath. Immune to the virus?

"You mean she'll never catch it? One day she'll die, and she'll stay that way?" Jane asked, still squeezing Jack's hand for all she was worth.

Mike nodded. "Never, Jane. Never."

Jane sobbed aloud. Freeing her hand from Jack's, she covered her face and cried.

Pulling a breath in through his open mouth, center hollow, Jack stared at the little miracle. "How?"

"We don't know. It could have been from the vaccine. It could have been from Jane being bitten, along with the vaccine, or some weird combination of the two. We don't know. Not without"— he stood, looking down at the baby—"more tests."

Jane stopped crying like a faucet had been turned. Sliding to the front of the couch cushion with a grimace, she held her arms out. "Give her back now."

Stepping away, he shook his head.

Jack's stomach dropped to his toes. Every fear he'd ever had, manifested in this moment. "Mike."

A thin string stretched out in the room. Time slowed to a crawl, the string taut. The future balanced on a razor edge.

"We need to do more testing," Mike said, taking another step back.

Jane stood. "Fine," she said, stepping toward him. "Give her back."

He shook his head. "I can't."

"Give her back, Michael," Jane repeated, taking another step toward him.

Mike balanced Katie with one arm and pulled his gun with the other. "I fucking know you, Jane. And you, Jack. You'll run. We can't let that happen."

Mike's use of his first name again socked Jack in the gut like a fist. Out of breath, every muscle in his body clenched, he pled with his eldest. "Mike, please. We'll cooperate. Let's talk about this."

The gun swung in his direction. "You think I don't know who you are. What you'll do, Dad. Like I haven't looked up to you my whole life. Tried to memorize everything you did. Tried to be you." He sniffled. "You'll take them both and leave. I know you will. This is the only way." Holding the gun on him, he inched around the coffee table.

Jack stayed in front of it, stepping between the gun and Jane when Mike came around. He held his hands up to either side of his shoulders. As much to show Mike he wasn't going to hurt him as to keep himself from reaching for his gun without thinking.

"It'll just be a few tests. I'll bring her back as soon as I can," Mike said, stepping toward the door.

"Who put you up to this?" Jane asked, hand on the back of Jack's shoulder. She stepped under his arm.

"Jane, don't," Jack said, reaching for her.

She stepped beyond his hand. "He won't hurt me. Tell me, Michael," she said, stepping closer still, "who was it? Your mom? The commander? Huxley? Who?"

His back hit the door. "Stop, Jane. Please. I'll bring her back."

"Tell me."

Mike shrugged, gun dipping. "Just stop, OK? Don't make me hurt you."

She stared up at him, shoulders relaxed. "You won't hurt me." She reached for the gun.

Though it had a vaulted ceiling, the room was still small enough to echo five or six times with the deafening explosion of a gunshot.

Jack's ears rang. As Mike opened the door and stepped backward through it, Jack heard nothing but cotton pillows in his ears. He wiped his face in the silence and glanced at his hand.

Smeared red with blood.

He glanced down, internal feelers inspecting every inch of skin. He hadn't been hit, but more blood stippled his shirt. "Ah fuck," he said, the sound echoing off the inside of his cranium.

From the floor, Jane's inarticulate screaming crept into his eardrums.

Scratch that. It wasn't inarticulate. She shouted for her daughter.

Kneeling next to her, he forced her to stop crawling for the door so he could figure out where she'd been shot. "Baby, stop. Let me look at you," he said, holding her arm. Most of the sound of his voice hit his eardrums from outside now, the cotton inside them beginning to wear thin. But the coppery scent of fresh blood crept into his sinuses.

Still, Jane twisted her arm. "Let me go, goddammit. I'll fucking kill him," she said, trying to crawl away.

"Jane, stop," Jack said, raising his voice. "Let me make sure you're not going to bleed to death first. Katherine needs her mother."

She rolled over and stared at the ceiling, eyes unfocused. "It doesn't hurt. I'm fine."

"That's adrenaline," he said, looking for the source of the blood. It splattered outward from high up on her shirt. Unsheathing his knife, he cut her sleeve, hoping to find the bullet hole before the cut got to her chest.

"Hey, if you wanted to undress me, all you had to do was ask," she said, giggling. "And wait four to six weeks. Ha."

Pressing his lips together, he continued the cut up to her shoulder. The blood thickened. Her quickening delirium not a good sign, he prayed to whatever god wasn't out there.

* * *

Sweat pouring down her face, cooling her already cold skin, Addy stumbled into Dean. "I don't know if I can go any farther," she said, resting her head on his shoulder.

Holding her up with the arm still planted around her waist, he hugged her with the other. "We can rest here. Just say the word."

"Word."

"Addy, no, you've got to hurry," Paul said, shuffling back to them.

Celia stood ten feet ahead, breath short, hands on her hips. "I've got a bad feeling about this."

Paul nodded. "We're not far. It's just down the culvert."

Addy shuddered. The dark, dank place was sure to be cold and wet and uninviting. Not to mention difficult as all hell to traverse, what with her legs made of wobbling jelly. "What's so important, Paul?"

He glanced around the street again. "I'd rather just show you."

Following his gaze over her shoulder, Addy eyed the empty street. Maybe a bush moved. Probably not. The cover on the street was scant at best. Unlikely anyone had followed them.

She gripped Dean's shoulder, and he helped her wobble off the street and into the backyard of the house where she'd first run into Renzo. On the dark side of town, where the houses were only full of drafts. But the trash cans still stood out back.

Paul and Celia dropped into the drainage ditch before her and held their hands out.

Clutching Dean, she half slid, half rolled down the steep concrete side. Her shirt lifted, rubbing a rash up about six feet of her abdomen.

The warm snap had melted much of the snow, and sure enough, the ditch smelled like wet earth and looked like the murder scene of a garden gnome. Dirt everywhere, fluids everywhere else. And for a reason known only to the ditch and the snow, broken pottery shards.

"Down here," Paul said, whispering. "Go careful. It's slippery. And. Well, you'll see."

Peering down the tunnel, Addy couldn't make out the end. The mid-afternoon sun didn't break through the cloud cover, and the light was thin down there. "You got a flashlight, Paul?"

"No, sweetie, I don't. It'll be alright. Just, like I said, be quiet. I don't know if…" He trailed off, glancing to the end of the tunnel again.

Something down there shifted.

"Fuck this," Celia said. She'd crawled a quarter of the way in, but when whatever it was started moving down there, she stopped and frowned in Addy's face. "You go down there. I'm waiting here. I'll keep watch."

Weak, little more than a whisper, a voice floated down the tunnel. Bouncing off the rounded sides as it came. "Celia, please."

Heart in her throat, Addy stopped. "Paul," she whispered, "who's down there? Are they alright? What's going on?"

He didn't answer, only crawled deeper into the tunnel. Sighing, Addy followed, Dean on her heels.

Celia sat on her ass, water splashing around her. Catching Addy's sleeve as she passed, she stared into her eyes. "Don't go down there. Please. Don't." Her hand shook.

"What else am I supposed to do? Come on," she said, crawling past.

Sniffling, Celia followed Dean in a crouch-walk. Whispering to herself.

As they reached the end of the tunnel, weak light outlined a shape lying on the other side of the cage-like bars.

"Celia?"

His red mustache bounced in her head, but there wasn't enough light to see it. Still, it could be no one else.

She shook her head. "It's Addy, Oren. Are you alright?"

"I'm cold. Where's Celia? Is she with you? Paul? You said you'd get her."

Paul patted one bloody arm sticking through the bars. "I brought her, friend Oren. She's here." He turned to the side and cursed in a fierce whisper. "Cee. Get your ass over here."

"No." Her voice floated from halfway back.

"Celia? I can't see you. Where are you?" Oren asked, pressing his face against the bars. A thinner cloud passed in front of the sun, and the shape of a bite on his cheek stood out in sharp relief. Beads of blood dried in his bouncing mustache. Grime, sweat, and more blood ground into the lines in his forehead, his neck, down his arms. He coughed with a wheeze.

"Celia, for god's sake," Dean said, crawling back down the tunnel.

They whisper-argued, the sharp inflections catching Addy in the ear, but the shape of their words eluding her. Then Dean's soothing voice.

Ye gods, it was like a balm to the spirit to hear him purr like that again. He'd been away too long. Again.

Avoiding Oren's bitten and bloody face, she glanced at Paul. "What the hell?"

Scooting over to her, he sat and leaned on a knee. "I haven't been able to get Oren or Ricardo on the radio for two days."

"Jesus, I didn't even know they were still out there this time of year. I thought maybe they'd gone back to Harkers."

"To be honest, I've been thinking about sending them back. Give all this intel to Scott. See if we can get backup." He sighed, glancing at Oren.

Eyes closed, Oren leaned against the bars and breathed. Heaving breaths, one too far after the other.

"Anyhow. Wanted to talk to you or your dad first. Figure out what we're going to do with reinforcements once they get here. But he was at the hospital and I couldn't get these guys on the radio. And you were gone. So. I waited."

"What about," Addy said, jerking her chin at the dying redhead.

"Came down here to try and get him on the radio again, once I saw you two coming down the wall. Found him like this instead. Had to get him awake, make sure he was still, you know, with us."

She nodded. Her eyes prickled. This damned virus. He should never have been out there in the first place. And what about Ric? Where was he?

Scuffling down the tunnel announced Celia and Dean before her eyes readjusted to the dark.

Celia breathed shallow. "Oren?"

His eyes popped open, and he lifted his head from the bars. Deep red marks where he'd leaned against them crisscrossed his face. "Celia. There you are." With his bloody hand, he reached for hers.

She twitched but let him take it. Grimaced. "You don't look so hot, buddy."

He coughed, blood tinging his lips in a fine spray. "Sorry. Sorry. No. I feel cold. It's so cold here. This is not where I wanted to die."

Celia shook her head. "You're not going to die. Hand me your dose. I'll give it to you. You're gonna be fine." She gripped his hand, wiping his mouth through the bars.

He closed his eyes. "I can't reach it. I don't think I have it. Something happened. I can't remember a lot. It's kind of a blur. There were five or six of them. Not many. Somehow they snuck up on us. I don't know. I don't know what happened to Ric. But here I am." He coughed again, more drops of blood sneaking onto his lips in a slow trickle. "Took me forever to get here. Days, probably. I don't know."

"Fine, I'll give you mine," Celia said, reaching for her dose.

He jerked her close to the bars.

She lost her balance, throwing her hand up at the last moment to keep her face from slamming into them. "Shit, Oren. Watch it."

"Sorry," he said, closing his eyes and stroking the back of her hand. "Celia. I don't know. What if. Listen."

"Just let me get you—"

"Listen."

She stopped and stared him in the face.

His crimson lips smiled. "I love you. Always have. Ever since we were kids."

"Oh hell, Oren. Don't start that shit."

"Really," he said, tugging her arm. "I'm sorry I never told you. I knew you wouldn't. Wouldn't want me to." He coughed again, blood dripping down his chin.

Wiping his mouth and chin again, she leaned into the bars. It was too dark to see if she was crying, but it was even money whether she was or not.

"You don't know that," she said.

"Your heart was always too busy for me," he said, laughing. Coughing and laughing. "You gotta promise me something, though." Pushing the other arm through the bars, he gripped her shoulder.

Wordless, she nodded.

"You open it up again. That pretty little heart of yours. And you go find somebody to fill it."

She shook her head. "You're gonna be OK. I don't have to promise any such thing."

Coughing, bubbling deep in his throat, he gripped both her shoulders so tight the ends of his fingers turned white. Even in the filtered grey light, they turned white.

"Oren," she said. "Just let me—"

Both hands relaxed and fell, one landing in a puddle and sending dirty water splashing onto Celia's neck and face.

Wiping it with her arm, she reached into a jacket pocket and extricated a small syringe full of amber fluid.

Gleaming, glowing, beautiful amber Cure.

Plastic tip between her teeth, she jerked the needle free and stabbed it in his arm, plunging the amber Cure beneath his skin.

Time stretched between breaths until at least a minute had passed. More.

His breath bubbled when his chest rose again, and a snarling growl began somewhere in the back of his throat.

He reached for her again.

Grasping hands reached for her, snarling bubbling lifting to a high, energetic pitch. He pressed his face into the bars and bit at them.

Paul leaned over to Addy. "Shouldn't it be working by now?"

Eyes glued to the new 'Head, Addy nodded. Her mouth opened and closed.

The syringe clattered to the floor of the tunnel. Celia hugged her knees to her chest, tiny pinpricks of light in her pupils the only thing lit on her face.

"Oren, you dumb son of a bitch," she said, unsheathing her knife. With a guttural shout, she rushed to the bars.

He grasped and clawed at her, biting the bars in front of him.

Pointing the knife between them, she pressed a palm to the end of the haft and stopped.

His grasping hands snared her jacket, and he pulled her into the bars.

As the syringe had before it, the knife clattered to the floor of the tunnel.

Addy's throat hurt, and she swallowed past the lump that had formed there while she wasn't looking. Her eyes stung, hot tears warming her cheeks as they fell.

Celia, eyes closed, let him pull her in.

Sliding in next to her, Dean snatched up the knife, and with a word of prayer, took careful aim. Apologized, and shoved it through Oren's eye.

And again, both hands relaxed. And fell.

* * *

Leaving Celia and Paul with the body, Addy and Dean struggled down the street.

Leaning on him with one arm and her staff with the other, all but ready to give up and ask him to carry her, Addy stopped. Tears drying on her cheeks had made them stiff. "What the hell happened back there?"

He shrugged, bouncing her shoulder. "I remember it being said that sometimes the Cure doesn't work."

"I don't know. I thought maybe that was a lie. One of those things Mom said to gain our trust."

"So?"

She frowned. "So, what?"

"So has she gained your trust? We haven't really had a lot of chances to talk about that since I've been gone so damn long." He closed his eyes and leaned against her, the two of them pushing each other over yet holding each other up.

"Tough to say," Addy said, eyes on the middle distance. "Back on Harkers, we had some really good times together. Just us two, and us with Mike. It was fun. And then she gave herself up to save Jane."

"How about since then? Since I was locked up?"

She shrugged, bouncing his head. "She's been working on the vaccine again. But she says she was forced by the commander."

"He's a tough case."

"He'd have to be," she said, laughing, "in order to have lived with Ella for so long."

Leaning back, he gripped her waist again so she wouldn't overbalance. "How's that going? The guys said something about you two hanging out."

Her stomach curled over itself, cheeks flaming. "Did they? What did they say?"

"Just that you must be very brave. Or stupid."

She exhaled a laugh. "Both," she said, grinning. "She's soft. And a bitch. But I guess she has her bonuses. She likes Trek, anyway."

Dean smiled. "Well then. It's not like you have nothing in common."

Eyebrows knitted, she opened her mouth to ask him what, exactly, he meant by that.

Echoing off the sides of the houses around them, slapping off the bark of the naked trees, a gunshot split the air ahead of them.

"Where was that?"

He narrowed his eyes. "Couple blocks at most."

"That's about how far Dad's house is," she said, limping forward. Clutching his shoulder, she dragged him with her.

He stumbled to catch up and hooked her arm over his shoulder again. They surged forward. Between breaths, he gasped, "There's no need to think it came from Jack's. Could have been anyone."

She shook her head. "You believe that?"

His silence was the same as an answer.

"Me neither. I'm fine, we can go faster," she said, limping, her ankle on fire.

Dad's house came into view, after what seemed like an hour of struggling down the sidewalk.

The front door stood open, light pouring out into the dim afternoon. Dad just inside, kneeling over someone.

"Dad!" Ducking from under Dean's arm, Addy threw down the staff and forgot about her ankle as she sprinted up the walk. Preparing to leap the three steps onto the porch, her brain hitched and she stopped. Grabbing the rail, heart skipping, she hopped on her good foot up the stairs and rushed through the open door.

Jane lay on the floor inside, unfocused eyes staring up at the ceiling.

Pressing a mountain of gauze into the hollow of Jane's shoulder, contents of the first aid pack splayed in the floor behind him, Jack grimaced at Addy. "Hey, baby girl. Glad to see you're in one piece."

She dropped to her knees next to them as Dean stepped into the doorway. "The hell, Jack?" he asked.

"Fucking Melinda. She's behind this. I know it," Jack growled, teeth clenched.

Jane sucked a breath through her nose, eyes skipping to Addy. "He took her, Addy. He took her."

"Who took who?" Addy asked, racing heart bouncing her eyeballs as they skipped from Dad to Jane.

Dad's arms trembled. "Mike. He shot Jane. Took the baby."

Confusion settled over her heart—when did they even have the baby?—and Addy shook her head to clear it. "How long?"

"Two minutes, maybe. Maybe more. Maybe less," Jack said.

Addy glanced at Dean. "We've got to go after her." She limped across the doorjamb.

Dean snagged her shoulder. "Let me."

"You stay here with Jane. Dad?"

"Dean," he said, glancing back down at Jane, "hold the pressure here. It went straight through, but we've got to get the bleeding under control."

"I've got it, Jack," Dean said, kneeling, "go with Addy." He glanced up, meeting her eyes. "Be careful."

Clicking her tongue, she flashed him a smile and a thumbs up. "Careful is my middle name."

He pressed his lips together and watched Jack kiss Jane on the forehead. "Watch yourself."

Gripping Dean's wrist, Jack squeezed and nodded.

Navigating the porch steps, Addy put weight on the ankle.

Not too bad. I mean, shooting pain up both sides but a broken bone would probably be worse. Probably.

"He's taking her to the hospital," Dad said, catching up to her about three-quarters down the walk.

"If we hurry, we should be able to catch him, then," Addy said, quickstepping on the bad foot.

"Baby girl, I'm gonna step it up a little." He broke into a trot.

"I'll be right behind you." With the blood flowing, adrenaline racing along with it, the pain in her ankle receded. She couldn't jog to keep up with Dad, but she could walk almost as quick.

Two blocks in, she began to sweat so much her shirt was soon soaked.

Four blocks in, Dad disappeared around a corner.

Five blocks in, a snowy mist began falling from the heavy clouds above.

Lungs burning, legs like rubbery stilts, Addy slowed as she trudged through the city center that led up to the hospital. Dad still too far ahead to see, she crossed her arms and lowered her head. Though the imperative to help Dad was strong, the need to collapse into a sleeping pile of goo held equal strength.

Someone shouted. Sounded like Dad.

Heart kicking it up again, adrenaline and lactic acid dumping into her legs, her eyes popped wide and she jumped to jogging. The screaming from her ankle receding once again to a dull roar.

The shifting, snowy mist obscured everything ahead of her, but as she rounded the corner, she picked out two men on the lawn of the hospital, the wall behind them twice as high as it'd been when she left.

As her eyes raced to take in the scene, she noted several changes to the hospital perimeter. And she didn't have time to ask Dad if he'd noticed the higher walls, the razor wire topping them, or the men in uniforms standing on perches behind them, aiming guns at the scene below.

Dad and Michael. Mike with a bundle in one arm, gun in the other. Dad with his hands held out, hair falling in his face, blood splattered all over his shirt.

Limping, stomach in a knot the size of Texas, she approached.

"Don't come any closer, Jack," Mike spat.

Addy flinched. This man, calling their dad by his name, edge of insanity on his voice. This wasn't her brother. It couldn't be.

"Mike?"

He turned, gun still pointed at Dad. "Bean?"

She smiled. "Why don't you give me the baby, huh?"

Clutching the baby, he squeezed.

The squalling wail of a newborn erupted from his arms.

"Please, Mike. She needs her mother. Her family," Dad said, inching closer.

"She was. I could've. I would've." He stopped and sighed, gun dipping. "I'm her family, too. She'll be fine."

"Mike, I don't know what the fuck this is all about, and I don't care," Addy said, stepping closer.

Though he flinched, he did not re-aim the gun. He may have shot Jane, but Addy was ninety-nine percent sure he wouldn't shoot her.

That one percent, though.

"She's immune, bean." He smiled, tears standing in his eyes. "Can you believe it? Immune." As he looked down, smiling at the crying baby, the tears fell in her face. He backed up a step. "We need to do more tests. She'll be fine."

Addy's lungs fought to pull in the next breath. A gust of frozen mist hit her in the face. "We?"

"We." Mom emerged from behind the barrier, Ella's armed and uniformed father following her.

As Jack charged them, Addy grabbed for his shoulder.

She missed, and he raised a fist at Burke.

"Dad, no." She watched the men standing on their perches around the wall. Each of them had trained a rifle on Dad.

"Jack, no," Melinda said, stepping between them.

He growled from deep in his throat. "Do you honestly think I won't hit you? I won't let you take my child, Melinda." He glanced around, taking in the men behind the wall. "You come at me with an army. I don't care. I won't let you."

Addy stepped up next to him. "Mom, this is ridiculous. Michael," she said, glancing at him, widening her eyes, "come on. What the hell, guys? This is crazy, you see that, right?"

"I see that you are standing in the way between humanity and the answer for this virus. Immunity," Melinda said, throwing her head back, "the greatest gift we could give them. But first, we must know how it works. And for that"—she nodded at Mike, who stepped behind Burke—"we need the child. It's nothing personal, Jackson." Her lips curved in a lupine grin. "The fate of the world rests on her tiny little shoulders. What did you name her?"

Jack cleared his throat. "Katherine."

Melinda sniffed. "Ah. Your mother's name. How…sweet." She nodded to Burke.

Before either Addy or Jack had time to react, Burke stepped around her and reached toward Jack with some kind of little black box in his hand. He touched Jack with it, and a crackling sound, not unlike a tiny explosion, emanated from it. Somehow twice as loud as it should have been.

Jack stiffened, eyes fixed to him.

After several seconds, Burke lifted the little crackling box.

Dad stumbled, rushing toward the ground without getting his hands out.

"Dad!" Addy shouted, jumping for him. Trying to keep him from hitting the ground, she twisted her ankle again and screamed.

Dad landed on the ground face-first and didn't move.

Heart beating in her ears, lungs burning for air, Addy hopped to her good foot and grabbed Melinda's arm as she turned to go back into the hospital. Clenching her fist, she dug her non-existent fingernails into Melinda's arm as hard as she could. The tips of her fingers burned.

Michael disappeared behind the barrier. With the baby. Burke waited.

Melinda waved her hand. "Go on. I'm right behind you."

"Mom, how could you do this?" Addy yanked on her, fighting to maintain her balance. Physically and mentally.

"Adelaide. We talked about this."

She shook her head. "We what? No we didn't."

"Oh yes we did. All those talks we had about space, about what humans are capable of when they work together. Now look at what we've accomplished. You should be proud."

"No. No, Mom. Not like this," she said, yanking Melinda's arm again.

Mom looked down at her hand. "Please, Adelaide, remove your hand." She frowned.

Another blast of snowy mist hit Addy in the face. She shook her head. "I can't let you—"

A fist like a brick hit her in the gut.

Coughing for air, she recoiled, her hand popping off Melinda's arm.

Another hit her in the nose. Warm blood spilled down her lip, over her mouth, and dripped onto the whitening ground.

Tears gathered in her eyes. A confusion so deep, so unyielding in its position over her mind, it could have been the Earth itself, staggered her. Her breath wouldn't come.

Melinda wiped her bloody knuckles on her crisp white lab coat. "I am sorry you don't understand. Your brother had a much easier time grasping this."

Tripping over her bad ankle, Addy landed on the cold ground next to her dad.

He groaned.

"No daughter of mine would fight something this important to the species. I don't know you, child," Melinda said. She spun on a heel and marched behind the wall.

The soldiers on the other side sealed the gap with a barrier almost as sturdy as the rest of the wall.

Crying, sniffling blood, Addy helped her dad to sit.

"I can't feel my legs, little girl," he said, glancing around the empty yard.

A dozen guards still watched them from the other side of the wall, gazes flat and empty. Guns trained.

He brushed hair from her forehead. "Are you alright? You're bleeding."

Shaking her head, the words stuck behind the breath caught in her throat, she leaned on his shoulder. The tears threatened, and her eyes hurt like they'd been pressed with red hot pokers, but they never fell.

CHAPTER 24

Jack's dumb legs tried to fold under him at each step. His mind swam.

"What was that Burke hit you with, Dad?" Addy, limping herself, still did her best to help him back to his house.

"Some kind of stun gun, probably," he said. Pins and needles tried to race through his body, but so many of his muscles continued to lock them out.

"What's a stun gun?"

"It's a little box with a big charge. Shocked the hell out of me. Locked up all my muscles, and I'm still having a hard time thinking straight. Watch this snow." Nodding at the sidewalk, he helped her sidestep the small mound that would become a drift if this kept up. He glanced at her. "Better question. Are you alright?"

She shook her head. "Yes. No. My nose is OK, anyway." Wiping her face, dried blood flaking off the inside of her nostrils, she frowned. "I thought. She."

"I know, sweetie. I know," he said, hugging her close. His poor little girl. Had her heart broken by her mom yet again. That woman did not deserve to call this brave, strong, loving, and courageous girl her daughter. Melinda wasn't half the woman Addy was.

"We'll figure this out, Dad."

"Of course we will."

Stumbling up the walk, he shivered. The shifting snow had dropped the temperature at least twenty degrees since they'd brought Katherine home.

Already seemed like a lifetime ago.

They hobbled up the stairs together, and he opened the door.

Bloody gauze on the floor, but no Jane. No Dean.

His stomach, one of the things that had unclenched first and threatened to spill its contents on the ground, did a backflip. "Jane? Dean?"

No answer. Only the ticking of the fridge from the kitchen.

Addy closed the door behind them and flopped onto the couch so hard it moved back six inches.

"I'm going to find Jane and Dean," he said, passing by her.

She snored at him.

Stopping, he took the full-sized blanket Jane had put together over the winter from the back of the couch and threw it over her. Poor, tired girl. With her ankle banged up like that, all this walking must have been killing her. Yet she hardly breathed a word of complaint.

Now, if he could just get the baby to grow up as well as she had.

He crept through the house. They must have been upstairs. Unless something had happened.

Oh good, Jack. Keep going down the rabbit hole. That'll help your nerves.

Bending his knees to climb the stairs got easier the more he did it. That stun gun had really taken it out of him.

A silhouette blocked the light from the top of the stairs. "Who's there?"

"Dean, it's me."

Rushing down the staircase to meet him, Dean grasped his shoulder. "Are you alright? Addy? Where's the baby?"

Jack shook his head, eyes prickling. "Addy's fine. She fell asleep as soon as her ass hit the couch."

Dean frowned, lines crossing his forehead. "And the baby?"

Opening his mouth to find no words, he closed it and shook his head.

"Shit. Well. We'll get it fixed. Don't worry," Dean said, squeezing his arm.

Jack nodded, less in agreement than to have something to do. "Where's Jane?"

Dean jerked his head. "Upstairs. She let me patch her up. The shot missed most of the important stuff. Could have been a lot worse. Got a few stitches in her."

Jack grimaced.

"She's in bed. I don't know if she's asleep. I waited on the top of the stairs for you to come back so I wouldn't bother her."

Stepping past Dean, he rushed up the rest of the stairs. Needed to see her.

Creeping into the bedroom, he turned on the dim bedside lamp. She lay on her side, every bit of her under the covers, curled into a ball.

Eyes hot again, stomach twisted in a slick knot, he kicked off his boots and slid in next to her. As he wrapped an arm around her waist, careful to avoid her injured shoulder, she stiffened. "Just me, baby," he whispered.

Nodding, she grabbed his hand and pulled his arm around, clutching it. Chin tucked into her chest, her whisper was almost too soft to hear. "You didn't bring her back."

And the moment he'd put off since Addy had dragged him to standing in that hospital yard overtook him. The black night of despair. The empty vacuum of failure. The bruises where his insides had been twisted and removed, stomped on, and put back.

He'd failed. He'd failed them both.

He shook his head against her shoulder blade. "I'm so sorry. So sorry, Jane. I couldn't. I tried. I tried." Releasing her, he rolled to his back. The tears, a never-ending waterfall of them, cascaded down the sides of his face, pooling in the cups of his ears before spilling onto the pillow.

Uncurling, she rolled onto her shoulder. With a quiet cry, she stopped and stared at the ceiling.

"But, are you alright?" She took his hand. Her eyes dry, she turned just her head and squeezed his fingers. "You look alright."

"I was hit with a stun gun. But I think I'm OK," he said, gripping her hand. "How's your shoulder?"

Her mouth creased, lips pressed into nonexistence. "Fine."

"I can't believe Mike—"

"I don't want to talk about it, Jack." She closed her eyes, fine line between her brows. "I just want Katherine back."

His heart twisted. So did he. His mind filled with her, her tiny little nose and fingers. The helpless way she squalled in Mike's arms. How she must be crying now, with all the needle pokes and god knew what else.

He breathed deep, all the way to his toes. "We'll make it happen, Jane. We'll make it happen."

* * *

With no memory of how she got there, Addy awoke in her own bed. Rubbing her face, she attempted to sit up.

Her ankle screamed it was having no such business.

"Ah, motherfucker." She grabbed at it.

"Addy, don't move," Dean said, sitting up on the other side of the bed.

Pain in her ankle giving way to happy zings of electricity, she rolled her head to look at him.

In the morning light, he rubbed his stubbled jaw, his bedhead less pronounced than it'd been the last time she'd woken up in the same house with him. His hair had grown out a bit. He ran a hand through it, standing most of it on end.

"Oh good," she said, smiling, "first night we sleep in the same bed together, and I don't even remember getting here."

Hand covering one eye, the other peeped at her. He grinned. "You're right. We've never officially slept together, huh?"

She crossed her arms, brow cocked. "I'm afraid I need a do-over. I don't even remember. That's not fair."

"I can't give you one of those right now," he said, sliding over, "not for sleeping." One finger traced her bicep.

It left a trail so hot behind it, Addy could all but see the smoke rising. Caught in his eyes, with his hand sliding down to her waist, her breath shortened. Blood rushed to her face.

Uncrossing her arms and grabbing the back of his neck, she shifted to get closer, pushing off with her bad foot.

Screaming ensued. Some cursing as well.

"Hell, sweetheart, I'm sorry," Dean said, sinking down beside her again.

Inhaling deep through her nose, she smiled. "It's alright. Really. Here, come here," she said, tugging on his shoulder.

He lifted up on an elbow. "Just tell me what you want."

With enough words and tugging, she maneuvered him so she could throw the ankle up over his shoulder.

Her long-winded explanation of how getting the thing elevated helped with blood flow and swelling became nothing more than a few brief sentences and mumbles as he took advantage of his position.

With a slow, gentle precision one would expect to be used on baby bunnies, he got her clothes out of the way. Her ankle never once protested. Once, when she tried to help, he grasped her wrist and kissed the inside of her palm.

"I got this."

Heart filled to bursting with love, body filled to bursting with desire, she bit her lips and waited for him.

And when they came together again, her mind lifted into transcendental. None of the things around her mattered. Not her ankle. Not the baby. Not her mom. Not the virus. None of it was important.

Just him. Just them. The rush of heat and light that rose inside her as she let everything fall away.

His hands slipped over her body, their skin rubbing together. The friction created heat, their sweat mingling as he pressed into her and she lifted her hips and arched her back to get closer. And when she couldn't take the distance anymore, she hooked her leg behind him instead, the pain from her ankle as distant as the horde out there in the valley, and pulled him into her. One arm around his neck, she linked her fingers through his, and when he brought her to the top of the mountain, she leapt with his name on her lips. Flying with him in a way she'd never known possible until he showed her how.

As they both descended the mountain again, sweating and out of breath, he nuzzled her neck and whispered how much he loved her. How being away from her had been nothing but pure torture from one moment to the next.

When she asked how he'd survived all those years before he met her, he kissed her and sat up to catch her eyes.

"Adelaide, I really do not know."

She smiled, blood rushing to her cheeks again. "I'm sorry they kept you in jail so long."

He shook his head, lying on the pillow next to her. Tracing a finger down her arm, he frowned. "I think it's time I told you a story."

Heart skipping, she put two fingers over his lips. Shook her head. Tapped her ear.

Come on, Dean. Get it. We can't talk here. They're listening. You told me that yourself.

Brows drawn into a V, he searched her face. Staring into the distance over her shoulder, his eyes widened. He frowned. "Where, then?"

She took his hand and tugged. "Let's go into the living room. Wanna show you a present Yaz brought."

"How is he, anyway?" he asked, pulling on his pants. He circled the bed to help her up.

She stood and leaned on him, locking a shout behind her lips. Her legs screamed from toes to hips. "You know, I haven't seen him lately. Hope he's alright. Slow down," she said, wobbling over her center of gravity. "Man, I have never been happier me and Cee chose a one-story."

"Yeah, maybe. But if something should happen, you know two stories are safer."

"Sure," she said, an image of Dad's stairs in Arizona, trip wires lining every other one, popping into her mind. She hadn't thought of those stairs in months and months. The first place she'd ever really called home, a distant memory, a dull ache.

"Here," Dean said, backing up to the couch, "you sit here and tell me what it is you want to show me." Sitting with her, he lowered her with careful precision.

Given his caution, her ankle didn't protest as they sat. Arms wrapped around his solid bicep, she laid her head on his shoulder and pointed to a table across the room with a wooden box on top. "That's what Yaz brought us. Check it out."

He moved to stand, and she tightened her grip. Glancing down at her hands, he grinned. "Can't get up if you're holding onto me, sweetie."

"That's true."

He cupped her jaw, drawing her close, and teased her lips with his. Light breath tingling across her mouth.

Goose bumps raced up her back into the nape of her neck. She shivered. Laughing, she released him. "Go on, take a look."

With a chuckle, he crossed the room and opened the top of the record player. He looked inside and laughed aloud. "Holy crap, Addy. I barely remember these. Don't they play music?"

"There's a door on the side with what Yasuo called records. Pick one."

He opened the door, pulling out the six records Yaz had dug up for her. All things he'd recommended since she had little to zero music knowledge. "I haven't heard music in way too…oh my god. Addy, no." He held up a record with a cream cover, marred by red streaks, scratches, and a giant black blob. All part of the aesthetic.

"Yeah. Yaz called it 'industrial' and thought I'd like it."

"And?"

"Haven't had the chance to listen yet."

"Hell," Dean said, unsheathing one of the two records contained in the sleeve, "my parents loved the shit out of this. You're in for a real treat." He lowered the record and looked for the button to push to make it spin.

"Yaz says use the 'auto' button," she said, watching his naked torso. The side of the silvery bite mark on his abs visible.

The music began and got loud right away. Dean turned it up even more and made his way back to the couch.

Yaz had been right. The music was loud and angry, yet lyrical with a comfortable groove. It was lovely.

Sitting and helping her raise her leg onto the ottoman before her, Dean leaned back and frowned. He kissed her neck and spoke in her ear.

"I think it's time to tell you how me and IRF became acquainted."

CHAPTER 25

The horde before Dean was big enough to call a horde but small enough that he and Cameron could have taken them all out in about five minutes or less. The kid had been so strong. So quick. So smart.

And now he was gone.

And there was a goddamned Cure. Of all things, a Cure.

Pulling his knife out of one side of his belt and the gun out of the other, Dean charged into the 'Heads, gun blazing. Probably have to reload at some point when he was right in the middle of them.

Something Cameron could have covered for.

As he stabbed the nearest one in the ear, jerking the knife clear before the 'Head could take it down with it, another gripped him from behind. Sweeping upward, he sliced the blade through the roof of its mouth. It fell, his knife cutting into his own shoulder.

Hopefully the virus couldn't be transferred from the blood on the blade to the cut on his shoulder. But even if it could, he had his dose. The stupid thing. The idiotic syringe that could have saved Cameron, if it weren't for an ill-placed rusty nail and a mere two weeks.

An image of a drop of blood glistening on the end of the nail, sun shining behind it, took up any room his head might have had for thought. As wave after wave of 'Heads stumbled toward him, some bubbling and gurgling, some buzzing like dirt across sandpaper, his vision blurred and all he could see was that rusty nail.

One.

Rusty.

Nail.

His leg screamed in tearing fire, pain shooting up through his back and into his brain.

Grunting, he glanced down.

A 'Head had gotten a hold of his knee and sunk its teeth into his thigh.

Hacking at its hands, he chopped them both off as two more jumped on his back. Elbowing them both, shooting one in the face and then hearing the click when he went to shoot the other one, he dropped to his knees. He stabbed the biter in the face and clocked the one still on his back with the butt of the pistol.

It fell, snarling, onto its back.

Dropping the empty clip, he slammed the reload home, chambered one, and ended it as it sat up.

Marked the spot in his memory. The one with the cut off hands splayed next to the spent clip. He'd have to retrieve it once they were all dead again.

Glancing up, he found himself surrounded. More upon more upon more came at him.

Maybe he should use these bullets on himself. Save them all the trouble.

The bite burned. If he didn't get that damn stupid Cure injected soon, he'd follow Cameron.

Follow Cameron.

He lay on his back and waited for them to come.

One by one, as they leaned over him, blackened fingers outstretched, he shot them between the eyes.

His ears rang from the gunshots. Aching arms. Burning bite. Face bloody and covered in tears and sweat.

What the hell. Let them come.

He dropped his arms.

Bullets mowed through the 'Heads. Some of them cut in half by the constant fire of what had to be a machine gun. Heads exploded.

His eyes tried to close as their ichor rained down on him.

Keeping them wide, his face, chest, his whole body drenched in their stinking, spoiled blood, he watched them all fall.

Some wriggled across the ground toward him. He could smell them more than hear them. His ears had become effectively useless after the machine-gun fire.

And so there he lay, covered in blood, his own and the 'Heads', when a face looked down at him.

The grey-eyed man with more pepper than salt in his hair popped a plug from his ear and spoke.

Dean couldn't hear him. He stared past him into the blue sky.

Someone poked him, hard, in the stomach.

Coming up swinging, he connected with bone. Gripping his stomach where he'd been poked, he felt something there besides shirt.

Glancing down, heart racing, he found a syringe sticking half out of his skin.

"What the hell," he said, yanking it from his hide. On the bright side, he could almost hear himself.

Sound oozed back into his ears, and around him, people introduced the remainder of the horde to the next afterlife with knives and handguns that *pop-pop-popped*.

The grey-eyed man held out a hand.

Dean took it and stood. Though his leg burned where he'd been bitten, at least he knew that wouldn't be what killed him. It should have. A month ago, it would have. But now. Well, now.

He held the syringe up at eye level. Glanced around at the dead. "Why?"

The man held out a hand. "Casey Burke. Because you looked like you could use the help."

Dean dropped the syringe. He stepped on it. "Thanks, I guess. I just gotta find that clip and pick up the brass and I'll be out of your hair."

"What's your name, son?"

"I'm not your son," Dean said, searching for the handless 'Head. He kicked over a body. Dammit. Not there.

"Sorry. I would like to know your name, though."

"Dean."

"Dean. If you come with us, you won't need to worry about collecting your brass anymore. Or your empty magazines. We've got plenty."

Unbidden, Dean pictured underground bunkers filled to the brim with both weapons and ammo. Something he and Cam had talked endlessly about. The super stash. Surely the military had bunkers like that. It was just a matter of finding them.

"What do you want with me?" He kicked over another body.

Ah, there it was. The one without hands. Now, where was that damn—

"I saw you fight," Burke said. "We could use a man like you."

For the first time, Dean looked up and took in the man's military fatigues. "Who's we?" The image of the super stash flashed through his mind again.

CHAPTER 26

"So he took me to their base, the place they called home," Dean said, gripping Addy's hand. His palm had begun to sweat at some point during the telling.

She clutched him anyway. He could've killed himself right then. And then she never would have known him.

Closing her eyes and breathing while he talked about Burke getting him cleaned up and settled in, she let the fear of never knowing him ride for a few moments. Once it had circled her heart a few times, she gathered it into a little ball, forgave it for existing, and set it free.

Opening her eyes to meet his emerald green ones, she found the fear had transformed into gratitude. Whatever might have happened, he was here, now. He'd touched her life. That could never be taken away.

He stopped, grinning sideways at her. "Are you even listening?"

She nodded. "Course I am."

"Sure. What did I say?"

"You liked Burke. He was nice but not too nice. Hard-nosed but lenient in the right ways."

He smiled. "Yeah. Didn't trust him any farther than I could throw him, but he kept us mostly clean and dry. He's the one who taught me how to weld and got me on the cell tower team."

"Did he send you to California when they got the first station up?"

"How did you know about that?"

"Mike told me. Like it was some big deal."

He nodded. "It was. It was a big deal. We were already in California at the time, and he wanted me to know how the whole system worked. Said I was the least fucked up of anyone he'd recruited."

Addy laughed. "Pretty low bar."

Pursing his lips, he elbowed her. "Hey."

She laughed again, leaning onto his shoulder. "Did you know he was here?"

"No. I'd been looking for him for a while, though. Part of crossing the country with you was to try and find him."

"Why?"

"Addy," he said, cupping her chin and lifting her head, "he's a good guy. He's got a good heart."

"But."

"But. He's driven. Once he's decided what he wants, he won't let anyone get in the way of that. I'd heard whispering IRF was working on some kind of vaccine. But there's more to it. I think they might actually be connected with Talus."

"Well yeah, they're connected. They're enemies, right? Opposition?"

He shook his head. "I think it's complicated."

Breath short, she sat up. "Do you think they're on the same side?"

"I don't know," he said, squeezing her hand. "I'd hoped he would tell me. He always seemed to like me. But he dropped off the radar about a year and a half ago. About the time I met Mike, I guess. I've been trying to track him down ever since."

"And now you have," she said, standing, "and he's working with my mom on this vaccine." Her gut twisted. Always her mom. Always back to that.

He crossed his arms. "God knows what your mom is really doing, who she's really working for. I hate to say it, Addy, but—"

"But my mom is slippery. I know." She rasped the side of her face with her palm and lifted her eyebrows. "Do you think he'd tell you what he knows?"

"I used to think so."

"But now?"

"Hell, honey, I don't know. He let me sit in jail for all that time. Never came to check in. Not once."

"And I saw him with my mom at least three different times. Including when they kidnapped my sister." Her stomach churned.

He hugged her again. "We could—"

A knock sounded at the front door.

* * *

Raising a fist to knock, Jack paused. The sound of gritty guitars and synth keys drifted through the door.

Addy and Dean must have been talking under the music.

He knocked anyway.

Dean, shirtless, answered the door. Flushed, he stepped back and opened the door wide. "Jack. Come on in."

Addy, ankle wrapped in a thick bandage, sat on the couch.

Dean turned the record player down. "Have a seat."

"Celia home?"

"No," Addy said, shaking her head. She pulled a blanket from the back of her couch and concealed her bare legs under it.

And Jack concealed a grin. He might be stupid, but he wasn't *that* stupid. He knew enough to know his little girl was all grown up. It was probably a good thing. The less she needed him for, the better. If he couldn't even protect a helpless, beautiful little baby…

Stop that right now, Jack. Just stop.

Dean sat. "The last we saw her was…" He trailed off, glancing at Addy.

She frowned, brow drawn into a sharp V, and her chin trembled. "Shit, Dad. Oren's dead."

Head expanding to balloon proportions, Jack stood, sending the chair rocking. He tried to catch a breath. Ask her to repeat herself.

It wouldn't come.

Hand held out, Dean half stood. "You alright?"

Head spinning, he sat again. Black spots blossomed in his eyes, and he leaned his elbows on his knees. When the black spots lessened but did not disappear, he leaned his forehead onto his knee.

Oren? Dead? He croaked out a word. "How?"

From beginning to end, Addy explained.

Listening with his eyes closed, something tugging in the back of his mind, his heart ached for Celia. She couldn't even Cure him before he died. One of the worst fates Jack could imagine was watching the world go dark through the crystal-clear vision of the dead.

"Jack," Dean said, "we forgot the thing."

He glanced at Dean.

Who pointed at the record player.

The little ping in the back of his mind jumped out and did a dance. *Told you you forgot something,* it said.

He shrugged. "Fuck it. Where's the damned microphone?"

Dean's mouth fell open.

Addy grinned. A fiery, unrelenting thing. She pointed just next to the record player. "That built-in bookshelf. There's a secret door. Here, I'll show you." Standing, she wobbled and threw out her hand.

Faster than Jack could see, Dean was on his feet and under her arm. He steadied her and helped her limp across the room.

He crossed the room with them, and when Addy slid the secret compartment door back, he reached inside.

Years of dust and cobwebs covered some long-forgotten doll hidden away. A yarn-haired girl with button eyes, she laid atop a stack of hundred-dollar bills.

Reaching past the useless memorabilia, Jack snatched at the microphone duct-taped to the side of the compartment. He yanked it and its wires from the wall, gripping the battery and the little transmitting unit in his fist.

"You listen to me, you bitch. We're coming for you. And you won't like it when we get there."

Dropping the unit, he stepped on it until it crunched.

An almost orgasmic wave of release washed over him. Clenching his hands and closing his eyes, he rode the wave. Savored the freedom of that broken little device.

He opened his eyes. "You two break the rest of them. These people are not controlling us. If they have to find that out the hard way, so be it." He headed for the door.

"Dad, what are we going to do?"

"You send Celia to me if you see her before I do. We're getting my baby back, for starters. After that," he said, mouth stretching into a humorless grin, "the sky's the limit."

CHAPTER 27

Jack stalked up the hill to the old part of town. The part his little girl had told him about but he hadn't bothered to come see himself.

He'd been too busy not thinking about the mess they were in.

Too busy allowing himself happiness, feeling like something was right with the world.

Being delusional.

Down here somewhere was the place Paul had always come to for his twice-weekly reports.

Down here also? A small faction of people who could be useful in this fight. That tiny vestige of the original residents.

Hips screaming from the cold, from the shock they'd taken yesterday and the fall after, he fought with a limp as he scanned the old houses. The broken windows in some of them loomed over him, their gaping maws jagged.

A bird whistled.

Two seconds later, his mind translated the bird call and informed him it was no bird. Paul had always been piss-poor at whistling.

He stopped, crouching, and peeked at the bushes to his left. "Paul?"

"How'd you know, friend Jack," came the whisper. Its owner invisible.

"Need to talk at you."

From the house next to him, wood creaked. Paul stood on the back porch, frowning. "Somebody else that needs to see you, too. Should probably ought to come in."

"In there?"

Nodding, Paul waved him up the stairs. "Seems like I'm not doing much good."

"What do you—"

"Just follow me, boy." He crossed the threshold into a mudroom.

A couple old plastic hangers still suspended above the washer and dryer caught Jack's eye as he followed.

Oh man, laundry machines. Easily one of the accessories of the old world he missed the most.

He followed Paul through the creaking house. Fading chem lights laid up against the wall in the darkened hallway.

"How's your woman?"

"Long story."

Paul grunted. "Ain't that always the case." He shuffled down the hall, dust swirling around his feet. "You out here making plans, what's she doing?"

Stopping beside the stairs, Jack frowned. "Getting some rest. She's had a hard couple of days. I can take care of this."

Grunting again, Paul led him through the door under the stairs. As they descended into the dank basement, the air closing in on them like a wet wool blanket, the temperature dropped at least thirty degrees. The walls hemmed them in. Grey light filtered into the room from the thin, ground-level windows.

A film of dirt covered the floor and crunched under Jack's bootheels as Paul led him across the basement to a closed-off room on the far side.

Paul opened the door and a wave of heat blasted them in the face.

"Shut it, for Chrissakes," someone said.

They crossed into the room and shut the door.

Nearly a dozen people filled the tight space. Some shoulder to shoulder, some napping on ratty couches. Two bunk beds against the far wall were full of people sleeping head to foot.

One woman lay on her side in the floor, curled into a ball with her face in the corner.

Jack sighed. Stomach knotting into itself, he sat down behind her and rubbed her back. "Celia?"

She shook her head, face hitting the floor, but didn't uncurl.

He gripped her shoulder and shook. "Celia. Look at me."

Again, she shook her head. "No," she whispered.

"Celia," he said, forehead tight, "I'm going to need your help."

"No."

"Addy told me about Oren."

She opened her mouth.

"You don't have to talk to me about it," he said, cutting her off, "that's not why I brought it up. But I need your help."

Sitting up, she brushed her shoulder and spun on her ass. She frowned at him. "You ain't never really needed me for nothing, Jack. Why should you start now?"

He sighed, backing up to the wall next to her. "That's not true and you know it. Who saved my ass during that monsoon that one year?"

She chuckled. "Pinned in a damned wash, rain coming down to beat the devil. You know a flash flood came through just a couple minutes after I killed all those damned 'Heads so you could escape."

"I would just like to point out I killed two of them myself." He paused, grinning. "What were you doing down there anyway?"

One side of her mouth turning up, she narrowed her eyes. "What do you need my help with?"

The grin slid from his face, eyes dimming. "She took the baby."

Murmuring around the room ceased. A quiet shuffling followed.

He didn't turn to look at the rest of them. Keeping his eyes pinned to Celia, he swallowed. "Melinda. She took the baby."

"What the hell? Why would she do that?"

"She's immune. My baby is immune."

A gasp went around the room, as Celia exhaled and hit the back of her head on the wall. "Of course she is," she said, half a smile curving her mouth.

"What makes you say that?"

She shook her head, standing. Offered him a hand.

He took her hand and stood. Arms crossed, he glanced around the room.

All eyes were pinned to him.

Fire rushed through him. More people, willing to put themselves in harm's way. Just because he'd asked. "If it was just for me, I wouldn't ask," he said, looking around at them all. "But it's for one of my children." He stared down at Celia. "For her, I'll ask for your help."

Celia glanced around the room and met his eyes. "Looks like we've got some plans to make."

* * *

Ella opened the door and frowned. "Adelaide," she said, "hello." She didn't step back from the doorway or move to open the screen. She did glance down and inspect a fingernail. "You're late for the party."

Arms crossed, Addy shuffled a foot. "Hi, Ella." Her own fingers crept to her mouth. Rather than clamp a nail between her teeth, she cleared her throat and re-crossed her arms. "It's good to see you."

The truth of that statement shocked her. She hadn't realized it until the words were out of her mouth, but she'd missed her.

"Fine, whatever. Come in," Ella said, stepping back. She disappeared down the hall.

Frowning, Addy let herself in and shut the door. This afternoon, when she'd gone to talk to Yasuo about Dad's plan, Yaz had reminded her about those amends she was supposed to be making. And then he'd asked if Ella would be upset that she missed the party. She'd shrugged and said, "Who cares."

The way her stomach churned as she followed Ella through the house answered the question.

Addy clearly cared very much.

By the time she limped into the kitchen, any hope of this being easy had subsided.

With the shades lowered over each window, the only light in the cold kitchen peeked from the hood over the stove.

Ella sat at the table, eyes narrowed, and opened her mouth. Only air escaped. She cleared her throat and tried again. "What do you want?"

Leaning on her injured ankle to make the limp more pronounced, Addy pointed at the closest chair. "May I?"

Ella shrugged and tossed a lock of honey blonde hair over her shoulder. Lacing her fingers together, she leaned on her hands and glared through the corner of her eye as Addy huffed into the chair.

"Screwed up my ankle," Addy said, trying on a chuckle.

Exhaling through her nose, Ella picked up a long-stemmed glass and took a sip. Today, the liquid was deep maroon.

Somehow it matched the dark kitchen.

Stomach churning, Addy tried again without the chuckle. "Dean got out of jail."

"Great." Sip.

Somewhere, the house ticked as it expanded in the afternoon sun. Outside, a small breeze moved the magnolia's branches across the roof. Scraping and scratching on the shingles.

This was pointless.

Tensing her knees to stand, Addy glanced at the side of Ella's face.

Mouth set in a frown, her chin trembled.

Dad had said to tell her nothing. Yet Yasuo had taught her amends had to be lived. You couldn't just say you were sorry.

And with a shock of dismay twisting her insides again, remorse coursed through her. She'd left Ella without so much as a goodbye, without any explanation, without any second thought. Deserted her for the party and for weeks after. Even knowing she had no friends except Matt.

Addy sighed. "I'm sorry I disappeared."

"Sure."

Heart thumping, she swallowed. "It's not because I don't care about you."

"Fine." Sip. Sip. Several blinks.

"I wasn't here, Ella."

For the first time, she turned. Eyes wide, she goggled. "What do you mean? No one saw you leave."

"No one…wait. How do you know that?"

Ella rubbed at a spot on the table. "I might have asked around." She shrugged. "People tell me things when I make them."

"And what do *you* tell them? Or your dad?"

She swallowed, glancing at Addy again. More fast blinking. Lowering her voice, she leaned across the table. "I haven't seen Daddy in days. I'm worried something has happened to him."

"Ella," Addy said, sitting back in the chair, "is that wine?"

She nodded, taking another sip and finishing the glass.

"Could you get me a glass, please?"

On stilted legs, she retrieved a glass from the cupboard and a full bottle of wine from the small fridge under the cabinet. Setting it down on the table, she uncorked it and, after a moment to let it breathe, poured them both a glass.

Swirling the bitter wine around in her mouth, Addy took a moment to clear her mind. She not only owed Ella amends, she also owed her an explanation. Mom had somehow gotten her daddy caught up in this mess, and while god knew Addy wasn't responsible for the acts of her parents, everything around her was still affected by their actions. Knowing she wasn't responsible and feeling it were two different things.

"What can you tell me about the history of this settlement?" she asked.

Ella frowned. "I don't know. Daddy brought me here about eight months ago. We already talked about this."

"Do you know about the people who built the place?"

She shook her head, taking a sip.

An empty feeling opened in Addy. She embraced it as best she could. "Your dad's company, IRF, gave the people who lived here the materials to build the wall. Once they were done, IRF kicked them out and brought the people who live here now. Stole these people from their homes and dropped them into someone else's."

Ella sat back, staring at the table. "That's ridiculous. Why would they do that? That's ridiculous."

Addy shrugged. "It all has to do with the vaccine, I'm sure of it."

"What about the vaccine?"

"My mom had been working on one with her company, Talus Crest. I think she's brought her knowledge to your dad in order to take over this operation. Remember that day we saw them in the lab?"

Ella shook her head and downed the rest of her wine. Fingers pinching the stem of the glass, she sat with her eyes closed.

Frowning, Addy studied her face. If there was one thing she'd learned about Ella in the time they'd spent together, it was that her eyebrows were like weather vanes. They could tell you which way the wind was blowing.

With them aimed down in a V, Ella opened her eyes. "This is ludicrous. You're telling me that my daddy, someone who has only ever wanted to help people, not only deliberately kidnapped people from their homes, he forced other people to give up their own so he could, what, work on some fake vaccine with your mother?"

"It's not fake. I saw Jane—"

"Oh. My. God. Do not get me started on her. Or *your* father."

Blood rushed to Addy's face, her forehead tightening. She shifted in her chair. "Exactly what is that supposed to mean?"

Through strained lips, Ella laughed. "Addy, your family could win the who's the most fucked up Olympics, you know that? My daddy is a *saint* in comparison. And now you're trying to tell me your mother, who, ha, if you knew what the guards said about her, you're telling me she's controlling my daddy as well?"

"Don't you talk like that about my dad," Addy said, standing. Using every inch her shoulders gave her, she loomed over Ella.

Unfazed, Ella stood and threw her head back. Her hair flew over her shoulder. Tears stood in her eyes. "Your dad, your brother, your mom, your friend, even your delinquent boyfriend. All of you. You're an embarrassment."

Red spots bloomed in front of Addy's eyes. Her heart thumped against her ribcage, and her breath came in short, sharp inhales. "What did you say about Dean?"

"Oh, Matthew told me all about him. The traitor."

The muscles in her arm bunched. Blood rushing down to her fingers, she curled them into a fist. Hitting Ella had been on her mind since the moment they'd met. This was going to be amazing.

Before she so much as twitched, her lungs filled with air. It traveled down to her belly, filled her torso with airy light, and exited the way it had come.

There was nothing in what Yaz had taught her that covered hitting people because it might make you feel better.

And that certainly wasn't a part of making amends.

Unclenching her fist, she pushed the chair under the table. "I'll see myself out, then."

Halfway to the front door, Ella shouted down the hall. "Get out then. I didn't want you to come back here, anyway."

As Addy opened the front door, she may have heard a sob. Then again, it was probably wishful thinking.

She saw herself out.

CHAPTER 28

Halfway back down the hill, Jack paused. "I want to see him, Paul."

Celia's breath caught in her throat, but she said nothing.

"What was that?" Paul asked, stopping next to him.

"I want to see Oren," Jack said.

"You sure, friend Jack? It's not pretty."

Silent, Jack stared at him. He bunched his jaw, his teeth squeaking against each other.

Paul held up a hand as though to stop Jack from speaking. "OK, alright. If it's what you wanna do. It's this way," he said, pointing back the way they'd come.

Following Paul, Jack felt the space beside him empty.

Stopping, he glanced back at Celia.

Her arms wrapped almost fully around her, she stood with her feet planted. She gave her head a curt shake.

Jack continued to follow Paul. Once they'd crossed the yard in front of them and slipped around the side of the house, he tapped Paul on the shoulder. "Tell me again what he said to her."

Frowning, Paul repeated the entire conversation. "I didn't really know either of them too great, Jack. But in this world, you get two people who feel like that, it's a damn shame to let it go to waste."

"What do you mean? She didn't seem to reciprocate."

"Yeah, sure," Paul said, shaking his head. "Anyway, the body's just down there," he said, pointing down a drainage ditch. "Probably get washed away before long, once all this really melts."

Climbing down the steep concrete side, Jack glanced up. "You coming?"

Paul shook his head. "I already climbed down there a couple times the last few days. My knees have about had enough, friend Jack."

Jack peered down the ditch as it disappeared under the wall. The dark seeping out into the grey day.

"You alright?"

"Yeah. I'd like to think this gets easier."

Paul sat on the edge of the concrete. "Which?"

"Saying goodbye."

A rueful grin crossed Paul's face, shadows from the thick clouds hanging over him. "Friend Jack, I am here to tell you, it don't."

Eyes narrowed, Jack ducked and crawled into the passage.

Scraping his knees against the gritty concrete, the palms of his hands growing raw before he was halfway down, he tried to crouch and duck walk.

His knees screamed at him that if given a choice between crawling and duck-walking, they'd choose to give up and die instead.

He pressed forward, the flat smell of stale water metallic in the back of his throat. And at the end of the tunnel, where the thin light filtered in, the grate squatted, blocked on one side by a body with its arms stuck through the bars.

Still. Silent. It had the taste of disease, and even the insects gave it a wide berth.

Just a day past its expiration date, the smell hit him when he was about three-quarters of the way to it. The sun broke through the clouds and bounced off one edge of the red mustache.

His eyes prickled.

Stopping to swipe at them, he swallowed around the lump in his throat. "Oh man, Oren. Damn."

Dropping back to all fours, he crawled. One knee to hand at a time, he took each step with care. Oren's face came into focus. Jack sat, avoiding the water, and studied the arms. They'd begun to bloat, and the skin puckered around the needle mark where

Celia had injected the useless Cure. His eyes dropped to the empty syringe.

How many times had Oren taken it over the years? How many times had he been bitten this time? How fresh was the 'Head doing the biting? What else went into that complicated math Melinda had spoken of?

Brow furrowed, one side of his mouth lifted as he thought of Oren's bouncing mustache. The way he'd stroke it when he was thinking, or when he was about to tell a joke. His clever wit and boundless optimism.

Reaching for his arm, Jack cleared his throat. "Gonna miss you, buddy."

Just as his hand landed on the cold, mottled skin of Oren's arm, the arm jumped.

Heart racing, tripping over itself, Jack fell onto his back in the draining water. Stifling a shout, he pulled air in over his teeth so hard it hurt.

"Mr. C.," a voice called.

Pitched low, it slid over his spine like a quiet centipede. But he processed who had spoken without thinking. "Ricardo, holy shit, where did you come from?" he asked, sliding back to the grate. Careful to avoid touching the body.

Rolling off Oren's back, Ric landed face-first in the water trickling out of the grate. "Mr. C., it's really cold out here. You gotta help me." His lips were blue, the skin around his eyes pale, so pale. Sticks and leaves stuck out of his matted hair, but he wasn't bloody. Showed no signs of bites.

Still. Couldn't be too careful. "Ric, are you bit?"

The kid shook his head. "I don't think so. We got surprised. I got away, and I hurt my arm." He held it up as if to illustrate. "I got all turned around in the woods. Took me forever to find this place again." He caught Jack's eyes. "How do I get in?"

Dammit, Jack. This kid is sixteen, at most. The hell were you doing, leaving him out there?

"There's a hidden door down the wall a bit. Head north, you'll run into it." Explaining how to find the small door as Addy had explained it to him, he reached through the bars to hold the boy's hand.

Ric snuffled, clutching at him. "I'm scared. Promise me I'll make it?"

Squeezing his hand, Jack nodded. "You'll be fine. Just go. I'll meet you there."

* * *

Leaving Ric in the basement with the others, Jack wandered home through deepening dusk, full of thoughts and lingering guilt. Arms crossed, one hand under his chin, he didn't notice Jane on the porch stairs until he almost tripped over her.

Feet on two different stairs, he paused with his hand out. "What are you doing out here? It's almost February. You'll freeze to death."

She pulled the blanket she'd knitted for Katherine tighter around her shoulders and glared up into his eyes. "I'll sit on the porch if I damn well please."

Vision narrowing to a pinhole, he didn't feel his hand dropping.

If she'd ever spoken to him that way, he couldn't recall the time.

Knees and hands burning from his trip under the wall, guilt over what had happened to the boy he'd left in the woods tearing at him, the patience he did have could be called thin at best. Still, he sat. Fought his voice to keep it low and modulated. "Something wrong?"

Eyes wide, she stared into the yard. "Something…" She trailed off, tugging at the blanket. "He really just asked me that," she said, voice pitched low. A small cloud of vapor puffed out of her mouth as she scoffed.

The heat began somewhere in his belly. Racing through his heart and into his face, tightening the skin across his forehead, it boiled and bubbled near the crown of his head.

Before he spat words he might not mean, he turned away from her. The spot in the yard where he'd taught her to build snow people homogeneous after all the new snow and time, he still tried to pick it out as he waited for the top of his head to cool.

But his mouth was quicker than his brain, despite his best efforts. "You're not the only one who lost a child, here, Jane."

She stood, throwing the blanket in his face. "Oh sure. I forgot how this is all about you."

Pulling the blanket down with slow precision and clutching it in his fist, he stood. "What exactly is that supposed to mean?"

She folded her arms between a belly that still hadn't really shrunk and her larger than usual breasts. Her nostrils flared, eyes blazing. "I woke up this morning and you were gone. Gone." She pointed away from the house. "I've been sitting around here all day, wondering where you were and if you were coming back, and what the hell were you doing?"

He opened his mouth to explain.

"You left me. Again." She pointed a shaking finger at the ground. "Just left me here. Again," she said, stabbing at the ground with each word.

Sucking a breath deep, still waiting for the top of his head to cool, he glanced at the bandage on her shoulder. "I thought you could use the rest. Not only have you just given birth, you've been shot." He glanced into the yard. "Or did you forget about the other child I lost during all this?"

As she inhaled a sharp breath, he processed the fact it was too late to take that little comment back.

"Don't you fucking talk to me about Michael."

"Why not? Why don't we talk about Mike? This whole thing with him is not all my fault. In fact—"

"I fucked up, alright? That what you want me to say? That I never should have gotten him involved? That it's really my fault? The hell do you want from me?"

Mouth still open, he drew in a breath. Now that the words were flowing, they refused to stop. But her admission of guilt slowed them long enough to get them to shift direction. He exhaled. "I don't understand why you let him hold her."

She backed into the handrail, mouth open. "Are you… Are you blaming me? For this?"

"No," he said before he thought about what he'd meant. His heart hammering the inside of his ribcage, he considered it. But before he got to the conclusion, his mouth had gone on ahead again. "I don't know. It just wasn't the best decision. He—"

"He was there for me, Jack," she said, crossing her arms again. "After…after the prison. And the hospital, the vaccine, your damned wife, I needed someone."

"You could have talked to me," he said, spitting the words at her.

"You ran away!" Voice rising, she stepped closer. "You weren't there. He was. He took me in, and he comforted me even though he didn't know what was wrong. You just. You just left."

"Don't try to pin that on me," he said, taking a step. "I only left after you rejected me. What the hell was I supposed to think?"

"The point is," she said, "when I needed someone, he was there. I wanted it to be you, but you weren't. Not after she showed up. You were already gone."

He flashed on the first night after they'd found out Melinda was still alive. Standing on the dune and calling Jane, but unable to raise his voice above the surf.

He hadn't really tried hard enough, had he? Had he even known if he wanted to?

She stepped closer again. "Don't you get my point? It was supposed to be him. We all knew that. I was supposed to be with him, and be happy and all that shit. And then you." Flushed, she stopped. Shifting from foot to foot, she lowered her eyes and sighed. "Anyway. You don't know him the way I do."

"No, I guess I don't," he said, top of his head cooling. Like molasses, the heated blood drained from his face.

What she'd said about being with Michael, though. That stuck in his brain and burrowed into his heart.

The truth of the matter was she'd probably been happier when she was with him anyway.

He blew a tight breath between his lips. "I guess I would've only lost one child if I'd let the other keep you."

"Keep me? Seriously?" She laughed. A humorless, colorless exhale. "You know good and goddamn well, I make my own decisions. Here's one, right now," she said, facing the door. "You follow me into this house, and it'll be the last time. You're so eager to leave. Then go."

As he stood, rooted to the spot, she slammed the door in his face.

* * *

Opening her front door, Addy limped onto her bad ankle. She raised a brow. "Dad, what are you doing here?"

He lowered his eyes. "Can't come see my kiddo?"

"Sorry," she said, stepping back and opening the door wider, "didn't mean it that way."

Crossing the threshold, he kept his eyes lowered. His shoulders curled in on themselves as he sank into the corner of the couch.

Unease fluttered across Addy's own shoulders, walking with goose feet down her back. She closed the door and limped to sit on the ottoman. As she did, she watched her dad's face.

Lips pinched together, hands folded between his knees, he stared into space.

"Dad? Something up?"

He continued staring off.

Shuffling in from the kitchen with two glasses and a pitcher of water, Dean glanced at Jack. Wide eyes asked her the silent question.

Addy shrugged. "Dad," she said again, laying a hand on his knee.

He started, eyes focusing on her. "Sorry, baby girl. What?"

"Is there something up?"

A ghost of a smile crossed his lips. "If there's one thing I should expect at this point, it's how quickly things can change."

"What do you mean by that, Jack?" Dean asked, perching on the opposite end of the couch.

Addy frowned. Dad had often been the serious, quiet man who raised her. But this distant silence set Addy's teeth on edge. Her nerves careened.

Jack stared through Dean and patted the couch. "Alright if I steal your bed here for a night or two?"

Dean cleared his throat and glanced at Addy. "I, um."

She flushed with such speed she got a head rush. Leaning over her knees, she tried to cough out some words. They almost stuck in her throat. "He's sleeping with me, Dad," Addy said, plunging ahead like diving into a cold pool of water on a hot summer day. "I mean," she said, glancing at Dean, "you know what I mean."

Jack's face clearing, he laughed. Not a full-on belly laugh, but a laugh all the same. "Sorry, sorry. I don't mean to laugh. I shouldn't be laughing. Feels nice, though." He peeked at them both, still smiling.

Dean shook his head, face like someone who'd been caught in a bear trap. By the bear they'd set it for.

Dad chuckled again. "I needed that laugh. Thanks. Dean, if you were still sleeping on the couch, I was going to have to ask what was wrong with you. Seriously though, could I steal your couch, little girl?"

And just like that, the unease sank back into her stomach. But she'd already asked him what was going on twice and he hadn't elaborated. Likely he wouldn't, not until he was ready.

She nodded. "Sure, Dad. I'll get you a blanket." She got halfway up before Dean stood, holding a hand out.

"Stop. Sit. I'll get it."

Sitting back down, she smiled and shook her head. "While you're at it—"

An insistent, fervent knock hammered the door.

Easing his gun out of its holster, Dean approached the door from the side. "Yeah," he said, voice deep. Commanding. "Speak up, who's there?"

"It's Yasuo. Dean, are Addy and Jack in there with you?"

Addy nodded at the door. "Let him in." She hadn't heard Yaz speak with such a high pitch in his voice in, well, ever.

Holstering his gun, Dean opened the door and checked the space behind Yaz. "Get in here," he said, glancing out the door one more time before he closed it. "What's going on? Sound like you're a rabbit with its foot caught in a trap."

He nodded, breathing hard and gripping Dean's shoulder. "Something like that. Addy," he said, spinning, "and Jack. I'm glad you're here. Jane said you would be."

Dad paled. "Sure. Did she?"

"Yeah. Listen," Yaz said, close to panting, "I have news."

Addy wobbled to standing. "Did you run here?"

Dean appeared beside her before she'd even seen him move. One arm around her shoulder, he steadied her.

Yasuo nodded. "Is that water?" he asked, pointing to the pitcher on the table. "Can I get some?"

Dad served him one, which he drank in one swallow.

While he drank, Addy's stomach crept up near her heart and tried to squeeze her throat closed. "Tell me what's going on. One of you." She glared at both Yaz and her dad.

Dad crossed his arms. "Yasuo," he said, angling his chin, "why don't you start."

He swallowed. "I think I was followed here."

She dragged Dean to the door and flung it wide. "Come out, you asshole! I'm sick of this shit!"

"Addy," Yaz begged, grasping her arm, "stop, please. There's more."

Glaring into the dark, she frowned. "What?"

"I," he began, glancing outside.

His nervous eyes jangled Addy's nerves. "This isn't like you," she said, leaning close. She lowered her voice. "What the hell, man?"

"Renzo got us on the radio just a bit ago," he blurted, eyes shifting. He squeezed her arm tighter. "The horde is coming."

A bush out front rustled with a soft clatter. A sharp intake of breath, all but inaudible, accompanied it.

Without a word, they all rushed into the yard. Addy snatched her staff from beside the door, quick-limped down the stairs, and wobbled toward the street as the guys surrounded the bush.

"Whoever you are," she called, "you've been following us for weeks. Might as well come out and say hi." She stood, as steady as she could, and planted her feet. "We know you're there. Just come on out. We'll talk. That's all."

"Hey!" Dean shouted, falling into a bush. "You son of a bitch, get back here. Addy, he's coming your way."

Just as she glanced in his direction, a shape burst from the hedges. Head lowered, he charged her. No doubt hoping to knock over the weak target and get away before the rest of them could stop him.

Breathing deep into her stomach, she glared as he rushed closer. Time slowed to a crawl. And when it seemed like he was too close, she stuck her staff straight out and directly into his solar plexus.

But rather than the stopping blow she'd expected, he bounced sideways at the last moment. Though his breath woofed out in a cloud, he grabbed the staff and her shoulder, pulling her down with him.

Snatching at his leg on the way down, she clutched the pants leg around his knee. She twisted and jerked.

He landed on her head.

She grabbed whatever she could reach and ended up with a fistful of hair.

A sharp exhale blasted her in the face.

She already had a pretty good idea who it was before Dad tackled him, forcing him onto his back.

Arm across the spy's throat, Jack pulled his head back to get a look at him. He scoffed.

Addy leaned up onto an elbow, asphalt grinding into the bone, and confirmed her suspicions.

"I can explain," Matt said.

CHAPTER 29

"So," Addy said, throwing Matt into a chair in her kitchen, "spill."

She, Jack, Dean, and Yaz leaned in a circle around the table. Glaring.

Staring up at the four of them, Matt licked his lips. "It's not what you think."

Addy slapped the table. "What is it we think, Matt?"

"You think I'm spying on you for the company." His wide, blue eyes stared up at them all.

Clenching her teeth, Addy grabbed the chair in front of her. It squealed across the linoleum, and she sat, hard. The chair rocked, and she threw her hands out.

Matt snatched one and pulled her down before she teetered over.

Yanking her hand from his grasp, she lifted her upper lip. "Don't. Just explain. You've got thirty seconds."

Lowering his head, he shook it back and forth like a pendulum. "It'll take longer than that." He glanced at her. "I've been dying to ask you a question, though."

"We ask the questions here, Matt," Jack said, looming over him. "I don't think you understand the predicament you're in."

He nodded. "No, I get it. I get it, Jack," he said, holding a hand up. "But look. It's complicated, OK? Just one question, please."

Dad leaned into his face and pointed his index finger at the ceiling. "One. One question."

Matt swallowed, the click in his throat audible. "I have a friend. I haven't heard from him since last year. I knew you guys' names because when you were coming east, I'd get radio reports from him, and I want to find out what happened to him."

Addy wrinkled her brow. "Reports? Like he worked for IRF too, or?"

Dad followed her question with another before Matt could answer. "Your friend? Who?"

It must have hit Dad at the same time it hit her because they spoke in unison. "Tim."

Matt flinched. "What happened to him?"

Dean sat across from Addy with a boneless thump. "You're kidding me."

His eyes darting between them all, Matt repeated his question.

"Ask Melinda," Dad said, voice gruff. He took the seat across from him and folded his arms on the table. "Think you want to tell us how you knew him?"

"I've known Tim for years," Matt said. He frowned. "Years. He was always kind of a dickhead, but—"

Addy snorted. "Yeah. You knew him."

The edge of a grin lifted Matt's mouth, one deep smile line next to it. "Addy, honey, it's a hell of a long story."

"Hey," Dean said, pointing, "you don't call her that."

"Sorry," Matt said, lifting a hand, "sorry. I didn't mean anything, Dean. I just—"

Jack sat. "Why don't you tell us, we've got time." He leaned on his elbows.

Glancing around the kitchen, Matt lowered his voice. "You guys destroyed all the mics, right?"

"How'd you know that?" Yaz asked.

With a start, Addy twisted around. He'd gotten so quiet she forgot he was there.

He stood, back in the corner between the cupboards and the wall, arms crossed. Eyes closed. "Let's find out what he knows." He lifted his lids and pinned his eyes to Addy. "Don't forget about the horde."

Stomach back-flipping, she nodded. "Hard to forget, Yaz."

Yasuo closed his eyes again and leaned his head against the wall.

"The microphones," Matt repeated.

"Yeah yeah, we got em all," Dean said, leaning back in his chair, green eyes flashing. "Talk."

CHAPTER 30

"Hey, little guy, I see you under there," the woman said, leaning down into the crawlspace and blocking out the sun with her head. "It's OK. You can come out now."

Hesitating, Matt brushed dirt off his eyelids. Sucking more dirt up his nose, he sneezed.

She stood. "Bless you." Her extended hand outlined in the sun, she curled her fingers.

He crept through the dirt. The crawlspace below this house had made a good refuge for the past couple days while the latest horde passed. The downside was, he'd lost his gang. They always scattered for big hordes. The better you were at either running or hiding, the longer you survived. He'd find them again.

He wiggled through the door and stood, brushing the dirt off him and the cobwebs out of his hair.

She held out a canteen.

He snatched it, spinning the lid off and downing the whole thing in three big gulps.

She chuckled. "Better watch it. You'll get stomach cramps like that."

"Thanks." He handed it back to her.

Her hand landed on his shoulder and gripped it. Stopped him before he started. "Hold up a sec."

The fingers gripping him didn't dig in, but they also didn't let him go.

Heart racing, he glared. There could be all kinds of reasons for adults to want a kid like him around. Not the least of which was fodder for the 'Heads. A kind of last-ditch escape plan. He'd seen it before. "What do you want, lady?"

Releasing his shoulder, she stuck out a hand. "Melinda Thibodeaux, at your service." Her brown eyes, tinged with green and sparkling into hazel, smiled.

Without thought, he gripped her hand. "Matt."

She shook. "Matt. Got a last name, Matt? Is that short for Matthew?"

"Lyburn. Yeah. Call me Matt." He pulled on his arm, but she didn't release his hand.

Just continued to shake it.

"Lovely to meet you. What are you, Matt, fifteen?"

Standing to his full height, puffing out his chest, he grinned. "No, ma'am. I'm just thirteen."

"Oh," she said, frowning. "I guess, if she's still alive, my daughter is about your age." She put her hands on her hips. "I wish I could remember what happened to her."

"You don't know?"

She lifted her face, smiling, and clapped him on the shoulder. "Why don't you come with us?"

His nerves told him to run. But she had cool water and a nice smile. What if she had food? It'd been almost a week since he ate. He shuffled a foot and looked over her shoulder.

"My truck is just around the corner."

Glancing up at the house, all its windows broken, its doors off their hinges, he considered the rest of the gang. They'd leave him behind for a pack of smokes and a loaf of bread.

He followed her around the side of the house.

A pickup truck waited, one kid already seated in the bed.

"Go on, climb up there." She pointed into the truck. "We'll take you home. Here." She held out a piece of what looked like beef but dried.

Taking it from her, he sniffed it.

Yeah, it was dried beef alright. His mouth watered. He bit into it and climbed into the truck without another thought.

The other kid grinned at him and took a bite of his own dried beef. "Pretty sweet, huh?" His long, scruffy curls bounced in the breeze.

Sitting next to him, Matt grinned back. Without answering, he took another bite and chewed, staring back at the house.

At least one of the guys had been trapped in there when the horde came. From the closed-up crawl space, breathing shallow, Matt could hear the kid screaming. Screaming for someone to save him. Eventually crying for his mommy.

If he remembered right, that kid made it less than six months without his parents.

Seemed there was no substitute for being smart. And lucky.

Matt glanced into the cab, stomach churning. "Hey man—"

"Tim."

"Tim. Do you think these people are OK?"

Tim chuckled. "Does it matter?"

Matt scooted toward the tailgate, watching the shadow in the front. "Yeah. Yeah, it matters. I think maybe I'll go."

The engine started.

Melinda walked around the side of the truck and lifted the tailgate, paying no mind to Matt trying to slide out.

"Hey," he said, "I think I'll take my chances."

She pushed the tailgate closed against his weight like he was nothing—man, she was strong—and grabbed him by the collar. She pushed him back into the bed, not unkindly, but with enough force to glue his ass to the metal. "Matt. It's OK. Promise." Swinging her hips as she walked to the door of the truck, she grinned over her shoulder. "We'll take care of you, alright?"

After she hopped in, they rode over backcountry dirt roads and tiny two-lane blacktop for the better part of an hour. A time or two, they passed lone stragglers in the woods, 'Heads who had gotten separated from the horde.

How did they know to stay in packs, anyway?

After riding for forever, they finally crossed through two chain-link fences, each surrounded on either side and topped with bales and bales of razor wire. Floodlights mounted at each and every corner of each and every fence.

"I've never seen fences like this, man," Matt said, leaning over to whisper as they parked next to a hill.

Tim shook his head, eyes wide. "Me neither."

The truck stopped, electric engine whine dying. Melinda stepped out and opened the tailgate. "Sorry, it's just you two and not more of your friends. But you're here now, so let's get you some clothes and beds." Sweeping an arm toward the hill, she smiled. One side of her mouth raised higher than the other. Eyes warm.

Matt slid out of the truck, Tim behind him. Walking close together, they followed Melinda to the hill.

As he looked around the enclosed yard, Matt's scalp tightened. Even if he wanted to escape whatever it was she was leading him to, he couldn't. There was no way out of this place.

She reached into the hill and opened a door set so far back it was hard to see in the gloom. "Gentlemen," she said, "welcome to the Molehill."

* * *

"Wait," Addy said, lifting a hand. "Are you trying to tell us you've been there? To the hospital where Mom woke up?"

Matt nodded, lines digging deep into his cheeks. "That's what I'm telling you. I grew up there, Addy."

Huffing out a breath, Addy sat back and glanced at her dad. "What do we do?"

He shook his head. "Let's finish the story," he said, blue eyes narrowed, "then decide."

"Make it good," Dean said.

* * *

Tim was in charge from the beginning. He always stood next to Melinda, looking over her shoulder at her papers when he could. As she collected young kids, he'd tell them how to address her and where to find towels and bedsheets and underwear. As she took him under her wing, so he took a few kids under his.

Then there were the younger ones, a small handful, no more than five or six years old. Melinda watched over them like they were her own babies.

Sometimes Matt thought about her saying she had a little girl his age. He wondered if she was alive. What had happened to her. Where she had gone.

Some of the kids took to calling Melinda "Mom," which she didn't seem to mind.

Years passed like that. Running up and down the subterranean halls. Playing games with the kids, learning to hit targets with a rifle. He'd lost his gang but found a new one, and Melinda was the head of it.

And it was OK.

The whole time, Tim stayed glued to her side as much as he could. He looked at her like some kind of goddess, eyes shining and wide, and as they grew older and Matt started to notice some of the girls they lived with, he also noticed Tim. Noticing Melinda.

Who, by this point, had become a colonel, in charge of an entire platoon of young people. Completely and totally loyal people. If she snapped her fingers, they'd follow any direction. Do anything she asked.

Matt had been called to her office one day when he was just barely eighteen.

"Matt," she said, motioning him to a seat across her desk, "thank you for coming." She offered him a piece of beef jerky.

It'd always been his favorite.

"I've got something very special I need you and Tim to do," she said, waving a hand.

The light from the door dimmed, and Tim walked through. He took the seat next to Matt.

Folding her arms on the desk, Melinda leaned forward. "Look. I'm being sent to the coast. They're making me a general and giving me my own hospital."

Tim sat forward. "That's amazing, general, ma'am! When do we leave?"

She shook her head.

The floor spun under Matt. She'd been the leader of his gang for years, and now she was leaving. And not taking them with her.

Abandoning them.

He looked around, but there were no crawlspaces to escape to. There was nowhere.

"Timothy, I need you, and Matt here, to help me with something far more important than the hospital."

"What could be more important?" Matt asked, voice flat. It didn't matter.

"I've remembered things. My family, for a start. I think they're still out there. I need you to help me find them."

Tim stood, chair flying. He slammed both hands on the desk. "I'm coming with you."

She smiled, eyeing Matt. "I want you, sweet, quiet boy, you and your mistrust. I want you to spy on our competitor. They're called Iridium Flare, and I'm sending you to California to hook up with them. Let them take you where they will, and I'll give you instructions on how and when to contact us." Standing, she held her arms out.

Stomach churning, the jerky sitting heavy at the bottom of it, he hugged her. "Will you find me again?"

Petting the back of his head, she pushed him back and nodded. "I'll never be far, sweetie."

* * *

"When I left, Tim was still arguing with her. Eventually, I heard she gave in, and he went with her to the new hospital for a few years. Then he left, and the next time I heard from him, he was on his way east with you guys." He glanced around the table. "IRF had been looking for a way to infiltrate Shanti Station. Burke was ecstatic about the chance."

Dean cleared his throat. "How'd you get hooked up with Burke and Ella?"

Matt shook his head. "I think that's a different story for a different time."

"You and Tim, huh?" Jack leaned back in his chair. "Best buds."

Addy sat and tapped her foot, chewing her lip. "Tim said he'd been working for IRF too. I didn't know what to believe, and I'm not sure I do now. Matt," she said, leaning forward and gripping his arm, "whose side are you really on?"

From under heavy lids, he frowned. "I don't know if you're going to believe this, Addy," he said, laying a hand over hers, "but I'm on nobody's side but my own."

Dean scoffed. "Yeah. That and a nickel will buy you a cup of coffee."

Jack laughed.

Brows knitted, Addy removed her hand from Matt's arm. "Whatever that means." She frowned and caught his eyes. "I don't believe you. Prove it."

He nodded. "You got it."

CHAPTER 31

Jack shook his head, hand to his mouth.

"What is it, Dad?"

His little girl, leaned forward in her chair, stared with her wide brownzel eyes.

He shook his head again, swallowing around the lump in his throat. He'd never really slowed down to think about what it must have been like for Melinda after she was cured. What could possibly have happened to the woman he knew that could have made her into the woman she was now.

"If what Matt here is saying is true, there's a lot of things we need to think about, baby girl."

"Such as?"

Dean shifted in his chair. "Anyone could be hers. Absolutely anyone." He glanced at Jack. "That's what you're thinking, isn't it?"

"One of the things," Jack said, nodding. "But that's not all. It's just the tip of the iceberg." He crossed his arms as Dean stood and paced.

Pulling a breath over his teeth, Jack glanced at Matt. "We have to assume she's prepared for us to find this out. Matt, I don't think you're safe."

The boy tensed to stand.

Dean appeared behind him so fast it was as though he'd been there all along. He laid a hand down on his shoulder. "Nope."

Glancing up, Matt frowned. Brow creased, he shrugged. "I can handle myself, guys. I've been doing it for as long as I can remember."

"One gang to another," Jack said. "Only this one has taken far better care of you. No," he said, shaking his head, "not only are you not safe from her, I can't trust you."

"Dad," Addy began.

"No, little girl. I don't know what he could say or do to make me trust him." Inhaling, he covered his eyes. "Not after the way Melinda corrupted your brother in so short a period."

"So you've given up on Mike," Addy said. Not a question. A softly spoken statement.

He sighed. Hadn't Mike given up on him first? Hadn't he been the one to desert them? What else could he possibly take it for?

And still.

"I'd never give up on either of you, Adelaide," he said, reaching across the table. Grabbing her hand, he squeezed. "Never. You get me?"

She nodded, eyes fixed on a point in the center of the table. As she blinked, tears splashed onto its surface. "I don't know what to do about any of this."

"Don't forget the horde," Yasuo said.

A truckload of bricks backed in and began dumping onto Jack's spine. As if what Melinda was doing with two of his children behind those walls, in that hospital, wasn't enough, there was a horde coming.

Backed by some very angry people.

Addy's head hit the table. Sobbing, her back shook.

Before Jack could move to stand, Dean knelt next to her. Wrapping his arms around her, he leaned his forehead to hers and closed his eyes.

It both filled Jack's heart and broke it, to see someone be such a comfort to her. It'd been a long time since she'd had that from anyone but him. Even though he'd known it was going to happen one day, he saw his last chance at being her rock slip away. Before he'd been ready for it.

He stood. "Walk with me, Matt."

Leading Matt into the living room, his mind racing, he went through their next moves. "Sit." He pointed to the couch. "That horde coming complicates things. Yaz is right. We can't forget about it." He paced, hands on his hips.

"Whatever you need, let me help," Matt said. "I can be an asset. I just don't want…" Trailing off, his gaze unfocused, he stared over Jack's shoulder.

"Don't want what?"

"I don't want people hurt."

"People are going to get hurt, Matt. It's inevitable."

"Ella," Matt said, swallowing. His eyes narrowed. "I don't want Ella hurt."

Jack nodded. "Care about her, do you?"

Matt frowned, lines framing his mouth.

"We'll do our best to not hurt anyone. No one at all," Jack said.

Red light bouncing through Oren's mustache colored the inside of his eyelids.

Insides twisted, he tried to put up a wall before his mind raced on, but he was too slow.

Tell that to Andrew.

"Dammit, we need a plan." Back to Matt, he crossed his arms. "Matt, does IRF know you've been helping the people who used to live here?"

The sharp inhale from the couch told him not only did IRF not know, Matt wasn't aware anyone knew.

Glancing over his shoulder, he shrugged. "Not hard to figure out. You've been following us around since we got here. You're good at keeping quiet. Someone has been helping those people. Someone good at keeping quiet. Someone"—he turned all the way back around as a light went off in his head—"responsible for setting guard schedules. Knowing exactly where they're all going to be at all times."

Though his face rippled as he fought it, a small smile touched Matt's lips. "Does make it easier to do whatever you want."

Jack nodded. "We can use that to our advantage. I hate to trust you, and to say I do would be taking it pretty far."

"But we don't have a choice. Do we, Dad?" Her face streaked with white, dried tears, Addy stood in the door to the kitchen.

Dean behind, with his arms around her, stared at him over her shoulder. "He could be pretty helpful," he said, glancing at Matt, "if he wants to. But I don't like it, Jack."

Jack sat on the couch next to Matt and caught his eyes. "Neither do I. So let me be clear. I'm not one to beat around the bush, Matt."

Swallowing, Matt nodded.

"If I get even the slightest hint of you betraying us, I'll kill you myself."

Addy gasped.

Cutting his eyes to her, Matt grimaced. "Understood. The general has treated me better than any other gang I was ever a part of." He dropped his gaze. "But she'd still leave me for a loaf of bread and a pack of smokes if it was the *right* loaf of bread." He looked back up, eyes scanning the three of them. "I'll do whatever you ask. I'll help you. Just remember what we talked about."

"I won't forget," Jack said. He held out a hand.

Matt shook.

Calling Yasuo to the war room, they got to planning.

* * *

"Adelaide," Dean said, closing the bedroom door, "you can barely walk on that damned ankle. I'm not going to let you traipse off into the woods on some stupid mission."

She stepped to the bed, suppressing a limp. "I'm fine, see?" Standing on one foot, she tried to do tree pose.

Her ankle screamed.

Pressing her lips together, she fought a grimace and lowered her other foot with as much control as she could muster.

Arms crossed, Dean leaned against the door and frowned. "If you think you're fooling me, I don't think this relationship is going to work out."

Chuckling through clenched teeth, she sat on the bed. "Dean, I've got to go. You know it has to be me."

"No, I don't know that." He crossed to her and leaned against the bed between her knees. Grasping one shoulder in each hand, he stared down into her eyes.

From the tips of her toes to the crown of her head, she tingled. Fell into his eyes and forgot everything but his face.

The corners of his eyes crinkled. "I know I love you. That's what I know."

Fighting the urge to pull him down into a kiss and then whatever else came after, she frowned. "I have to go," she whispered, "they trust me. Some of them. It can't be anyone else. We need their help."

Before he could open his mouth to continue arguing, she did pull him into that kiss.

For a bit, legs locked behind him, she floated away from the mess this had become. The horror of what her mother and brother had turned into. The stinking horde on its way.

When he stood again, brow creased, she put a finger to his lips. "Look, you're not going to convince me not to go out there. We need these people. But at least this time you can come with me."

One side of his mouth turned up as he pushed her away from the edge of the bed and followed her onto it. "I'd like that," he said, hands sliding under her shirt.

His rough hands gripping the soft skin between her hips and her ribs, he kissed her neck until he hit the collar of her shirt. When he moved to take it off, she offered no resistance.

With their clothes littered in a pile on the floor, they slid under the sheets together, skin touching. A wave of gratitude gripped her, holding her like she'd been suspended in a pool of warm water.

No more microphones to intrude on them.

Safe under the sheets with him.

Tight in his arms, a perfect feeling of security like she hadn't felt since she was a child.

Without warning, she saw the last night she'd cuddled between her parents. The next day her mom had been gone.

She'd never returned.

Snuggling deeper into Dean's arms, into his scent, the heat of his skin, she tried to scrub her brain of the fear.

"Hey," he said, lifting her chin with a finger, "you OK?"

She nodded, kissing the soft spot under his jaw. And she got lost with him for a few minutes, in the rhythm they created, the warmth surrounding them.

But when he lay next to her again, eyes half closed, smile touching his lips, her mind spun.

"This is a terrible plan," she said, whispering in case he was asleep.

Sucking a breath in through his nose, he rolled over and stared at her. "Besides the part about you going off into the woods when we know good and damn well there's a horde coming?"

"Yeah, all of it. I think it's a mistake to trust Matt."

"We don't trust him."

"But we do, Dean," she said, turning her head. "He's as much a part of this plan as anyone. If that's not trust—"

"I won't turn my back on the guy, alright?"

Heat flushed her cheeks. Pleasant just a moment before, it tingled and pinched now. "No, it's not alright."

He sat up on an elbow. "You don't trust him. That's fine. But trust me on this. He's good people, Addy."

"Oh, good. He's a good guy because you said so. Well, that makes it all OK," she said, flipping onto her side and showing him her back.

"Addy," he said, sliding a finger down her spine. "Don't be upset. Come on. You know as well as I do, we don't have a choice."

A pleasant shiver worked its way down her spine with his finger. She buried a smile in her arm and shook him off. "I don't like it at all. And to leave him alone with Dad while we go talk to Mann…"

"Your dad can handle himself, sweetie."

"Sure." Neither agreeing nor disagreeing. But as a thought raced through, she flipped back over. "What do you think happened with him and Jane? Why is he sleeping here tonight?"

Dean shrugged. "Who knows? People get mad. People fight."

"Seems like a bad time to fight."

"My love," he said, smiling and laying his head on his arm, "you were yelling at me not two seconds ago."

"Whatever," she said, bumping him with a hip. When she went to tweak his cheek, he caught her hand and kissed her palm.

Butterflies raced through her. Pressing against him, she kissed him with all she had.

He leaned back to take a breath and grinned. "Round two?"

She did a better job forgetting the world this time.

* * *

A soft knock jolted Jack out of sleep.

Rolling from the couch, his knees the first to complain as he tottered across the room, he lifted his knife and stood just away from the door. "Yeah."

"It's Matt," he said, pitching his voice low as Jack had.

"Stand away from the door," Jack said, exhaling. They'd taken a chance letting him leave with Yasuo last night. And though Jack had no reason to trust him, he had no reason not to. Not yet.

He opened the door and checked outside.

From the corner of the yard, Yasuo waved a hand and disappeared.

Otherwise, the street stood silent as the grave. The sun hadn't yet shown its face.

Waving Matt in, he shut the door behind him and made his way back to the couch in the glow of a single lamp. "Good lord, it's early, boy."

"I thought you said—"

"Yeah, yeah," Jack said, rubbing his face. "I know what I said. Still early. I don't have a watch anymore. Jane hates them. What is it, four?"

"Yessir."

One eye popped open. "Don't sir me, Matt."

"Yessi— Um. OK."

A mix of chuckle and breath, Jack huffed through his nose and smiled with one corner of his mouth. "You're an interesting one."

In the dim light, his laugh lines ran deep beside his mouth. "Appreciate that. You and your family are, too."

Jack scoffed. "Not going to get on my good side like that," he said, standing. "But, it's a start. Let's get the coffee."

Still covered in darkness, they picked their way through light snow, stopping every few blocks for a swallow or two of coffee.

Licking his lips and handing the thermos lid to Jack, Matt frowned. "How do we even still have this?"

Knowing full well what he meant, Jack asked anyway. "Have what?"

"Coffee. I mean, I read it was pretty hard to grow. And harvest. And it only grew in certain places in the world. Shouldn't we be out of it by now?"

"So you read," Jack said, picking his way forward again. Off the sidewalk, no early risers were likely to see them, and Matt had assured him the guards were elsewhere at the moment.

"Yes, Jack, I read. Books we have plenty of."

Jack glanced over his shoulder. "You continue to be a surprise, boy."

Clearing his throat, Matt spoke in a stilted voice. "I'm the same age as your daughter, Jack. I'm not a boy."

"She's still my little girl," he said, not turning.

"Yeah, OK. But she's not a little girl. Besides, isn't Jane—"

"I get your point," Jack said, stopping. He clapped Matt on the shoulder. "You're right, Matthew. Apologies."

"I'll let it go if you stop calling me Matthew." He shuffled a foot and pointed with his forehead. "She's the only one who gets to do that."

Following his gaze, Jack found they'd stopped across from Ella's house.

Turning back to him, Jack watched Matt's face as he watched the swaying magnolia.

He'd crossed his arms, and his jaw bunched and released over and over. He took a step toward the sidewalk.

Jack laid a hand on Matt's chest. "Whoa there. No can do, not right now."

Glancing down at his hand, Matt nodded. "I know. Sorry. Just." He sighed. "I miss her."

"Don't you see her all the time?"

He shook his head. "No, man. I haven't seen her in days. All this spying on you takes up a lot of time."

Jack grimaced and wished he had time for a full report of what Matt knew.

But Matt went on. "Not to mention keeping the damned people over by the wall hidden. Most of the time, my guys follow their routes. But sometimes"—he grinned, glancing down—"when they want to do something they'd get in trouble for, well."

"Sneak a drink or a smoke?"

Matt nodded. "Sure. Then I've got to make sure they don't go somewhere they'd find all these extra people." He turned the side of his face to Jack. His lips curled in a rueful smile. "It's freaking exhausting."

"You're not alone anymore," he said, narrowing his eyes. "Why do you do it, Matt?"

"Do what?" he asked, still staring across at Ella's.

"Hide the people."

"Oh, that," he said, sliding his eyes to the side. "I don't know. I met them all, you know."

"Who?" Though he thought he knew.

"The people who used to live here. I was with the first group from IRF to come here."

"Did you help relocate them?"

Rather than answer, he stared at his feet and kicked at a root.

"You know what happened to them out there," Jack said, eyes pinned to Matt's face, waiting for his reaction.

Matt swallowed. His Adam's apple bounced three times before he spoke again, voice just above a whisper. "Yeah."

"You have a hand in that."

"I know," Matt said, voice rising. He took a step toward Jack.

Jack fought his hands. They wanted to raise. Rather than cross them and send the wrong message, he stuck them in his pockets.

Looking from his face to his lowered hands, Matt deflated. "I know," he repeated. "I wish I could fix it. I'm telling you, when we got here, I didn't know what they were planning."

Either this kid, this *man*, was a great actor, or he really didn't know. And it ate him up.

"Come on, let's get this done." Without waiting, Jack continued toward the wall.

CHAPTER 32

"Addy, I'm not going to lie," Yaz said, as he and Dean helped her through what Dean had called the Alice in Wonderland door, "I've never seen a horde that big. I stay away from the mainland most of the time because of the one there." He frowned, brushing a leaf from her hair. "Not everyone was so lucky."

"Someone you knew?" She wobbled, throwing a hand out.

Dean caught it before she wobbled back the other way.

Frowning, Yasuo planted his staff. "Which way are we going?"

Addy lifted her eyebrows at Dean. "Directions?"

"Well, we know Renzo was on the radio," he said, pointing into the hills. "I think our best option is to try and find him, get whatever intel he's got about the horde and about the Magnolia people, and see what shakes loose."

With a nod, Addy leaned on her own staff. Tested the ankle.

It held, and as the morning let go of the scent of darkness and invited the light into the naked branches, they made their way up the hill. The snow hadn't touched too much of the space beneath the trees, and Addy skimmed across the frozen ground as best she could. Dean told her the cabin was probably about seven miles, but it seemed like so many more. So many.

She couldn't smell the horde. Not yet. But as the morning wore on, the air changed. Some sort of heaviness lay on it, not unlike fog. She pulled each breath in with effort.

"You guys feel that?" she asked, closing her eyes and sniffing.

"Feel what?" Yasuo asked, staff lifted. He glanced around.

"Yasuo," she said, peeking from under a lid, "I can't handle you all nervous. It's not good for my calm."

Yaz took a breath, puffed out his stomach, and exhaled between tight lips. "Sorry, Addy. I don't know why I'm letting it get to me like this." He chuckled. "Been a long time since anything has."

Dean shook his head. "It's a lot of 'Heads, Yaz. Addy told me about the size of it. It's probably something like none of us have ever seen." Licking his lips, he met Addy's eyes. "It's alright to be scared."

One side of her mouth lifted. "Sure. If you're a bitch," she said, spiking her staff into the ground and moving off before either of them could disagree.

Sticks breaking behind her, she stayed ahead of them for as long as she could. With her ankle hobbled, it wasn't long.

"Adelaide," Dean said, one hand on the small of her back, "you're going the wrong way."

Rolling her eyes, she stopped. "I knew that."

He grinned. "Mm-hmm. Sure. This way, sweetie," he said, pointing over her left shoulder.

After what probably could have taken them half the time if she wasn't broken, they found the cabin. Sitting in the woods, no driveway, no old power lines, no nothing.

Addy led them in. "Ever wonder who this belonged to before?"

"No," Dean said, waving Yaz in and closing the door. "Does it matter?"

Addy shrugged and took a seat on the bed.

Dad had mentioned the place, that they'd been staying there on and off while surveilling the settlement, but he hadn't said much about it. Not that it mattered, but now that she was here, it felt…cozy. One small cupboard crouched under the sink. Must've been dishes or something in there, because there were none on the counters. A couple pans hung up over the stove, an old woodburning thing. Something she could really get behind, burning wood for fuel.

Swinging her feet, she sighed. "Where's the radio, Dean?"

"Here," he said, approaching the bed. He leaned over her and reached above her head, his shirt hiking up and exposing the skin between shirt and pants.

Reluctant to move her eyes, she looked up.

Fumbling against the wall, he pushed a piece of the paneling that looked no different than any of the rest of it. But this piece slid over, not unlike the hidden door in her bookshelf back in Emerald Hills. Magnolia. Whatever it was.

He slid the radio out. "Can't just leave it lying around. Never know who might come by."

"Uh, Dean," Yaz said, from the window where he stared into the midday woods, "I hate to point out the foolishness of this plan, but do you have more than two radios?"

Dean smiled and sat next to Addy, the bed depressing and rolling her into his leg.

"No, we don't, Yaz. But we do have this," he said, flipping the radio over. A screw held the battery compartment closed. From his belt, he freed a small tool and flipped it open. An assortment of screwdrivers and knives nestled themselves inside the handle. Picking a screwdriver head, he spun the screw off the radio and bumped Addy's arm.

She stuck out a hand, and he dropped the screw into it.

"I was about to make a screw joke, but we've got company," he said, voice low.

"Yeah, I can still hear you," Yaz said. His voice bounced off the window where his breath fogged the glass.

Smiling, eyes crinkled—god how she'd missed that while he was in jail—Dean pulled the battery door off the back.

A small, folded piece of paper nestled between the batteries and the wall of the compartment. It wouldn't interfere with the operation of the radio, and it was only something you'd find if you were looking for it. Or changing the batteries.

Either way, Dean plucked the note free and unfolded it. "Ah, see," he said, pointing, "he's left us a map."

On silent feet, Yasuo left his vigil at the window and crept across the room. "What sort of map?"

Renzo had drawn it himself, or at least someone had drawn it by hand, and it showed a rough illustration of the cabin, the woods surrounding it, and at the very edge, it said "MAGNOLIA." A green circle between the cabin and Magnolia bore the label "US."

She grinned. Data was somewhere in that "us" circle. And the little girl he'd grown attached to.

Dean's finger moved over the map.

She followed it, brain shuttering after his fingernail bumped over the crease running across the cabin and down the hill behind it.

Dean breathed shallow.

Wobbling, Yaz sat on the bed.

Though Addy had seen the horde already, it was a new thing altogether to see the red circle envelop the rest of the map.

In large, bold, black letters, the circle was filled with "HEADS."

* * *

Creeping through the streets, out onto the icy sidewalks, Jack and Matt picked their way toward the house where Jack had left Ric. He stopped two blocks away and pointed to a side yard. "In there."

Following his finger, Matt slipped next to the house and crouched beside the lower split-level window. A scruffy evergreen bush covered it. "This where they are? I thought—"

"No. You're not coming with me to the house," Jack said. "You stay here. I'll circle back soon." Glancing into the silent street, sunlight beginning to brush against the upper shingles of the houses, he stepped out.

"At least give me a weapon," Matt said. He lowered his voice to a fierce whisper. "I'm naked out here, man."

On one slow heel, Jack turned. "I don't. I'm not. Let me back up. Do you know what your friend Tim was up to? With us?"

He shook his head. "I didn't even know who you were until after you showed up here."

Jack chuckled. "For someone so well informed, you're going to have to do a better job convincing me of that one." Covering his mouth, he laughed again. "Really. What a whopper. Wanna try again?"

"I really didn't, Jack. I mean, I knew your names. Tim told me about you, like I said. But I didn't know *who* you were. Not until I really got a look at Addy." He smiled, one corner of his mouth turned down. "She really looks a lot like your wife."

"Do I have to get papers or something? Ex-wife, Matt. Ex."

Shrugging, Matt sat back on his heels. "Sorry. Besides the daughter she mentioned, I didn't even know she had a family until the day she sent me away. I thought we were her family."

Jack crossed his arms. "I'm starting to think she doesn't have any family. Not anymore. Just people she uses to get what she wants."

"Was she always like that?"

Head snapping up, Jack frowned. "Of course not. The woman I knew was kind and warm. Sure, she had a cold streak. She got what she wanted. There was no arguing with that. She always got what she wanted." He stopped, casting memory back to that bowling alley when he'd walked in and laid eyes on her for the first time. Pink neon from the bar glowing in her hair.

She'd pinned her eyes to him, marked him as her own, and pursued nothing but him until she'd won.

His mouth turned up in something like a grin. "I spent so long making those memories of her perfect, maybe I forgot a few things. But she had warmth. It's something she's missing now." He shook his head, clearing the memories like cobwebs. "No weapons, Matt. You plant your ass," he said, pointing at the ground, "and be here when we come back."

"Yes, sir," Matt said, sitting. He cocked a leg out and leaned against the house, half-behind the bush. "Sorry. Yes, Jack. 10-4."

Jack checked the street again.

Still clear.

Heading down the street alone, he crouched across from the house and watched. The rising sun melted snow still trapped on the rooftops. Slow, cold droplets slipped into the gutters. Nothing else moved.

He snuck in the back door. Creaking down the hallway, he Listened as the rest of the house woke with the sun. Old wood stretched and whispered. Dust danced in the shafts of light falling through the windows. And a low murmur that could have been water dripping off the roof but came from the basement below his feet.

He descended the basement stairs in darkness. Last time he'd been here, Paul led him down these stairs with confidence. Though it was close, and dank, and quickly became the kind of darkness that swallowed you whole before you could reason with yourself that it was just a basement, his nerves hadn't buzzed like they were now. They hadn't screamed at him to take a deep breath, hold it, and run for the top of the stairs. Burst out of the staircase like a moth emerging from its cocoon. Run down the hallway and escape. And never come back.

Not that they said anything like that this time. Not at all.

He crept into the inky basement where the west-facing, ground-level windows sat dark. The barest hint of sunlight on the grass outside had not yet permeated this room. Crossing, stepping neither quick nor slow, he tapped twice on the inner door.

The movement behind the door had been all but inaudible until it stopped. Then it sounded like elephants standing on cotton balls. There but not there.

"Yeah," someone whispered.

"It's Jack," he said, raising his voice through the door.

"Mr. C.," Ric said, opening the door, "it's early. Everything OK?" Bruises marked his neck and the side of his face. Undoubtedly where he'd tried to escape the mini-horde that had gotten Oren.

Behind him, Celia and Paul stood. They'd agreed to spend the night with Ric, make sure he was alright.

Jack stepped in and closed the door, glancing at the half dozen people also crammed into the room. "Listen, guys. We have a plan. It's time for me to ask for that help you offered."

CHAPTER 33

Hidden in the frosty evergreen bushes across from the jail, Matt leaned into Jack's ear. "We can't get the whole town in there, Jack."

He nodded. "I know it. But we can get what, three-quarters of them in there?"

"Crammed in like sardines, sure."

"It's a start, then. We'll find a place for the rest of them. Ric is scouting the city, trying to find a good spot. A warehouse. Apartments. Anything. Somewhere we can keep them safe. Just in case."

"In case the horde gets in, you mean, don't cha friend Jack?"

"That's what I mean, Paul," Jack said, frowning at him. "Addy's trying to keep them out. But with a horde this size, it's best to plan for the worst."

"Those people have never seen a single 'Head, Jack. They don't even carry weapons," Matt said, narrowing his eyes. "They're like fluffy baby sheep."

Celia snorted. "You got that right. Lily-white baby sheep."

"Cee," Paul said, "what did we talk about?"

"Don't want to hear it, old man. Not now."

"Keep it down, guys," Jack said, looking back at the jail. "First thing's first. We have to get the guards off the streets. Melinda gets wind of this, we're crashed before we begin. Let's go." He crouched and slipped from cover.

The rest followed, and he angled off to the side of the building before the camera on the front door could catch him in its glassy gaze. "Matt," he whispered, angling his chin, "get us in there."

As per their plan, Celia clasped her hands behind her back and let Matt take her upper arm. The two of them approached the door as guard and prisoner.

Unease bubbled up in Jack, starting at his toes. Like he was a pitcher of cool water, being filled with a trickle of electricity.

Like when he'd been hit with that stun gun and his muscles had locked up. Only much slower.

The door buzzed to let Matt open it.

First thing Matt and Celia had to do was take care of the men inside. Matt had assured them there'd be four at the most. Given their guard would be down, and the fact Celia was practically a one-woman army, four should be easy. Round them into a cell and go from there. Two by two, Matt would bring the rest of the guards in from patrol with some bogus call. Put them up in Club Med and repeat. Matt explained there was a squadron at the hospital, inside the barrier wall, but there was nothing they could do about them. Getting the rest of the guards would have to do, for now.

"You alright, friend Jack?"

"Sure. Tough couple days, Paul," he said, crouching next to the building. Leaning in the cool shade, he rested the back of his head on the wall.

"Rough couple days, huh," Paul said, leaning against the wall next to him. "Anything you want to talk about?"

Shaking his head, scraping the back against the bare brick, Jack closed his eyes. "Not really."

"Where's Jane, Jack?"

His eyes popped open. "Don't beat around the bush, do you?"

Paul chuckled. "Ain't got time for any of that, no."

Heart racing, Jack looked down at his hands. Picked at a nail. Made an attempt to squash the butterflies fighting inside. "I'd guess she's at home. But she might also be gone. I don't know."

"What do you mean, you don't know?"

Good old guilt, coming to lay its blanket across his heart and lungs, put up its feet for an extended stay. Maybe he ought to start charging rent.

Swallowing, he explained the awful things he'd said to her.

The blame he'd tried to lay at her feet.

"I don't know," he finished, "maybe she and I aren't such a great idea." He leaned his head back again, but rather than close his eyes, he stared at Paul through slitted eyelids.

This would be the part where his dad would break out some weed and tea and try to Zen it all away.

Paul stared into the distance. "You ever lose a child before, Jack?"

"No."

The elder man exhaled a laugh. "Lucky."

"Yeah. I know."

"You don't know," Paul said, turning to him and spitting venom. "You don't." His mouth twisted into a cruel bow. "And that woman you got, she's the only one who you can lean on right now. You're the only one she can lean on. You both lost that baby."

Warmth blossomed in Jack's midsection like a horse had kicked him in the torso.

And for no reason at all, he remembered both Ger and Liz had lost their kids early on.

God, no wonder she'd connected with Ger. Jack was clueless. Had no idea what it felt like to lose a baby to the world.

Now here he was, pushing away the one person who knew just what he was feeling. Which she had tried to tell him, and instead, he'd pushed Mike off onto her.

"Fuck's sake. I'm an idiot," he said, frowning.

"No kidding," Paul said, leaning an arm over his knee and grinning. "No one ever questioned that."

Jack laughed. "Watch it, old man. I can still kick your ass."

"Like to see you try."

"Hey," Matt whispered over the intercom, "door's open. Let's do this."

Jack moved to stand, but Paul caught his arm. "You fought for her before," he said. "I remember. You drowned yourself to save her. You gotta fight again, alright? But this time, it might not be so easy."

"That wasn't—"

"Listen to me, son. Don't interrupt."

Jack zipped it.

"There ain't a lot of women like her," Paul said, smiling into the distance. "We all only get so many chances. I reckon you know that by now."

Jack nodded, but Paul continued staring into the distance. He was looking at something only he could see.

"You can't let her go. Not if you can help it." Glancing at Jack, he narrowed his eyes and returned from wherever he'd gone. He gripped Jack's collar. "You hear me, boy? Don't make my mistakes."

Though the question came to his lips, Jack didn't ask it. Now was not the time for questions. "Yes, sir."

"Don't sir me," Paul said, releasing Jack's collar and smoothing his shirt. "Just you remember to be grateful for what you got."

"I will. I am." Standing, he held a hand out.

Paul took it, putting most of his weight in Jack's arm to pull himself up. "Forgive me, friend Jack. Old knees. Old heart. I get a little melancholy sometimes."

"It's forgotten," Jack said. "Let's go."

Easing to the door, Jack didn't jump this time when it buzzed to admit them.

* * *

Addy stopped, hand on Dean's shoulder. "Is that them, up there?"

"I don't see anything, sweetie," Dean said, squinting into the trees.

A bird called.

Odd, considering most of them had gone south for the winter.

Glancing at her, eyes crinkled just a bit, he called back.

Renzo stepped around a tree fifty feet away, naked branches between them shifting shadows across his face. He picked his way to them.

Nodding to Dean and Yaz, he knelt in front of Addy, where she'd taken a seat. The ankle was not getting better after walking about ten miles on it. Why did she have to jump out of that damned tree?

"You alright?"

"I'll be fine. What do you have for us, Zo?"

Eyes bouncing back and forth, he leaned close. "These people, they're not sure what to do. They're scared of the horde—"

"Who's not," Yaz interrupted.

Renzo frowned. "Right. But they're leading it anyway, because Mann says so." He shook his head. "I don't think most of them want to do this, but they don't see what choice they've got."

Addy smiled, corners of her mouth turned down. "Perfect. That's perfect, Renzo. Can you bring some of them here? Maybe the girl, too?"

Dean side-eyed her.

"What? I want to see my dog."

"Let me round them up, Addy. I'll be back."

Dean stood. "I'll come with you."

Addy's stomach flipped. Not that she couldn't handle some 'Heads if they came, and Yaz was still here, but having lost him to the jail for so long, she hated letting him out of her sight.

Renzo held up a hand. "I'd love to have the help. But Mann is observant. She sees someone wandering around she doesn't know, it could cause all kinds of hell. No, let me do it. You guys hang tight."

"Whatever you say," Dean said, sitting next to her.

She leaned on him. Breathed deep. He smelled of the woods and the dust in the homey cabin. Cold seeping from the ground through the ass of her pants, she shivered.

He put an arm around her and rubbed her arm. "We gotta get you out of these cold woods," he said. "Keep you off that ankle."

"I'm a big girl, Dean," she said, frowning yet snuggling closer. "I'll be fine."

"None of us should be out here," Yaz said.

"What was that you told me last summer? There are no accidents? We're right where we're supposed to be, Yaz," she said, closing her eyes. "The people Renzo's bringing back can help. Maybe divert the horde. Maybe at least buy us some time to get everyone safe."

Time they needed to rescue her new sister. And her brother.

Yasuo huffed out a breath. "Turning my own words against me. The pupil becoming the teacher, I see."

"No, just reminding you what you already said."

Leaves crunched, and Yaz sat on the other side of Dean. His face pinched in on itself, high brow sweaty even in the cold.

"Yasuo," she said, sitting up, "anything you want to talk about?"

He shook his head. "We've all got dead people, Addy. There's nothing to talk about."

"Doesn't seem that way," Dean said. "But if you don't want to talk about it, I get it. I do." He clapped a hand on Yaz's knee. "If Cameron were here, he'd make you talk about it, though. Tell you it really does help."

Frowning, Yaz lowered his head. "That mainland horde ate my parents. No big deal, OK?"

And though Addy had nothing to do with the horde directly, guilt still threw a party whenever anyone mentioned something for which her mother had been responsible. Because apparently guilt didn't need an invitation to come over.

"Hordes aren't really anyone's thing," she said, instead of the 'I'm sorry' that wanted to pop out. "Pretty sure most of us have a story or two."

"Exactly. We've all got dead people," Yaz said, staring at her from beneath his brow.

"Doesn't make them any less important," Dean said, wrapping both arms around Addy. "It's OK to miss them."

Trying on a smile, dimples appearing in his cheeks, Yaz nodded. "Anyway. I don't want that to be the story for those people in the city."

"Yasuo, I think I can get the horde diverted," Addy said, sitting up straighter. Saying it out loud helped it to be true. Solidified her belief in the allies they'd made among these people. "If nothing else, I can get them to help. Get them to come over the wall before the horde gets there, help us get into the hospital. Help us evacuate everyone. We can all get out together."

The plan they'd cooked up with Dad seemed so impossible then. But now, hearing the words come from her own mouth, watching Renzo return with a whole group of people—Mason and Data and Dora among them—made the whole thing so much more likely.

"IRF got them there, they can get them out," Dean agreed. "Might need helicopters or something, but I bet Burke can get it."

"We need to get into the hospital," Addy said. "Get Burke to listen. He needs to know about the horde. And…" she stopped, staring off through the trees and watching Renzo get closer with her dog.

"And what, Adelaide?" Yaz asked.

She focused on him again. "And he needs to know about my mother. What she's done, what she's capable of doing."

Dean rubbed her arm. "You think it'll be enough?"

"If we can't get that horde turned, it'll have to be."

* * *

Addy sagged against Dean's side. "I don't think I can climb that wall again."

"Don't," he said, kissing her on the cheek. "I'll go over. Get the Alice door open. You wait outside of it." Disentangling his arm, he steadied her, kissed her, and started to climb.

Turning her face up to watch him climb, she frowned. Stomach in knots. What if he went over that wall and never came back? "Dean," she called.

He stopped, peeking under an arm to smile down at her. "Addy."

"Be careful, alright?"

Raising one hand above the other, he grabbed the next handhold and began climbing again. "You got it."

Yaz helped her around to the Alice door. "You seem a little nervous about leaving him."

"How could you tell?"

"My finely tuned sixth sense."

She nodded, grinning. "It's been a long year." Eyes on the door, she sat with her back against a tree. Poking at the ground with her staff, she stirred brown leaves with snow. Soggy, they didn't break. Just turned into some kind of dead paste. "This time last year, Jane and I were talking about getting our own place." Her smile turned down, something inside shriveling. "I don't think I apologized to her properly, Yaz."

"You know what we said about living amends. Sometimes you can't just say sorry."

"Yeah, I fucked that up, too."

Ella's shout at her retreating back echoed in her head.

She swallowed, dry eyes prickling with heat. "I feel like Dean is the only thing that's going right. And I keep feeling like I'm going to lose him, too."

"Adelaide, he'd sooner take a bullet than leave you. Haven't you seen the way he looks at you?"

Flushing, cheeks burning, she peeked at him through the side of her eye. "That's what I'm afraid of."

"Do something for me, Addy."

"What?"

"Pick a time, every night, when you think about what happened throughout the day."

Chuckling, she sighed. Swiped at her freezing wet eyelashes. "Think about what? All the shit I fucked up?"

"And all the stuff you did right. Don't forget about that."

She laughed.

Yaz smiled. "Remember about the control thing. We can't stop that bullet. All we can do is choose our reaction to it. And you don't always do it wrong."

"I don't always do it right either," she said, snuffling.

The door opened, Dean on the other side.

Yaz didn't move. "Just think about it, OK? Every day. What you can do better next time, and what you did better already."

"Made you forget about that horde, didn't I?" she asked, winking. She crawled through the door. Standing in the garden beyond it and waiting on Yaz, she brushed the knees of her pants. "I wish we could use the phones."

Dean shook his head. "You know IRF can listen in."

"I know," she said, hooking an arm around his shoulders. "Do you think Dad and Matt got phase one wrapped up yet?"

Dean watched Yaz come through and close the door. Its thick metal clanged against the wall, sealing it shut from the inside. "Probably. Unless they ran into problems."

"Hey, Addy, check it out," Yaz said, pointing across the garden. Without waiting for her to ask, he leapt over the closest row of dried, dead watermelon stems and picked his way across the rows that, in the spring, would contain everything from corn to carrots. He disappeared around the tool shed.

"Come on," Dean said, wrapping an arm around her waist and tugging.

She followed, using one foot to hop over the rows.

Yaz wandered out from behind the shed, wheelbarrow squeaking in front of him. "Your chariot," he grinned.

Laughing, she let Dean settle her into the bucket. Though her cheeks flushed and her insides cringed, she wasn't about to let embarrassment stop her from not walking on the damned ankle for a while.

Like a load of mulch, Dean wheeled her through quiet streets. A few times, he let gravity take them down a hill, laughing behind her as her hair flew away from her forehead and whipped at him. She gripped the sides, fingers wrapped around the cold metal. His knuckles white around the handles, he never let her fly uncontrolled.

Stopping a few blocks shy of the jail, they stashed the wheelbarrow next to a hollowed brick building. Insides floating after her flight through the streets, Addy all but bounced on her feet. Her ankle forgotten in the adrenaline racing through her.

"How do we know who's in there?" Yaz asked, angling his chin at the four-story building ahead.

"Hang on," Dean said, producing a flashlight. "It's a regular Bat Belt over here," he mumbled.

Addy grinned. She hadn't forgotten the education she'd gotten about Batman, but it bugged him to no end when she pretended not to understand his pop culture references. "A what?"

"Don't give me that, woman," he said, flashing the light at a third-story window.

The window flashed back.

An exchange of flashes followed, a flurry of Morse code.

He slid the flash into his pocket and took her arm again. "All clear. Come on, let's get inside."

CHAPTER 34

Raising his hand to knock, Jack lowered it and looked at his fist.

The next few sentences he uttered could determine whether he spent the rest of his life alone or not.

Eyes closed, he tried to form a picture in his head of what that would look like. Instead, white noise, like the static on a TV, played across his mind. Shifting shapes inside the buzzing noise.

Static. Unchanging. Deadlocked.

He whispered to himself. "Just knock, Jack."

He raised his fist again and the door flew open.

She stood on the other side, both knitting needles held in one hand, her arm drawn across her shoulders. Nostrils flaring, eyes aflame.

Without so much as a breath of hesitation, he met her eyes. "I'm an idiot, Jane. Forgive me."

Squinting, lips twisted into a frown, she lowered the needles a fraction. "Come in."

Rather than the annoyance that wanted to bubble up, he let her conditional acceptance of his apology flood over him. Taking a breath, he crossed into the house and sat as she closed the door after him.

He flipped on the lamp next to the couch. "Kinda dark in here, isn't it?"

She sat, stabbing her needles into the coffee table. "Don't really need light to knit." The needles vibrated as she sat back.

He stared at her, the line between her brows, the way she curled her arms around herself, her hair in her face. He grasped at the straws of what he needed to say.

Curling a leg onto the couch, she hooked her elbow around it and sank into the space between the back and the arm. "You waiting for an apology?"

He faced her. "No. Just trying to figure out what to say."

"You're leaving." It was a statement, not a question. She stared at a nail.

He slid closer. Close enough to feel the warmth of her leg on his knee. "That's not what I came here to say. Is that what you want me to do?"

Glancing into the hallway, she shook her head. "No. But you can't keep blaming me for shit that's not my fault."

"Jane," he said, laying a hand on her raised knee, "I didn't mean to say those things. I don't know where it came from."

"You resent me for it. That's obvious."

Claws ripped down the inside of his chest. He opened his mouth and inhaled.

"Don't try to deny it. If you didn't, you wouldn't have said it. The question," she said, facing him, "is are we moving past this or what?"

"I'd like to. It was horribly complicated. With Melinda and everything. But it's not anymore." He took the hand on her knee and squeezed. "I have to ask you one question, though," he said, swallowing.

Meeting his eyes, she frowned and raised her eyebrows. "This sounds like a great idea. Ask away."

Trying on a grin, the corners of his mouth turned down. "It's a bit hypothetical."

Fine line between her brows, she waited.

"If the last couple days hadn't happened, would you want to be with Michael? You said it should have been him. Maybe you're not wrong."

Tugging her hand free and taking a little piece of him with it, she lowered her leg and leaned toward him. Gripping both sides of his face, she forced him to look at her.

And look at her he did. Drinking in her eyes like he'd done so many times. Falling in love with every line, every inch of skin.

"The universe in which I'd say yes no longer exists. I love you. You're the only one I love. Jack," she said, calling his attention away from her mouth and back to her eyes, "I've never loved anyone else. Not ever. And I never will."

Butterflies rippled up his backbone, flitting over his chest. If someone had asked him a year ago if he could ever feel something greater than what he'd felt for Melinda, he would have asked them what kind of drugs they were on. But now, as she spoke, he discovered not only was this different, it was altogether more engulfing. He'd never once questioned his love for Melinda, but as he looked into Jane's eyes, he knew nothing would ever top this.

Sinking a hand into her hair, he pulled her close and kissed her silky lips. Just like the first time, white light exploded across his senses, filling every nerve ending.

As she sat back, smiling, he laid his head sideways on the back of the couch. "We can't let the hurt we're feeling right now cloud this," he said, pointing a finger between them. "We've got to be together in this."

"The first of many hurdles, I'd guess."

He laughed without humor. "I wish it wouldn't be, but I'd be willing to bet there'll be one or two more."

"Jack, listen," she said, leaning forward, "about Michael."

"I thought—"

"No, not that. Listen, he's. He wasn't. Oh god, what am I trying to say," she said, slapping her leg. "When he took Katherine, when he came over. He was Mike. I know he looked bad, he looked awful."

Nodding, Jack stayed quiet. Mike had never looked so bad, not even when he'd come over and kicked his ass.

"But it was him, Jack. Not the confused guy I saw that day he, well. Last time he was here."

Slight grin lifting his lip as Jane hit on exactly what he was thinking, he nodded. "What are you getting at?"

"I mean, if he hadn't been, I don't know, Mike, I wouldn't have handed her over. But he was OK. I was sure of it. I *am* sure of it."

"Clearly, you were mistaken."

She shook her head. "No, I wasn't. I don't know what's going on with him, why he did that, but we're not dealing with a stranger Melinda has corrupted. I'm telling you."

Jack considered her words. Her intuition. "If that's true, then what are we dealing with here? Do you think Katherine's really immune?"

Her face lit up. "She is. He was telling the truth. I'm just as sure of that."

Without a chance to really think about it, Jack had pushed that detail to the side. Now it hit him with the full force of a truck. The newest addition to his family was immune. Never to catch the virus, never to become one of those things. Never have to suffer the way so many had.

What a goddamned miracle.

"If you're feeling up to it, we've got a plan to get in there."

"Of course I am. Tell me." She said, sitting up and sliding closer.

Nodding, his gaze turned inward as he remembered all the steps. "First thing you need to know, there's a horde coming. It's bigger than anything we've ever seen."

"Right now?"

"Yes. It'll be here in just a few days. Oh! We found out about the guard."

"Who?"

"Matt."

"That makes sense. Who else would know just when and where the rest of the guard would be? Who could control them? We probably should have known all along."

She was right. They should have.

He went on. "He's helped us round up the rest of the guards, except the ones at the hospital. They're cooling their heels in the jail right now. We'd like to divert the horde, but Addy doesn't think that's going to work."

She grabbed his wrist, squeezing her nails into the soft skin on the underside. "What about all these people, then? Jack, they don't even carry weapons for Christ's sake."

"We're going to try and get them into the jail. It's stocked, and secure. Bulletproof glass, reinforced walls, the works. Matt says they built it for just such an occasion."

Laughing, she shook her head. "That IRF. They think of everything."

"I hope not. Because the other part of this plan is getting us into the hospital. Matt thinks he knows how, and the original residents of this place can help."

Her eyes lit up. "Me and you?"

"All of us. Look, there's one more thing, though," he said, frown returning.

His stomach balled into knots as she nodded the go-ahead.

He swallowed. "Matt was raised by Melinda. Tim was practically his brother."

"You're shitting me."

Shaking his head, stomach roiling, he told her the story.

"So we're trusting him for all this stuff," she said. Again, a statement, not a question.

"Only as much as we have to. But yeah. Some of it we have to take on faith he's not lying."

Ruthless little sprite that she was, she eyed the knitting needles. "I can make him talk, if you want me to. Make sure he's telling the truth."

Jack chuckled. "I won't stop you. But you probably shouldn't."

She nodded, grinning. "Let me know if you change your mind, love. In the meantime, let's start getting these people rounded up."

As she moved to stand, he laid a hand on her leg. "It's dark and cold out there. We have to start in the morning. Besides," he said, frowning, "I'll once again point out you just had a baby and you've been shot."

"I can handle myself, Jack."

"I know." He shook his head. "I know it. But I need you for the hospital. I want you to sit out for the rounding up phase, alright?"

She kissed him on the cheek. "I'll think about it."

* * *

Matt leaned in the jail doorway. "I know this is probably going to weird you out, Addy, but you look so much like your mom when you hold a clipboard like that, I had to do a double-take."

"Inappropriate, dude," she said, staring at the paper. Two more checkmarks as they brought in the last of the people from beyond Seventh Street.

"I know. Sorry. Just an observation." He stood.

Snaking out a hand, she grasped his arm. "Wait." She swallowed, butterflies telling her she probably shouldn't ask this question. What could it matter? What could it change?

Head shaking, she let him go but plunged ahead anyway. "What was she like? When you met her? When you were a kid?"

"What do you mean?" He leaned in the door again and crossed his arms. This time the parentheses around his mouth pointed down, eyes cast at his feet.

"I don't know, was she…" Eyes glazing, Addy stared into the past. An image of a smiling woman helping her pick raspberries sprang into her mind with such alacrity it brought tears with it.

She swiped at her eyes. "Was she kind? Did she like, I don't know. Did she like looking at the stars?"

"Oh yeah." Matt straightened. "She loved the stars. Took us up on top of the hill every chance she got. Told us about the constellations, and about how when she was a girl, people had rockets they used to try and reach them." He smiled, eyes dancing. "She was pretty passionate about it, to tell you the truth."

"That's my mom," Addy said, frowning and scraping a toe across the linoleum. "And the other part?"

"Kind?" His brow drew together. "What do you want me to say, Addy?"

Her heart twisted into a knot. "Just the truth, Matt." *No matter what I want to hear.*

"Not really. I guess she could be. Especially—" He stopped, swallowing. "Especially when she dealt with the younger kids. She kinda coddled them. But I always got the feeling it was just a show."

"Maybe that was just you." Addy raised her brow, meeting his eyes.

He frowned, gripping her shoulder. "Sure. But you and I both know that's probably not true."

Nodding, Addy glanced down at the clipboard. The letters there made no sense when there were three of them.

She blinked, the paper soaking up a tear before she could stop it falling. "I'm sorry," she said, swiping her face again.

"It's your mom. You don't have to apologize to me. I don't remember mine." He gave her shoulder a squeeze, his thumb moving in a circle.

Her throat burned. Glancing up, she wrinkled her brow. "Sometimes I think—"

"Sweetie," Dean said, walking around the corner, "we've got at least a hundred more on the next block we've got to get in here today. Hey Matt," he said, stopping next to Addy and looking him up and down. "Uh, I'm glad I ran into you." Though he sounded anything but.

Matt dropped his hand and backed up a step.

As Dean leaned closer to Addy, the air in front of him crackled. She'd never seen him give some other guy a death glare. It was interesting.

Floating just off the ground, she smiled. "What's up, Dean?"

"That last block," he said, glancing at her, eyes crinkled, "Ella's house was on that block." Looking back up at Matt, his eyes uncrinkled. On and off like a light switch.

Speaking of Ella, the feel of the first night they'd met hung around in this room. Not that she could pin down why.

Matt stiffened. "So then, where is she?"

"We weren't sure exactly how to handle her."

Eyes wide, Matt's mouth fell open. "You left her there?"

"Look, we're short-staffed as it is," Dean said, chest expanding. "There's a lot of people in, but there's so many more to go. We didn't know what to do about her. I mean, can she get in touch with her dad? If she blows this for us, well. We couldn't take the chance."

"Dean," Addy said, touching his arm.

He deflated, a smile touching one side of his mouth.

"What do you mean we're short-staffed? Didn't Renzo bring some people in?"

"They're not here yet, Addy. I don't know what's going on with them. Your dad said to go ahead without them, so we're doing our best."

"How far is that horde?" Matt asked, chewing a nail.

"Day and a half, tops," Dean said. "It's not turning now. How long will the walls hold?"

Matt sighed. "They're built to last for months against a horde that size."

"How do you know they'll hold?"

Folding his arms, Matt shook his head. "To be frank, we don't."

"So, back to the problem. More people to get in, less time to do it. And very little help. You've got to handle Ella, Matt."

Addy glanced at the clipboard. "Looks like we've got…" She added in her head, a questionable concept, and flipped the top page over. "About three-quarters of them are in already. The rest have to go to the warehouse Ric found downtown." She nodded at Dean. "Can we get it done?"

"It's gonna be close, honey," he said. "If Renzo would get here with those people, it'd sure go a lot faster."

"Well, he's not." She handed him the clipboard. "You take this. Come on, Matt. Let's go get Ella."

* * *

Addy crossed her arms. Nodded to Matt. "Well? You gonna knock?"

He shuffled his feet. "I haven't been over in a couple days. Been busy, you know."

"So."

"So. She's gonna be mad at me."

Addy tapped her foot, huffing out a breath between her teeth. "I should care because?"

"Just thought you should, um, thought you should be prepared." Holding the screen door open, he used the giant brass knocker to make their presence known.

The curtain over the front window twitched.

Before Addy could turn to get a full look at it, it'd fallen back into place and stopped moving. As though it'd never moved, it hung still as a windless day.

Thirty seconds passed. Long enough for Ella to go from the front room to the door.

A minute. Long enough for her to come all the way from the kitchen.

Closing in on two minutes, Addy trying to bore a hole through the door with her eyes, the doorknob finally twitched.

Matt let out a breath like he'd been holding it the entire time.

Ella opened the door. One hand on the door, the other on her hip, her eyes flashed over them both. "Matthew." She looked Addy up and down. "Adelaide."

"Ella, pumpkin pie, we need to talk," Matt started, sticking one foot in the threshold.

Sucking in a breath, one slender brow raised, she took him in again. Eyes flicking between him and Addy, her mouth twisted.

For just the barest of moments, Addy caught her chin tremble.

Throwing back her shoulders, hair flying, she slapped Matt across the cheek with a resounding crack. "You've got to be kidding me." She slammed the door, and he pulled his foot back just in time.

Rubbing his jaw, he glanced at Addy with wide eyes. "The hell was that all about?"

Addy shrugged. "Got me."

As the red oozed out from under Matt's fingers and flushed the rest of his cheek, an idea oozed out from under its door in Addy's mind and came around to say hi.

"Oh," she said, glancing at his feet. "Oh!"

"What?"

"She thinks we're sleeping together," Addy said. Without asking, the blood rushed up her neck and into her face.

Matt scoffed. "That's ridiculous." He picked up the knocker again.

The heavy wooden door, reinforced with steel, clanged and echoed with the knocker's strikes.

"Go away, Matthew," Ella said. Her muffled voice came from just inside the door.

Addy took a step off the porch. "I don't have time for this. Come on."

The screen slammed behind her, and Matt's hand encircled her bicep. "Addy, wait." He tugged her arm. "I know she's a pain in the ass. But she's *my* pain in the ass. Please, help me. We can't leave her here."

The last conversation she'd had with Ella replayed itself. Ella, hurt over Addy's unexplained disappearance, had driven her away by insulting her family.

Naturally, the quickest way to Addy's heart.

But those words, they still had barbs. Still stung.

"Addy, she's never even fought a Dead Head outside a closed range," Matt said, pulling her close and whispering.

"A what now?"

"A range. It's. I'll explain it later. Help me now, please?"

She shook her head, freeing her arm. Ella had all but told her to get out and not return.

But it was out of pain and fear, not anger. She hadn't meant it. And she couldn't be left here to die.

Sighing, Addy approached the door. "Ella," she said, leaning on it, "I'm not sleeping with your boyfriend. I wouldn't do that." She glanced at Matt.

He stood, one arm crossed around his midsection, the other elbow resting on it. Taking a nail off at the base with his teeth.

Addy grinned sideways. "I've got my own handsome man. Why would I need yours?"

"I haven't even met him," Ella said. "You could be lying."

"Come and meet him, then," Addy said, laying her forehead against the door. The pain, the rejection in Ella's voice unmistakable, Addy's heart ached for the lonely girl. "I'm your friend, Ella. I don't care that we fought. I love you, I hope you know that."

And as she spoke, she found the words rang true. The girl was a pain in the ass. But she was *her* pain in the ass.

Without warning, the door opened. Leaning on her bad ankle, Addy fell over the threshold and into the hallway.

Ella exhaled a laugh through her nose. "Adelaide. Your coordination really could use some work."

"So I've heard," she said, holding out a hand.

Glancing at it, Ella narrowed her eyes. But her eyebrows lifted. "You really don't hate me for all the terrible things I said?"

Addy waved her hand.

Ella took it, helping her to her feet. She frowned. Her eyebrows scrunched together, high on her forehead.

Ella's worried face.

Smiling, still amazed at the way she'd let the truth fall out of her mouth without thinking about what it might be, Addy grinned. "No, Ella, I don't hate you. Come on, let's go meet Dean."

CHAPTER 35

Jack stood on the roof of the jail, watching the street.

Dead quiet, snow melting in the midday warmth, the only sound reaching his ears that of dripping water.

Clenching his jaw and fist, he sucked a breath in through his nose and pictured his son. Not as he'd last seen him, but as a boy.

What a happy, smiling little elf he'd been. Always bringing him gifts, laughing when he was startled, learning weapons so fast Jack couldn't believe this bright and joyful little dude was his own son.

He'd always been a better person than the one raising him.

Shaking his head, Jack closed his eyes. If what Jane said was true, Mike needed help. He couldn't handle his mother alone. Not the way she was now.

"Think we're about ready, friend Jack."

Jack didn't jump, but only because he locked his abs against it. "You move awful quiet, old man," he said, a grin lifting his upper lip.

"You would be so lucky to get as old as me." He thumped him on the shoulder. "And to be half as quiet."

Opening his eyes and turning, Jack nodded. "Right on both counts. You coming too?"

"No way you're leaving me out of this party," Paul said. "I couldn't get my own kids back. Helping you get yours is second-best."

Eyes stinging, Jack clapped him on the shoulder. "So, everyone else is ready?"

They left the roof and descended into the cool dark of the jail. "Everyone's gathered on the ground floor."

"We hear from Renzo yet?"

Paul shook his head, white hair bouncing as he rounded the banister and stopped on the landing. "No. What do you make of it?"

"He's not the same guy that locked me in a lonely cell to die. He would have gotten in touch with us no matter what. Something must have happened."

"Hm. Yeah. Kinda what I figured."

Meeting Addy, Dean, and the rest of the group on the ground floor, Jack took Addy aside.

"Listen, kiddo, maybe you should try and get in touch with Renzo." And stay out of the hospital.

"I'm coming with you, Dad," she said, grinning. "I know what you're trying to do."

Frowning, he nodded. "Let me explain something, Adelaide. I don't know what we're going to run up against in that hospital. Your mother could be just as much a prisoner as anyone."

"You don't believe that, do you?"

"I don't know, honey," he said, glancing at his feet.

"What happened to her, Dad? Why is she like this?"

He shook his head. The note of sadness in her voice tugged at his heartstrings. Twanged them like a rubber band strung across a jar lid. "I don't know. She was always one to get what she wanted. I don't know how that got so twisted up."

She glanced at him from under her brows, eyes shifting. "We're not going to hurt her, are we?"

And though every fiber of him wanted to answer otherwise, he looked her in the eye and was as honest as he could be. "Not if we don't have to."

Throwing her arms around his neck, she squeezed. "I hope we don't have to," she whispered.

Hugging her back, squeezing his little girl for all he was worth, he tried to hope so, too.

She stepped back, frowning.

"Everyone's in, yes?"

"Yeah," she said, holding a hand out to Dean.

Dean reached over the desk and pulled up a clipboard. Without a word, he handed it to her. The smile she laid on him could have made flowers bloom, it was so bright.

Ah, to be young and in love.

"The checklist Matt gave us looks complete. We ended up fitting about sixty percent in here and moved everyone else downtown to an old warehouse. There's a few guards down there, the folks from Magnolia. No one should be out and about."

"And Ella?" He glanced at Matt.

Addy rolled her eyes. "She's good. For now. She's in the penthouse upstairs."

"Penthouse?"

"We have a kind of officer's quarters up there," Matt said, stepping away from the desk. "She's got the run of the place."

Jack frowned. "Can she get in touch with her father?"

Matt shook his head. "Not from here. Why? Do you want her to?"

Scratching his chin, the stubbly beard he'd been working on tickling his neck, he shook his head. "No. Not right now. But could she, if she had to?"

"Of course. I don't know what he's up to in that hospital, but he'd never leave her without a way to get in touch."

"Right. Well. We'll keep it in mind. It might come in handy." He clapped Matt on the shoulder. "Thanks for taking care of that."

Matt grinned. "Wasn't me. Talk to your daughter."

"Good going, kiddo." Jack flashed half a grin in her direction.

Hair tied up with her needles, armed to the teeth with at least twelve visible and gleaming knives, Jane stepped out of the door behind the desk. "We gonna jaw all day or are we doing this, Jack?"

Taking in the glint in her eyes, his misgivings about her coming along dissipated like cooled steam. Of course she should come. That he'd ever considered otherwise was not only a slight to her character, it was a foolish proposition. No one was better suited to stand at his side through this.

He fought the urge to sweep her into his arms in front of everyone and instead met her fierce grin with one of his own.

* * *

After lifting a manhole cover three blocks downhill from the hospital, Matt waved Addy over. "You're sure you want to do this?"

Swallowing around the lump in her throat, the look on Dad's face when she'd asked whether or not they would hurt Mom stamped on the inside of her eyelids, she nodded. "We have to." Shifting her eyes to Dad as he and Jane crossed the road to meet them, she swallowed again. "We're not going to hurt her, OK? You'll back me up on that?"

"She's a cold bitch, Addy. But she *is* the only one who ever took any kind of care of me, before Ella." He laid the manhole cover down with a metallic clang and stuck out a hand. "I'll back you up on that."

She shook his hand. "Thanks."

Crouching, he lowered his foot to the first rung of the underground ladder. He smiled up at her, blue eyes sparkling, dimples framing his mouth. "Sure thing."

As he descended, Addy knelt next to the hole. Her ankle had healed enough to use a ladder again without looking like a frog. The ladder wasn't a huge deal.

It was the smell.

The smell wafting into her face wasn't as bad as a horde, its rotten and filthy stench, but boy was it close.

She held the back of her hand to her mouth and nose and glanced up at her dad, who'd joined her. "We really have to go down there?"

He frowned, wrinkling his nose. "Afraid so." He smiled at Jane as she joined them.

Good to see they'd made up from whatever it was they'd fought about. Though Addy couldn't have imagined it before, seeing them apart now was unusual. They really were better with each other.

Jane took his hand and lowered into the hole. Before she followed the ladder down, Jack tugged on her.

"You sure you don't want me to go down first?"

Fine line between her brows, she glanced below her. "Honey, if you think I can't handle some skinny kid, think again. I got this," she said, winking at Addy.

Addy grinned. "I'd let her go, Dad."

Kissing the back of her hand, he released her and knelt next to the hole. "I'll be down right after you."

Without stopping her descent, Jane nodded.

"How is she?"

Still smiling down the hole, he shook his head. "Tough as nails."

"Duh," Addy said, "isn't that what you used to say to me? Duh?" The stench wafted up again, and Addy idly wondered what exactly had to die to make that smell more pleasant.

He grinned up at her, lips pursed. "Yeah, that's the word. You're right. She's good, I think. Ready to fight. I'll have to keep an eye on her, though. She's a little hot under the collar."

The question popped from her mouth before she considered whether it was appropriate. "That what you fought about?"

Face reddening, he shook his head. "I fucked up. I know you think I'm perfect—"

Addy scoffed.

Eyes widening, he stared at her.

"You're only human, Dad." To say it out loud, and to him, lifted some kind of weight she hadn't known had been sitting on her shoulders all this time. Ever since she'd realized whose baby it was, in fact.

Smiling again, he nodded. "It's true. Painfully so. Anyway. I said dumb shit. She forgave me. Simple as that."

Jane's voice floated up from the bottom. "You guys coming or what? This stink does not get any better."

As Jack swung a leg into the hole, Addy frowned. "I'm sure it's not as simple as that, but I'm glad you guys worked it out."

He shrugged, pausing with just his head sticking out into the street. "It's been a long time on my own. I'd forgotten. When someone means as much to you as Jane and I do to each other, you're a team. You work together, not against each other. You don't have to be alone in things. Having a partner, it's a big deal." He frowned. "I really had forgotten what it was like, having someone else help carry some of the weight. It doesn't lessen the burden, but it makes it easier to lug."

Glancing over her shoulder, Addy found Dean over by the trees. Since the day they'd met, he'd been trying to help her carry her load. She probably hadn't been doing a good enough job helping him with his.

Before she had the chance to shout his name and ask what was taking so damned long, Paul, standing next to him, lifted the radio to his ear.

His voice, raised a notch, floated across the road to her. "Say again?"

The radio crackled, but she couldn't catch the words.

His face pinched in on itself, lines between his brows and lips pressed so tight they formed a white line. "10-4." Tapping Dean on the shoulder, he pointed across the road to her.

Dean looked up and caught her staring. "Adelaide," he said, jogging over.

Her heart jumped into her throat. "What's going on?"

"We've got a problem," he said, kneeling next to her and glancing down into the sewer.

His shaky voice sent her heart into overdrive. Her nerves clanged like a thousand cymbals. "Well?"

"Renzo finally got in touch. They're blocked outside the wall. Something about the ladder being gone and the Alice door stuck shut. But Addy, that's not the worst part."

She swallowed, her face going numb. "There's worse?"

He nodded, glancing into the sewer again. "The horde is here. And somehow, they're getting in. Addy"—he clenched her shoulder—"they've breached the wall."

THE HOSPITAL

CHAPTER 36

Dean's voice followed Jack down the ladder.

"They've breached the wall."

Stopping halfway down, heart sitting like a stone in his gut, he glanced down.

Jane and Matt stood, side by side, staring up. Jane lifted a fist to her hip. "What's wrong, Jack?"

Rather than jump far enough to hurt himself, he descended the ladder and stepped off. Kept one rung in a fist, though. Something to grab onto as he told them about the horde.

"Oh my god, Ella," Matt breathed, looking up the ladder.

Jack followed his gaze. One round patch of blue-grey sky stared back, soon blocked by an Addy-shaped silhouette.

"Dad? What do we do?"

He glanced at the others. While Jane held his eyes with a laser focus, Matt stared up the ladder.

His eyes wide, sweat popped out on his upper lip. Deep frown lines pointed down. "Ella. She needs my help."

"Let them go, Jack," Jane said, laying a hand on his arm. "We can do this."

Her calm, sure voice soothed nerves that had jumped up and twisted themselves into a ball. He breathed deep. The smell didn't get better, but it did help clear his head. "Matt, tell us one more time how to get in the hospital. Then get up that ladder, close us in, and go to your girl."

Rooted to the spot, Matt stared up the ladder.

Jack clapped.

Matt started, glancing back at him. "Right. Right. OK, go down this way." He pointed behind them. "You'll come to the T intersection. Then it's a left, and you'll come to the Y junction. It's going to get smaller here." He frowned.

"At the Y, we take the right fork," Jane said, eyes half-open, "then at the five-way, we take the second from the right."

"That should bring us up in the basement," Jack said, sliding an arm around Jane. "From there, it's up to us."

"Right, right," Matt said, ghost of a smile touching his lips. "You guys are quick. Here, take my key card. It'll get you in wherever you need to go." He unclipped it and held it out to Jack.

He clutched the plastic rectangle. "Matt. We get caught, the commander is going to know you gave this to us."

"Just say you took it by force. Besides, don't get caught. You have the map Paul drew?"

Jane tapped her hip pocket.

The light dimmed again. "Dad?"

"Matt," Jack said, glancing up, "go. We'll be fine."

Matt ascended. At the top, he mumbled to Addy. Jack caught snatches of the words Y and basement.

"Are you sure, Jack?" Dean called down. "I could come with. You might need backup."

One corner of his mouth lifting, he held Jane close. "I've got backup. Go. Before the horde comes. Get inside. Stay there. We'll be back in two shakes."

"Whatever that means," Addy said, as the cover slid across the hole and blocked the light.

As it formed a half-moon, then a crescent, he pulled the flashlight from his belt. Jane dug a tiny LED one from her pocket.

"Wait," he said, as the darkness shrouded them, "don't turn it on yet." In the full dark, water dripping and trickling around them, most of it snowmelt but not all, he faced her and pulled her in close. Even as his eyes adjusted, the dark consumed him and Jane. "No matter what happens here, know I love you. Never have I felt about anyone, the way I feel about you." Sliding his fingertips up her neck, he found the bottom of her chin and tilted her head back. "I meant it when I said I want you to be my partner in all this. No one else."

"And I meant it when I said yes," she said, breath tickling his chin.

With a smile, he eased his face toward hers until their noses bumped. He kissed her like it was going out of style.

When she pulled away, he could hear the smile in her voice. "Come on, lover boy, we're in a sewer. Very romantic and all, but let's get the hell out of here and rescue our baby."

* * *

"Adelaide," Celia hissed as Addy, Dean, and Matt crossed the road, "what the hell are we doing?"

"We gotta get back to the jail," Addy said, stepping light on the weak ankle. The last couple days had healed it nicely, but there was no reason to re-injure it by running. "You heard what Renzo said on the radio."

Lips pressed together, she looked over Addy's shoulder. "We can't let them go in there alone," she said, angling her chin at the manhole cover.

"Cee," Dean said, "we have to." He gripped her shoulder. "They'll be fine. But we gotta go. Come on," he said, tugging her arm.

Backing up, eyes on the street, she glanced at Addy. "Say he's gonna be OK."

Addy frowned, following them deeper into the trees. "He's gonna be OK."

She stopped, ripping her arm free of Dean and clutching both of Addy's. Leaning into Addy's face, her eyes flicked back and forth. "You don't believe that."

"He has to be. Come on, Celia. We gotta go."

"Addy," Matt said, "we can go a different way to get back. Less chance of being taken by surprise than the way we came."

Dean drew his gun and pointed the barrel through the trees. "Lead the way."

"Can somebody give me a damn gun or something? There's a horde coming."

Biting her lip, Addy squinted. "Sorry, Matt, I don't think so. Not yet."

He sighed. "I don't know what Tim did to you, but it must've been bad."

"I'd rather not get into it."

"I'm not him, Addy."

"No, you have a different suitcase full of lies." She crossed her arms.

"You don't get it."

"Oh, sure. Tell me again what I don't get. How you're working for my mom? Or how you're spying on all of us for the commander? I mean, he's basically your father-in-law."

"Addy," Dean said, voice pitched low.

She took a breath. Her voice had been rising. And there was a damned horde, probably just around the corner.

"Another time, sweetie," Dean said. "We need to go."

"Yeah, yeah. Don't give him any fucking weapons." Drawing her machete, she stalked five feet and stopped. "Which way?"

Brushing past her, Matt started down the same path they came up but veered left through thick undergrowth until they met another path.

The new path through the trees curved behind a mall, where they found railroad tracks. Following the tracks west, they headed for the jail.

Addy sidled up next to Dean. "Where's your train, do you know?"

He shrugged. "It's theirs, really. Probably already drove it away."

"Not true," Matt said, stepping up on the other side of Dean. "It's actually just behind the…oh look, here."

They rounded the bend behind the overgrown and crumbling mall. The gleaming silver train sat on the tracks, engine pointed south. Like it was ready to leave, waiting for them to get on and go.

Addy entertained the idea. Just drive away from all this bullshit. Just her and Dean. Get on the train and leave, and ride it back across the country. Like the first time she'd seen it. Spend weeks alone with him in the train. Only this time, take advantage of that alone time, especially since Mike was—

Right. Mike. With Mom. Shooting people, kidnapping babies. God knew what else. If nothing else, someone had to help him. Before they'd gone, Jane had dropped a hint or two that she thought he needed help. That he was not what he appeared, and that maybe his hand had been forced.

Just because he was older didn't mean Addy hadn't always felt like she needed to help look after him.

"Now we know where she is." Dean bumped her shoulder. "When we're ready, we can make our speedy getaway."

A clump of a dozen or more 'Heads wandered onto the tracks a hundred yards away.

"Incoming, twelve o'clock," Paul said. He pulled a weapon, some kind of blade Addy hadn't seen in forever. Looked almost like something Mom had once pointed out in a book and called a cutlass. Almost as short as her machete, it widened and curved before coming to a deadly point.

"Get behind me," he said, pushing through the middle of them all and leading with the tip of the sword.

"Don't be stupid, old man," Celia said, pulling her own long-handled knife. "I'm not letting you have all the fun." She glanced over her shoulder and flashed a wicked grin at Addy. "Been wanting to hit something."

The grin touched Addy's lips, whether she liked it or not. Things were about to get brutal, bloody, and messy. Just like they were meant to be.

"Guys," Matt said, "a weapon would be great."

Narrowing her eyes, she shook her head and glanced at him. "Just stay back. Let the grown-ups handle it."

"The grown." He stopped, pinching the bridge of his nose and closing his eyes. "Good lord, Adelaide. Please."

"No," she said, Tim's grin floating, unbidden, in her mind. Like that cat Mom had told the story about. The one and the same story with Alice, if she remembered right.

No time for disappearing cats, Adelaide. Fight.

Raising the machete, she blew past Paul and Celia and deep into the thick of the approaching 'Heads.

Some of them had stumbled over the tracks, rolling around on the ground next to them. Goose-stepping past them, she swung with two hands and sent a 'Head's head flying into the air, its buzzing cut in half. The body crumpled to the ground, clotted and rotten blood oozing from the neck in clumps.

Fighting the dry heave, she struck another before everyone else caught up. The blade hit sideways, and the 'Head stumbled.

Dean took her back. "Why'd you leave your staff behind again?"

"Didn't think I'd need it in the sewer, Dean. Your ten," she said, nodding.

When he'd switched his gun for his own giant knife, she didn't know. In an energy-conserving swing, he rammed the knife through the side of the approaching 'Head's skull. Grabbing it by the shoulder as it fell, he pulled the knife clear and backed up to her. "Addy, on your left."

"We could use a third," she mumbled. Without room for a full swing, she made do by using the machete as a stabbing blade. Up through the soft skin of the 'Head's chin, she fought to free the blade as it fell.

Missed. It dropped with the blade still lodged.

"Dammit," she said, falling to a knee to yank at it.

Dean stepped off to deal with a 'Head of his own, his blade thwacking into its skull.

Down here, at ground level, the buzzing cacophony of them and the stink of their blackened feet surrounded Addy in a cocoon of death. Dry heaving again, she yanked at the stuck blade. It popped free, sending her sideways.

Right onto that damned ankle. The pop as it gave under her audible, she locked the scream behind her lips and fell to her side, clutching it.

A shadow fell over her. Blackened feet filled her vision. Like the never-ending tide, they came on and on. She'd never be free of them.

Gritting her teeth, she reached for the machete. The one lying just out of reach.

Before she could launch herself for it, stomach clenched in an iron fist, someone thumped down next to her. She felt the tug on her belt but didn't have time to look around before Matt unsheathed her Bowie knife and, on his knees, sliced through the 'Head's Achilles tendon.

It fell right in front of her, snapping at her nose.

Springing over her, he buried the knife hilt-deep in the side of its skull. As he did, he landed on her hip and drove her other one into the gravel between the railroad ties. It ground into her bones.

She clenched her teeth, but it wasn't enough to keep the groan back.

Grinning, Matt sprung up and offered her a hand. The knife still in the other.

Taking his hand, she stood on the good foot and wobbled. As Dean appeared from nowhere to steady her, Matt stabbed the only remaining 'Head in the eye. Behind his back. Without looking.

She frowned. "Fine. Keep the damn knife."

* * *

Between Addy and the jail, a street full of 'Heads bumped and buzzed.

The others grouped around her, crouched together in the bushes.

Dean leaned down, warm breath tickling her ear. "You gonna make it on that ankle?"

She grimaced. "Probably. Come on," she said, tensing her legs to stand.

Matt caught her arm. "Wait."

Brow drawn into a V, she glanced at his hand and up at his face. "What?"

"I don't have my key card. We can't get in."

"You don't. You what?"

"What the hell, man?" Dean asked, speaking at the same time.

Matt swallowed. "I gave it to Jack. They needed it to move around the hospital. I'm sorry, I didn't think it through."

Addy gaped. Still, his logic was sound. "No, but you're right. They needed it more than us."

"We need it pretty bad right now," Celia said, heavy-lidded eyes on the crowd of 'Heads before them. "Even once we clear that group, how are we supposed to get in?"

"Someone will have to open the door from inside, of course," Paul said. He pulled the radio from his belt and spoke into it. "Yasuo, this is alpha team, over."

"Come in, alpha. Where are you?"

"Across the street."

The radio whined as he released the button. A couple 'Heads stumbled in their direction.

Addy lifted her machete.

Dean put a hand on her shoulder. "You stay here. Matt," he said, standing into a high crouch, "no sound. Quiet as mouse farts."

"Got it," Matt said, grin dimpling one cheek. With Addy's knife raised, he stepped away with Dean, their feet silent on the dry, brown grass.

"Need you to open the door for us, Yaz," Paul said. He spun the volume down and pressed the speaker to his ear.

All Addy caught was a mumbling response and a bit of static.

"How long?"

Mumble. Static.

"10-4." Paul clipped the radio back onto his belt and jutted his chin at Celia. "Thirty seconds. Help me with Addy."

Teeth clenched, Addy stood and wobbled. "I'm sorry I'm so goddamned clumsy, you guys."

Chuckling, Celia dipped under her arm. "No apologizing for who you are, Addy. We love you anyway." She lifted her long knife with the arm not around Addy. "We got you."

Unexpected tears stinging her eyes, Addy nodded. "Dean," she hissed.

Stabbing the 'Head in front of him, he looked over his shoulder. "I got her, Cee."

It crossed Addy's mind to argue. Weighing him down, adding potential for him to be bitten, it wasn't on her to-do list for the day.

What Dad had said about letting him help shoulder her weight popped to mind instead. Of course, this time, it was literal weight, but the idea still held. And to tell the truth, it sometimes seemed like he was still trying to make it up to Cameron for not being able to help him. He put everything he had into helping everyone else. Especially her.

It probably made him feel better, in a way.

She threw her left arm around him and patted Celia. "Help us clear the path. I'll stick with this handsome man, here."

"Bet you will," Celia said, grinning.

Matt took down the other 'Head that had wandered their direction, with calm, clinical precision.

"If you taught Ella how to do that," she said, as he joined them, "she ought to be fine. Even in a horde."

He shrugged. "Rather not find out."

"Come on," Dean said, "let's get to the door."

As they stepped from behind their cover, more 'Heads turned and wandered their direction. Mostly buzzing but some gurgling. Some bubbling.

"There's some fresh ones here," she whispered.

Dean nodded. "What do you want to do with them?"

"Do we have extra doses inside?"

Matt shook his head. "One thing we didn't stock."

As Dean lopped the head off of the closest one, she frowned. "That's the dumbest thing I've ever heard, Matt."

Driving the knife through the temple of another, Matt shrugged again. "I don't know, Addy. I just follow orders."

"You have this 'pristine population' as you call it, and you don't keep enough Cure in the fortress you built for them?" She twisted, holding Dean's arm with her left hand and slicing halfway through the neck of a 'Head with the other. "That make any sense to you?"

"What did you want me to do," Matt said, stabbing another through the eye, "just go get a bunch and haul it over here on my own?"

"Yes," she said, pulling closer to Dean as he missed the head of the one next to him and instead buried his machete in its shoulder.

In one large step, Matt faced the 'Head. Holding the haft of Dean's machete, he pulled the 'Head close and sank the knife through its nasal cavity. "That makes no sense. Do you hear yourself right now?" Freeing both weapons, he flipped the machete and held it out to Dean.

One arm around her waist, Dean squeezed her and took the machete. "I think she's right, Matt, but maybe we can talk logistics later. The point is—"

Matt pointed over his shoulder. "Six o'clock."

Whipping Addy around, Dean sliced through the neck of the one stumbling toward them. It bubbled from the wound as it went down, blood that had been congealing over just a few hours pouring onto the ground in a hot puddle.

"Damn," Addy whispered. "That was one of Mann's. I think I knew her."

"The point is," Dean said, resuming hauling her toward the jail, "we could have saved that person if we had extra. But we don't. So let's just get the hell inside."

The heavy jail door swept back, Yasuo holding it open. "Get in here, you guys," he said. "There's too many of them."

Addy glanced around. Easily fifty more had filled the space where they'd been hiding just a couple minutes ago.

Machete clattering to the ground, Dean picked her up in a full cradle hold and rushed the door.

She wrapped her arms around his neck and buried her face in his shoulder. She couldn't fight his playing the hero right now, so she may as well enjoy the moment.

Two of her favorite scents mingled on his jacket. Blood and musk.

CHAPTER 37

Jack lifted the grate above his head and peeked from beneath it. Sparse lighting scattered through the basement, showing him piles of old, busted hospital detritus. Beds, bent wheelchairs, and the like.

No movement in sight.

Pulling a silent breath through his nose, he clicked on his penlight and swept the room in front of him.

"It's clear," he said, pocketing the light. "You stay down here, Jane. Let me check it out." He pushed the grate aside, a whisper of metal scraping the concrete, and began to climb out of the hole. Squeezing his shoulders together, he just fit.

"The hell I will," she mumbled. She tugged his pants cuff. "I'm not leaving you alone."

Half a smile crossing his lips, he climbed out of the hole and lay on his belly, sticking a hand down. "Come on, then."

She followed, replacing the grate. "Pfft. Leave me down there to wait. Who do you think I am?"

Smile broadening, he helped her stand. His back complained, but he told it to piss off. This was no time for it to give up on him. "I'm sorry, sometimes my mouth runs off without me."

Standing on her toes, she kissed the corner of his mouth. "I know." She slid Paul's map from her hip pocket and smoothed it on her thigh.

Jack pulled the penlight out again and shone it at the map. "Alright, so we should be here." He pointed the light at the bottom left corner. "And Paul says he thinks we need to get here." Moving the light diagonal, he aimed it at the very top corner on the right. "He says this is a suite above their test facilities, and it's the nursery."

"Being Melinda, I'm a little surprised the nursery isn't dead center in the test lab," Jane said, voice stretched thin over her vocal cords.

His throat bunched. Though Jane was right, it gave him no pleasure to realize it. To feel it. "Mm. Yeah. Well. Katherine should be there." He traced the stairwell. "We can't take the front stairs."

"What about this?" Jane knelt and laid the map down.

He knelt next to her and followed her finger with the light as she traced a solid line from the top floor to the basement.

"It's a good try," he said, brow tight, "but that's the service elevator."

"So, what's wrong with using that? It's a straight shot."

"Well, now that it's just you and me, we don't have the manpower. We—"

A noise across the basement, what could have been the sound of a heel scraping over the concrete floor, echoed through the room. He froze, hand falling to his knife.

The needles in her hair glinted in the flashlight beam as she spun toward the sound.

It came again, a low scuffle.

"Rats," she whispered.

Jack's stomach turned. He shuddered.

She chuckled, turning back to the map. "My love. Rats? Of all the things to be scared of."

"Rabies," he countered. "We don't have the cure for it anymore. Have you ever watched someone die from rabies?"

"No. Have you?"

"Once." Pointing the flashlight back at the map, he sighed. "Anyway. The service elevator is out. There's not even a car in there."

She leaned against him. "That's perfect then. We can just climb up that way instead of sneaking through halls."

He swallowed. Not that he wanted to say it, but… "Jane, it's been just about a week since you gave birth. Four days since you were shot. I don't know if you're ready to climb six flights up a ladder." He met her eyes in the dark. "Assuming the ladder is even complete."

Exhaling through her nose, short and sharp, she slid an arm around his thigh. "We'll just pretend like you didn't just say that." She sniffed. "Except the ladder not being there part. That, we should worry about."

"I don't want to get halfway up and be stuck. Plus, how would we come down with the baby?"

"They call it babywearing, honey. Surely you've seen it before."

An unbidden flash of Melinda wearing Addy around in a sling popped through his head.

A thousand tiny little knives stabbed through his heart.

Clearing his throat, he turned his attention back to the map. "Look at these stairs here," he said, following them up with his finger. "Paul says there's only two key card doors. One at the bottom, one at the top. Otherwise, it doesn't pass through anything secure, so there's not a lot of activity. I think that's our best bet."

She pulled the map up and folded it back into a small square. Kissing him on the cheek, she moved to stand.

He tightened his grip on her arm. "Wait. Just. Jane," he said, sighing.

"Jack."

He hesitated. For all the times she'd made him feel like he could fly, he couldn't seem to get his feet off the ground. Fear gripped him, constricting his lungs and weighing down his heart.

"Jack, what is it?"

"What if this doesn't work?"

"That's not an option."

"I know that. But." He clicked the light off, shrouding them in the soupy dark. Hiding his face. "I'm scared, Jane."

She stood, tugging his hand until he stood with her. Leaning into him, warm and soft, she wrapped both arms around him and pulled him in. "You're not alone in this. Remember? Maybe if it was just you, or just me, maybe it wouldn't work. Together," she said, warm breath tickling the underside of his beard, "we can do this. We will do this."

* * *

The door behind the desk slammed open, and Addy caught a blur of color as Ella streaked across the room.

Had she ever moved that quick? She didn't even know the girl had a fast speed. Seemed like she flounced everywhere.

Though she flew across the room like she'd been shot from a cannon, Matt caught her without a stagger and wrapped her in both arms. Cradling her, he kissed her with the passion of the dying.

As he did, Addy turned away and asked Dean to set her down.

"Watch the ankle, sweetie," he said, setting her on her feet, one arm around her waist.

She opened her mouth to thank him for carrying her, or ask him why he'd dropped his machete, or some other thing, but Ella's shrill shout drowned out her thoughts.

"What the hell happened out there, Matthew? Have you seen that horde? What are we going to do?"

"Ella, sweet pea," he said, letting her go and raising his hand, palm out. A stop sign.

Not that Ella paid attention to stop signs. "Don't you sweet pea me! You tell me how you're going to fix this."

"I always do, baby. You know I do. I'll take care of it."

The calm in his voice surprised Addy. She had already tried to slap Ella at least sixteen times in her head.

"Tell me what happened," Ella said, voice rising again.

Addy slid her arm from around Dean and tested her ankle. It held. She hadn't sprained it as badly as before. "Ella," she said, crossing the room. "We don't know exactly. We don't know where they came from, but we're safe here."

"I know that," she said, throwing her head back. "Daddy always said if anything happened to stay in the house. But if I couldn't," she said, glancing at Matt, "the jail was the second-best place to come."

"Shit, shit-shit," Celia said.

Addy spun.

Cee leaned against the wall beside the door, bleeding from her hip. Paul stood next to her, leaning down to check the wound.

"Celia?" Addy stepped closer.

"It's a bite," Paul said, standing. "We need to get that clean. We need a dose."

Celia slid down the wall. Sitting, knees raised in front of her, she covered her face with her arm and leaned on her knees.

Addy's heart lurched. Celia had given her dose to Oren. The dose that hadn't worked.

Crossing to her, Addy sank down onto the floor and laid her hand over Celia's. "Let me get it."

Balling one hand into a fist, Celia struck the floor. Face still buried in her arm, she lowered her voice. "Don't you let me die like that, Adelaide Cooke."

"You know I won't," Addy whispered back. Pulling her own dose from her pouch, she tapped the syringe. Amber liquid floated inside. "Where do you want it?"

Sitting back against the wall, Celia rolled up her sleeve with three sharp twists. The frown she wore could have cut brick it was so hard.

Addy saw no need to mention the tear glistening in the corner of her eye.

Instead, she removed the plastic cap from the syringe and sank the needle into Celia's bicep. Jamming down on the plunger, she injected all the amber liquid under her skin.

Eyes closed, Celia nodded. "That's only the second time. We should be good. Oren had taken it at least seven times. Maybe eight. He was always taking bites for me."

Stomach twisted, Addy looked down at the syringe and slid the cap back on.

"I should have known," Celia said, opening her eyes and smiling at Addy. The tear slipped down her cheek. "Should have known. He was so..." Trailing off, she glanced across the room and swiped at her face with her arm. "Idiotic." She stood, pushed off from the wall, and disappeared up the stairs.

Dean sat next to Addy. "Take this," he said, holding out a syringe identical to the one she'd just emptied into Celia's arm.

Addy shook her head, turning the empty syringe in her hand. "No."

He continued to hold it out.

She continued to stare at the empty she held.

Grasping her hand, he pried her fingers open and laid the full syringe in her palm. "I'd just give it to you anyway. There's no sense in you not having it."

Half a frown dragging her lips down, she tucked it into the pouch. "Don't be surprised if I give it back to you," she said, leaning on him.

He threw his arm around her and pulled her in close. "Addy."

Closing her eyes, she let her head ride his chest up and down as he breathed. Rather than answer, she sighed.

"Adelaide," he said, squeezing her tight.

Without leaning back, she raised her head.

"Don't you give me that dose if you need it. Don't you do that."

Shrugging, she leaned back into his chest and closed her eyes.

"Promise me, Addy. You'll take it if you need it."

Again, she shrugged. He had no right to tell her what to do with the dose. He'd given it to her, and it was now hers to do with as she pleased.

He pushed her away. "Adelaide," he said, catching her eyes and holding them with his own.

Her stomach lurched and fluttered. Looking in his eyes was like electric fire dancing across old power lines. Sparkling and crackling, it had a life of its own, that gaze.

"Please. Don't give me that dose if you need it," he said, cupping her chin. "I don't want to live in a world where you sacrificed yourself for me. I won't. You hear me?" The edge of his emerald eye sparkled.

And that was it. That broke the spell. The implication of what his brother had done for him, and the fact he couldn't live with himself if she did the same, it brought her out of her stubborn reverie.

A tear fell from her eye, and she nodded, wiping the corner of his eye with her thumb. "I won't, Dean. If I need the dose, I'll take it. I promise."

"I'm going to remember your word." He kissed the inside of her palm.

"You hold me to it, then."

He nodded, looking around at the rest of them.

Matt and Ella sat on the desk, holding hands. Yasuo still stood by the door, staring out the one-way window. He could see out, but the 'Heads couldn't see in. Thankfully.

Dean raised his voice. "Who else has a dose?"

Everyone else still had theirs. Ella didn't carry one.

"Mann's people don't have enough to go around," Paul said. "If y'all would excuse me, I've got to get Celia's wound clean." He disappeared up the stairs.

"Most of it is kept at the hospital," Matt said, crossing to Addy and Dean, Ella attached to his hip.

"I've got about two hundred doses in my basement," Ella said, lips pulling away from her teeth. Something like a grin.

"It's a start," Addy said.

* * *

Stopping on a dark, damp landing, Jack waited for Jane to catch up. "You alright?"

"Fine," she said, panting from somewhere below him. "Forgot about the elevation is all."

Stuffing a grin, he sat on the stairs and waited. He couldn't pinpoint the leaky pipe, but the *drip-drip-drip* was a constant companion as they climbed. The sporadic, blinking fluorescents lit the stairs enough to not trip over the one in front of your foot. Barely. So different from what they'd seen of the rest of the hospital, Jack's unease mounted.

Jane rounded the banister below him and trudged up the stairs. "Lot of steps," she said, out of breath. She sat between his legs on the step below him and leaned, looking at him upside-down.

Smiling, he brushed the hair from her face. "Glad we didn't take the broken elevator?"

"I'm not saying you were right," she said, teeth peeking from behind her lips, "but if you were, I'd say yes, I'm glad."

"These stairs remind me of that place," he said, glancing at the walls. Running his hand over the banister, peeling paint under his palm, sent a shiver up his spine. "Smells better. But gives me that sick feeling anyway. Like the last time I saw Andrew."

Not that he'd meant to bring up his old friend. But he'd popped up anyway, likely because he'd been killed in a hospital not unlike this one. Twisted and broken.

Sniffing, Jane stood. "I sometimes like to think he's still with us," she said, brushing her fingers across his. "You know I'm not much on that spiritual crap or whatever, but he was a brave soul, Jack. If anyone could stick around and lend a hand, it'd be Andrew."

Jack nodded, eyes full. "I ever tell you why he called me Jackie?"

Grinning, she shook her head.

A door slammed open on the next flight down.

Jack's heart stopped. And restarted, at a rolling gallop. He mouthed the word "go" to Jane and tugged her hand.

On silent toes, she took the last two stairs to the next landing and started up.

Feet trudged up the stairs below, one clomping up after the other. The rasp of a lighter echoed off the walls.

Rolling his feet heel to toe, Jack crept onto the landing and edged around the banister. Fighting the urge to look down, lest whoever was down there look up at the same time and spot them, he started up the next set of stairs. He pulled Matt's key card from his pocket and held it toward Jane.

Snatching it, she waved it in front of the door's sensor plate. The door lock beeped, the light on the sensor plate turned green, and she yanked it open.

"Who's up there?" Following the voice, tobacco smoke wafted up the staircase.

Something Jack hadn't smelled in ages.

Even after more than twenty-five years, some part of his hindbrain cried out. Begged for just one drag.

A sharp intake of breath in his face pulled him up short.

As he turned, his nose almost touched the end of Mike's.

Mike's eyes wide, his mouth moved up and down without sound.

"I said who's up there," the voice repeated from below, heavy feet stomping.

Grabbing Jane's arm, Mike pulled her through the door.

Jack balled a fist.

"Just me," Mike called down, releasing Jane and wrapping a hand around Jack's bicep. He tugged.

His strength unexpected, Jack almost lost his footing as Mike shoved him through the door and put a foot out on the landing.

Mouth and eyes as wide as his son's, Jack glanced at Jane. His breath had caught somewhere around his collarbone. It didn't want to move up or down.

But Jane, Jane crossed her arms and smiled. Winked.

He stepped next to her as Mike called out to the person on the stairs. Chastising them for smoking in the stairwell.

Taking her hand, Jack laced his fingers between hers and put one hand on his knife.

"Don't," she breathed.

"I don't care how cold it is out there," Mike said, retreating back through the door, "next time go outside. Some of us don't like smoke, alright?"

"Trust me," Jane said, squeezing against him. "It's OK."

Uncoiling the spring inside, he let his hand fall away from the knife and watched Michael as he pulled the door closed.

If she wasn't right, they were both probably doing more than getting shot in the shoulder.

Door latched, Mike faced them. With a sigh, he crossed his arms and shook his head.

"You two are fucking crazy."

CHAPTER 38

Addy knocked on the door of what Matt had called the suite. "Ella?"

"Addy," Ella said, swinging the door wide, "please, do come in."

Addy limped through the door, the ankle healing fast this time, and entered the large, blocky room.

"Forgive me, I haven't had the chance to decorate," Ella said, waving Addy into an adjoining, also blocky, room. "I guess the guards use this as their break area and hang out. Some of the decor may be…" She paused, tugging a sock from under a sagging couch and tweezing it between two fingers. "Hm. May be not up to my standards."

"It's OK, Ella, really. I mean, that sock is rank. Put it down," Addy said, grinning, "but it's OK. Don't worry."

Nose wrinkled, Ella tossed the sock behind the couch. She led Addy across the room, pulled a pitcher of water from the fridge, and began opening cabinets.

Taking a seat at a small, wobbly, scratched table, Addy stuck a hand under her chin and waited. It was always best to let Ella finish bustling before talking to her. Nothing ever sank in. Couldn't penetrate the cloud of "busy."

Once Ella had found a cupboard with glasses, she sat two on the table and sniffed at the kitchenette. "There's barely any way to even cook here. This is awful."

"Not really what I wanted to talk about, Ella," Addy said, pouring the water. She'd hardly removed her hand from the pitcher when Ella grabbed her fingers with both hands and squeezed.

"Adelaide, I am so sorry," Ella said, lowering her voice. She swallowed. "I didn't mean to assume. I mean, it was wrong of me to think. Ugh." Letting Addy's hand go, she pushed it away. "It's so much easier to just be right all the time."

Chuckling, Addy took a drink. "Yeah, well, it's fun to watch you try to apologize. I don't think I've ever seen you do anything so tough."

Ella picked at a nail. "I said some pretty mean things," she said, eyes fixed on her own hands.

"You did."

"I didn't mean them."

"Good."

Ella shrugged, balling up her hands and pulling them to her breastbone. She crossed her arms and tightened them as far as they'd go. "I was scared," she whispered.

So Ella had called her family a disgrace, Dean a traitor, and accused her of sleeping with her boyfriend.

All in all, not the greatest things to say.

But hell. Forgiveness was supposed to be the thing to do. So said Yaz.

She leaned over the table and gripped Ella's shoulder. "I get it. It's OK."

Ella nodded, not looking up.

"Ella," Addy said, shaking her shoulder.

She looked up, holding eye contact with Addy. No tears wet her cheeks, but both eyes sported red rims.

"It's alright. I understand. I forgive you for the completely baseless accusation and all the mean things you said. I understand being scared."

"You do?" Her eyes wide, Ella both looked and sounded like the child none of them had ever gotten to be.

"Sure. Course I do. Look." She lowered her eyes. "I've lost a lot of things. I haven't had many friends. I'd sooner not lose any I do have."

Ella peeped at Addy from under her brows. "You just never seem scared of anything."

Addy laughed so loud she thought her vocal cords might burst. Glancing at Ella, whose face contorted into a confused half smile, sent her over the edge.

By the time her laughter tapered off, her abs hurt and she'd almost fallen from the chair. Twice.

"I needed that laugh," she said, wiping her eyes.

Ella frowned. "I'm sorry. I don't really understand what was so funny."

Addy shook her head. "I'm scared of literally everything. I was so scared of Dean at first I ended up believing some lies about him, and instead got myself into a heap of stupid trouble I could have avoided." As the words fell out of her mouth, she did what she could to block the feel of Tim's hand covering her mouth and nose. His tongue rasping up the side of her face.

She shuddered. "Anyway. Fear has gotten me into some pretty tight spots."

Shrugging, Ella took a few sips of water. "You just seem to always know what to do. You never look scared."

Opening her mouth to repeat how she was always terrified, Addy instead took a moment to consider things from Ella's perspective.

She'd just blasted through two mini-hordes on a busted ankle. Yeah, she'd had a couple close moments. Sure, she'd dry heaved her way through one fight. But she never paused to worry about it.

Come to think of it, save for a couple times, she hadn't operated based on fear in months. Instead, she'd practiced what Yasuo had talked about. Intention. The knowledge that things were out of her control. The trust that all she could do was choose her own actions.

It felt like a light had shone down on her head. Like the sun had come straight through the roof.

He'd talked the fear right out of her. All this work he'd had her do. The meditation. The exercises in powerlessness. Working out her part in it. The amends.

Not that those were all finished. But still.

It'd all been engineered to flush out the fear, face it, and let it go.

Sneaky bastard.

Grinning, she downed her water. "First thing's first. I think we need those doses in your basement."

"Addy, you're insane," Ella breathed. "There's a whole horde out there. Haven't you seen? You'll never make it."

"We can make it. I've been through worse."

* * *

Jack shifted from foot to foot. There had to be some words to say to Mike. Something that could fix everything in one fell swoop.

As he stood, fingers laced between Jane's, mouth flopping up and down like a carp, Mike stepped across to him in one giant leap and grabbed him in a tight, encompassing hug.

After a moment of pure shock, Jack dropped Jane's hand and hugged his boy. Wrapped both arms around him and closed his eyes, breathing through his nose and swallowing tears.

"I'm so sorry, Dad," Mike said, voice muffled by Jack's shoulder. "I don't know what else to say."

"There's nothing that needs to be said, son," Jack said, gripping the back of Mike's shirt. The boy'd always been a hugger, but he hadn't wrapped him in this kind of bear hug in longer than Jack could remember. Jack allowed himself to leave everything to the side and savor the white light coursing through him.

Letting him go too soon, Mike stepped back. His wide smile faded as he glanced at Jane. "Um. Jane. I, uh." He faltered, shoving his hands in his hip pockets and staring at his toes.

She stepped next to Jack. "You shot me, Michael."

His skin, already pale and slick, turned green. "I'm so sorry, Jane. About that."

Jack waved a hand. "Are we in a good place to talk?"

Nodding, Mike looked around the room. "This wing isn't really used much at the moment. It's kind of been my getaway the last few days. My place to think."

"Think about what?" Jack asked.

And Mike, normally the diplomat, didn't even pause. "What I did to you."

Jane chuckled under her breath.

Before she could get a word out, because those were sure to be some fiery words, Jack grabbed her hand and laced his fingers through hers again. "Can we sit?"

Mike held a hand toward the other end of the room. "Sure, over here."

Weaving through old hospital equipment, busted monitors, IV poles with cracked machines attached to them, and miles of discarded plastic tubing, they found a couple couches tucked into a corner of the room.

"I guess this was some kind of old storeroom," Mike said, patting the couch.

Jane sat next to Jack, leaning back into the uncomfortable plastic couch. "Michael. You shot me."

He flinched. "I know, Jane. I'm sorry. I had to."

Before he could take in Mike's apologetic, well, everything, the despair in his voice, the defeat in the set of his shoulders, Jack's blood heated up. "Had to. So you could kidnap your little sister."

"If I hadn't been the one to do it, Mom would have," he said, peeking at Jack from under scrunched brows. He swallowed, Adam's apple bobbing. His eyes glistened as he looked at Jane. "In that moment, she would have killed you both."

Exhaling through his nose, the breath hot on its way out his nostrils, Jack sat back and put an arm around Jane. Of course. Of course Mike was right.

Remember the look on her face after the baby was born, Jack? It wasn't pain or sadness. It was murder.

Mike went on. "When she found out the baby was immune, she wanted to take her right away. I could hardly talk to her. She started loading her guns," he said, rubbing his arms. The dark circles under his eyes made them look sunken and small as he leaned back into his own couch. "I've never seen a look like that on her face, Dad. She's said a lot of things to me over the past few months. But that." He swallowed again. "I was scared."

Leaning forward, Jack put a hand on his knee. "It's OK, son. It's OK to be scared."

"She was going to kill you. Shoot you both in the head and take the baby. I mean, I get she needs to know about the immunity thing. She's not wrong, it is important."

Jack nodded. "It's not nothing. I'll agree with that."

"Fucking miracle, is what it is," Jane said, rubbing the side of his leg.

Half a smile lifted Mike's mouth. "It is. But she really meant to do it. She didn't care what I said. In the end, the best I could do was convince her it'd be easier for me to get through your door, and that I'd bring the baby back. Whatever"—he swallowed, glancing at Jane's shoulder—"whatever that took." Staring at his shoes again, a tear fell from one eye. "I'm sorry, Jane. I didn't want to. But it was the only way to get out of the house. You never would have let me leave."

She chuckled. "You know me well, Michael."

He shrugged. Glanced between her and Jack. "You still surprise me sometimes."

Her cheeks reddened. "I'm not going to apologize to either of you. But if I had it to do over, I might handle it different." Sliding her cool hand into Jack's palm, she laced her fingers through his again. "Probably would have been a bit more upfront with you, Mike."

"Well now that we're agreed everything is a convoluted mess," Jack said, "where is the baby and how do we get to her?"

Mike frowned. "It's not going to be easy."

"When was anything good ever easy?" Jane asked.

Jack squeezed her hand. "Where's that map of Paul's?"

"Speaking of," Mike said, glancing around, "where is the old guy? I would have thought he'd come with you."

"Probably dealing with the horde," Jane said, staring down at the map as she unfolded it.

Mike's breath stopped.

Jack's heart skipped. "Mike, don't tell me you don't know."

"Dad. What? What horde?"

* * *

"Addy, sweetie, I love you, but this is a bad idea," Dean said, peeking out the fourth-floor window.

She huffed a breath out through her nose. "We need those doses, Dean. We have what, three between us? What are we going to do when those run out? When the food is gone? No," she said, joining him at the window. Her breath fogged the glass as she watched the street undulate with the mass of 'Heads below. "We need to be proactive. We go now, while we can plan. Not when we're desperate."

Tugging her hand free of her crossed arms, he curled her fingers around his. "You've got a point." He kissed her fingers. "There's not any way I can talk you into staying here, is there?"

She laughed, throwing both arms around his neck. "You're a funny man, Dean Ross." Kissing him on the neck, she whispered in his ear. "Are there any quiet corners left in this building?"

Pushing her hip back with one hand, he chuckled. "Sweetheart, there's people sleeping in the damn stairwells."

"So, no, then?"

"I'm coming, too," Ella blurted, her voice echoing off the walls.

Everyone stopped. Except for Yasuo, all the men spoke at once.

"Ella, pumpkin," Matt began.

"Now, I don't think that—" Dean said, stepping toward her.

"Little girl," Paul said, still seated on a couch. The one with the rank sock stashed behind it.

Addy glanced at Celia, half a grin curling her mouth.

Celia gave her the same look back, dark eyes laughing. She shook her head.

Yasuo continued to pace, ripping at a nail. Picking up Addy's tricks, it seemed.

Ella pushed her chair back from the table, finishing her water and slamming the cup down. "I want to come, too," she repeated, throwing her hair over a shoulder. "It's my house. I have the key—"

"Sweet pea," Matt interrupted, "you can give us the key."

"Don't. Interrupt. Me. Matthew." Crossing her arms, her eyes flashed bright blue. She always carried an air of beauty, but she looked downright regal as she defied everyone to contradict her.

Addy couldn't help but be impressed. And a little frightened.

"It's my house. I have the key. I know where the doses are. I can get into Daddy's safe. I can, and will, help you. But I want to come, too."

Against logic, Matt stepped up next to her. He gripped her shoulder. "I don't want you to get hurt, Ella-belle. There's thousands of them out there. You could die."

"Only so many of them can get to us at once," Ella countered, smiling. "I can fight. You showed me how."

"Ella, that was a closed range. The 'Head was hobbled. Me and Burke were right there next to you. Do you honestly think we would've let it get to you?"

"Give me a weapon. I'm coming."

Celia chuckled. "You boys better listen. The girl wants what the girl wants."

Matt shook his head. "I only have the one knife, honeybunches."

"You know where the weapons are, Matt. Don't pretend you don't," Paul said. "We appreciate you playing along, but we all know you know."

Addy could have slapped herself in the forehead. Of course he knew. Why she hadn't considered it until right now was beyond her.

Dean turned back to the window. "I told Jack we needed that grenade launcher."

CHAPTER 39

Mike pointed at the map. "Dad, this hallway is too busy for us to use," he said, fingernail trailing down a line from the room they were in. His brow furrowed. "How is this even on here? I didn't think civilians were allowed in that part of the hospital."

"They're not," Jack said, grinning. "Paul is an expert in getting into places he shouldn't be. Kind of his thing."

Nodding, Mike pointed out another corridor. This one wasn't complete on the map, but Paul had drawn a dotted line where he thought it went. "This is almost correct. Why didn't he finish it?"

"That's the hallway where he was picked up. We were going to avoid it, knowing someone found Paul there."

Mike shook his head. "No, that's the perfect way to go. It goes around behind the nursery. Probably got caught the same way you almost just did."

Jane folded the map. "Aren't we going to the nursery, Michael?"

He sighed. "She's not there."

"Then where is she?"

"Mom has quarters, and a separate lab, on the other end of the hospital. There's a skywalk," he said, motioning with his hands, "we'll have to go through it to get there."

"I saw that from outside," Jack said, crossing his arms. "Seems kind of exposed. There's no other way to get in?"

Mike shook his head, skin turning green again. He opened his mouth but didn't get a word out before Jane grabbed his arm.

"What is my baby doing in your mom's private quarters?"

He frowned, swallowing. "She's immune, Jane. She's the first person who's ever been. Do you think Mom would let her out of her sight? It's almost as if…" He trailed off, glancing at Jack.

Jack thought of Mike as a baby. How Melinda sometimes slept in the floor next to his crib when he was sick. How she fell asleep in the rocker while nursing him. How she followed him around and picked him up every time it looked like he was even going to trip.

And it came to him what Mike was going to say. As much as he wanted Jane not to hear it, he couldn't insulate her from the world. He couldn't insulate her from anything.

"It's as if Katherine is her own baby," Mike finished. He grimaced, watching Jane flinch.

She paled, covering her mouth with the back of her hand. "We've got to get her out of there, Jack," she said, laying a hand on his bicep and staring up into his eyes.

The floor spun under him as every thought he'd had about Melinda in the last year coalesced into this one drumbeat. Whoever she'd been before, she could not be trusted with his children. Her single-mindedness about the virus was a danger to anyone near her.

He gripped Jane's hand. "You couldn't be more right. Mike, show us the way."

Mike led them out of the room. "This hallway branches off up there. What we'll have to do is follow the left fork and head around behind the nursery. We can take the stairs at the other end. They're private and lead directly to the skywalk." Stopping, he glanced at Jack. "How did you open that door? Do you have a keycard?"

"We do. Will it get us into Melinda's quarters?"

A door to their right opened, and Burke stopped with one foot raised. His mouth fell open.

Dropping Jane's hand, Jack slammed his forearm against the commander's neck and backed him into the room. At the same time, he drew his gun and pressed it into Burke's temple. Mike closed the door behind them, and Jack kept pushing until the larger man backed into a table full of test tubes. Glass tinkled.

"Watch the samples, dammit," someone said.

"Sorry, Hux," Mike said, righting a couple of the tubes that had fallen. "Nothing spilled."

Without lowering the gun, Jack peeked around Burke. Dr. Huxley sat at a microscope, wholly intent on what was in front of his eyes. He likely didn't even know who'd come into the room.

Glancing at Jane, he angled his chin at the doc.

With half a grin, she slid her needles out of her hair and shook it out.

She could do that a dozen times a day and he'd never get tired of it.

Burke shifted.

Tightening his arm across the commander's throat, Jack glared into his grey eyes. "Nice to see you again, commander."

"I've been expecting you, Jack," Burke said, eyes narrowed.

"Bet you have." He pressed the sight of his gun into the commander's skin and glanced around him again.

Jane leaned on the table next to Huxley and tapped his shoulder with a needle.

"Yes, Michael, what is it you—" Huxley glanced up from the microscope, slightly buck teeth hanging over his lower lip as he stopped and stared up at Jane. "Oh."

"What shall we do with him, honey?" she asked, tracing his arm with the deadly point of a needle.

Huxley swallowed.

"Mike, cuffs," Jack said, arm pressed into Burke's throat.

Michael took a pair of cuffs from Burke's belt and clipped the commander's wrists together.

Jack led him to a chair next to Huxley and pushed his shoulder until he sat.

"Listen, Jack," Burke began.

"Pretty sure it's your turn to listen, Burke," Jack said. "I don't care what you think of Melinda, I don't care what you think about what she's doing. Or what she's done. Or any of it."

Burke opened his mouth.

Jack held up a hand, palm out. "I just want my baby back. No one has to get hurt. Honestly, I'd rather not hurt anyone."

"I could kill the bitch," Jane said, fingering the point of her needles. "Sorry, Michael."

Sliding an arm around her waist, Jack went on as if she hadn't spoken. "I'll do what I have to, though."

"Mr. Cooke," Huxley said, "you have to understand. Her immunity isn't just a rarity. It's unheard of. I told you I'm one of the foremost experts in NMZM."

"You did."

"It's never happened. Not once. No one has ever shown immunity to the virus. I don't know if you understand the significance."

"And I cannot explain to you what this virus has taken from me," Jack said, for a moment carrying the weight of his little girl as they ran from the back of that sporting goods store. Shaking his head, he squeezed Jane. "I won't let you take my baby, too. I can't."

"Listen, Jack." Burke shifted in his seat. "If we can recreate the conditions under which your daughter gained immunity, we can let her go."

Corners of his mouth turned down, Jack lifted his lip. "Let her go? I don't think you have a choice," he said. "You're going to take us to Melinda's quarters, and you're going to give Katherine back to us. End of story."

* * *

"Are you sure leaving Huxley back there was a good idea?" Jane whispered, hooking her arm into Jack's.

He glanced at her. She'd tied her hair back up and stared up at him with round eyes.

"We already have to keep an eye on Burke. I didn't want to have to split our attention," he said, nodding at Mike and Burke. They walked ahead, Mike with a gun in the small of Burke's back.

Jane sniffed. "I will kill her if I get the chance, you know that, right?"

Swallowing, Jack nodded. Any argument he could come up with to sway her from murder smacked of sentimentalism.

Instead, he went with neutral agreement. "I can't argue with you, Jane."

"Addy would never forgive me, though," she said, tugging his arm. "Guess I'll just play it by ear."

Something inside uncoiled. She might be a pitiful excuse for a human, completely fixated on "curing" the human race of the virus, but still. She was the mother of two of his children. She'd been by his side for almost two decades. No matter how much it hurt to admit it, that couldn't just be erased.

"So, Burke," Jack said, "what are we walking into here?"

"Whatever you might think of your ex-wife," Burke said, "she's an incredible woman."

Jane scoffed. "That's not your brain talking, commander."

Burke, to his credit, flushed. Two high spots of color appeared in his cheeks. "Do you know what kind of physical and mental fortitude it must have taken to survive such an early dose of the Cure?"

"She said several other people took it as well," Jack said. The first night they'd all been back together repeated in his mind.

"They didn't survive, Dad." Mike pulled Burke into a hallway to their left. "This way."

The lights overhead flickered, the hallway dark and closed in. The antiseptic, clean smell that permeated the hospital receded.

Jane squeezed up next to Jack. "What do you mean, Michael? What happened to them?"

Burke answered. "There were at least half a dozen in that first test group. They all survived the dose, but once they returned to IRF's test facility, the results were... Well, they varied."

"Wait." Jack reached out for Burke's shoulder and stopped them all in the middle of the hallway. "IRF? I thought she worked for Talus. I thought they were the ones that found her."

"Seems like there's a lot of things you thought," Burke said, leaning into his face, his grey eyes alight. "That she was dead, top of the list." He loomed.

Jack stepped back.

Half a grin curving his mouth, Burke blew air out his nose. "You left her there to die. But she's stronger than you think. Too good for you." He pulled back up to his full height and looked down his nose.

Air knocked out of his lungs, Jack backed into the wall. Not that he believed what Burke was saying, but the shift in the IRF/Talus Crest paradigm had thrown him into an unexpected loop. Who were they, really?

"Jack, I'd like to get out of this hallway," Jane said.

He closed his eyes and swayed. The IRF thing would have to be sorted out later. The baby was the only thing that mattered right now.

Priorities aligned, he opened his eyes and followed Jane to the end of the hall. Removing the keycard from his pocket, he glanced at the picture.

Matt's unsmiling face.

"Hey," Burke said, bumping Mike with his shoulder and looking down at the keycard, "where did you get that?"

Jack frowned. "None of your business." He swiped it in front of the pad, unlocking the door.

"Tell me he's alright," Burke said, face twisted. "He's…" He paused, swallowing and glancing at Jack with his brow furrowed. "Just tell me he's alright."

Jack grabbed him by the arm and pushed him through the doorway.

"Don't tell me you give a shit about him, sweetie," Jane said, chuckling as she pulled the door closed.

The dark hallway threw deep shadows onto Burke's face. He shifted from foot to foot and cleared his throat. "It's just. He's the captain of the guard. And he's supposed to be keeping an eye on Ella. If you have his keycard, where is he? And"—he swallowed and glanced at Jack—"where is Ella?"

* * *

"No, Ella, stay behind me," Matt said, hacking at the Dead Head reaching over his shoulder.

"I can help fight, too," Ella said, dropping her arm. She slapped her leg with the flat side of a long-bladed knife.

Addy sighed, rolling her eyes sideways at Dean.

He grinned, corners of his eyes crinkled, and ended the 'Head in front of him. He pointed ahead of them with his forehead. "We make those trees, this'll get easier."

Kicking an approaching 'Head in the knees, Addy knocked its legs from under it and drove the machete through the side of its skull. "Yeah, just waiting on those guys to open up a hole."

Yasuo, Paul, and Celia spun like a top ahead of them. Though they'd chosen the area with the sparsest groupings of 'Heads, a horde was still a horde. With Ella in the middle of their circle, Addy and the others couldn't move quite as quick. But as Yasuo knocked them down, Celia finished them. And Paul kept his side clear so they could do the work of opening the path for both groups.

The three of them worked together almost as well as she, Jane, and Michael had, once upon a time.

"Six, Addy," Matt said.

Taking a large step away from Ella, her ankle twinging but doing well, all things considered, Addy swung for the 'Head's neck. With a clean sweep, she separated its head and stepped back into the circle.

"You need to teach me how to do that," Ella said, bumping her shoulder. "You look so cool."

Blood rushing to her cheeks, Addy glanced over her shoulder.

Sweating and flushed, Ella grinned. Her blue eyes sparkled, high forehead glistening. She'd never looked more alive, more energized.

Addy grinned. "It'd be my pleasure. But for now, stay between us, OK?"

"You got it. Behind you," she said, jutting her chin.

Spinning, Addy hit the next one in the forehead, end of her machete sticking halfway in.

The 'Head dropped, taking the damned blade with it.

"Why do these things always have to be so greedy with blades," Addy said, mostly to herself, as she worked to free it.

"Maybe they were knife collectors in their— Shit," Matt said. Bumping Addy's shoulder, he stepped over the 'Head and drove her Bowie knife, the one she'd let him keep, hilt-deep into the skull of a 'Head reaching for her.

Throwing one hand to the ground to steady herself, tiny pebbles and dried grass digging into her palm, Addy scowled. "Appreciate the assist, but maybe try not to knock me over while you're helping."

Matt backed up to Ella again, frowning. "Sorry. I— Yeah, sorry."

As her blade popped free, Dean grabbed her under the arm and hauled her to her feet. "We're gettin' left behind, sweetheart."

She glanced ahead. Three or four 'Heads had wandered into the space between their group and the others. "Do you and Matt have those? I'll stay back with Ella, cover the rear. We need to catch up."

Rather than answer, he kissed her on the cheek and stepped away.

Matt shadowed him, and they took down two at a time.

That didn't stop three more from popping up before her.

Addy's heart rate ratcheted up. This horde was getting out of hand and fast.

"Addy," Ella whispered, "what do we do?"

Without looking, Addy reached behind her and grabbed Ella's hand. She squeezed. "You stay between me and the guys. You'll be fine. Let us handle it."

Dropping Ella's hand, she beheaded one 'Head and drove her blade into the skull of another.

Its buzzing didn't stop. The blade thrummed as it tried to keep pushing forward.

It pushed against the blade in its head, and Addy stumbled back a step, fully expecting to run into Ella.

The air was empty behind her.

Glancing over her shoulder as she pushed back against the 'Head, she caught Ella stepping to her side and holding the long-bladed knife with both hands. A 'Head stumbled toward her, bubbling, gurgling, fingers still red.

Too fresh, too fast.

"Guys," Addy hissed. Her blade popped free, and the 'Head surged forward. "Ella, get behind me dammit," she said, swinging the machete like a baseball bat. She buried it in the cranial cavity of the same 'Head, which finally stopped its buzzing and drooped.

And the fresh one reached for Ella, muscles still mainly intact. The stupid thing wasn't even past its sixteen-hour expiration date.

If they'd had more Cure and more time, Addy would have tried to save them. But as it was, its teeth chomped and bit, closer and closer to Ella. There was only time to save one of them.

Before Addy could make a move to help, Ella closed her eyes and swung the long blade upward. She stifled a cry behind her lips.

A 'Head grabbed Addy's shoulder.

She swatted at it like a fly, taking one of its hands off at the wrist.

Ella's wild swing hit home. The blade curved up through the bottom of the 'Head's jaw and poked out the top of its skull. She yanked the knife free and squealed. Blood splattered into her face as she smiled from ear to ear. "Did you see that, baby?"

Addy punched the 'Head trying to bite her in the face and glanced around.

Matt stood grinning, breathing hard, eyes locked on Ella. "I saw it. I saw you kick its ass, sweet cakes," he said, crossing to her in two giant steps. One arm around her waist, he swung her in a circle and kissed her. Horde be damned.

"You want me to get that one," Dean said, hand on the small of Addy's back.

The one that had tried to bite Addy at least four times while she watched Ella worked its way back to its feet.

Grinning, Addy ended it and caught Dean's hand in hers. "Let's get to the trees. Come on, guys," she said, tugging Dean behind her.

Setting Ella on her feet, Matt took her hand, and the four of them dashed into the trees where Yasuo and the others waited.

CHAPTER 40

From the greenbelt across the street, Addy watched Ella's house. "There's at least two hundred 'Heads between here and there," she whispered.

Dean crouched next to her, peering through the same tree. "I don't know if there's gonna be a good time to do this."

"Now or never, kinda thing?" She gave him a side-eye.

He frowned. "I don't see what choice we have."

Addy nodded, stomach clenched. She ground her teeth together and swallowed. The stink of the horde surrounded them like the air they breathed. Permeated everything. Stuck to her nose hairs like it had been painted on.

She swallowed again. "How do you propose we get in once we get there?"

"How do we know it's locked?" Matt asked, kneeling next to them. Ella knelt as well, stuck to his hip like a binary star.

Addy pointed at the front windows. "Watch."

Narrowing her eyes, she stared at the front of the house and waited for what she'd seen earlier.

It didn't take long for Data's brown snout to reach up and sniff at the inside of the window, sneeze, leave doggie snot all over the glass, and wander off.

"See that," she said. Less of a question, more of a statement.

Ella was the first to nod. "Probably all over the furniture as we speak. Getting hair everywhere."

Addy shrugged. "He doesn't shed that bad."

"Still, do you know how hard I worked to find appropriately clean furniture to begin with? How much effort I put into keeping it clean?"

"Babycakes," Matt said, encircling her shoulders with his arm, "let's don't worry about that right now. OK?"

She nodded, laying her head on his shoulder. "It's my house, Matthew."

"Mann might argue that," Dean said.

"She might indeed," Paul said from behind them.

Heart leaping into her throat, Addy spun on a knee. "Damn, Paul. You sure can move quiet for an old guy."

Half his mouth raising, he bowed at the waist. "I'll take that as a compliment, little girl."

She grinned. "You're like the grandpa I never had," she said, standing. "Do you have any suggestions?"

He shook his head. "I can tell you Mann lived in that house first. She feels it's hers. She feels that way about the whole town."

"What about the others? The ones back at the jail, at the warehouse? They helped us," Addy said, stomach suddenly full of knots. If those people truly felt the way Mann did, they could turn on them at any time. Run the Emerald Isle people out into the streets and leave them for the horde to devour.

Closing her eyes, she shook her head and waited for Paul to answer.

He clicked his teeth. "Most of them would rather not see anyone hurt. If they have to, they'll live side by side with the new folks. They're as horrified about the horde being here as anybody."

"I thought she was their leader," Dean said, folding his arms. "Did that change?"

"Not overnight," Paul said. "But even they can't believe Mann would be this reckless."

Addy sighed. "So, back to the question. How do we get in if the doors are locked?"

Ella chuckled.

A 'Head stumbled in their direction.

Hand on the haft of her machete, Addy waited for it to approach. They'd have to let it into the trees before they killed it. If they stepped out, they'd be found by the horde.

As it was, they were pushing it. According to Mom, they could smell food. Didn't matter if they were hiding in the trees, eventually, they'd be sniffed out.

Addy tugged one of Dean's arms over her shoulder.

Wrapping her in it, he spoke to Ella. "So. What's so funny?"

Ella smiled. "It's my house, Dean. I don't know how many times I have to tell you that."

"Oh. Duh," Matt said, rolling his eyes. "You mean the tree."

Blushing, she dropped her eyes and smiled. "I mean the tree, baby."

Their grins catching, the corners of Addy's mouth raised. "Somebody want to clue me in?"

Matt glanced at her, blushing himself. "Her dad lets her walk with me at night. But she always has to be in right after."

"I remember the night walks," Addy said. "The first night I met you was on one of those, Ella." She shook her head as Dean pulled his arm loose and approached the 'Head. It had wandered into the trees. Buzzing with a loose rattle in its chest.

Probably its wasted lungs were in pieces by now. How they continued to drive the body was beyond explanation.

Ella watched Dean as he took care of it. "Me and Matt installed a window in the attic you can unlock from outside. You have to climb the tree to get to it."

"But you just climb the tree, zip on over to the window, and you're in," Matt added.

"Good lord, Ella," Addy said, the sound of Dean's knife popping through the brain of the 'Head too close, "you're a full-grown adult. Why wouldn't your dad just let him stay?"

Ella smiled with the corners of her mouth turned down. "Daddy is a bit old-fashioned."

"Daddy is overprotective. Even with me," Matt said, meeting her frown with one of his own.

"Bottom line," Paul said, holding his hand up, "is we have to climb that monster Magnolia."

Addy glanced behind him.

Celia sat with her back against a tree, covered in blood splatters and bits of rotted flesh. Poking at the ground with the tip of her knife.

Yaz stood next to her, leaning on his staff and glaring at the horde. When Addy caught his eye, he shook his head. "I shouldn't have come, Addy."

She patted Dean's shoulder as he joined her again, cleaning his knife. He caught her hand and kissed the inside of her palm.

Butterflies rushing through her belly, just like every time he did that, she stepped next to Yaz and lowered her voice. "What do you mean, Yaz?"

He glanced at her but couldn't keep eye contact. He swallowed, dimple in his cheek deep. "I'm— I'm scared." He shrugged. "I guess I don't do well with hordes." The nervous laugh that followed was something Addy had never heard issue from his mouth.

"Remember, Yaz, you're powerless over all this."

He nodded, eyes cast down. "While I realize that is fundamentally true, and the only thing I have control over is my actions," he said, nervous chuckle popping out again, "the only thing my actions really want to do is pee themselves and run away." He met her eyes and gave her half a pained smile. "I'll try."

She clapped him on the shoulder, and when he met her eyes again, she forced him into a hug.

He stiffened, then hugged her back. "You're right."

"I learned it from you," she said, stepping back.

Grimacing again, he turned his eyes to the street.

Celia stood, brushing off the ass of her pants, and frowned. Wiping some of the blood and bits of flesh off her face, she shrugged. "How are we doing this, Addy?"

She glanced at Ella. "You get between us again, alright?"

Ella nodded, raising her knife. She'd clenched both hands around it once more. "Got it."

"No heroics," Addy said, frowning at the knife.

Throwing her hair over her shoulder, Ella nodded again. "No heroics. Got it."

She did not "got it." But what could you do?

As she turned to address Dean, he wrapped an arm around her waist and buried his face in her neck. "Be safe, Addy."

"It's not a Sunday stroll, but I'm sure it'll be fine." She squeezed him back. She inhaled the scent that screamed Dean. Part man, part magic. Filled her lungs with it.

Would rather that scent overpower the stinking horde out there for as long as possible.

"Are we ready?" she asked, stepping back.

"Waiting on you," Matt said, Ella already behind him. Her fist balled in his coattail.

* * *

Jack stared at the skywalk.

Grey sunlight peeped through the glass surrounding the walkway. The walk itself held no cover. None. Not a stitch.

"I hate this," he said, gripping his knife.

"It's not ideal," Jane peeked over his shoulder, "but it's the only way to Katherine. We don't have a choice."

He nodded, frowning. Of course they had no choice. Didn't mean he had to like it. All that exposure. Being out in the open. Nothing to hide behind.

"Make it like a Band-Aid, Dad," Mike said. "Like you used to tell me."

"Painful but fast," Jack said, nodding. "You're right, son. Let's get this over with."

He glanced at Burke, who'd chewed his lip into a furrow after they'd told him Ella was at the jail. He'd insisted the house was the best place for her and had let them in on the tidbit that beyond the hospital, the bulk of the Cure was stored at the house. Not at the jail. And rather than continue his speech as the leader of Melinda's fan club, he'd been mostly silent since they refused to tell him how they'd acquired Matt's keycard.

He caught Jack staring and widened his eyes. "Don't look at me. I can't help you. It's long. It's exposed. It's hot. But it's the only way into her quarters from here."

Jack sighed, stomach one large, painful knot.

Jane kissed him on the cheek. "Come on, love. Let's get this done."

Nodding, using the spot where her lips had touched his cheek as a grounding point, he pushed the commander in front of him into the skywalk.

Burke was right. It was hot. It didn't take long for the chill to work its way out of his bones and float off into the air. Sweat popped out on his forehead before they'd crossed half of the walkway.

"Don't walk like you're a prisoner, dammit," he whispered.

Burke talked out the side of his mouth. "And how am I supposed to do that?"

"Straighten your shoulders," he said, hand itching to yank his gun from its holster and force the man to comply. "Walk like normal."

"That's difficult in handcuffs," Burke said. But he pulled his shoulders back and walked tall.

Jack grunted. It was the best he could expect.

Movement out of the corner of his eye.

Two guards sauntered in from the wall, heading under the skywalk.

"Jane," he whispered, "try to hide behind Burke. It's best if they don't see you."

She nodded, making herself small as she ducked behind the larger man. Burke had at least a hundred pounds on her. He made good cover for her.

Turning his face away from the guards below, Jack widened his eyes at Mike. "Wave."

Nodding, plastering a smile to his face, Mike lifted a hand as the guards passed under their feet.

Jane switched sides.

Jack continued to stare forward but let his peripheral wander as the two guards came back into view.

One of them raised a hand back to Mike and said something.

But it wasn't loud enough to hear, and Jack couldn't turn his head to read lips. "What'd they say, Mike?"

"Pretty sure they called me a spoiled brat."

Jane chuckled.

Jack's brow furrowed. "A what? Why would they say that?"

Three-quarters through. Almost there.

"My guys live like the military," Burke said. "Not in fancy houses like you people."

Jack eyed his back. "You've got a military background, then?"

Burke nodded. "It's served me well these last twenty-five years. No reason to abandon it now."

Reaching the door at the other end, sweat rolling down his back, Jack pulled Matt's keycard out again.

"That won't work here," Burke said.

Before his words had taken the time to find themselves a home in Jack's head, he'd swiped the card.

The pad beeped and turned green. The latch let go, and Jane pulled the door open.

Burke's jaw dropped. Eyes red, he glanced at the card in Jack's hand. "How'd— What— Matt?"

Shoving him between the shoulder blades, Jack pushed him through the door and followed. "We can discuss that inside," he said, eager for cover.

Mike followed and closed the door behind them all, sealing off the light and the heat.

The latch re-engaged.

Jack breathed deep, filling his lungs with cool, dark air.

Before he exhaled, Burke bumped him with his chest, backing him into the wall. "You tell me how that keycard works on this door," he growled. "I might be cuffed, but I can kill you six ways without my hands."

"Try it," Jane said, her silver blade appearing in front of his throat.

All Jack could see of her was a slender fist wrapped around the haft of her knife. But the way Burke's torso arched told him another knife had poked into his back. Maybe hard enough to draw blood. The commander sucked a breath over his teeth.

"OK, OK. I'm not going to hurt him. Please. Just tell me," Burke said, both trying to glance over his shoulder at her and not move at the same time.

"Well, Casey, it's a hell of a story, if you've got time," Melinda said.

Jack closed his eyes. This was about to get ugly.

* * *

Keeping an eye on the house while fighting 'Heads and making sure Ella didn't die was a touch more than Addy had signed up for today. She did the best she could with it.

At the very least, only Paul was bitten before they all got in the tree.

He hadn't cursed or shouted, and the only way she'd even known he was bitten was when Dean climbed up after helping him onto the second-lowest branch.

She frowned at his hand. "You've got blood on your hand, Dean. Are you alright?"

Wiping his palm on the tree, Dean inspected his hand and arm. "Not my blood." He glanced under his feet where Paul sat, panting and leaning against the trunk. "You bit?"

Paul nodded. "Just a touch."

"Take your dose," Addy said, pitching her voice low. The horde couldn't reach them up here, but Mann could still stick them in this tree forever if she caught them out here. Clenching the scratchy bark, she leaned as far as she dared.

"Once we get inside. I'm fine." He flapped his hand at her.

"Dad would kill me if something happened to you. Take your damn dose."

"Addy," Dean said, pointing over her shoulder.

Ella had climbed out onto the roof, and Matt had followed. Holding her fingertips, he walked on the downhill side of her as they crossed the porch roof.

Walking on her toes, Ella wobbled a few times. Her feet never slipped, and Matt made her stop more than once to get her bearings.

Addy couldn't hear him from here, but his lips moved the entire time. Talking her through it, most likely.

Yasuo and Celia followed them onto the roof once they had the attic window open. Matt climbed through first and leaned out to help Ella through the tiny opening.

"Come on," Dean said, "let's get inside."

Addy climbed. Her heart pounded against the inside of her ribs hard enough to crack them. She didn't climb often, and when she did, it was generally something more solid like a ladder. The last time she'd climbed a tree, she'd all but broken her ankle. And if something happened inside, they had a few hours before Paul turned. She'd be happier if he got the Cure sooner rather than later.

Without warning, Oren's bouncing red mustache appeared in her head.

She stopped, breathing hard, and closed her eyes. Hands wrapped around two branches, she let the sensation of the dry bark bite into her palms. Let it erase the memory of his last moments. His cheek pressed against the grate. Red mustache grinding into his face, blood glistening on his whiskers.

"You alright, sweetie?" Dean climbed up next to her.

"Fine." Lips tight, she climbed onto the roof. And when her ankle went out from under her, he was there to catch her. She kept one hand locked in one of his, and they crossed the roof together, Paul bringing up the rear.

She climbed into the window. Yasuo grabbed her under the arms and pulled her in.

Sitting next to the window, she watched Dean and Paul as they climbed through. Dean slipped in sideways, and Paul locked more than one groan behind his lips, but it seemed they all crossed into the house without being found out by the inhabitants below.

Addy glanced around and whispered at Dean. "Where's Ella?"

Dean closed the window and looked around the room. Half a grin on his face, he took Addy's hand and hauled her to her feet. "Not right now, man," he said, speaking low over his shoulder.

Matt and Ella appeared from the shadows.

Using a thumb to wipe the corner of his mouth, Matt smiled. "Right. You're right." Two spots of red on his cheeks, he held Ella's hand. "What now, Addy?"

"We need to get downstairs and get control of Mann and whoever else is here. We know"—she glanced at the group—"there's at least one child here with her."

"Dora," Celia said. "She comes with the dog."

"Exactly," Addy said, nodding. "I have no idea how many other people there are, or even how many rooms there are. Ella?"

"I can navigate this house with my eyes closed, Adelaide Cooke. I can certainly tell you where all the rooms are." Throwing her shoulders back, she sniffed.

"Course you can," Addy said. The same knee-jerk of slapping Ella in her head threatened to pop up, but she cut it off. Ella didn't deserve to be slapped.

Paul grunted.

Addy caught him pulling an empty syringe from his arm. Thank god.

"Right as rain in a minute," he said, capping the hypo and pocketing it. "So, groups of two?"

Addy nodded, glancing at the others. "Except Matt and Ella. Cee, you wanna go with them?"

Ella frowned, eyes cast down. "You don't want to come with me, Addy?"

"Course I do," Addy said, touching her on the arm.

Addy and Jane had always been close. Jane had always given a shit. But she'd never acted like she needed Addy. She probably did, but she'd never let the walls down enough to show it. Having Ella show her heart so clearly took Addy off guard. Knocked the wind out of her a bit. But right now, she wanted to be with Dean. There was a damned horde outside, and she'd never been closer to losing him as she had in the last few minutes. She played a good game of steady and fearless when they were fighting, but it was too hard to shake the fear of losing him.

Now, how to tell Ella that without making her upset.

Ella grabbed her hand and glanced at Dean. "You don't have to explain, Addy." She leaned in, whispering, "He's damn pretty. I hope that's alright to say."

Addy grinned, cheeks hot. She lowered her voice to match Ella's. "He's a hell of a guy, too, Ella. So is Matt. We're lucky girls."

Nodding, Ella stepped back and hooked an arm into Matt's. "So, you're with us, Celia?" She threw her hair back again. "You're so good with that blade. You're all such good fighters." She looked around at them all. "I hope I don't get in your way."

"You're not so bad, muffin," Matt said, squeezing her. "Now, are you going to show us around the house, or am I going to have to do it?"

She nodded. Pointing down the stairs, she explained the four rooms on the second floor and reiterated the layout of the ground floor.

"But the Cure in the basement, that's behind two doors. Both of which are locked by combination and fingerprint scan."

"Shit, Ella," Dean said, "are we going to be able to get in those doors?"

"Of course," Ella said, straightening. "My fingerprint will open them both. Daddy wouldn't leave me in this house alone without a way to get to the Cure." She sniffed. "What do you think my daddy is, some kind of monster?"

Celia opened her mouth.

Addy stepped between them. "Let's just go. Once we clear the top floor, we'll get downstairs and get the Cure. Remember, don't shoot anyone unless you have to."

Yasuo lifted his staff. "I won't be shooting anyone, that's for sure."

Addy grinned. "Wish I'd brought mine. It's pretty useful for non-lethal."

Nodding, Yasuo glanced at her machete. He opened his mouth, breathed in, and closed it without a word. Neither smiling nor frowning, he peeked at the window. "I'm not looking forward to taking it back into that horde, I can tell you that."

Brain twisted, Addy couldn't decide how she was supposed to feel. Normally annoyingly confident without being full of ego, Yaz had never shown as much fear as had been oozing from his pores since they left the jail.

No, since before that. Since they'd found out about the horde. He'd been more skittish than a mouse in a cage full of cats.

And not that it threw everything he'd taught her into question, but how was she supposed to process this? Everything he'd taught her had been with the intention of conquering fear. How many times had he told her "if it's not love, it's fear"? And told her she needed to let go of the anger, the sadness, the fear?

Shaking her head and shelving the doubts for a better time, she stepped to the top of the stairs and looked down.

"Let's do this thing."

CHAPTER 41

Jack opened his eyes in time to see a knife sail across the room.

It buried itself in Melinda's left shoulder.

Grunting, Melinda lifted her right arm, a snub-nosed .38 peeking out of her fingers.

Jane raised another knife and took a step toward her. "Go ahead," she said, nodding to Melinda's shoulder. "That was a freebie. The next one will be in your cold, black heart."

"Oh sweetie," Melinda purred, "you have no idea how black my heart is. I was going to give you the chance to find out," she said, glancing down at the hilt of the knife protruding from her shoulder, "but you know what?" She aimed at Jane's forehead and pulled back the hammer.

Shoving Burke out of the way, Jack jumped between them and raised his hands. "Look, stop. Alright?" Catching Melinda's eyes, he stared.

She narrowed her eyes.

What Mike said about her wanting to kill them both flashed through his mind.

Crap, Jack. Probably not such a great idea to step in front of this gun.

Better me than her.

He took another step toward Melinda. "Can we just fucking talk about this like grown-ups?"

Melinda's thumb remained on the hammer. But she eased her finger off the trigger. And slapped him in the cheek with the gun.

As his head exploded with red light, Jane shouted from far away. Mike, too.

Probably best for Jane that Mike got to Melinda first, ripping the gun from her hand. "Mom, stop."

Melinda sighed. "I feel better already." Giving the knife a quick tug, she dropped it to the ground. It splattered blood in a semicircle, and she walked into the room beyond the entryway. "Let Casey out of those cuffs, Jackson."

Opening and closing his jaw, the joint on the side she'd hit threatening to lock up, he shook his head. "I don't think—"

The baby began to cry. Long, loud wails.

Before he even had time to reach for her, Jane had taken off at a sprint. The front of her shirt wet.

Curling up in a ball and waiting for Melinda to murder them all might be preferable, but he had a baby to protect. A woman, and a grown son, too.

"Don't let him out of those cuffs, Mike," he said, following Jane. "Let's go talk to your mother."

The hallway opened into a large living space. It still had the same faux-tile floor coverings the rest of the hospital had, but area rugs had been lain over most of the floor, so they absorbed much of the sound. It had the feel of several rooms being combined into one. What looked like it could have been a doctor or nurse's break area spanned part of one wall, with a sink, a fridge, and some cabinets. A stove had been moved in.

All this made up like a one-room apartment.

Jack edged over next to Jane.

She stood five feet from Melinda, who was holding the squirming baby. Tears welled in Jane's eyes. "Give her back, Melinda. Please," she said, leaning against him. Shaking, she vibrated in waves.

"You know nothing of what it takes to be a real mother," Melinda said, lip curling, "but if there's one thing I can appreciate, it's wanting to hold your baby in your arms. And since I don't have a bottle ready," she said, trailing off. She took two steps toward Jane.

Jack held his breath. There was so little he could do to protect either of them. Anything could happen.

Melinda laid the baby in Jane's arms and stepped away.

Jane's tears fell in Katherine's face as the baby stopped crying and rooted into Jane's chest. Crying freely, Jane turned her back on Melinda and found a place to sit.

Lip still curled, Melinda watched as Jane sat and nursed the baby, her silent tears still flowing.

And Jack still didn't let that breath out. It was too easy.

"There, everybody's happy," Melinda said, peeking up at him. Eyes red-rimmed, she glanced at Burke. "Now that she's got what she wants, could you please release those handcuffs? Then we can all sit and talk." She sniffed. "Like fucking adults."

Jack sat next to Jane and let the barrel of his gun drift toward the commander. "I wouldn't try anything."

"I just want to get her cleaned up." Burke pointed to Melinda with his forehead. Leaning forward so Mike could release his hands, he kept his eyes on her.

Jack glanced at Melinda. "You have a first aid kit?"

She took a step toward the kitchen area.

"No. Stop," Jack said, standing. "I'll get it. Sit," he said, pointing at a chair with the gun.

Frowning, Melinda sat. "Do what you like, Jackson."

He found the little white box with its red cross under the sink. Handing it off to Burke, he sat and watched as Melinda unbuttoned her shirt enough to pull down the bloody shoulder.

Burke drew a breath across his teeth and glared at Jane. "You're lucky those knives are sharp. Doesn't look like you've caused any permanent damage."

"So what you're saying is, *she's* lucky they're sharp," Jane said, without looking up. She continued staring down at the baby and stroking her chubby little cheek with one finger.

The tiny, blue-eyed baby stared up at her mother as she suckled, kicking her little feet.

Before he could be overtaken with love for them both, Jack glanced at Burke again.

He'd cleaned the wound and was taping gauze down.

Mike sat on the arm of the couch where Jane had parked herself. Planting himself on the same side of the room as she and Jack. Picking a side without speaking.

Melinda frowned. "Your sister has already proven her disloyalty, Michael. I didn't expect it from you as well."

"I love you, Mom. You know that."

Burke grunted. "Got a funny way of showing it, kid. Leading your dad here."

"It's his baby, guys. You can't keep her from him. It's wrong." Arms crossed, Mike slid down to the couch cushion next to Jack.

Jack's heart soared, to have both Mike and the baby back.

Of course, that feeling could never last.

Smirking, Melinda waved a hand in the air.

A door opened, and no less than six guards entered the room. Rifles drawn and aimed.

Jack sighed. "Are you going to kill us now and take the baby back, Melinda?"

She stood and leaned on the back of the chair. "No, Jackson. Michael was right to keep me away from you for a few days. I would have killed you, and her"—she jutted her chin at Jane—"and that would have ruined my chances at more complete research."

Stomach sinking, Jack slid closer to Jane and put an arm around her. He lowered the gun. It'd do him no good now.

Without warning, he flashed on Andrew. Poor Andrew. Half 'Head, half human. There'd been enough of him left to save Jack, but most of his humanity had been stripped away by Melinda and her "research."

Jack grimaced. "What kind of research?"

She smiled. "There are so many unanswered questions. Was it the vaccine that created baby Katherine's immunity?"

One of the guards gasped.

"Yes," Melinda faced the boys, "that baby is immune. The first of her kind. Thanks to me." She bowed.

The guards shifted on their feet, a couple of them smiling and staring at Jane.

Like maybe they couldn't wait to have their own immune babies with her.

Sliding his hand from around her, pausing to slip his fingers into the patch of hair at the nape of her neck, Jack fought the sudden, overwhelming urge to kiss her like there was no tomorrow. Because there might not be.

He stood, putting himself between Jane and Katherine and the guards. A couple of them, not the ones grinning at Jane, had lowered their rifles.

"Don't think I don't appreciate what you've done for us, Melinda," he said, glancing over his shoulder. Jane and their baby, both never to catch the virus. Never to turn. One death was all they owed. "But we aren't going to just stay here and become your lab rats." Keeping his body between the guards and Jane, he inched toward the closest one, a steady stream of words flowing from his mouth. "There's a horde outside, you know." He angled his head at the window. "I don't know how they got in, but they're here now. And we've all got to go. It's only a matter of time before they overrun this hospital of yours."

A couple more of the boys lowered their rifles. Not completely, but their guard was dropping, one by one.

"Besides, don't you have all the samples you need? You kidnapped my baby," he said, glancing at the guards. One of them openly glared at Melinda. Must have been a father himself. "Don't tell me you didn't almost drain her dry over the past few days."

Breaking off from whispering in Burke's ear, Melinda sat up.

Burke stood and left the room, exiting through one of the three doors along the back wall.

"We'll soon know more about this horde you're talking about. If it's not just some trick you're using to scare me."

Jack edged closer to the nearest guard. "You can't seriously expect me to believe you don't already know about the horde. Thought you were better informed than that." He could no longer keep himself between Jane and them, not all of them, but he glanced at their feet, getting a good look at each position. Hoping to keep them distracted with the words.

He marked the one who'd glared at Melinda. Making no plans to kill any of them, he didn't fool himself into thinking there would be no casualties. He didn't want this young father to be one of them, though.

"Besides, you don't scare that easily, Melinda," he said, taking one more sliding step.

Melinda waved a lazy hand over her shoulder again.

The guard closest to him jerked, raising his gun into Jack's face. "Step back, sir."

Surprised the boy's voice didn't crack, Jack grinned with one side of his mouth. "Sure."

He put one foot behind him and dropped his weight back.

The boy stepped forward.

Grabbing the end of the gun, Jack pulled.

Helped along by the forward momentum, the guard flew into Jack. Spinning, Jack bucked at the hips and threw the boy to the ground. He ripped the rifle from his hands, planted a foot in the kid's chest, and opened fire on the rest of them.

* * *

"Matt," Addy whispered, "how many?"

Peeking around the bedroom door, Matt flashed five fingers twice.

She turned back to Dean. "If there's almost a dozen up here, we have to assume there's at least that many downstairs."

"Plus your very quiet dog and one little girl," he said, glancing down the stairs.

"Guys," Matt said, dashing from the bedroom on silent toes.

How did he manage to make combat boots so stealthy?

"Two of them are bitten. We had to give them our last two doses."

Addy frowned, stomach churning.

The woman she'd met in the woods, she was driven. Bitter. Bent on revenge. But to put her own people in such danger. To march alongside a horde of literal thousands, without extra doses.

When had Mann become so broken? And why hadn't someone stopped her?

Swallowing, she glanced down the stairs. "Are they secure?"

"They're tied. And Celia's holding them. I'd say so," Matt whispered, a smile in his voice.

Shoving her gut down, Addy put one foot on the stairs. "Get Ella. And Yaz. Paul and Cee can handle those guys while we get this done."

Matt trotted off, feet still silent, and disappeared into the second room.

The hall clock downstairs *tick-tick-ticked*. It would have driven Jane nuts.

Of course, if it was her dad's hall clock, it would have been ticking, but not because it was telling time. The proximity alarm had been buried deep inside his grandfather clock, and it would be playing hell with them right now if this was his house.

It seemed more 'Heads arrived every minute. Soon there'd be hundreds, just around the house.

"It's a little exciting, isn't it?" Ella said, ducking in behind her.

Addy glanced at her.

Ella's whole face flushed, and she smiled. High cheekbones red under her flashing blue eyes.

Keeping her gorge in check, Addy nodded. "It can be. I guess." She pointed to Dean.

He crept down the stairs. Gun aimed, he crouched to look below the banister.

Holding her breath, Addy waited for him to signal.

After sitting still for at least thirty seconds, Dean waved her down.

She crept down six stairs until she could also see under the banister. Mouth open, she drew in a breath to speak.

Dean glanced over his shoulder, eyes wide.

She closed her mouth and frowned.

OK, maybe talking isn't a great idea. But why hasn't Data noticed we're in the house?

The boards in the living room creaked with footsteps. Mann said something about getting water.

Rushing down the rest of the stairs, Dean spun around the banister and disappeared from sight. As Matt blew past Addy on silent feet, she dashed after them both.

Yasuo and Ella plastered to her back, they rounded the banister and took the hall to the kitchen.

Low murmuring drew them closer, whoever was talking unaware they weren't alone.

Listening, Addy flashed three fingers over her shoulder. Putting one finger down, she made eye contact with Yaz. Forked her fingers at the kitchen. Then lowered one more finger, pointed to Yaz, and aimed him to the left. One more point, at Ella, to the right, and at her own chest.

Yaz nodded, lifting his staff.

Ella shrugged.

Rolling her eyes, Addy took Ella's hand with her left and hefted the machete in her right. She flipped the handle so the dull side would hit her enemies. These weren't Dead Heads. They were people, and they didn't deserve to die.

Staff at the ready, Yasuo leapt forward when she nodded.

Stomach in her throat, Addy jumped into the kitchen after him. Taking in the scene with as little thought as possible, marking Yaz fighting one already, she dropped Ella's hand, hit the man closest to the door in the shoulder with the dull side of the machete, and followed with a left-handed jab to the nose.

He stumbled, hands clapping to his face. Nose spurting blood.

Yasuo absolutely danced, even in the small space. With economy of movement, his staff spinning, he attacked and defended in equal parts, striking blows with only enough force to injure. Watching the grace with which he fought, the calm center within the whirling staff, brought tears to Addy's eyes.

When the one bleeding from the nose came at her again, she stuck her left arm up. Dropping the machete, she blocked his incoming punch and delivered an uppercut of her own at the same time. It hit him right in the "go to sleep button," and he fell to the floor like a sack of rocks.

But the third one. The third one came out of nowhere.

Something, a freight train maybe, hit Addy just behind the ear. A cracking sound, it might have been her skull, echoed.

She stumbled, flashes of light behind her eyes and thunder in her ears. The train hit her in the back, and she fell to her knees, gasping for air.

A boot drove itself into her stomach, knocking out the rest of the air and sending her to the floor.

Closing her eyes for the next hit, she tried to both catch her breath and hold it at the same time, sucking her abs in. Her back, her front, her head, all screamed in pain.

The next hit didn't come.

And didn't come.

She opened her eyes.

A face swam into focus, lying on the floor just in front of her. Blood dripping from the corner of their mouth into the floor.

"Mumble mumble?"

Addy rolled over and looked up.

Ella stood over her, holding a wine bottle by the neck. It floated over her shoulder like a baseball bat. "Mumble mumble?" she asked again.

Addy shook her head.

Dropping the bottle, Ella stuck out her hand. She hauled Addy to her feet. "Is he breathing?"

Addy glanced down. Her ears rang, but at least English was making sense again.

The man's chest moved up and down in slow, steady waves.

"He's breathing," she said. Her voice coming from far away, it echoed off the inside of her skull. "We secure?"

Stepping between them, Yasuo tied the man's wrists with a rope, finishing it in some kind of knot Mom had tried to teach her on a long-ago day of beach fishing.

"We're secure," he said. With a small bow, he thanked Ella for her help.

"You son of a bitch," a strident voice called, "get your hands off me."

Dean stepped into the kitchen, pushing a tied Mann before him. Matt followed, Dean's gun trained on her.

"Sit," Dean said, pointing at the table. "Is this everyone?"

Mann sat, glanced around the kitchen, then made eye contact with Addy. "You. I should have known it'd be you." She glared at Matt. "And this one. Always saying he wanted to help us. I knew it was too good to be true. Can never trust a man."

Grimacing and holding her side, Addy knelt next to her. "No, no, you can't. Ms. Mann. What have you done to your people?

How many of them are part of that horde out there now?" She waved an arm in the vague direction of outside.

Mann's chin jutted, her nostrils flaring. "Oh, look at you on your high horse. Friends with this girl," she angled her head at Ella, "who looks like she thinks she owns the place."

"This is my house," Ella said, standing up straight.

Mann moved to stand.

Matt shoved her back in the seat. "Stay right there, please, ma'am."

"Or don't," Dean said, leaning on the table and looming over her. "We can do it either way, really."

Addy fought a grin. Watching them play off each other entertained her in a way she'd never really thought of. Something Dad had once called "good cop, bad cop."

"Laurel," Addy said, "we can talk about all this later. Right now, we have to get our doses of Cure. Help the rest of your people. And get us all the hell out of here."

"We're not—" Mann began.

Data's barking interrupted her.

While she ought to be glad to hear him, Addy's nerves started jangling.

And why hit home two seconds later.

"Addy," Dean said, "it's coming from outside."

CHAPTER 42

Jumping up so fast she knocked the chair over, Mann shoved Matt with her shoulder and ran to the window. Her throat worked, but all she did was whimper.

Helping Matt up, Addy glanced at Dean. "Which way?"

He smoothed his face and closed his eyes. "West." He flashed those emerald gems at her and joined Mann at the window. Encircling her forearm with a hand, he guided her back to the table.

"We'll get her back," Addy said, insides jittering. She patted Mann on the shoulder and walked past her to the window above the sink. Leaning across the sink, she looked out back.

While they'd been inside the house, the horde had probably doubled in size. They buzzed like a beehive, rocking and rolling into each other.

There'd only been two other times she'd seen anything close to this.

"They stink more than the ones on the mainland," Yaz said from her elbow.

With a start, she looked down.

He crouched against the smooth cabinets, staff in front of him. His head hung. "Maybe the ocean makes everything smell better."

Crouching next to him, she shrugged. "I dunno. The sound still smells pretty damn bad. And so does that horde."

"I've seen them out there a couple times," he said, lifting his head and staring at the opposite wall. Eyes unfocused. "I'd almost hoped they'd been on Emerald Isle when you guys killed so many of them." He stopped, looking at his shoes.

When he glanced at her, a tear fell from each eye. He sniffed. "They were good people, Addy."

"I'm sure they were, Yaz. I'm sure of it." Her throat burned, but she blinked fast, and the tears evaporated.

"Anyway. I've seen them since then. Did you know—" Breaking off, he wiped his face and made a sound in the back of his throat. Like a rabbit caught in a trap. "Did you know I always see them together? Like they somehow know to stick together. Like they know"—he swallowed, staring at the ground again—"like they know who they are."

Addy blinked fast again, all but fanning the tears away with her lashes. Still, one crowded the inside corner of her eye. "We have no way of knowing. After sixteen hours, we lose our chance to find out."

He nodded, cheek dimpling. "I know. They're long gone. It's been years," he said. "Years. How are they even still there? Don't you think they'd just decay to nothing while their blood all dried up?"

"Addy, I think your mom has theories about that, if, you know, you were interested," Matt said.

Her head snapped up so fast she smacked it on the cabinet. "We need to get the girl. Yasuo, you bringing that staff or what?"

He shook his head, not watching her stand.

"You. No. Do you need a gun or something?"

Shaking his head again, he slid the rest of the way to the floor and sat, legs splayed in front of him. He laid his staff on the ground. "I can't go out there again. I'm staying here."

He could've picked up that staff and slammed it into her rib cage. It would feel better than whatever just happened.

She knelt next to him again and whispered. "What do you mean, you can't go out there? Come on, Yaz. No fear, remember? If it's not love—"

"Adelaide," he said, looking up. No anger tinted his voice, but the edge of it held tears. "I cannot go out there."

Addy's mouth flopped open and closed three times before any words followed. "Are you sure?" The best she could do.

Watching him and understanding that she could become this unshakable entity, just like him, had sometimes been the only thing to keep her going after the prison. Besides working the fear out of her, he'd taught her to believe in herself again at a time when she hardly believed in anything. Her mom's "resurrection" had shaken her into dust. And Yaz had built her back, piece by piece.

But how was she supposed to move forward if he couldn't do that for himself anymore? Was it even worth it to keep going down the same path?

She shook her head. Better to mull this shit over later. Right now, a little girl and her dog needed her. But before she stood, Yaz grabbed her arm.

"You take it." He held the staff out to her.

Stunned, her mouth dry, she couldn't even ask him if he was sure. She just took it and met Dean by the door.

Matt stepped up next to him. Addy's Bowie knife in hand.

Next to him, Ella held a handful of his shirt. Long-bladed knife in the other. Eyebrows arched, daring them to question her.

The three of them spoke at the same time.

"Ella, I don't think—"

"Listen, you're—"

"Pumpkin pie, I wouldn't—"

She pointed the knife at Matt. "I love you, baby. But I want to come." Pulling her shoulders back, she lifted her brows higher and stared at him with wide eyes.

Before he or Dean could open their mouths and insert their feet, maybe with a nice side of salt, Addy grabbed Ella's arm and asked her to join her. She led Ella out of the kitchen and stepped just inside the hall.

"Listen, Ella, I want you to come. I do. You're not fearless, or really that great with a blade, or terribly calm under pressure, but—"

"That's a nice string of insults, Addy," Ella said, frowning at the floor. She kicked at an imaginary rock.

"But you've got incredible determination, and you're loyal and trustworthy. Once you get past that hard shell," she went on, pretending Ella hadn't spoken. Addy poked her in the shoulder, inexplicable butterflies flitting about her insides. It'd been hard to know the girl, and harder still to open up to her. But now that she had, there was no turning back. "That shell of yours is just a show, you know." She pointed her thumb back toward herself. "I've got one of my own. You think I'm all strong." She stopped and chuckled. "But it's just an act. Just like your hard shell."

Frowning, Ella swiped at her eye. "What's your point?"

Addy gripped her shoulder and waited for Ella to make eye contact. "I love you, and I need you to stay here. Besides, we haven't gotten you to open up the basement yet. We need that Cure, and we can't get it without you."

Ella shifted like she wanted to crush Addy in a hug. After taking a step toward her, she stepped back again and smiled. "I'll do that while you're gone. You're right." Looking down, she did crush Addy into a hug, pushing the wind out of her lungs. "I love you, too, Adelaide Cooke. Get back safe."

Without making eye contact, Ella handed her the long-bladed knife and opened the door to the basement.

* * *

Shooting the one in front of him in the arm, Jack aimed low and squeezed off another round before they even thought to fire those weapons they'd brought.

The next one went down with a bullet in his thigh, and Jack clocked the one on which he stood with the butt of the rifle. Then he dropped, rolling back to the couch and crouching behind the coffee table.

Michael and Jane had already sheltered behind the table. Jane cradled the baby between her raised knees and her body, hunched over her. Knife in one hand.

Again, he fought the urge to kiss her. Their time together from here on could be as short as forever or as long as a moment. He suddenly needed it to be a good moment.

Wood splintered in front of her face, chunks of it flying toward her eyes.

She closed her eyes and ducked as Michael fired back. The couch jumped back an inch when the bullet that'd torn up the tabletop slammed into it.

As Jack flipped the table up with one arm, he glanced at the guards.

The one he'd clocked, the young father, still lay in the floor, unconscious. The two he'd shot also lay in the floor, writhing through the pain those bullet holes transmitted to their brains.

Melinda had disappeared.

Peering out, heartbeat in his throat, Jack caught sight of her shoes on the other side of the chair she'd been sitting in.

"Jackson, this is ridiculous. We don't need to fight," she said. "I just need to run some simple tests. Study some things."

"If it were really that simple," he said, covering behind the table again and watching his boy, "you wouldn't have brought in all these kids with guns. No. You're lying."

Dropping the magazine, he estimated it was about a quarter full. For a half second, he wondered where the rest of the bullets had gone.

Slamming the magazine back into place, he lay on his belly and crawled past Jane.

She squeezed his shoulder on the way.

He never should have brought her. He should've insisted. Forced her to stay back. If he couldn't get her out of here, anything that happened was on him.

"Jackson," Melinda said, sighing, "it's no lie. I'd really rather not hurt anyone. They were a precaution against you going all hero. Looks like a necessary precaution."

Jane chuckled. "You're a terrible liar, Melinda. Must be where Addy gets it. She can't lie to save her life." Holding the baby close to her body, she put her back to the table. "You'd like to hurt us both, like you did when you had Mike take the baby. So you've gotten what you wanted. How much more blood do you want to try and squeeze from this stone?"

"At least a few more vials."

She'd moved closer.

Jane pulled a long length of fabric from her waist, wrap after wrap of it falling to the floor. Once it was all loose, she began to twist it around herself and the baby.

Mike pointed two wide blue eyes at Jack. Mouth clamped shut.

They'd need Jack to cover their escape.

"Melinda," he said, turning back around, "what do you need from me to end this? I don't want to kill all your men."

Silence.

"You know I could. To protect my children, I'd do anything."

She sniffed. Closer still.

Between Jane and Mike, he sat and faced the table. Aimed the rifle low and to the right of where it sounded like Melinda was.

Taking a breath and hoping his aim was true, he exhaled and squeezed off a round.

It slammed through the table, pushing it back half an inch. Jane didn't so much as flinch, but Michael let out a whimper.

Melinda, on the other hand. Melinda screamed. A deep-throated, scratchy, red scream.

But she moved away as she did. No doubt taking shelter behind the chair again.

"Surrender yourself, Jack," she said. "I can pull the same trick you just did. I know where she is. I know where you are. Surrender yourself, and I'll leave them out of it."

And even though she wasn't to be trusted, his legs tensed to stand. He laid the rifle on the ground and began to raise his hands.

It was him she wanted all along. That had to be it. She'd let Jane and the baby go if he gave himself up.

Jane grabbed his half-raised wrist and clenched. Hard. Her nails dug into the soft tissue below his palm.

His tendons popped. The pain centered him, and he stopped. Took a breath. Looked at her.

Her narrowed eyes shone. Her lips clenched in a frown, she shook her head twice, side to side. Nostrils flaring, she gripped his wrist with a steady hand and cradled the baby with the other. Though he hadn't heard it fall, her knife lay on the floor next to her foot.

Taking another breath, he raised her wrist to his mouth and kissed the tips of her fingers. Gave her a single nod.

She released him.

"I can't do that, Melinda. My kids need me," he said, glancing at Mike.

Michael nodded. "He's right, Mom. I need you both."

Melinda laughed. "And so you shall have us. I promise I won't hurt him."

Jack shook his head.

But Melinda spoke before he had the chance to scoff. "Much."

He picked up Jane's knife and handed it to her, catching her eyes. He opened his mouth to speak...

A door on the other side of the room crashed open. Burke spoke, voice thick. "Mellie. There's a horde. We have to go."

...and saw red.

It engulfed his senses. Though Melinda spoke to Burke, confirming the size of the horde and whatever else he knew about it, the sound was nothing but a murmur. His ears rang, and vertigo gripped him. Without breath, he sat on his ass and closed his eyes.

Look, Jack. You don't even want her anymore. She's not your Mellie. Your Mellie is dead and gone. This woman can be anyone else's Mellie.

Eyes wide, he glanced at Jane.

The smallest of smiles turned her lips up, the very beginning of lines beside each corner. She whispered, "I know, baby. It's OK."

He inhaled as deep as he could.

"We'll be fine here, Casey," Melinda said. "Just get IRF to send some troops. We'll push the horde back and get our test population back in place. It won't be a total loss."

"But—"

"Grow some balls, Burke. Call your boss, get the men. I'm handling something here." She raised her voice. "Right, Jackson?"

"Mellie, I need to find out where Ella is," Burke said, his voice growing faint. The door slammed.

Kneeling, Mike leaned close and whispered in his ear. "Dad, what are we doing?"

He shook his head again. "Melinda, I—"

Heat flared in his hip, as though someone had hit him with a hard fist. He had time to ask himself why his leg should be so hot before the sound of the shot hit his ears. No searing pain swept through him, just a hot streak running from his hip to somewhere down his thigh.

His ears began to ring, even as Jane shouted. Screamed. Drew three knives and crouched, facing the table.

"I'll fucking kill you, I swear to god," she said, peeking over the table.

"I was aiming for you," Melinda called. "But I didn't want to hit that precious baby."

"So you hit Dad instead," Mike said, rising up on the other side of him.

Jack shook his head and grabbed for Jane before she made the top of her head a target.

His hand was covered in slick, red blood.

Wait. What's that from?

Oh hell. She shot me.

His eyes blinked heavy, like his lids weighed a hundred pounds if it was an inch. Still, he grabbed Jane's wrist and tugged.

She glanced at him. Panic raced through her green eyes, those expressive and beautiful eyes of hers, and she ducked again. Cupping the back of his head, she helped him lay over sideways. "Ah. Dammit, Jack. You're gonna be alright. We're gonna get out of this. Michael," she said, reaching over him, "give me something to press this wound with. Fuck."

"Jane, orphan child, give him to me," Melinda said.

Her voice wobbled in and out like one of those toys he used to have that had sand in the bottom and you punched it and it fell down and back up. Like that. Wobble, wobble.

Jack closed his eyes. "Jane."

"Jack."

"How bad is it?"

"It's fine," she said, taking something over his head. "You got us covered, Mike?"

Now the pain seared, burning his side. He clamped his lips over the groan.

His boy knelt over him, his weapon drawn, eyes everywhere at once. "I'm going to keep talking to Mom."

Michael's voice receded to a dull murmur as he talked to his mother. Tried to get them out of here.

While the pain became a screeching banshee.

"It doesn't feel fine," he said, trying to open his eyes and lift his head.

"Ssshh. It's fine." Pressing his forehead, she leaned so the baby warmed his back. Little Katie wiggled but was otherwise quiet. Probably just happy to be smelling her mother again. "I think it's in your thigh."

He whimpered as she pressed a spot like an anvil in his leg. He couldn't stop the cry. Through the pain, he began to drift. It was warm, but so was the baby. And Jane's hands. And the bullet, lodged next to his femur. Pressing on the long bone when she leaned into him to staunch the bleeding.

But like some surprise ending, the twist you didn't see coming, Burke popped over the back of the couch like a Jack-in-the-box. Pop goes the lapdog. "Look, people, I think working together is in everyone's best interest," he said.

Another of the boys with guns popped up next to him and leveled a rifle at Jane. Burke aimed at Michael.

"We're not afraid to shoot them, Jack. But it's you the general needs right now. Well. She needs your lady, too, but first, she'll need to take some pills."

"I'm not taking any of your fucking shit," Jane spat.

With a threat on his lips about what would happen if they hurt Jane, Jack began to sit up, attempting to draw his gun. It stuck in the holster, the bullet shifted in his leg, and the pain that shot up the nerve into the base of his skull knocked him on his ass.

The last thing he saw before losing consciousness was the side of the old, scratchy couch.

* * *

Swallowing, holding Yaz's staff at the ready, Addy glanced over her shoulder. Dean had tried to get in front of her, but she insisted she go first. She was the best at Listening, and the very first thing they had to do once they stepped out on the wraparound porch was find out where Data's barking was coming from.

Paul, Matt, and Celia frowned at her. Dean squeezed her shoulder.

She frowned and spoke around them. "Ella, will you be OK here?"

From the table, she sniffed. "I have a dozen doses here waiting for you, Addy. I won't go near the door, you have my word."

"What about Mann?"

"Addy," Dean said, leaning into her ear and sending butterflies up her spine, "not only are Mann and her people tied up and locked in one of those safe rooms of Burke's, Mann is desperate for us to succeed. That's her only family. She'll behave. Stop stalling."

Addy kissed him before she had time to think about it. Someone said something to her, but she neither heard nor cared. For that golden moment, she and Dean were alone in the world.

Breathless, she stepped back and faced the door again. Staff raised once more. "Ready?"

"Ready as we'll ever be," Paul answered. "Let's get that baby back in here."

Pressing her lips together, Addy inhaled through her nose and sent the breath to the bottom of her lungs. It filled her abdomen, and she pushed it out through her mouth. A circular breath Yaz had taught her through yoga, it centered her. She took one more, and as she released it, she opened the back door.

None of the 'Heads milling in the yard had found the porch stairs yet. Wandering with an aimless sense of half-realized purpose, they bumped into each other as the never-ending stream of them coursed through town. Somehow, they seemed to be headed somewhere.

The team crept onto the porch, Celia bringing up the rear. She eased the door closed and latched with a faint *snick*.

One of the 'Heads might have turned their way. But its cloudy eyes never settled on them.

Addy reached behind her and held out an empty hand. Dean took it, kissed her palm, and then wrapped it in his own fingers. He squeezed as she closed her eyes to Listen.

Data's shrill barking continued. Unbroken, uninterrupted, each woof as desperate as the one before it. Both terrified and defiant. He sounded like he'd tear each of them to shreds if they touched his girl, until he was unable to fight anymore.

Addy crept along the porch, one soft foot falling after the other.

Dean followed close behind, clutching her fingers. One of them had begun to sweat, and her fingers slipped as she tugged.

But if it weren't for his grip, she wouldn't have known any of them were behind her. The others were all dead silent.

A hollow thumping preceded a brief pause in Data's consistent bark.

Addy held her breath.

As he began again, she exhaled and opened her eyes. Just around the corner of the house, she'd be able to see where it was coming from. She tugged Dean with one hand, staff in the other.

She stepped around the corner. Her eye fell on a small shed about a hundred feet from the end of the porch, surrounded by 'Heads that bumped into it every few moments. There were three or four that could be construed to be actively trying to break down the door.

"Jesus, Addy, that may as well be ten times as far away. I don't know if we can make it," Matt said.

She peeked around Dean.

Matt's back pressed against the house, his chest rising and falling in short bursts.

Next to him, Celia crossed her arms and leaned a shoulder against the wall. "You scared?"

He stared out at the horde. "Yeah. I am. This is a big damned horde, lady."

"And that's a little bitty girl out there," Paul said, gripping Matt's shoulder. "If you're not sure you can help her, stay here. Go back inside. Whatever you think you need to do, friend. But don't get in the way."

Matt shook his head, eyebrows meeting in the center. He brandished the Bowie knife and straightened his shoulders. "No. I can do this. We can do this."

Celia smiled with half her mouth. "Ah. There's that backbone I thought you had."

"Sweetheart, it's now or never," Dean said. "Some of them are taking notice."

Addy glanced into the yard. Indeed, a handful of the ones milling about the porch railing had looked in this direction. One or two of them bumped into the porch, reaching for the banister. Black fingers hooked into claws, they reached for the food they had scented.

"Five-sided diamond, like we talked about," Addy whispered.

They got into formation, Celia and Dean on either side of Addy. Matt and Paul to her back.

"Keep as close as you can. As we get nearer, get ready to go in. We all go in, we all come out. I'll handle Data."

"I'll get the kid," Dean said. "But don't you for a minute think I'm getting her back into the house without you, Adelaide Cooke."

She flushed. That'd been exactly what she was thinking, if it came to that.

Rather than admit it, she shook her head, mouth drawn into a frown, and headed off the porch.

Data's barking continued, and Dora's small whimpers sounded in-between them.

Poor kid was terrified. She'd probably watched her whole family die in this horde, and now she was out in it, too.

And for the slimmest, barest of moments, Addy considered letting the kid go. I mean, her life would never be the same after her parents were dead. She'd keep everyone at arm's length. Take forever to get involved with a boy. Fuck up all her friendships. Cry all the time.

Have a little too much fun mowing down the 'Heads in front of her for Dean to slice up.

Grin as his blade popped out and sprayed clotted blood all over her. Covering her in its stink of old blood and death.

"There's so many of them," Matt murmured.

Glancing over her shoulder, she watched as he stabbed the one reaching for Paul. The knife dug into its eye socket. Too wide to slide all the way through the small hole, it stuck about halfway in. Enough to stop the 'Head, drop it in its tracks.

"Addy," Celia said, no louder than a whisper.

Without looking, Addy swung the staff and crippled the one in front of her. It still grasped her shoulder and pulled with alarming strength.

"Need me?" Dean didn't turn from his own kill, but he asked from the corner of his mouth.

"Nah," she said, grinning and knocking it aside with the staff. Stepping away, she got a good two-handed grip and swung so hard, the 'Head fell with its head on sideways, the neck cracking like a crushed pack of crackers. "I got it."

He nudged her with his shoulder and took on another.

She glanced behind her again and counted living people.

All four of them were still with her. None seemed to be struggling too hard. Though they were neck-deep in the biggest horde she'd ever seen, Ella had been right. Only so many 'Heads could come at them at once. If they'd had to fight their way to the edge, they wouldn't have made it. Exhaustion would have taken over long before they did.

As it was, they were mere feet from the door to the shed.

"Celia, get the door," she said, jabbing the one in front of the smaller woman. "I've got this one."

Celia grabbed the door handle. "Little girl," she said, speaking through the door, "is this barred?"

No answer, only Data's barking.

"Dora," Addy called, "open the door!"

Data's barking ceased.

Metal scraped inside.

A tiny voice called out. "It's open!"

Addy nodded to Celia, who yanked the door. She stood behind it as the others rushed in, only pulling it closed as Paul tripped through the doorway. Two 'Heads got in with them, and Celia booted one in the chest as she yanked the door. It fell outside the door, and she kicked its feet out of the way to get it closed. Matt lowered the bar, and Dora screamed.

Data, mouth full of the other 'Head's pants leg, growled from deep in his wide chest.

"Dean," Addy said, angling her forehead at the 'Head.

Without a word, he stepped behind it and wrapped an arm around its shoulders.

"Matt, knife," she said, holding her hand out without looking.

He slapped the haft into her palm.

Wrapping her fingers around the warm handle, she pushed it through the 'Head's ear until she heard the pop.

It slumped.

She turned to the child, scratching her dog behind the ears. "Dora, what are you doing? I saw you in the house."

The tow-headed girl's mouth dropped open. "You did?"

Kneeling, she hugged the kid to her. "I did. Are you OK? Are you bit?"

"I'm OK, Addy. I was trying to come see you."

Closing her eyes tight over the threatening tears, Addy squeezed her closer. "How did you know where I was?"

The girl shrugged as best she could in such a tight squeeze. "I didn't. I thought Data might help."

As though he'd received an invitation, Data's cold nose sneaked under Addy's arm.

She jumped, smiling, and sat in the dirt floor of the shed.

Data buried his head in her lap and lay on her legs. Stupid dog still thought he was a puppy.

Warmth spreading through her, she glanced around at the faces looking down at them. "Dora," she said, "I'd like you to meet some of my friends. Celia you know." She paused long enough for Cee to nod. "And this is Dean, Paul, and Matt," she said, pointing to each of them in turn.

Dora grinned. "She talked a lot about you, Dean. He's just as handsome as you said, Addy," she said, blushing.

For what it was worth, Addy blushed, too, as Dean shuffled his feet.

"No descriptions could do you justice, Dora. You're cuter than a button," he said, kneeling. "What do you say we get you back in the house? Can you come with me?"

Nodding, Dora glanced at Matt. "My grandma talks about you," she said, pointing.

He grimaced. "Oh yeah?" He swallowed and glanced at Addy. "What does she say about me?"

"That you're nice, but ineff…ineff…useless."

He choked, coughed, and turned a deep shade of brick red. "Well. We can talk about that later, I guess. Let's get you inside."

Addy handed him the knife back. "You're not entirely useless," she said. "Not all the time."

"Addy," he said, meeting her eyes for a brief moment, "that's the nicest thing you've ever said to me."

"Don't get used to it," she said. "Dean, you got her?"

He hefted Dora onto his hip. "Yes. Come on. Don't let go of me, Dora, no matter what, OK?"

She nodded, face buried in his shoulder.

Spotting a length of rope under the workbench, Addy wrapped some of it in a fist. "You stick with me, boy," she said, kneeling to tie the other end to Data's collar. He licked her face and wagged his tail.

Once Celia opened the door again, their journey back into the house became a memory she wouldn't let go of for years. It stuck in her brain, like the few times they'd found popcorn and she'd gotten kernel skins stuck in her teeth for days on end. Impossible to loosen, it just had to wear down enough to slip out on its own.

Dean and Dora in the center of the four-sided diamond, a 'Head got past one of them and headed straight for the kid. Dean swiped at it, but the angle was all wrong. It bit him on the forearm. He shouted but kept his grip on the girl with his other arm.

Matt knocked it off him, and Celia jumped on it. It bit her too, and as it tore at her hand with a rabid growling, Addy remembered a smiling game of rummy with such clarity she could almost taste the bacon.

Mason, with his light brown skin and bright green eyes. Though less bright now, covered in a white film and staring. He bubbled, fresh, with the strength and speed of about a day past the turn. One of those doses Ella had on the kitchen table could be for him.

But he'd already bitten both Dean and Celia and Data yanked and pulled at the leash. Mason gouged him in the side with his red and black claws.

More stumbled into their broken circle.

Shouting, Addy hit Mason low on the legs, taking them both out from under him. Shoving the staff into his neck and standing on one of his legs, she held him down, her other hand fighting with Data's rope. "Matt! Tie him!"

With the Bowie knife, Matt sliced through the end of the rope. Celia covered him.

Paul yanked Dean to his feet and pushed him toward Addy. "Get that girl in the house. Now," he said, spinning back toward the horde.

As Paul raised his hands above his head, the memory of Addy's mom running across the sporting goods store superimposed itself over him.

Knowing what he was about to do shook her to her core. She wanted to scream for him not to do it. That Dad would kill her if she let anything happen to him. That she didn't want her honorary grandfather to run headlong into a group of 'Heads just to save their skins. That they'd all make it back together.

But it all stuck in her throat as Matt got the rope tied and rushed back into the horde, he and Celia clearing a path to the house. Addy dragged Data and Mason with her, unable to breathe around the tears collecting in her throat.

And Paul, he wailed. Louder than should have been possible. Kicked 'Heads out of the way, threw rocks at others, took bite after bite after bite.

Addy and Dean stumbled behind Matt and Celia, Data running ahead and Mason fighting the restraints. His teeth inches from her ear.

She fought every instinct she had to get the gnashing teeth away from her, to end his struggling, glad, for once, that she'd left the machete behind.

The rest of the horde funneled toward Paul as he ran out of the yard, banging some trash can lids he'd found god knew where.

Three 'Heads milled on the porch, the only ones who'd noticed the house, and as the group mounted the steps, Celia ended all three. Matt shoved the door open and herded Dean inside. Data followed.

And as Addy tripped through the doorway backward, dragging Mason with her, the banging stopped.

Paul still screamed, but it wasn't the same. It was the high, desperate keening of an animal. Brief glimpses through the thinning crowd afforded her more than she needed to see.

Any thoughts of him escaping the suicide run ended as he gurgled his last, blood drenching the brown grass.

Addy shouted for Ella to bring a dose, and Matt barred the door behind them all.

CHAPTER 43

Jack swam up from the depths of a well with stone sides, fingers slipping over the moss growing there. Flashes of red light called him from above the surface of the water. And though he held his breath until his lungs ached for air, he did all he could to make himself heavy.

But the pain won, and he opened his eyes with his teeth clenched.

His whole side screamed as he tensed against it. A paper blanket scratched his legs.

"Hey, take a breath," Melinda said. "Don't fight the pain, that'll only make it worse."

Pressing his teeth together so hard he thought they might crack, he loosened his chest and sucked a breath in through his nose. When he tried to raise his head and look down at the wound, a strap dug into the skin above his eyes.

He jerked his arms. Restraints held them, too. Breath coming shallow, he tried to pull his knees up. While both stayed static, pain radiated from his right hip down as he jerked. The red flashes of light appeared before his eyes again. The pain tasted like blood.

Stilling his legs and taking another deep breath, he tried to find Melinda with his eyes. "What did you do to me?" he asked, teeth clenched around the words.

Her boot heels clacked around the table he found himself strapped to. "We had to stitch up that nasty bullet wound. You're lucky. It missed the bone. But the bullet was too deep in your thigh for us to retrieve safely. The equipment we have just isn't good enough. And our surgeons at the Molehill are much more qualified."

Pain or no, he jerked against the restraints. "You're not taking me there. Where's Jane?" Though it did no good, he jerked his head to try and move it side to side. Tweaking a muscle in his neck, he opened his mouth and shouted for her as loud as he could. "Jane!"

"Jack!" Her voice came from far away, on the other side of a wall somewhere.

Pain screamed all the way up his right side as he tried to thrash. He got very little movement for his trouble.

Melinda laid a hand on his chest. "Jackson. You're just going to hurt yourself. She's fine. I'll let you see her soon enough."

"Let her go, Melinda. You have me now. Just let her go."

She breathed on the side of his face.

He cut his eyes as far as he could to find her.

Leaning on her elbows, she cupped her chin in her hands and smiled at him. "Would you like something for the pain, before we get started?"

He answered yes before he thought about the whole question.

Appearing above him with a syringe, she pulled a small amount of clear liquid inside. "Not too much," she said, tapping it and peeking at him through the side of her eye.

"Get started with what?" he asked, eyes on the syringe. Possibilities screamed at him from the dark. Almost all of them involved some kind of torture.

How the hell did you let yourself get into this position, Jack? She could pull every single one of your nails out one by one. Go all Gitmo on you. Good lord, she's got you at the worst disadvantage. It had better be worth something.

"You at least let Mike and the baby go, right?" He watched her lower the syringe.

Cold air struck the side of his throbbing thigh. She wiped his skin with something. Probably alcohol.

Closing his eyes, he exhaled. Tried to relax.

The needle stabbed him, but at least it didn't feel like she was trying to send it into next week.

Standing, she rubbed the spot. "How was that?"

"For a moment, I forgot you wanted to kill me."

Her lopsided grin made an appearance. "That was brief. And irrational. I'm glad Michael stopped me."

He snorted, relaxing his neck and staring at the ceiling. "Well, that's a line of bullshit. Good try, though."

"Really," she said, bustling away. Metallic clinks echoed off the ceiling. The rustle of fabrics. Hollow, plastic *thunks*. "That immune child of yours is so interesting. Michael isn't immune. I have to assume Adelaide isn't, either, though I'll need some blood to test."

"Melinda," he said, tears collecting in the back of his throat, "please. Leave Addy out of this. Don't drag her into it."

"Jack," she said, leaning over him again, "she's my favorite too." She dropped her voice to a whisper and leaned close enough to tickle his nose with her hair. "Don't tell Michael I said that." She stood. "I wouldn't hurt a hair on her head. You can depend on that."

A fear so intense gripped him, he thought he might throw up. Which, considering he couldn't turn his head, could prove fatal. He swallowed, the antiseptic stench of the hospital cloying. "Melinda. She's probably going to come after me. Please. Don't hurt her."

"Oh babe, I'm sure she will. But I swear to you, I have no intention of hurting our daughter. We were talking about your other one, anyway. The one you had with that child."

He swallowed again, closing his eyes. "She's not a child, Melinda. And I love her. I'm sorry you can't see that."

Her laughter grew from nothing to so loud it hurt his ears in less time than it took to register she was laughing.

Squeezing his eyes closed, he waited for it to pass, heart pounding against his back on the cold metal table.

"That child, the baby I mean, we don't know what's caused her immunity. The fact is, if it's due to our, to *my* research, we need to find out how to recreate it." She walked away again, still talking. "I mean, I had high hopes for Jane when she survived the vaccine trial. I followed you all to that island so I could keep an eye on her." She stopped. No sound. Pulling a sharp breath across her teeth, she hissed. "Then she turned up pregnant. I'm not an idiot, Jack. I saw the way you looked at her." Her boot heels clacked across the floor again, echoing off the ceiling tile.

She stopped and sighed. "When I had Timothy round her up for the vaccine trial, I had little clue what a fortunate turn of events that would be. We've never seen immunity before. We have to believe the baby is unique. I decided to bring her back here, but I knew you'd never cooperate." She paused, sighing. "Michael convinced me not to kill you, so I convinced Casey to release Dean from jail."

The table squeaked as she leaned on it, but he couldn't catch her in his peripheral.

"I needed to distract our daughter, and my little birds told me she'd come back." Leaning over him, she frowned. "Anyway, in order to do our research more completely, we must recreate the conditions under which little Katherine was conceived as fully as we can."

He flashed on the cell in the prison where he and Jane had consummated their love.

Melinda chuckled. "I see you blushing, Jack. I know what you're thinking. But that's not what I mean. Exactly."

An unpleasant thought crept into the edge of his mind. One he couldn't look at except sideways.

He jerked against the restraints again. But the pain didn't shoot up his leg.

A hand reached under the paper blanket covering him and stroked his thigh. "Ah, there. See? Not too much, not too little. Feels better already, right?"

The best he could do was try to shake his head no. The thought that'd been in the edge of his mind just a moment ago had come creeping closer.

She leaned over him. "So, the first step in our new research study. We need fertilized eggs. Eggs with your genetic component. And hers, if we can get them, of course. That's a fairly delicate and time-consuming process. You, on the other hand," she said, sliding her hand farther under the paper blanket.

"Melinda," he breathed. He cleared his throat and tried again, building a brick wall around the thought trying to freeze him out. "Melinda, stop. I won't cooperate."

Laughing, a throaty chuckle, she stripped away the blanket and laid him bare.

The cold room was less of a shock than the implication.

He treaded water in sludge, trying to get his brain to move. "You can't, Melinda."

Resting her chin on his chest, she smiled at him. Showed him all her teeth. "You can claim you love her all you want. I've no doubt you've convinced an innocent child to follow your every whim. But you can't fool me, Jackson," she said. Without warning, she gripped his cock and yanked. "We both know you're *my* man. You always have been. You always will be."

Locking the shout in his throat, behind teeth he was certain he'd already cracked, he couldn't stop the hot tears from rolling down the sides of his face. He tried to shake his head again when words failed.

And with her extensive knowledge of him and everything he'd always liked, a book she'd practically written herself, she began to caress him.

Which was foolish. He'd never cooperate. She couldn't force him to do something he didn't want to do.

And yet.

And yet.

His body disagreed.

A fear he'd never even considered to be real stole over him. Like someone had poured a bowl of ice-water in the center of his forehead. His eyes glazed. He opened his mouth and someone else's voice spoke.

"Mellie, please. You don't have to do this. If you love me, don't do this."

Leaning into his face, her hair framing it, a smile lit her eyes. "Oh, Jack. I'm doing this because I love you. You're going to be immortal, baby." She glanced down. "Besides," she said, looking back up and catching his eyes, "you can talk all you want to, but this little guy here ain't listening."

And, for the love of god, it was true. His body, the one he'd lived in for forty-seven years, the one he thought he knew inside and out, it had turned on him. He could feel the blood rushing down at her urging, getting him ready even as he denied it in his head a thousand times over.

He opened his mouth to scream for help.

Jane had called to him from just the next room. She'd come.

Oh god. She'd come in. And she'd see him like this. And she'd think…she'd think.

He couldn't lose her again over assumptions and bad decisions.

And besides, would she be wrong?

Melinda laughed again. "Fuck the samples. I'll get it later," she said, stopping the torture.

He breathed a sigh of relief. Told his body to behave. And wished she'd pull out his finger and toenails. He could feel himself cooling, and hot tears tracked down his face again, pooling in his ears. He wanted to thank her for stopping, but at the same time, she'd already proven her point, hadn't she?

Without warning, she climbed onto the table. She'd stripped as naked as he was, the latticework of scars on her torso and legs bright white in the glaring lights.

"Melinda, what the hell are you doing?" He yanked at the restraints again. "Let me go," he said, mustering all the command he could.

Small smile playing across her lips, she began to move her hips back and forth.

Nothing could stop him from hating himself when his body began to react again. He told it to stop in a million different ways. That other person's voice begged her to stop. He bucked and convulsed and did anything he could to get her off of him, and she laughed. He did all he could to escape, to turn it off, to make her stop. Nothing.

As his body turned traitor and he knew, without doubt, there was no way to stop what she was doing to him, his mind curled into a little ball and hid. He couldn't call for help. They wouldn't understand.

He didn't want this.

So he ran away, found a dark pit in the corner of his mind, and pulled the dirt in over top.

At least once, he began to ask himself just what the hell he'd ever say to Jane.

Stopping mid-thought, he threw her name as far as it would go from this. Before she could be tarnished by it.

When he felt the beginning of the end coming, the final and ultimate betrayal of his body, he bit the insides of his lips. His back arched. He turned as far away from it as he could get. From somewhere else, he felt the pressure on him ease, but it was too late.

"Now, see," Melinda said, smile in her voice, "you obviously enjoyed it. And I got my samples anyway."

With a rustling of fabric, she clacked away. Leaving all the lights on, and with him exposed to the world, a door slammed behind her.

He crawled back into the hole in his mind and shut it all out.

CHAPTER 44

Ella held a tray in front of Addy's nose. Seven champagne glasses rested on it.

Addy took one. "Thanks, Ella. This is a terrible idea."

"Nobody's twisting your arm, Adelaide," Ella said as she shoved a glass in Dean's face.

He took it, frowning. "Ella, sweetie, Addy's right. I don't know if this is the best idea."

It didn't matter how many times he said the words, "Addy's right," it thrilled Addy to the core each and every time. She sipped the mimosa. The alcohol bit into her tongue on the way past. She opened her mouth to tell Ella maybe she'd made them a little strong.

"Pretty strong, baby doll," Matt said, sipping his own.

Ella sighed at him, one eyebrow cocked, and delivered a glass to Mason, who reclined on one of Ella's giant couches. His face ashen, he smiled and nodded at her, tweezing the fragile stem between fingers that were still red and raw on the tips.

She set the tray on the coffee table and picked up her own. Flipping her hair over her shoulder, she held the glass aloft. "First of all, we're supposed to toast *before* we drink. Not after. Second, don't you notice we have an extra glass? I thought we'd invite one more to the party." She nodded to Celia, who stood leaning in the door to the hallway, one boot crossed over the other.

She nodded and spun around the doorjamb.

After she'd disappeared into the hall, Addy set her glass on the table. "What are we doing, guys? It's been two days. We have to make a move at some point. We can't stay in this house forever."

Dean set his glass next to hers and hugged her knee. "I've seen him out there, too, Addy."

She shook her head. Nice of him to bring up Paul. Out there, blue eyes fading, wispy hair caked in blood. Bumping into the other 'Heads. The ones he was now part of.

There'd been a few moments, hours, to tell the truth, when she'd looked for him out the window with the thought of saving him. They had all this damned Cure in the basement, after all.

But the few times he'd wandered close enough to the house to see, the extent of his injuries became clear. He'd lost too much blood. The only hope for him would have been the hospital. Not only would they have had to capture him, they also would have had to transport a fresh 'Head through a horde of them, just to get him to a threshold they didn't even know they'd be able to cross.

And Yasuo hadn't come up from the basement since.

Everything felt broken. Like she'd failed. Dad and Jane hadn't come back. Hadn't radioed or called or anything. No indication of their presence in the hospital had been made. No one said or did anything.

Just these damn 'Heads. They'd taken over most everything. They were all that moved out there.

Celia tromped back into the room, footfalls preceding her, dragging Mann behind her. "Sit," she said, shoving the woman at a chair.

Mann sat, hands tied in front of her, and eyed them. "Addy," she said, glancing at her from under her brow, "I hadn't had the chance to thank you yet."

In her mind, she kicked over the drinks, flipped the table, screamed at the woman, and left the room. Maybe punched a wall on the way by. Probably tripped over her feet at some point.

"You're welcome," she said, sitting back and crossing her arms.

Dean opened his mouth.

"Ladies, gentlemen," Ella said, snagging the last glass and handing it to Mann. "A toast." She tilted her glass at Addy and widened her eyes.

Exhaling through her nose, Addy grabbed the glass in front of her and held it up as Ella had. She nudged Dean.

He picked his up, too, lowering his head and lifting his glass above it.

Ella waited until everyone had done the same, including Mason, from the couch, and Celia from her spot in the doorjamb.

Matt stared up at her with half his smile turned down. Eyes shining. The past two days, he'd stolen time with her whenever he could. He'd spoken right when he'd said she was a pain in the ass, but she was *his* pain in the ass. Seeing them together these past couple days had lightened Addy's heart.

That he could have grown up the way he did and still treasure someone the way he treasured her had to be some kind of miracle.

Ella raised her glass just a bit higher. "To old friends, new friends, and getting the fuck out of this mess," she said.

Matt chuckled and stood to tap her glass.

Addy and Dean joined them and turned to wait for Mann.

Who grimaced and stood. With her hands tied, she still toasted.

They all drank.

Addy's head took a wobble and settled back on straight. Gripping Dean's shoulder, she pulled him back down to the couch with her. "We need in that hospital. Laurel, where are the rest of your people?"

Mann shrugged, glancing at the four of them.

Celia retreated to the doorway again. "Half of 'em in that horde out there, aren't they, woman?"

Hanging her head, Mann nodded. "Getting back in, it was chaos. I don't know what happened. I don't know how the horde beat us in here. The ladder was destroyed. We ended up coming in the main gate, which the horde must have torn down."

Dean sat up. "Tore down?"

Mann shrugged again. "I think some of my people are still out there, in the woods. I really don't know. I just kept thinking, if I could get here"—she paused, glancing around the living room— "to this house, everything would be OK. Somehow. I'd figure it out."

"Did you?" Addy asked.

Shaking her head, Mann stared out the front window.

The angle allowed them to see the tops of the heads milling about out there. Not much more. Except Data's nose prints all over the bottom.

Addy reached down and scratched him behind his warm ears. His tail thumped. "So here we are. Our friend is dead because you couldn't just talk to these people. Because you thought you could use a horde of Dead Heads to win some kind of pissing contest."

"A pissing contest?" Mann stood, her mouth twisted. "That's what you think is going on here?" She tilted her head at Matt. "Ask him. Ask him what really happened. You've heard it from me, hear it from him. They tricked us. They kicked us out in the cold. Left us out there to die. Fuck them all," she said, spitting at Matt's feet.

Matt stood.

Ella was faster. She jumped between them, hands on her hips. "We're never going to figure this out if you keep acting like such a bitch."

Addy gaped. It might have been what she was thinking, and it might have been what needed to be said, but nobody would have said it. And certainly no one would have said it better than Ella did.

Mason sat up on one arm and stared at her. "Laurel," he croaked.

When she didn't answer, he went to speak again but instead started to choke and cough. Ella, who'd taken to nursing like she'd done it all her life, stepped over and held a tissue to his mouth, one hand cradling the back of his head. He finally worked out a large chunk that splattered into the tissue. Lip curled, Ella dropped it into the trash can next to him. She turned back to Mann and caught her eyes.

Mann lowered her head. "You have a few of my men in the basement. It's all I can give you."

Nodding, Addy glanced up at Ella. She opened her mouth, and the front door rattled.

Dean slipped into the hallway, knife drawn.

A beat passed.

"Shit," he said, voice muffled. "Addy, it's Renzo," he said, flipping all the locks.

She jumped, air escaping like she'd been punched in the gut. Sprinting into the hall, she cleared the corner just in time to see Dean push the screen door open and usher Renzo and five other people inside.

About a dozen 'Heads followed them up onto the porch. Dean didn't have to tell Renzo and the others to hurry.

Addy glanced over her shoulder, heart in her throat, to tell Matt to lower the shades in the big room.

He was already on it. Ella clutching the back of his shirt.

"Addy, I'm so glad you're here," Renzo said, grabbing Addy's shoulder. "Have you seen Laurel?"

"I'm here, Renzo," Mann said, stepping into the hallway. "I'm glad to see you made it. Who's with you?"

"Julia stayed behind with the others. They fell back. Not far, but far enough."

Dean cleared his throat. "Great, we're all here. Now what, sweetie?" he asked, finishing up the locks and meeting Addy's eyes.

She glanced around at them all. "Now, we break out my dad."

* * *

Two days. Two days Jack had been in this room.

Hands and feet freed at some point, he'd rolled off the table into the floor and lain there until someone, some stranger, had forced him to a nearby chair.

Curling his legs into it, that stupid piece of shrapnel still lodged in his leg and screaming, he covered from head to toe with a real blanket they'd given him.

The first time Melinda came back, she at least turned the lights off. Told him he looked cold. Offered a drink, a blanket, some food.

Cheeks stiff, he closed his eyes and said nothing.

In the dark, she kissed him on the earlobe, sucking it for a moment, before she clacked away again and slammed the door.

He wished she'd just waterboard him.

The second time she came back, she leaned over him with a clipboard. "Jackson, thank you for your contribution to my research. For a man your age, your spermatozoa are highly motile. No wonder you were able to impregnate the girl. Good job," she said, patting his crotch.

He whimpered at the touch. Regaining his bearings, he considered telling her off. Realized she could tell Jane anything she wanted to. He could only deny so much. She had gotten her samples, after all.

"We may need more," she said, rubbing his thigh.

This was before that stranger had let him off the table.

Probably.

It was all mixed up.

He tried to shake his head. It was bound to the table, strap pressing into the skin above his eyebrows. A tear snaked down his face, following canyons made by the rivers that had come before it.

"The process of extracting eggs isn't dangerous," Melinda said. This was the third time she'd come back. Maybe. Maybe she'd never left.

He was in the chair.

"Listen," she said, "we are definitely going to need more. You choose. The easy way, or the hard way." She purred in his ear. Hot breath. If his ear had been glass, like the glass he was now made from, it would have fogged.

His voice floated out around a catch in his throat, asking her to stop. Asking her not to hurt Jane, or the baby, or Mike. Asking her again to leave Addy out of it.

All of which she promised to do if he continued to "contribute."

She reminded him of his obvious signs of pleasure. Implied the threat of telling Jane.

From under the blanket, he found his voice. "What's the hard way?"

Had he been here two days? Or two years?

A whole team of people came in, setting up things. Wearing face masks and latex gloves, they shoved a pill down his throat and waited.

He didn't even try to bite the fingers reaching down his gullet to cram the pill in. When they left, they gave him so much morphine he thought—maybe even hoped—he might OD.

Lowering the blanket, he looked around the room. Alone in it, he eyed the doors. Two of them on opposite sides.

He glanced under the blanket and found they'd given him his clothes back at some point. He was wearing them.

One of the doors stood ajar.

Bunching the blanket in one hand, he dropped silent feet to the ground and stood.

The bullet ground into bone.

Though it would have eased the pain, he never wanted to take painkillers again in his life.

Jane's voice floated through the open door. She was singing Billie Holiday to the baby.

Longing punched him in the gut so hard, he flopped back into the chair.

Cold winter days, snow piled up outside, record player spinning. Twirling her around the living room, pregnant belly between them. Tiny little baby kicks, sympathetic heartburn, and warm snuggles under the covers.

He snatched the blanket from the floor and, curling his screaming legs back into the chair, covered himself head to toe.

* * *

"Listen, Addy," Zo said, taking her aside, "Ricardo is still out there. He found grenades."

She grinned. "Dean wanted grenades," she said, peeking around Zo's shoulder.

Dean, Mason, and Celia sat on the floor, Dean watching as Celia changed Mason's bandages, whispering something Addy couldn't hear.

"Yeah, so he's out there with that stuff, and with my girl Julia," Renzo said. He snagged a small walkie from his belt. "I can get in touch with them. Just say the word."

Nodding, Addy let her eyes drift. Unfocused, she stared at the wall. "Ella," she called, still staring at the wall.

Ella breezed over. "You called, my dear?"

"Can you get in touch with your dad? Matt said you could." Focusing on Ella's brows, she watched them contort.

"Oh he did, did he?" A hand high up on her waist, she glanced at him. "I do know how to get in touch with Daddy. The question is if I want to. Addy"—she lowered her voice and clutched Addy's arm—"why hasn't he come to get me? What's he doing with your mom?"

"Dammit, Ella, how am I supposed to know?" The mention of her mom sent her blood racing through her brain.

She took a few breaths to cool it off and completely missed what Ella had said.

"Sorry, Ella, repeat that?"

She sighed. "Nothing. I'll call him. Give me a minute." She pulled the middle drawer of the hall table out and reached back into the depths of it. Most of her arm disappeared. "Now I'll need a new hiding place for"—she paused, grunting—"this."

Only the third smartphone Addy had seen in operation slid from under the table. Most of them had cracked, gotten dirt inside, and ceased to be of use a decade ago. Long before they'd gotten the towers back on line.

As Ella turned her back to dial, Addy turned to Renzo. "Zo," she said, "do you know how the horde got in?"

He shook his head. "No idea. We didn't let them in, I can tell you that. Even she had nothing to do with it," he said, jerking his chin in Mann's direction. "I think she really only meant to use them for a siege. I don't think she meant them to come inside the walls."

"That's not what she told me when we met," Addy said. Sitting atop that hill, gazing down into the stinking valley, the woman had threatened every man, woman, and child in this settlement.

"You got to her," Renzo said, tapping her knee. "She'd never say so, but you did."

Addy couldn't help it. She smiled. Dad would be proud. The Mom she used to know would have been, too.

Celia sighed. "That's all well and good, but how does that help us now?"

Mason shook his head. "It doesn't. But it's nice to know, right?"

Cee shrugged. "You say so."

Addy laughed and scooted to lean against Dean. He wrapped an arm around her, and she peered down the hall.

Back to them, Ella gestured with the hand not holding the phone. A few shrill snatches of words floated down the hallway. She sniffled and threw her hair back four or five times.

Impossible to judge how the conversation was going since she couldn't see Ella's eyebrows, Addy exhaled and leaned back. Closing her eyes, she fidgeted with the handle of her machete. It would be nice to be doing something. Going somewhere. Have a plan. All this waiting, at this stage of the game, was driving her bonkers.

Yasuo burst through the door to the basement.

With a yelp, Addy sat up. "What the hell, Yaz?"

"Sorry. I'm sorry. I thought you'd left. I didn't hear anyone."

Squeezing Dean's knee, Addy stood. "I kinda thought you wanted to be left alone."

Yaz nodded. "Kinda. But not really. I've been thinking about it," he said, swallowing, "and I think if you're going back out there anytime soon, it's best if I come with you." Though his face read anything but, his voice remained steady.

"Sure, if you're sure. We could always use the extra hands," Addy said. She leaned closer. "Are you sure?"

"I'm sure. I may not want to, but honestly, I've got to get out there. I can't sit around in fear all the time."

Half a smile curved Addy's lips, but as she opened her mouth to respond, to share her relief with him that he'd begun to see past the fear, Ella charged up the hallway.

"Daddy says he can get us in, but we need a diversion. He says we have fifteen minutes." Shoving the phone in her pocket, she held a hand out.

Matt appeared from the great room and took it, folding her fingers inside his. He kissed her cheek. "You're the best, Ella-belle."

Cheeks reddened, Ella grinned and peeked at Addy. "Can we do it?"

Addy glanced at the group. "Mann, we need your people. How many of us are there?"

Mann glanced around. "I've got fourteen in the house. Plus myself."

"There's eight of us," Addy said, glancing at her friends and including Mason in the count, "plus the others who came with you, Zo."

"That's a pretty good group, Addy. I think over twenty of us could come up with something," Dean said.

"Not everyone," Addy said, shaking her head. She clenched her teeth.

Several feet shifted as everyone tried to figure out who she intended to leave behind.

Addy savored the moment. All eyes on her, not something she ever really wished for before, but something that had turned out to not be as bad as she thought it might be. As long as she wasn't tripping over things.

"Laurel," Addy said, turning to Mann, "you have to stay here with Dora."

"Please, child. You can't force me to do that. I'm not going to abandon my men to you," she said. She might have been trying to cross her arms, but with her wrists bound, she couldn't bring them up.

Addy crossed the hall and began untying her ropes. "You have to stay with your grandbaby. You're all she's got, Laurel. No heroics," she said, catching Mann's eyes and holding them. "Just watch after her."

Mann sighed. "You could sell heaters in hell, Adelaide Cooke."

Grinning, Addy took her hand. "Whatever that means. Does it mean you'll stay here? Take care of your family?" She turned to the rest of them. "Because that's what I'm doing. I'm taking care of my family. If any of you don't want to be a part of that, tell me now. You're welcome to stay here with Laurel." She turned back to Mann. "I'd like to give your men the same chance. They can stay here if they want."

In the end, half of Mann's guys stayed with her and the girl.

Addy hugged the girl and the dog and told them to take care of each other. Data's fur was wet with tears when she stood and glanced around the group.

"Alright. We're going to make three groups. Ella, you get behind me, Matt, and Dean. Zo, did you get in touch with Ric?"

"He's going to meet us near the hospital. He's got the grenades ready."

Flashing a fierce grin at Dean, she opened the front door.

CHAPTER 45

Traveling to the hospital went faster than Addy thought it would. But given everything that came after, the memories of the journey got shoved to the back, unimportant.

What she did remember of it was Dean's shoulder on her right and Matt's on her left. Ella gripping both hers and Matt's shirts in the back and whimpering when either of them had to move away. She had her long-bladed knife, but she never used it. The one thing she did do was stay out of the way and not get bit.

Both Dean and Matt saved Addy's ass more than once when she was protecting Ella. They made a good team.

Otherwise, it was a blur of blood and blades.

All two dozen of them made it to the hospital, and as they approached, Renzo's radio buzzed.

"Go," he shouted.

A small explosion rocked the air on the side of the hospital.

Keeping one eye on the wall guards and the other on the 'Heads in front of her, Addy prayed they'd move.

The guards shifted, aiming their guns in the direction of the explosion. But they didn't move. Some of them even turned their heads toward Addy and her group.

A bull horn whined from behind the wall as another explosion sent 'Heads into the air about fifty feet away.

"What are you waiting for? Get over there and check it out!"

The helmeted heads disappeared from behind the wall in front of her.

Shoving 'Heads to the side, moving as quick as they could, the three hexagons made their way to the wall.

A section slid back, just wide enough for everyone to squeeze through, one at a time.

Burke stood behind it, sweating in the cold winter afternoon, holding a hand out. "Ella, sweetie!"

Ella shook her head. "Addy, get in there," she said, yanking Addy's arm.

"Come on," Addy said, waving her other arm, machete spraying congealed blood all over. "Everybody in!"

Dean and Matt stayed behind with her, a wall of flying blades before she and Ella. Celia covered her side until Addy shoved her through the hole.

But when she and Ella tried to get the men to go in first, they pretended not to hear. With their backs to them, they walked backward until Addy and Ella had no choice but to go through the slim opening.

Heart in her throat, Addy waited for Dean to come through the hole.

He and Matt squeezed through one right after the other, and they both pushed the barrier closed.

Leaning against the concrete barrier, Addy sighed. "Thanks, Burke," she said, eyes on Ella's dad.

Ella hugged him, both arms flying around his neck.

He smiled, closing his eyes and kissing the top of her head. "I'm glad you're here." He glanced at Addy, Dean, and Matt. "Thank you for taking care of my little girl."

Arms crossed, Matt nodded. "Of course, sir."

Addy cleared her throat. "Alright, now that we're—"

"Look out," someone shouted.

Cold engulfed Addy as 'Heads came around the corner of the hospital. Something must've happened to the barrier on the other side.

Dozens had spilled in and now headed toward them.

"Inside," Burke said, shoving Ella toward the hospital and pulling his sidearm. With impeccable aim, he took down half a dozen before moving.

Ella, screaming for her daddy, ran toward the hospital and yanked the door open. The group of them piled inside, Burke bringing up the rear.

After pulling the door closed, he rounded the front desk, shoved the kid there out of the way, and reached under.

Something clicked, and the lights in the room turned red.

Holding her breath, Addy waited for sirens. None came, and she exhaled. The alarm was silent.

"It's transmitting to headquarters," Burke said. "We need to get to the escape coordinates."

"Not without my family," Addy said, heart in her throat. "You take me to them now, commander."

"We don't have time—"

"Daddy," Ella said, "I'm not going anywhere until Addy gets her family back." Standing straight, she pulled herself up to her full height.

Addy had seen her do it a hundred times if it was one, but watching her stand toe to toe with her dad was somehow more impressive than any of those hundred times.

And like a man practiced at losing to her, he agreed with surprising speed. He glanced at Addy. "I'll take you there. But you're going to have to get them away from Melinda. I can't help you with that."

"You get us there," she said, glancing at her friends, "and we'll do the rest."

* * *

When the lights turned red, Jack dropped the blanket to the floor.

The red lights had to indicate something was wrong. It had gone past time to get his woman and daughter out of here. And his son. He'd been curled up in this chair long enough, feeling sorry for himself. He still had a responsibility to those people, and he needed to see it through.

He crept toward the door through which he'd heard Jane singing to the baby. Whenever that had been. Hours, days, or years ago.

He pressed his ear to the door, and muffled voices snuck through.

"We need to get out of here. Where's Jack, Michael?"

"Mom didn't tell me."

Rustle. Soft baby cry.

Jack closed his eyes and listened to his littlest as she cooed at her mother. He clutched the doorknob.

"I'll search every fucking room in this hospital if I have to, Michael. I'm not leaving without him."

"I know, Jane. I know. Do you have any weapons?"

"Just my needles."

Sounds of rummaging. "How do they always miss those?"

"No idea." Smile in her voice.

Jack found himself smiling with her. They did always miss them, until they became a deadly problem. Sometimes it was almost comical, the way everyone underestimated Jane. She was one of the most ruthless people he'd ever met.

The need to be enfolded in her arms, with her telling him it was OK, overwhelmed him.

He began to twist the doorknob. It turned in his hand.

Hands he'd pollute her with if they touched her. His inability to control his own body couldn't have been anyone's fault but his own. He was supposed to be a man, after all. If he couldn't even control himself, what good could he be to her?

Maybe he should just lock this door and wait for her to leave.

Backing away, he crossed the room to try the other door.

Shouting permeated the far wall and door.

With a start, he crouched and snuck back to the table, where he ducked under and waited.

Raised voices talked over each other. Occasional shouts punctuated the conversation. Several more people had entered the other room.

Melinda's distinct shrill shout.

Adelaide's pleading voice.

Oh hell, little girl. Get the fuck out of here.

More shouting. Dean, Celia, Mike, all shouting.

Burke's deep baritone.

A gunshot. Followed in quick succession by two more.

He shrank under the table as an unfamiliar female screamed. Screamed for her daddy.

The door opened.

"What do we do, Ella?" Matt asked, his voice thick and high-pitched.

Someone sobbed outside the room.

Tree-trunk legs stepped in. "Jack, you in here?"

Renzo. The man who'd once been a prison guard, antagonizing him every chance he'd gotten, come to save him from the depths.

Jack peeked from under the table and lifted his eyebrows.

"He's in here, guys," Renzo called over his shoulder.

Before he had a chance to get out of the doorway, Jane blew past him. Baby strapped to her chest, she knocked the larger man into the door.

"Jack," she said, falling to her knees in front of him.

"Jane," he said, breathing her name through his lips. He reached to take her outstretched hand.

"Are you alright?" She searched his face.

He dropped his hand. "No. I— You go on," he said, glancing down. "My leg. It'll just slow us down. You go on. I'll be right behind you."

She shook her head, cradling Katherine. "I'm not leaving without you." Before he could stop her, she grabbed his hand from the floor and squeezed. "You'd never slow me down. With you, I fly. Come on, honey."

"Dad," Addy shouted. She ran into the room, sliding on her knees to him. She opened her mouth, and someone shouted from the other room. A gun fired again.

"Daddy!" Scuffling. More shouting. "I'm going to fucking kill that bitch!"

"Addy," Matt said from the door, "Ella's going after your mom. I can't let her go alone." Feet pounded away.

"Renzo, help Jack, he's been shot," Jane said, squeezing his hand before she released it and stood.

Before he could stop her, Addy took off, back out of the room. Presumably after her mother, Ella, and Matt.

As Renzo pulled him from under the table and supported his weight, Jack found Dean standing in the doorway.

"Don't wait on me, Dean. Get after her," he said.

In silence, Dean disappeared.

Jack watched Jane and Renzo, the only ones who were still here. The rest had gone after that woman. The one who only looked like someone he used to know. She'd killed everything inside him that made her who she'd been.

And had killed everything inside that made him who he'd been, too.

"What are we doing?" Renzo asked.

Jack shook his head. He needed to protect his eldest kids from their mother. She'd already ruined him. He couldn't let her destroy them.

"We've got to go after them. Jane, you—"

"I'm coming with you," she said, slipping under his other arm. "You can't tell me otherwise." She kissed him under his jaw.

As the familiar electricity zinged through him from her touch, his stomach curled. Twisted in on itself. His eyes stung.

Shoving it aside as best he could, he nodded. "Let's go after them."

* * *

Burke had taken a moment to embrace Matt before leading Addy and the group through the hospital. He'd whispered something to him, something about taking care of Ella. Matt had smiled, nodded, and clapped Burke on the shoulder.

They stopped in front of a large lab.

The commander took a breath. "Ms. Cooke, there is research here we cannot lose. I'd like to request your help in gathering the most important bits of it. Including blood samples from your little sister and other samples from your family."

Addy swallowed. Now might not be the time, but something about that baby having been put through having her blood taken, and the blood Mom had shown her under that microscope all those months ago, it made her reconsider.

Though she hated Mom more every time she thought about that snowy day on the lawn of the hospital, she had to admit, immunity was nothing to sneeze at.

"What do you need, Burke?"

He nodded at the group behind her. "Can some of your men help gather research? My research team can direct them."

Addy looked over her shoulder. "You guys, I can't force you. But could some of you stay and help?"

A few of Mann's people stepped up, including Mason. And Yasuo. "Don't worry about us, Addy," he said, "go get your dad."

"Thanks, Yaz," she said, hugging him. She squeezed him tight.

"Thank me later." He hugged her back. "Get out of here."

With the group mostly halved, they moved on through the hospital until they reached the skywalk she'd seen from outside.

"Your mom's quarters are through here. Your dad, your brother and sister, and your mom, plus some of her men, are in there."

"Well, let's go," Addy said, starting across.

Dean and the others followed her, but Burke grabbed Ella's shoulder. "Ella, I don't want you coming in there."

Matt stopped, frowning, and turned back.

Addy met Ella's eyes.

Whose brows curled into a V.

Grinning, Addy continued down the walk. The drama could play itself out behind her, she knew how it'd end.

Reaching the door at the other side, she tried to open it.

It remained shut.

"Need a keycard," Matt said, catching up with Ella in tow. "Pops," he said, "keycard."

Slight grin turning his mouth up, Burke pushed past and scanned his card.

As the key plate beeped green, Addy pushed the door open and stepped to go through the vestibule.

Burke grabbed her arm. "Let me go first," he said, drawing his sidearm again. Holding it at shoulder height, he spun around the doorjamb. "Clear."

Addy stepped in, her eyes landing on Jane and Mike.

Jane had been laughing at something he said and wrapping the baby to her body.

"Oh my god, you guys, are you OK?"

Jane stopped, eyes wide. Mike crossed the room and swept Addy into a hug. Just about knocked her off her feet.

"Bean, it's so good to see you."

"Whatever, jerk." She closed her eyes.

"I'm sorry about all the dumb shit I did," he said, releasing her.

"Later. Jane," she said, hugging her over the baby, "where's Dad?"

"Oh, he's not far," Melinda said.

Addy spun, heart tripping. She hadn't seen Mom since she'd punched her in the gut and socked her in the nose. Time hadn't yet healed that wound. Flames curled in her gut.

"Let him go, Mom." She took a step toward her mom, even though Melinda had raised a gun and pointed it at all of them.

A tall man with dandelion hair and wearing a white lab coat stood next to her, holding a satchel. Must have been the doctor Dad mentioned. His eyes red, he could hardly make eye contact.

"Jack wants to stay with me, sweetie," Mom said, taking a step.

Before anyone could say anything or think to stop her, Melinda grabbed Jane's shoulder and pulled her into a stranglehold, pointing the gun at her head. "Gotta take this one with me, too."

While bright white fear and anger in equal portions froze Addy, rooted her to the spot, Dean, Celia, and Matt all shouted.

Mom waved the gun at Burke. "Thanks for calling the helicopter, Casey. Don't hate me for taking it and leaving you here."

"Don't take the girl, Melinda." He smiled. "Besides, it's not IRF I called."

The end of the gun dipped. "What do you mean?"

"Talus is coming. They're the ones I called." He frowned. "There's so much you don't understand. But I imagine they're going to wonder why you've been developing the vaccine for IRF." As the barrel of the gun dipped farther, and Melinda's grip relaxed on her, Burke snatched Jane's arm and shoved her behind him. "I'll explain everything to you, Mellie, just—"

Melinda shot him. Once in the gut.

Breathless, he stumbled backward.

Melinda shot him again, once more in the gut and once in the leg.

As Ella screamed for her daddy, Addy watched him fall. His mouth and eyes wide, one hand gripping his stomach and the other still gripping his sidearm. He'd never had a chance to take a shot with it.

Like a felled tree, he crashed to Earth. Bubbling and wheezing from what sounded like a sucking chest wound.

Something Addy wished she didn't know what it sounded like.

Heart in her throat again, she looked for her mother.

Melinda and the doctor had disappeared.

Ella sank down next to her father. Her honey-colored hair hung in sheets over her face. "Daddy?"

That reminds me.

"Renzo, go and look for my dad," Addy said over her shoulder.

Matt fell to his knees on Burke's other side, hands in his hair. "What do we do, Ella?" The lines around his mouth pointing at the floor. Chin trembling.

Burke grabbed him. Wheezing. "You take care of her, Matt," he said, air sucked out of his words.

"He's in here, guys," Renzo said.

Addy backed toward his voice, watching as Burke put a bloody hand to Ella's cheek and told her he loved her. Forever and ever. As she cried, he reached for his sidearm.

Jane all but sprinted past, into the room Renzo had entered. Burke raised the gun to his own temple.

Addy trudged through mud. This whole thing had turned into such a nightmare. And just what had Burke meant about IRF and Talus?

Her foggy thoughts cleared as she laid eyes on Dad. He seemed in one piece. A small favor. She rushed to him, falling to her knees and sliding. As she opened her mouth to say something, anything, who knew what, Burke pulled the trigger.

"Daddy!" Ella's heartbroken shout, more out of control than Addy had ever heard her, sent Addy's heart into overdrive. Tears threatened.

"Addy," Matt said from behind her, "Ella's going after your mom. I can't let her go alone."

"Renzo," Jane said, squeezing Jack's hand, "help Jack, he's been shot." She stood.

Watching her, and her dad, she listened to the sound of Matt's footsteps pound away. Jane had Jack. The strongest man Addy knew. She'd be alright.

Ella needed her.

And as much as she despised her mother in this moment, she still didn't want to see her dead. Which Ella would do, if she had the chance.

Without so much as a word, she dashed off after Ella. Past Dean, past Burke's unarmed body, down the hallway opposite from which they'd come.

CHAPTER 46

The pain in Jack's leg wasn't unbearable. He was able to keep up fairly well.

Addy seemed to like Ella. Seemed to care for her. Here he'd been pressing her to make smart alliances, but Addy wasn't built that way. She loved everyone she got close to, whether she wanted to or not. And it always showed.

And Matt. In the short time they'd spent together, he'd come to care about the kid. Man. Whatever. He seemed like a decent sort of fellow, and he'd just lost the man he considered a father.

"Renzo, can we go faster?" he asked, limping less. "I'll be alright."

Renzo grunted. "Sure thing, Jack."

Jane held his hand, one arm around the baby strapped to her chest. "Are you alright?"

Grimacing, he swallowed. Lied. "Yes."

It didn't seem like enough.

"Just worried about Mike and Addy. Their mom is—" He stopped again, letting his feet slow. "She's unhinged."

"I gathered," Renzo said. "She shot her closest ally."

Jack shook his head and began walking again. "She doesn't have allies. She doesn't have anything." He swallowed again, forcing her face from his mind. "She'll kill them if they get in her way."

Celia ran around the corner ahead of them. "Jack, the helicopter is coming in. She's getting away." She glanced behind them. "There you are, kid."

Following her gaze, he found Ricardo catching up to them. "Ric," he said, "I'm glad you're alright."

"He was our diversion," Celia said, throwing an arm around his shoulders. "He took some pretty big risks for us." She shook him back and forth.

Brown eyes grinning, he glanced at his feet and shrugged. "Just a few grenades and stuff," he said. "Least I could do."

"Here," Celia said, pointing and pulling Ric along, "we go out this door." Shoving the door open, she pulled him out into the bright afternoon.

Jack, Jane, and Renzo followed.

Helicopter blades whirred, approaching. Beating the air, slapping it into submission.

Two gunshots cracked the air, louder than the blades.

Though the bullet rubbed up and down inside his thigh, Jack released Renzo and Jane and broke into a trot. Celia and Ric on his heels. Stomach in his throat.

Could have been one bullet each for Mike and Adelaide. He wouldn't know till he got there.

Though he tried to ball the fear up and shove it down, it did nothing but bloom in his chest. Working to stop his breath.

He pressed forward, toward the place Celia pointed to and shouted it was the landing pad.

Three small buildings stood before a flat spot on the ground, a giant H painted in the center. Mike and Addy stood, thank god, Dean with them, and Matt with his arm around a crying Ella. They surrounded the woman standing apart. Doctor Huxley stood with her, though he looked ready to bolt. Kept glancing side to side.

As Jack slid between two of the buildings, Celia and Ric ahead, Jane and Renzo behind, he finally caught snatches of conversation.

"This research is more important than you can possibly imagine. Just let me leave with my samples, my work," Melinda said, snatching the case from Huxley and pushing him into Addy. Eyes falling on Jack and the others, her brows lifted and her mouth fell open.

He couldn't look at her. Couldn't maintain eye contact. It was like being hit with the stun gun.

Ella pushed Matt's hands away and lifted a handgun. With the helicopter landing, her blonde hair flew back from her brow as she stood straight, aiming for Melinda's heart like she was standing on a gun range. Her father's bloody handprint emblazoned on her cheek like it burned from the inside out.

Diverting his eyes from Melinda, Jack caught sight of Matt's face.

Stunned. Like he'd been punched in the gut. Mouth and eyes wide. All the blood draining from his hairline down.

Jack followed his eyes.

To Ricardo.

The truth of it, what Jack should have seen earlier, what he should really have known all along, especially once they found out about Matt's upbringing, unfurled in Jack's mind like one of those giant American flags that used to hang above car dealerships.

He glanced back to Ella, aiming her gun at Melinda.

And before either Matt or Jack could shout at her, tell her to watch out, Ricardo shot her.

Blood and bits of bone, spraying away from Ella under the force of the helicopter blades, showered Matt in a misty cloud. Like something out of a dream, Matt screamed Ella's name and caught her before she hit the ground. The side of her head pushed out at an unnatural angle, her limbs flopped.

"Ella-belle," Matt shouted again, gathering her into his arms.

Ricardo threw his arm around Melinda and guided her to the landing helicopter.

The helicopter blades drowned out everything. Except Matt trying to shout Ella back from the afterlife.

Jack's heart broke for the boy. He'd just lost everyone he considered family. Even the leader of his gang.

Speaking of the woman, as she climbed onto the helicopter, she glanced back at them all. A tear might have fallen, but the wind from the blades whipped it away from her face.

He looked away again. Found Addy, stunned, staring at Ella and crying. Tears streaming down her face in an unending waterfall. And though she sobbed aloud, her lips forming the word "Ella" over and over, Jack couldn't hear a word over the blades and the wind.

The helicopter's engine whine increased, and the blades teased it into the air.

Covering his face from the sandblasting as it took off, he took a step toward his little girl. His living, breathing little girl.

CHAPTER 47

Melinda watched her children. Having taken what she could gather of her research and samples from that spineless bastard Huxley, she clutched the satchel to her chest.

Ella held a gun to her heart. And why shouldn't she?

Jack came charging onto the helicopter pad. He'd lost something in the last few days. A trickle of unease filtered into her mind, but she allowed it no headspace.

And she caught sight of one of her boys. Little Hector, all grown up now. Mean as the world that'd spit him out, she'd wondered if she'd ever see him again, or if his cold little black heart would get him killed. It was nice to see him. She'd taken quite the shine to him before renaming him Ricardo and sending him off with Tim to try and keep the elder boy in line.

She kept the smile off her face as she turned back to the unsuspecting girl. Though in her peripheral, she could see recognition reach that traitor's face.

Her pretty little Matt. He'd turned on her for this girl and her tricky father. The one who'd told her lies about IRF. Lies upon lies upon lies.

She had some questions to ask that son of a bitch Anthony when she got back.

Her ruthless Hector killed Ella with less hesitation than a rattlesnake. Then he put his arm around her and guided her to the waiting helicopter as Addy exploded into tears.

That she was essentially responsible for the heartbreak on Addy's face did not sit easy. It crept up her throat with a squeeze.

But it was a necessary evil. This research was more important than any of their lives, save the baby.

"Mama," Heck said, "it's so good to see you." Shoving her into the helicopter and following after, he wrapped his arms around her and buried his face in her shoulder like a five-year-old.

As the helicopter lifted from the ground, she watched her babies fade into the distance. Grow smaller and smaller.

If all had been right with the world, they'd be on the helicopter with her. And so would Jack. Why he refused to admit he still loved her was beyond her comprehension. Especially after their recent night together.

But it was as it was. She had chosen to save the world. He had chosen to fuck a twelve-year-old.

C'est la vie.

"Did the horde work good? It was hard getting them in. But I did it," Hector said, flashing a wide smile. "Nobody even knew it was me."

She smiled, half the words hitting her ears. The other half floating off into the ether with the helicopter blades.

"Mama, are you alright?" Heck asked over the whirring.

She shrugged. "I still need the girl for her eggs. But I can get along well enough with what I've got," she said, lifting the satchel.

"No, I mean, did they hurt you?"

Opening her mouth to say no, she pictured Addy's face. Weeping for her murdered friend.

A tear collected in the edge of her eye. She swiped at it and shrugged again.

His face hardened. Those flat murderer's eyes of his deepening till they were almost all pupil. Mouth set in a cruel twist, he pulled a little ball of metal from his pocket.

Yanked the pin out.

"Last one," he said, flipping the spoon away from the body of the grenade.

Before she could shout, stop him, he flung it out the side of the helicopter.

She leapt over him, trying to catch it. And do what with it, who knew. But she had to stop it.

He caught her, and she watched, helpless, as it fell to the earth. Just next to Mike, Addy, and the others.

The sound of the explosion, the heat from the fire, none of it reached her ears up here.

Only the light and the smoke.

Heart going triple speed, she leaned back into the seat and motioned to the pilot. "Take us home," she mouthed.

He nodded, pointing the helicopter south.

CHAPTER 48

Addy couldn't feel the ground beneath her feet. The air in her lungs, if there was any. The wind rippling her clothes as the helicopter took off.

What the literal fuck had just happened?

Matt, covered in a sheen of blood, cradled Ella in his arms. Lifeless, limp Ella.

Before he'd scooped her up, Addy had seen the side of her head. The wrong shape, size. Bits of brain littering the edge of a hole in her skull.

She expected to dry heave. But nothing came. Because there was nothing.

Movement caught her eye.

She glanced up, and there was Dad, taking a step toward her.

God, at least he was OK. He didn't look so hot, but he didn't have any new bullet holes.

His head snapped up, and he tracked something in the sky.

The sky falling wouldn't be entirely unexpected at this point. Her face a mess of tears, snot, and maybe blood, she turned to follow Dad's eye.

Before she got all the way around, Dean tackled her. Forcing her to the ground with a grunt, he lay on her as the world went white.

She closed her eyes, turning her head away from the light and the heat.

The force of the explosion pushed itself up her sinuses. Jiggled her eyeballs in her head. The hearing loss was instant. Her lungs compressed, squeezing her insides with a hammer fist.

It ended, and as Dean leaned back, all she could think was she hoped she'd be able to hear again.

He took in her face and glanced over the rest of her before catching her eyes again. "Are you OK?"

Only she couldn't hear him. Just watch his mouth move. She still wasn't great with lip-reading, but she could see what he was asking.

She nodded, unsure if it was true or not.

He stood, holding a hand out to her.

She took it, standing and looking to find her dad. And everyone else, make sure they were OK. Before she did, Dean touched her on the shoulder.

She turned, ready to give and receive a relieved embrace. A kiss or five.

"Addy?" His eyebrows lifted, asking her a question.

Not that she could hear him. But the way he said her name, she'd hear it in her dreams for months.

His legs buckled, and he dropped.

"Dean!" Her voice echoed off the insides of her cranium.

Kneeling next to him, she looked him over as he panted, leaning on his elbow. His legs twisted beneath him.

There, inside his thigh, a patch of blood grew at an alarming rate. It began to soak through his pants and drip to the ground.

Reaching for her, he fell to his side.

Her ears still ringing, she shouted. "Dad! Oh fuck, Dean. God, please!"

Straightening his leg, she found a rip in his pants just along his inner thigh. Gripping both sides of the tear, she tore his pants open. The inside of them absolutely soaked in blood that squelched between her fingers.

Dad appeared next to her. "What happened?"

At least she could hear something now. She shook her head. Her vision doubled. "He's bleeding out, Dad."

Jack whipped his belt off and started a tourniquet.

Hands covered in blood, soaked in his life, she gripped the sides of Dean's face. "You stay with me, baby. Don't you leave me, I won't allow it."

He nodded. Patting one of her hands with his pale, limp fingers, he gave her a weak smile. "You're OK, though," he said, eyes unable to focus on her.

At some point, she'd begun crying again. Everything hurt. Inside, outside, mentally, emotionally. A raw bundle of nerves gripped the sides of his face and forced him to look at her.

He did, through half lids. Emerald in his eyes fading. He opened his mouth and pulled in a shallow breath. Just the one.

She shook him. Couldn't see his face through the tears. Opening her mouth to say his name didn't work because she couldn't speak around the ache in her throat. Instead, she snaked a hand down his neck and felt for his pulse.

It wasn't there.

She glanced at the pavement.

His life's blood lay in a spreading pool around him. Drying on the ground.

At least Dad had gotten the tourniquet on.

Rather than sink into a puddle of despair, laying her face in his blood and waiting for him to spring to life and kill her, because why not, at this point, she looked up. All of them, including that doctor, stood around Dean in a circle. All except Matt.

And Ella. Ella-belle. Of course.

She turned to her brother, who knelt next to her. "Michael," she said, gripping his shoulder, "and Dad, help me. We've got to get him to the train."

Mike sniffled. "Addy, he lost too much blood. We can't—"

"Don't you say we can't to me. Not right now. We can. Help me get him to the train, goddammit. We haven't got much time." She found Renzo. "Do you have rope or something?"

He nodded, eyes drooping.

"Good. Tie his hands. Do it now."

Without slowing to think, she stood and walked to Matt. Kneeling down beside him, she avoided looking at Ella's misshapen head as he rocked her. A piece of shrapnel had traveled up his back, ripping through his jacket, but the wound appeared only a little more serious than a scratch. Likely he didn't even feel it.

"Matt," she said, hand on his shoulder, "we gotta go now."

He shook his head. Leaned farther over Ella's lifeless body. "I can't leave her, Addy."

Choking on the words, Addy cleared her throat. "She's gone. She's not coming back." More tears fell. Good lord but she'd need to drink a gallon of water to replace them. "She's gone. We gotta go."

Again, he shook his head. "You go. I can't leave her," he said, voice lowering to a whisper. "She was the only one that ever really cared. Don't you get that?"

"Look at me," Addy said. When he didn't, she repeated herself.

He looked up. Eyes bloodshot, face swollen, cheeks wet, he looked at her.

"We care, Matt. Come with us now. There's nothing for you here." She tugged his arm.

He looked down at Ella, smoothing her hair off her high, clear brow.

Addy thought of her arching those brows, looking annoyed. But really, it was all just an act. That's all it ever was. Her defense mechanism.

Her eyes stung. Again.

Matt lowered Ella's head to the ground with care, smoothing her hair one more time, and wiped his nose with the back of his hand.

Standing, he offered Addy a hand up.

She took it and glanced around.

Jane, Dad, Renzo, Mike, the doctor, Celia, and Matt. They'd all fit on the train. The rest of Mann's folks could stay here and deal with IRF when they came to rescue them. Or Talus, or whoever. It didn't matter, they'd be fine.

"Come on," she said, pointing at Dean. "We've got to get him on the train. Doc," she said, clapping him on the shoulder, "I've got a special job for you."

CHAPTER 49

Addy wasn't sure how they got to the train. All she knew was someone else did the slicing and dicing, while she helped support Dean's limp body.

As Dad, Mike, Renzo, and Matt loaded him onto the train, she pulled everything from the cabinets in search of the damned first aid kit. It just would not show itself.

Smacking herself on the forehead, she remembered the compartment behind the Captain's Chair.

"Mike, get up here and drive this thing. Get us home."

He shuffled to the front and sat, slouching in the chair. "Addy, he's gone. He's lost too much blood."

Arching her brows, pushing away the visual of Ella doing the same, she didn't look up. "Get the damned train started, Mike."

As they thumped down the tracks, Addy glanced out the window once or twice. Most of the horde must have been called to the hospital, with all the commotion. The tracks held a sparse population of 'Heads.

What was Mann going to do about what was left of them? Could she plug the hole? Would any of them survive? Would Data be alright?

Too many questions. Not enough time. Dean had sixteen hours before the Cure was useless. If she didn't get him back to Harkers in less, she might as well not even bother. As it was, he'd lost too much blood.

"Doc, get your ass over here," she said, kneeling next to Dean. He'd already begun to stir, but his eyes were still closed.

She popped the first aid kit open. Dean was well stocked, with needle and thread balled into its own little compartment. Pulling it from the case, she shoved it at the doctor. "Sew him up."

Dean began to gurgle around the blood in his lungs.

Thank god his eyes were still closed.

The doctor choked and coughed. "You want me to sew up the tear on this man's femoral artery, on a moving train, while he is himself newly infected with the live and active virus? I think you've misunderstood my capabilities, young lady." He gave her a crooked smile, slight buck teeth hanging over his lower lip.

Brows drawn into a frown so hard her forehead hurt, she held her bloody machete under his chin. "Sew him up, or I'll cut your throat and throw you off this train."

The doctor gulped. Nodding, he bent over the first aid kit and pulled out a pair of scissors. Cutting away the rest of Dean's pants leg, he looked up. "I need some water. Sterile, if you have it. Alcohol as well."

"I got it, Addy," Celia said.

With a start, Addy glanced around. There were still other people here.

Matt sat on the bed, face in his hands, just his bloodshot blue eyes peeking out from between his fingers.

Renzo sat in front of the cabinets, watching as Celia looked for water and rubbing alcohol.

Dad and Jane cozied into the far corner up front, both curled around the baby. Jane grinned. Dad did not. It was almost as though he was looking past them both, off in his own thoughts. His expression inscrutable.

Celia set the supplies down and put an arm around Addy. "It's gonna be OK, girl."

The doctor shook his head, threading the needle. The train bumped, and he missed. "Miss, my name is Doctor Huxley, and I'm an expert on neuro…this virus." He got the thread through the needed and tied it off. "I've never seen anyone lose this much blood and recover."

Through stinging eyes and a gripping band around her throat, Addy watched Dean's face. Waiting for his eyes to open. "Sew him up, doc."

"I need someone to hold him down."

Renzo eased over, kneeling at Dean's feet. Holding his ankles, he nodded. "I got 'im, doc. Do what you need to."

"Could someone wash the area, please. I need to be able to see what I'm doing. This tourniquet was well applied. The leakage of blood has stopped, but I can't see through the spent fluids."

Celia jerked her chin. "Keep his hands out of the way, keep him from sitting up, Addy. I'll help the doctor here."

Nodding, Addy crept up next to his head.

Growling emanated from deep in Dean's throat. Gurgling around the fresh blood, what there was of it.

He began to stir, moving his arms.

Holding her breath, she pressed down on his shoulders.

* * *

In a fog, Jack helped carry Dean through the horde, the leg in his hands growing colder by the moment.

Jane never left his side, fending off any 'Heads that even looked at him cross-eyed. And all she had were her needles. That woman could fight through anything with nothing but spit and determination.

Occasional flashes of love fought their way to the surface when he forgot to feel awful.

But he focused on carrying Dean as much as he could. There was no way the man would make it. He'd lost almost all the blood a body could lose. He was gone.

Adelaide insisted on Jack's help, though, so he helped. Losing Dean would never sit right with Addy, he was her first love. But she'd kill herself if she didn't do everything she could. If it'd make her feel better to try this, Jack would help.

Once they'd gotten onto the train, he laid Dean in the floor and retreated to a corner, watching Addy give directions. She was focused, determined, and unwilling to admit defeat.

He'd been that way once.

Jane settled down next to him, unwrapping the baby and pulling one of his arms around her shoulders like a shawl. "Finally," she said. "Together again."

Tears stung his eyes. He blinked them back. Every word he thought of inadequate, he ended up just nodding and laying his head on her shoulder.

Trying to stare at the baby, he pushed all thought away and concentrated on her pretty little face.

Now that they'd gotten through the horde, Michael steering them back toward the island, and Addy focusing all her efforts on poor, doomed Dean, he had a quiet moment to himself.

Not something he wanted.

The kind of violation Melinda had visited on him, well, he'd never even considered it a possibility. Did women always live with this fear? It had never occurred to him that someone could do that to him. Never, not once. Not that kind of invasion.

He couldn't look at it straight on.

He couldn't stop visualizing what had happened.

His mind spun in such a circle, anything else would have been preferable.

"Hey," Jane said. She'd been staring up at him for longer than he'd realized.

He tried on a smile. It didn't work out, but he gave it every effort. "Yeah."

"You alright?"

"Fine."

She bumped him. "You don't look fine. Wanna tell me?"

That long-ago night on the truck, when he'd told her she needed to talk about what had been bothering her, it flashed through his mind. It'd been good advice.

He opened his mouth to say something. Maybe not to tell her, because hadn't he technically cheated? But to say something. Anything.

Only breath came out. He tried on a smile again. "No. I just want to get out of this place and get home."

She nodded, kissed him beneath the jaw, and went back to the baby. "She seems OK. Do you think she's OK?"

"I think she's perfect," he said, a real smile finding its way to his lips as he gazed down at her. He wrapped the other arm around them both. The promise to keep them both safe on his lips, he paused.

He couldn't follow through on it, so it was best if he didn't promise.

They got past the outer wall of Emerald Hills and began their cruise out of the mountains. It'd take probably six hours to get back to Harkers, and about twenty minutes by boat to get across the sound. Maybe less if they could get Scott on the horn and have him meet them with a motorboat. Then they'd have to get Dean to the infirmary and get some blood in him. Then administer the Cure and wait. All told, if Addy could pull off the impossible, Dean would be dead only about eight hours.

If any obstructions came up, though. If something had happened to the tracks between here and there.

It was a long shot anyway, bringing him back.

He glanced over at Matt. His destitute face said it all.

Leaning his head against the wall, the gentle rocking of the train lulling him, Jack fell into something like meditation. Watching Matt fight sleep, he did the same.

Jane's bony elbow snuck between two ribs. Hard.

His eyes popped open. "What the hell, Jane?"

She pointed her forehead toward the center of the train. "The fuck is she doing?"

Following her gaze, he watched his eldest daughter. Still his little girl.

They'd patched Dean up as best they could, and she'd held down his shoulders as they did. Staring into his face.

Now they were done with the sewing, they'd tied his feet together. He could do nothing but bubble and gurgle, teeth gnashing the air.

Adelaide sat over him, lowering her forearm to his mouth.

* * *

Holding down his shoulders while the doctor worked, Addy prayed Dean wouldn't open his eyes.

The bubbling emanated from his lungs. Wet, sticky, gurgling growled from his throat and through his mouth. His jaw worked, his nose scenting the air.

She wanted to close her eyes. To look away from this wreck happening in front of her.

Managing a moment of distraction, she glanced at Matt.

He still watched from between his fingers. Nothing showing but two spots of blue.

Lungs in free fall, she considered asking him to do this. So she could be the one curled up on the couch, watching through her fingers.

But she couldn't. Couldn't leave Dean. She looked down into his face again.

His eyelids fluttered. Beneath them, his emerald eyes had grown a thin, opaque coating. He stared at her, nose scenting again, and lifted his head from the ground. With the strength of the newly dead, he tried to lift from the floor and tear her face off.

She held him. She held him down and watched as he snarled and bubbled, the virus twisting his features into an unrecognizable monster. Breath coppery from the blood pooling in his lungs.

How they didn't choke on the blood and die again had always been another mystery that'd made her wonder just what the hell this virus did. How it survived once its victims were dead.

He popped a few inches from the floor, teeth snapping at the underside of her chin.

"Hold him steady," Huxley said, drawing breath across his buck teeth. "I'm almost done here."

Addy pressed Dean's shoulders with all her strength, pinning him to the floor. Her stomach did a complicated little dance where it thought about losing its contents. She swallowed, saliva drenching the inside of her mouth as she fought her gorge.

Dean's struggling quieted. His filmy eyes staring up at her, he moved his jaw up and down. Almost like talking.

Mom's words screamed into Addy's brain from nowhere. Crystal clear.

And what Elizabeth had said. Like the kind of nightmare where you know you can't run fast enough, but you can't even make your brain *think to move*.

Dean was there, now. If she could get him back, this was what he'd remember. He'd remember being pinned down, in pain, not knowing why. Just that she held him to the floor while someone hurt him.

From miles away, the doctor spoke again. "I'm done. Finish tying him up. If he moves that leg too much, it'll rip the sutures."

As they tied him, he didn't struggle. Just continued to stare up at her through those filmy eyes. Mouth moving up and down.

Dear god. He was all alone in there. Unable to scream. Unable to want to scream. Alone.

Alone.

When Cameron had died, and he'd been alone, he told her he'd tried to commit suicide by horde.

When Addy had been bitten, and he'd been faced with being alone again, she'd ended up with his dose in her own veins instead of his.

When he'd seen the sky falling, he'd thrown himself over her to protect her. Rather than protect himself.

All the times when he could have helped himself, he helped everyone else. Just so he wouldn't have to be alone.

Yet here he was. Tied at the hands and feet, laid in the middle of this train car.

Alone.

Celia sat up front with Mike, one knee cocked in the air. Her arm wrapped around it. Doctor Huxley with them, blood cleaned from his hands.

Matt curled up on the bed, fighting sleep. Renzo already passed out in the bouncy chair that'd always been Dean's favorite.

Jack and Jane rocking with the train, hugging each other while curled around the baby.

Yet, here Dean was. Tied at the hands and feet, laid in the middle of the train car.

Alone.

If by some miracle he pulled through this, he'd look back on this and that's what he'd remember. That's all he'd remember. That they left him alone to die.

Sadness, utter despair, overtook Addy. Her insides crushed into each other, as though a giant hand had reached into her chest cavity and squeezed until they were all one mass of blood and bone.

He couldn't be left alone like this. It was the last thing he'd want.

As she wept, tears falling onto his face and running down his cheeks, an idea so perfect in its form hit her, she couldn't believe she hadn't thought of it sooner.

Of course. Of course. He could bite her, then she could turn, then he wouldn't be alone. She could be with him. When he looked out on this memory with the crystal-clear vision of the dead, he'd see her with him.

Oh, it was so perfect. She should have thought about it before.

Brushing his hair from his sweaty, cold forehead, tears obscuring his features, she lowered her forearm to his mouth. If he got her in the fleshy part of her forearm, she'd turn before she lost too much blood. Then she could—

Dad tackled her, her head bouncing off the floor of the train. He ran into her with such force, they finished up against the cabinets.

Her shoulder took the brunt of the impact, and something inside popped. Head swimming, she shoved him. "What the hell, Dad? What are you doing?"

"Adelaide, stop," he said, gripping her wrists. "What were you thinking?" Strong as a rock, he held her down.

She struggled, heart tripping into double-time. "He's all alone, Dad. He's all alone! You can't. We can't. I can't let him be alone. He doesn't want to be alone," she said, yanking her hands.

Dad held onto her wrists. "Addy, look at me."

Shaking her head, she closed her eyes.

"He's not alone. We're still here," Dad said. Voice soothing the ball of nerves in her chest. "You can't go with him where he is. You might not come back."

She opened her eyes and looked at her dad. "I'd be OK, Dad. I've only taken the Cure once. I'd be OK." She tried to push him off, watching as Dean struggled against his bonds.

Brows raised, Dad put his face between her and Dean. "Adelaide, listen to me." Little more than a whisper.

His calm began to rub off. Easing her fight, she stopped trying to free her wrists and listened to his voice as he soothed her like a child. Told her everything was going to be alright, and even if it wasn't, they had each other. Just like always. "I can't let you follow him, Adelaide. I can't let you take that risk. Stay here with us, little girl."

More hot tears spilled down her cheeks. As if she hadn't already cried them all over Ella. As if she hadn't already lost them all over Mom leaving, again. As if she still had tears left to cry over Dean. They just kept coming. An unending river of them. Lakes could be filled. Hydropower could be created. And still, the tears would come.

She leaned into her dad and let them.

After enough of them fell, and she could see through them again, she found a piece of cloth and handed it to Dad. "Gag him," she said.

Stroking the side of her hair, Jack took the gag and tied it around Dean's mouth.

Sniffling, Addy crept back to Dean's side and pulled her knees up to her chest.

He turned his filmy eyes to her, trying to bite through the cloth in his mouth. Jerking his bound arms and legs.

Eyes peeping over the tops of her knees, she whispered. "You're going to be OK."

THE END

A SPECIAL NOTE

If you are a survivor of sexual assault, please know you are not alone, and that no matter who you are, it was NOT your fault. It does not matter your sex, sexual orientation, or gender identity, if you have been in that position, and you feel alone, please contact someone. Below are some resources where you can reach out for help. Please, when you are able, ask someone for help. You can recover from this.

National Sexual Assault Telephone Hotline: (800)656-4673
https://www.rainn.org/about-national-sexual-assault-telephone-hotline

Information about Male Survivors of Sexual Assault:
https://www.rainn.org/articles/sexual-assault-men-and-boys and https://firststep.org/education/sexual-assault-topics/male-survivors-of-sexual-assault/

Websites and Other Online Resources:
https://www.nsvrc.org/sites/default/files/2014-09/nsvrc_publications_resource-list_online-resources-for-survivors.pdf

National Sexual Violence Resource Center:
https://www.nsvrc.org/

Acknowledgments

Special thanks, as always, to my incredibly patient beta readers and writing partners. You guys have seen all the ups and downs and stuck around anyway, and I'll be eternally grateful for that.

I basically disappeared from family life while writing this trilogy, and for their unending patience and support, my family deserves the world. If it weren't for how awesome they are, this story wouldn't exist.

Bonus thanks to M.A. Roberts for the "heaters in hell" line. That was way more clever than what I could have come up with.

And special thanks to my editor, Michelle Rascon, for helping me make it shine again. Any mistakes are mine, come at me with those, not her. She's a special gem and puts up with a lot of crap from me!

Huge, huge thanks to Jonas M. Steger for creating yet another gorgeous cover. You have the absolute best eye in the business.

And thanks to you, readers, for coming along on the journey. A story isn't complete without readers.

ABOUT THE AUTHOR

Bethany has had many lifetimes—one in the American South, one in the American West, and one both before and after sobriety. She's always had a passion for reading and writing, and when she's not working, hanging with her kids or partner or pets, she's likely at the computer, writing. Poetry, horror, fantasy, sci-fi, you name it. If it's got an off-beat twist, she's probably into it.

Her debut novel, and book 1 in the Reclamation Series, *Reclamation*, is available wherever books are sold. Book 3, *Reconstruction*, is slated for release in 2021. She also has a contemporary fantasy novel tentatively entitled *Give Me Grace* coming from NineStar Press in late 2020.

If she were in front of you, she'd tell you to read a book. But also that a little TV is OK, too, as long as it's *Supernatural* or *Star Trek*.

Visit her website and sign up for the mailing list. You'll receive ONLY news about upcoming releases.

bperrywrites.com

Reclamation 3:

Reconstruction

Excerpt

CHAPTER 1

The helicopter touched down, and Melinda's feet hit the soil above the Molehill for the first time in five years.

"Good to be home, huh, mama?" Hector bumped her with his shoulder, black eyes smiling. All his dark hair stood on end.

She glared, clutching the satchel. "It is. I wonder if it's changed while we've been gone."

He shook his head. "What would they do different?"

"You got me, Heck. You got me."

Grinning, he ignored the path and ran down the hill through the tall grass.

That evil little imp hopping through the sunny grass could have killed her whole family. And what would she have left? Just what was in this satchel. Pieces of Jack.

"Let's go, Mama!" Hector waved from the bottom of the hill, smiling into the sun.

Following the brick path down the hill, taking the steps one careful foot at a time, she descended. Wouldn't do to get sloppy and lose the samples now. Or the research.

Warmth spread through her. The research.

She smiled.

Heck opened the door within the hill. "What's that smile for?"

"My research. From Shanti Station. It should all be here," she said, shaking her head. "I told Tim I deleted it, but in reality, I transmitted it all here. I'd forgotten." Her smile grew. So many things to be happy about. Before walking in, she met his eyes. "You were instrumental in that. I don't know if I ever thanked you. Releasing those remnants was a stroke of genius."

His lips split in a smile that rivaled the sun. He waved her in.

The door closed behind her, locking them into the earthen smell she'd been away from for so long. It didn't really feel like dying, here, and yet it didn't feel like living. But it did smell like wet earth, and there could be few more pleasant scents in the world.

He followed on her heels. "You think they still kept our rooms?"

Nodding, she led the way through the labyrinth of tunnels. "I do. Our things are probably still there as well." She smiled. It would be something to see her old music collection again. The DVDs she'd somehow located over time. Her telescope.

But first.

"I've got to report in, Heck. Why don't you go ahead and see if your room has changed."

Without another word, the boy ran off down another corridor. The dark swallowed him.

Sure, the hallways were lined with tile and brick. But the electric and phone cables didn't have conduit, and the lamps only shone in a three-foot circle. Spaced at least five feet apart as they were, it didn't make for the brightly lit hallways she'd become accustomed to back in Magnolia, or in Shanti Station, for that matter. And the light always seemed to taper off entirely about twenty feet out. Something about all the earth surrounding them, most likely.

Compared to this place, the Big House on Harkers was nothing as far as confusing hallways went. But her feet found their way. Tapping on the door with her knuckles, she clutched the satchel in the other hand and waited.

Swinging open, the heavy metal door creaked. A full-figured woman revealed herself behind it, nodding to Melinda with a sideways smile. "General. So good to see you again."

"Ilasha, your perfect hair has not changed," Melinda said, brushing through the door.

Ilasha closed the door, smiling. Leaning out of a shadow, her dark brown skin and high cheekbones shone. "You wouldn't believe the hell I go through to keep it that way, ma'am."

Melinda snickered. "Ma'am. Please, Lash. Don't start with me. Where is he?" Eyes wide, she glanced around the room as though the man she sought would somehow reveal himself. Like a magician under a cloak of invisibility.

Lash held out a hand. "Where else? Things don't change much around here, Em."

"After you."

Affecting a stronger Southern accent than the one she already had, Lash glanced over her shoulder. She fluttered the long lashes that framed her deep brown eyes. "Don't you be lookin' at my ass, white woman," she said, swinging her hips as she led Melinda across the anteroom where Lash's desk and a couple chairs sat. Before leading her into the office beyond a second set of doors, a nameplate reading "Charles Anthony" glued to the center, she leaned over and lowered her voice. "He ain't been in the greatest mood lately, hon. Watch yourself."

Melinda nodded, swallowing. She'd been able to handle him before she left. Shouldn't be any different now, even though it'd been a few years.

Clearing her throat, Lash stepped into the room, tugging Melinda's elbow. "Look what the cat dragged in, sir," she said. Fingers in the small of her back, she gave Melinda a gentle push.

Stumbling, Melinda glanced back at Lash.

Who'd already disappeared.

She swallowed. "Mister Anthony, sir, I can't believe I'm standing here again. After all these years, I—"

"Are you bringing me a vaccine, general?" Behind a great oak desk, he sifted through papers. Mounds and mounds of them.

"You received my transmission from Shanti Station?"

He snorted. "Your own Tranquility Base. Yes, my dear. I did. That was nearly a year ago." Laying a paper down, he glared over the top of his glasses. Hawkish blue eyes, set wide in his pale face, pierced her, pinning her to the spot. "Are you telling me you've made no progress since then?"

"I— Yes. I have." She held up the satchel and cleared her throat. "Using my test vaccine, we may have synthesized immunity."

He stood so fast the chair rolled into the wall with a bang. "You what?" With three large steps, he rounded the desk.

She straightened her shoulders and held the flinch inside. "It's not a hundred percent," she said, the satchel falling a tick, "but I witnessed it, Charles. Immunity in a living, breathing person." She cleared her throat again.

Arms crossed, he leaned back against the desk. "Immunity. Huh. And what is it you have there?" he asked, bony finger pointing at the satchel.

She clutched it close. "My research. Samples. Half the clean biological component from the immune person. Some of their blood."

"Half. Some. Samples. Doesn't sound like much, general," he said, removing his glasses. Cleaning them on his shirt, he glared. "What can you do with this half-assed science you've brought me?"

Her stomach curled. Shoving the collection of the samples to the side, she grimaced. "Give me a few hours, a couple days probably. We need human eggs. I can synthesize some embryos."

"Ah. So that's the half you've brought? The father of this immune person? Is this person a child?"

"A newborn."

"Even better," he said, slapping the desk. The flat of his hand echoed off the wood.

Melinda jumped, clutching the case. "I am almost certain this was the first human born with it, sir."

Waving a hand, he slid the glasses up his nose. "Do it again, Melinda. Then we'll talk."